Andrew MacAllan is the pseudonym for James Leasor, whose Dr Jason Love adventure novels have been published in nineteen countries. He is also well known for his factual books, such as *Green Beach* and *Boarding Party*, filmed with Roger Moore and Gregory Peck.

Under the name of Andrew MacAllan he has written three previous epic sagas, *Succession*, *Generation* ('an epic success' *Sunday Express*) and *Diamond Hard*, which are all available from Headline.

Fanfare

Andrew MacAllan

HEADLINE

First published in 1992
by HEADLINE BOOK PUBLISHING PLC

First published in paperback in 1992
by HEADLINE BOOK PUBLISHING PLC

10 9 8 7 6 5 4 3 2 1

ISBN 0 7472 3823 5

Phototypeset by Intype, London

Printed and bound in Great Britain by
HarperCollins Manufacturing, Glasgow

HEADLINE BOOK PUBLISHING PLC
Headline House
79 Great Titchfield Street
London W1P 7FN

FANFARE

A flourish, call, or short tune, sounded by trumpets, bugles, or hunting-horns.

The Oxford English Dictionary

From the Writer to the Reader

As a small boy, I was intrigued by a picture that hung on the wall of my bedroom. This was 'Remnant of an Army', a famous Victorian painting by Lady Elizabeth Butler, who specialised in military subjects. It showed an exhausted rider on a weary horse approaching Jalalabad, near the Afghan/Indian frontier.

This rider was William Brydon, a Scottish surgeon and distant relation of my mother's family, and the sole European survivor of a British and Indian force, forty thousand strong, that had occupied Kabul. The army retired, under promise by the Afghans of safe passage to the border. This promise was not honoured. Forty thousand set out – soldiers, wives, children and camp followers. Only one man came back. Everyone else was massacred or died of exposure on the terrible journey across frozen mountains.

My novel stems from this melancholy footnote to imperial history, which underlines the truth of the Psalmist's sound advice: 'Put not your trust in princes, nor in any child of man.'

Fanfare describes what happened to some who did . . .

A.M.

Chapter One

Sometimes, even now, when winter winds breathe down the chimney to set the fire agleam, and the Scottish Grampians wear capes of snow, I remember other, fiercer winds that howled across higher, more hostile hills. Instead of logs crackling in my homely grate, I hear an angry rattle of muskets and the wild cries as Afghan brigands surged down the mountains to pillage the dying and the dead.

This was, of course, in another time, another world, now all but forgotten. Everyone I knew then is dead long since, save for one other person who survived with me. And this is his story, not mine.

As I sit in the chimney corner, seeing pictures of the past in the dying embers of the fire, I sometimes examine a small silver case I had made in the Street of the Silversmiths in Delhi. It contains a single lock of hair, red as the flames before me. I marvel anew at the difference between what was and what might have been, the vast aching chasm between loneliness and love. But, as a man grows old, is not this a universal regret?

Time, I know now, can never be easily or accurately measured. When I was a schoolboy, a week seemed an eternity. But as I grew older, this changed; now, what happened when I was twenty-five seems, nearly half a century on, more vivid than events of last week.

1

In the United States I am told that they still commemorate Custer's last stand, which cost 276 lives. But who in my country can call to mind even the briefest details of our army's retreat from Kabul in Afghanistan in which nearly forty thousand died, men, women, children? And I marvel how I, Douglas Kintyre, a Scottish physician attached to this doomed army, survived. The only other who lived was a babe then, newborn. I brought him into this world, and at the hour of his birth I helplessly watched his dear mother die. But more of that later. For sometimes, even now, I can scarcely bear to dwell too closely on the memory.

In my undeserved deliverance I see the merciful hand of the Almighty. Why is one taken and another left? There may be a reason, but I have never discovered it. Sometimes I wonder whether I have used to best advantage, or indeed to any advantage, these years vouchsafed to me by Providence, when so many others, more worthy than I am in every way, were cut down in all the vigour of youth.

But I am rushing ahead. How had I come to join this force, so far away from the hills and glens of my native Perthshire? And why did so many die so needlessly in such misery and humiliation and defeat?

People who ask this question often expect a simple, comprehensive answer in a few words, just as patients invariably expect a quick cure from me, regardless of the complexities of their ailment.

A patient suffering, perhaps, from a poisoned leg may not realise that this started with something else that seemed totally unimportant and unrelated; perhaps a scratch by a briar or a thorn. With the gravest catastrophe that ever befell British arms, the roots go back a long, long time; in one sense, to Columbus.

Christopher Columbus discovered America by mistake. He was not searching for a new country, or a new world in the West, but for a new and safer route to the very rich old world of the East. The Indies and the East were at that time an irresistible magnet to enterprising British, French and Portuguese traders. They constantly sought to find quicker ways to reach Sumatra, China, the Spice Islands, for one voyage out and back could make them a fortune; the profit from two could buy a title and a great estate.

In those days, the only means of keeping beef edible during the long cold winters of northern Europe was by salting it heavily. Spices could add flavour, and at the same time disguise the taste of rotting, rancid flesh. Spices were thus in great demand to grace the kitchens of the rich. But voyages to the East to collect them were as dangerous as they were long. Sea captains lacked compasses, proper charts or accurate maps, and a round voyage might take them a year, continually dependent on the winds of Heaven and on the mercy of the Almighty to preserve them from shipwreck or pirates.

The prices merchants could charge for cargoes of spices were high, but so were the risks they faced. Apart from the natural hazards of such a long voyage, ruthless pirates in heavily armed ships would intercept homeward-bound vessels and kill their entire crews to seize the cargo and sell it as their own.

Gradually, European merchants came to private arrangements with local Indian rulers to rent or buy enclosures of land along the Indian coast. Here, on the edge of the sea, they established outposts, called factories – actually, only godowns or warehouses. Ships could unload spices here and sail back East for more, while other larger, and faster vessels carried the cargoes on to Europe.

To guard these enclaves, the trading companies recruited local Indian men, known as sepoys, from the

Persian word *sipahi*, meaning a soldier. Each company dressed their guards in uniforms, based on the soldiers' uniforms of the country concerned. Retired drill sergeants would sail East to bring discipline to these company guards as the factories grew in wealth and importance.

Soon, the original handfuls of sepoys, wearing English, French, Dutch uniforms, became private armies. Local rulers, wishing to subdue a troublesome neighbour, would engage their services, perhaps with the threat of cancelling the company's concession if they refused permission.

The British Honourable East India Company was the most successful of all these commercial concerns. Gradually, it came to control huge areas of India, without initially intending to do so. But in order to remain profitable, it was forced increasingly, and unwillingly, to become a political power in the land.

At the time of which I speak, in the 1830s, the East India Company, controlled by twenty-four directors in London, each annually elected by shareholders, governed what were known as presidencies: Calcutta, Bombay and Madras. Here they administered justice, set taxes, collected revenue. So rapidly did the Company's responsibilities multiply that, in addition to their own army, they would sometimes need to hire from the Crown regular British regiments on their tour of foreign service to ensure that insurrections or local wars did not interfere with the Company's primary purpose: to make a profit.

In Addiscombe, near Croydon, the Company founded a military academy to train British cadets for service in their army, and a college in Haileybury, Hertfordshire, to train other recruits as civil servants. The brightest volunteers studied Eastern languages so that they could draft minutes and negotiate treaties in native tongues. All this showed the Company's determination to achieve political stability in India and so ensure financial success and a correspondingly satisfactory dividend for their shareholders.

The British Government became alarmed at the Company's constantly increasing power. What had started as a purely commercial venture had become unwillingly, almost unwittingly, an arm of British policy in India.

This was the situation when I joined the Company's Bengal Army. I had recently qualified at the University of St Andrews, and after some time accompanying my local doctor on his rounds, I decided to go East.

My father was a Presbyterian minister, and we lived in a manse near his small church. I was his only son. My mother had died some years earlier.

A woman in her thirties lived in the attic: Bertha was our housekeeper, a dour, pasty-faced spinster, given to smacking her lips and shaking her head over what she considered the wickedness of the world. It never struck me then that she might resent her position and hope to become my father's second wife, but I was young and unfamiliar with the wishes and wiles of women.

We were short of money, but because our life was quiet we never really noticed this. Money has never been important to me; I have not worshipped the golden calf. I went East because I wanted colour and fun and laughter in my life, to do things I had never done: to drink wine under bright and southern stars; to ride fast horses; to know pretty women who wore beautiful clothes of silk and satin; to live life in prime and vivid colours. I was tired of the chill and mist and pettiness of a small Scottish village. Bertha would call such wishes sinful.

I had no idea of seeking my fortune, which is just as well, because I never found it. But several contemporaries of mine had already taken employment with the

East India Company and wrote back glowing accounts of life in seemingly perpetual sunshine, of being waited upon by servants, and enjoying all manner of sport – riding, shooting, hunting. As with other young Scots whose lives have been regimented from childhood by the strict bonds of religion, I wanted to escape; I wanted to be free.

I sailed to Bombay, and then went on to Calcutta. I did not know then how little friendship existed between the Company's Bombay and Bengal Armies, or that their commanders watched each other suspiciously. If they could impede a rival's promotion, they would never hesitate to do so. Nor did I know of the coolness existing between officers of the Company's armies and officers holding commissions in the regular British Army, who considered themselves to be socially superior.

I was not impressed by Calcutta, which struck me as a filthy city, but I admired the splendid houses that rich English merchants, the nabobs, had built overlooking the *maidan*, a wide expanse of grass between the city and the Hooghly River. What depressed me was the dirt and squalor just behind this theatrical façade of white pillars and porticoes.

Once, at dinner in the home of a wealthy surgeon, I enjoyed a plate of succulent, over-sized prawns. But next morning, on the river bank, I saw some Indians trying to haul in a corpse. They had secured ropes to the rotting trunk, and in pulling it ashore, the body keeled over. Underneath, it swarmed with greedy prawns, feeding on the dead. I have never eaten Calcutta prawns again.

The incidence of cholera, typhoid and other unknown fevers was so high that the average life span of Europeans in India was barely two monsoons, about eighteen months. Every summer, after the rains abated, it was the custom for Europeans to visit neighbours and leave their calling card. This was not simply a social duty: it was done as proof that they had survived another spell of heat and humidity.

I had only spent a few weeks in Calcutta when I was unexpectedly posted to join a column going to the north-west frontier of India. Normally I would have been too new and too junior to be invited to undertake such a journey, but the surgeon who should have accompanied them had fallen ill with one of those fevers of the East that defy both diagnosis and treatment.

I felt sorry for him, but glad for myself, and so, as one of the least distinguished members of what to me seemed an important band, I set off from Calcutta. I knew nothing of the customs of the country, and was surprised to receive orders that I should grow a beard and a moustache. The Pathans regarded clean-shaven men with contempt or suspicion. A smooth chin was the sign of a eunuch, or at best a man totally lacking in virility; it was not the mark of a warrior.

I had no clear idea why we were undertaking such a journey, nor, I suspect, had most of the other people in the long column; we were only told it was of great importance to the Company and therefore to our country.

I rode next to a lieutenant in his thirties. He had been passed over for promotion time and time again because he lacked money to buy a captaincy. All commissions were bought then, and the more money a man could spend on his own career, the higher the rank he could reach. Without private means, an extremely able officer could stay a lieutenant for twenty or thirty years or even throughout his entire army career.

This lieutenant was Ben Bannerman. He knew exactly where we were ultimately heading and why.

'Afghanistan,' he explained drily. 'The anus of the East. And we're going several hundred miles up it to the capital, Kabul. Our aim is to secure the overland route from Europe to India, and to keep out the Russians and the Persians.

'Our country controls every ocean through the power of our navy. But an invading army could still seize India through Afghanistan, unless we go there first and prevent them. The Persians and the Russians are both envious of our position and already have their agents in Kabul trying to win concessions for them. The Persians actually seized the town of Herat in the north to show they were serious in their intentions. Then the Afghans, under the leadership of Futteh Khan, the Afghan king's chief minister, drove them out.'

'So why are we on the march?'

'In case they come back. Afghanistan, Doctor, is the roughest, cruellest, most barren country in Asia, probably in the world. There is little there but mountains up to fifteen thousand feet high, covered by snow feet deep in the winter, and bare rocks baking like oven bricks in the summer. The people are just as harsh and unpredictable. Life isn't simply cheap: it is free. You doubt that? Then let me tell you how the Afghan king Mohammed rewarded Futteh Khan when he reported his victory over the Persians.

'First, he was scalped. Then he had his eyes pierced by the point of a dagger, and, finally, the King's men killed him – slowly, very slowly. One man cut off his left ear, another his right. Then his nose and his hands. The poor wretch was still conscious, but he did not cry out until the last insult of all – they cut off his beard. That is about the worst thing that can happen to a Muslim. Then they hacked off each foot with a sabre and finally, mercifully, cut his throat.'

'But why?' I asked him. This treatment made no

8

sense to me. After all, Futteh Khan had not failed in his mission; he had succeeded.

Bannerman shrugged. 'The King was jealous of him. Futteh Khan had shown how good a general he was. He might become too powerful and be a threat to him. So the King killed him. The womenfolk are just as cruel. If an enemy soldier is wounded in battle and left behind, they come out and cut off his cods as a warning to other soldiers to keep out of their country.'

Bannerman took an extremely harsh view of life, I thought then. But I knew so little of life that this was too easy a judgment. I liked him. He was a character. He was honest, never a time-server. He said what he thought, a quality rare among the military, and one that had not helped him to overcome the impediment of not being wealthy.

'If the Persians are out of the running, how will we persuade the Russians to keep on their side of the frontier?' I asked him.

'The Commander-in-Chief thinks that we will frighten them off. But he should know that the Russian bear does not scare easily,' he replied. 'No one who knows the country would entertain this mad scheme that takes us to Kabul, but we are ruled by people who *don't* know the country.

'In Lahore, a former King of Afghanistan, Shah Shoojah, Mohammed's brother, lives in exile. Mohammed kicked him out, and we have given him a safe haven for the past thirty years. Our plan – if anyone can dignify such muddled thinking by the name – is that we will escort Shah Shoojah to Kabul and put him back on his brother's throne. Then, out of gratitude, Shah Shoojah gets rid of all foreign emissaries, spies, agents, and whoever else whose presence could in any way detract from the size of the dividends paid to

9

the shareholders of the most honourable East India Company.'

'Will this work?' I asked.

Bannerman shrugged. 'It should not be too difficult to put him on the throne. But keeping him there, if the other chiefs don't want him, will be a totally different matter. The Afghans have similarities with you Scots. They are divided into clans, each with its own leader. And even if they rarely agree among themselves, they will always unite against strangers. And we are strangers. So I say that this plan is bound to fail. But then, apart from you, Doctor, no one has asked for my opinion.'

Bannerman told me more about the background to our involvement. In 1807, Napoleon and Tsar Nicholas I of Russia made plans to invade India. This was part of a far more ambitious proposal in which, by joining forces, they hoped to conquer the whole world and divide it between themselves as they pleased.

Napoleon would provide an army of fifty thousand French troops to invade Persia and Afghanistan, and then, united with the Cossacks, they would cross the Indus into India. But he had totally underestimated difficulties of terrain and climate: enormous mountain ranges, freezing cold, burning heat. The East was not Europe, but he did not accept that conditions were totally different. The British knew almost as little about Afghanistan. They had come to India and the Far East by sea, not by land. Belatedly, they set out to map the unknown, to pinpoint passes where enemies could gain access to India.

The British Government was alarmed by the fact that for the previous four hundred years the Russians had been increasing their empire at the astonishing rate of fifty-five square miles every day, twenty thousand square miles every year. At the start of the nineteenth century the British empire in India and the Russian empire in Asia were two thousand miles apart. But this frontier grew closer every hour; it was imperative from our point of view that they should never touch.

As we rode on, I felt a growing sense of foreboding, especially when we reached the foothills.

The sun scorched us with the focused heat of a giant burning glass, but somehow a chill remained at its heart. The warmth felt false. These valleys and mountains had seen centuries of treachery and violence. They had not forgotten a single cruelty out of thousands. The people who lived here were as cruel as their climate, and had been so since the time of the Mongols. In battle, they would herd prisoners – men, women, children, the old and the ailing – in front of their advancing troops in any attack on a moated stronghold. When they died, their bodies would fill up the moat and the Mongols would simply ride on over them.

After any victory they would seize the defeated leaders, strip them, and bind them naked on wooden planks. On top of these boards they placed other planks to form a stage or platform. Here they would set out their tables for a victory feast, slowly crushing the bodies of the vanquished beneath them as they caroused. They had never been conquered. We were from the West, infidels, people without the faith. I could only guess at our fate if they united against us and defeated us.

I did not consider that I personally might be wounded or even killed, but gradually my confidence in our leadership diminished and died. It soon became clear, even though I knew nothing of strategy, that no serious plans had been made for this invasion.

The Company's Bombay Army, 4,500 strong, went by sailing ship to land five hundred miles north-west in Karachi, which was not then British territory and was ruled by the wild Amir of Sind. The troops landed under fire from the Amir's army – simply because no one had thought to inform him of their arrival. The troops then marched three hundred miles in heavy serge uniforms, enduring temperatures so great that water spilling on the burning rocks boiled immediately. Finally, they met us in the Bengal Army, 9,500 strong.

We had meanwhile marched six hundred miles south-west from our depot in Ferozepore, which was actually only four hundred miles from Kabul. So we all marched one and a half times this distance *in the wrong direction* before we both headed towards our objective!

Shoojah's personal levies, cavalry, infantry, and horse artillery, possibly six thousand men, meant that our total force, under the splendid title of Army of the Indus, was about twenty thousand men, and twice this number when camp followers were added. We could not rely on finding provisions in this bleak and hostile land and so had to drive enough meat on the hoof to last us for two and a half months, and in addition we needed to carry one month's supply of grain for our horses.

Shoojah decided he required one thousand camels simply to carry his personal belongings and those of his courtiers. Our general used a further two hundred and sixty camels for his luggage and that of his immediate staff. Brigadiers made do with sixty camels each, and colonels, fifty. As a surgeon, I was allowed five to carry my medical stores.

Bannerman and I obeyed orders to travel light. Most other officers did not. They took with them such impedimenta as ceremonial swords, dressing cases, crystal bottles of eau de cologne and perfumes, Windsor soap in silver caskets. One regiment demanded two camels simply to carry cigars for their officers' mess.

Other camels were loaded with jams, pickles, meat and fish in hermetically sealed glass jars, and table linen. Of course, every officer had his own tent, which meant that more camels were carrying tables, chairs, carpets, rugs, even sideboards. We had a total of thirty thousand camels bellowing in rage every morning at the indignity of being loaded with kit and supplies.

'You know what's really wrong?' Bannerman asked me as we rode side by side. 'Apart from taking along all this totally useless junk, there is simply not enough fodder for our camels to eat on the way. We're going through hills, valleys, deserts, plains – very little there but bare lava and dust. Thousands will starve to death.'

This is exactly what happened. Camels proved to be terrified of heights, and would not venture up the slightest slope, even if this presented the possibility of grazing. Many died through eating poisonous plants and weeds alongside the rough track we followed. Instead of these useless animals, we should have taken mules and donkeys, or local ponies known as yaboos, hardy beasts that could march for thirty miles a day carrying three-hundredweight loads and still not tire.

In the furnace-like heat, wearing shakos and scarlet serge coatees with swallowtails, and tight serge trousers, our troops presented easy targets for roving bands of robbers who followed us, high up on the hillsides, out of range of our old-fashioned muskets. They killed in the hope of looting a few trinkets or coins from a dead soldier.

Political officers attached to our column bribed local rulers to sell us food, but Shoojah's troops also needed food. Soon our two forces were bidding desperately against each other for the same crops. We thus paid possibly ten times the price for fodder not worth buying at any price.

The country was barren; locals lived at starvation

level; it was impossible for them to feed forty thousand strangers. Even when we reached Kabul we would still be locked in the heart of a maze of hostile mountains, deserts and plains. Our nearest British outpost would be the mud fortress town of Jalalabad, 110 miles away.

On the march, our column stretched for forty miles. When the head halted to pitch camp for the night, the tail had barely moved off from the previous night's camp. Worse, it soon became clear from Afghans we met that virtually all held Shoojah in total contempt. They had driven him out once thirty years ago; they did not want him back now.

'Our king is Dost Mohammed,' they told us time and again, and laughed at our claim that Shoojah was really their rightful monarch.

The earth was harsh and hard and dry and so mixed with salt that it crackled like glass under the feet of the horses. Camels died by the thousand of hunger, dropping without warning, scattering their loads, which robbers rode down from the hills to seize as they fell. We could not spare time and energy to fight them off; it was all we could do to keep going. We had to let them loot as they pleased and hope they would go away. They didn't. The Bolan pass, sixty miles long, took us six days to go through, and all the time robbers on sure-footed ponies rode above us, on either side, firing down on us indiscriminately as we forced our way through piles of tents, chairs, carpets and the corpses of the camels, abandoned by the leading troops in the column.

As we approached Kabul, we expected a set battle with the forces of Dost Mohammed, King of Afghanistan, but to our amazement the Afghans melted away. What persuaded them to retreat was a charge by five British officers leading a unit of native cavalry.

Quite unexpectedly, they had come across a detach-

14

ment of Dost Mohammed's army, and rode right at them, believing that their troops would follow. Instead, the native cavalry slowed to a trot, then to a walk, and finally turned and fled. The Afghans instantly cut to pieces all five officers, but their heroism had greatly impressed Dost Mohammed. If five British riders could fight so bravely against hopeless odds, how ferocious would a whole army be? He surrendered, and our generals foolishly thought we had won without a fight. In fact, we had only won time. Dost Mohammed now was technically our prisoner; in fact, he was our guest, and treated as such, although accommodated some miles from the capital.

To achieve this so-called victory, we had lost hundreds of men, British and Indian, and twenty thousand baggage camels on the march, with everything they were carrying. I was assured that such losses were acceptable, and our arrival was hailed as a great victory and celebrated by a peerage for the general, with baronetcies and knighthoods for less senior officers.

To my surprise, the Afghans in Kabul appeared friendly to us. We played cricket matches against them. As the weather changed, and lakes froze over, our regimental blacksmiths made skates and we taught them to skate. We enjoyed amateur dramatics together and organised horse races. The 16th Lancers even brought along their pack of foxhounds. In the middle of all these amiable diversions, our army commanders quite forgot the reason we were there – to keep our sponsored King, Shah Shoojah, on the throne and hold Afghanistan against any foreign invasion or infiltration from Persia and Russia.

We needed to find more permanent quarters for our troops; they could not live in tents in freezing winter temperatures. The best site was Bala Hissar fortress, so large that it was really a small town, set on top of a hill overlooking Kabul. This could easily be made impregnable, and at very little expense.

But Shoojah objected. He pointed out that since the fortress physically looked down on his palace, it would demonstrate to all how totally he depended on the British for survival. Largely to humour him, it was agreed to build a cantonment elsewhere, where we could be quartered.

The site finally selected was the worst possible choice: a swamp two miles north-east of Kabul, with the Kabul River on one side and a wide stagnant canal on the other. It measured about 600 yards by 1,000, surrounded by a ditch, and quite indefensible. It lacked space for the commissariat, so all stores – food, ammunition, and everything our army needed – were kept in an old fort two miles away.

Orders were now given that wives and families of the British and Indian troops could be sent for. They all duly arrived in Kabul, and the Afghans realised with a shock that we were planning to stay indefinitely, not simply for a short time, as for some reason they originally imagined was our intention.

Many British officers had begun liaisons with Afghan women which were precipitately abandoned when the officers' wives arrived. There is no greater coward than a philandering husband who fears that his wife may discover his infidelities. The Afghan attitude towards sexual matters is summarised in their saying: 'A woman for children, a boy for pleasure, a melon for sheer delight.' I need not go further into what this meant for young and amorous Afghan women married to homosexual husbands. They had been delighted to take their pleasure with the vigorous young men of our army.

When the affairs ended so suddenly, the women needed convincing excuses why it would be unacceptable to continue to entertain British officers in their homes. For the most part, the Afghan husbands had no idea their wives had been unfaithful. The wives therefore concocted plausible reasons for not inviting the officers to their homes. The easiest explanation – and always accepted – was that the officers had somehow insulted them or their families or Islam, or all three. This naturally increased hostility to all of us.

I had not seen much of my travelling companion Bannerman since we reached Kabul. His duties took him outside the city, but in the week after the first of the wives arrived, he came over to my quarters. I was smoking a cigar, feeling at a loose end, and out of sorts. The presence of other men's womenfolk makes a single man feel uneasily conscious of being unloved and alone.

'Join me in a whisky,' I suggested to Bannerman, very pleased to see him.

'No,' he said, shaking his head. 'You come over to my place. Have supper with me.'

We walked over to his quarters on the far side of the cantonment. The night was warm. In the sudden rush of the dark that ends each day in Afghanistan, the hills stood out for an instant like a towering black line of rock against the dying sun. Then darkness swallowed them up.

Bannerman had a small three-roomed house. I remember this as clearly as if I had visited it only yesterday. Dark red rugs covered the floor, and brass oil lamps, wicks neatly trimmed, cast a gentle glow on the simple furnishings.

And coming from an inner room to welcome me was the most beautiful woman I had ever seen.

She wore a long white dress. Her red hair was piled high on her head with a tortoiseshell comb, in the fashion of the time. Her face was sensitive, alert. I was

17

so astonished to see such a lovely person there, so incongruous in her beauty in that primitive place, that I simply stood and stared at her, almost in disbelief that she could be real.

'Darling,' said Bannerman gently to her. 'I would like you to meet the physician and good friend I have told you so much about. Dr Douglas Kintyre. My wife, Anna.'

'My pleasure, ma'am,' I said, and as I spoke I hardly recognised my own voice. I was not simply looking at her; I was devouring her with my eyes. I had never seen anyone so lovely.

'I didn't even know you were married,' I found myself saying rather ungallantly.

'Ah,' Bannerman replied, grinning. 'I thought we might be parted for years. There seemed no point in talking about a wife when she's not with you.'

'How long has there been a Mrs Bannerman, then?'

'We met and married before we left Ferozepore. Just before you and I met, in fact. Anyhow, enough of that. Do come in. A sherry? Madeira? I have them both.'

You have everything now, I thought enviously. I sat down in the shadows where I could see his wife more clearly in the light of the lamps, without my scrutiny being apparent. I don't know what we talked about, but I felt we were talking on two levels. I know I was thinking on two levels. I had been in Ferozepore for a month. Why hadn't *I* met Anna, instead of this passed-over lieutenant? I knew at that moment of first sight Anna was everything I would ever want in a woman. And at the same time I sensed she was someone I would never have.

I must have taken part in the conversation, but what we talked about eludes me now. All I can remember is this remarkable woman, and the radiance that surrounded her, like a halo.

From that first evening spent together, the three of us would meet frequently, either in their house or in my quarters. Bannerman, despite his knowledge of the cruelty of the Afghans, soon became friendly with several of the King's relatives. I also met them frequently at his house. My bachelor quarters were so small they were not suitable for any sort of social gathering.

Their manners were civilised and courtly. They spoke English well and it was difficult to believe they could be compatriots of the Afghan robbers who had ridden alongside us on the way north, sniping at stragglers, robbing the dead, the dying, and any who fell behind on the march.

One impressed me especially. He was a cousin or some equally close relation of Dost Mohammed, named Akyab Khan. He was an extremely good chess player, and would sometimes partner Bannerman against Anna and me. Invariably, they would beat us.

He was cultured, and knowledgeable about all manner of unexpected matters, such as herbal remedies, and the way Afghan physicians had of treating illnesses, not with physic, but simply by pricking the patient's skin with a sliver of bamboo or a golden needle.

I thought this ridiculous, until I saw that it worked, and my respect for Akyab Khan increased accordingly. It was almost impossible to imagine that only months previously we had been on opposite sides, and might have killed each other on sight. War and death seemed far away now; these people were not our former foes, they were our new friends.

Anna Bannerman loved flowers and birds. She would often ride out for miles with Akyab and an Afghan groom, or sometimes only with a groom, and bring back strange exotic blossoms which faded almost as soon as they were cut. I am not a poetic person by nature, but it seemed to me that these swiftly dying flowers symbolised human feelings that so often change or die with equal speed. Somehow, this thought depressed me, but why, I knew not, and I did not mention my feelings to anyone else. Perhaps it might have been better for us all if I had. She pressed the petals between the pages of books, and explained their significance to her husband and to me, where she had found them, and how they differed from plants in Britain.

Anna was confident that no harm would come to her on any of these rides, and indeed none did. But this did not mean that harm was not just over the horizon for all of us.

The general who had commanded us on the march to Kabul was replaced by Major-General William Elphinstone, of very different calibre. I had to visit him on the day he came to Kabul. He was sixty years old, fat and crippled by gout and dysentery. What concerned me most was that this weak and enfeebled man was in supreme command of our army. Our lives were literally in his hands.

I prescribed what treatment I could, and had just returned to my quarters when Anna Bannerman came to see me.

'A social visit?' I asked her hopefully.

She had never called on her own to see me, always with her husband. It was not the custom for any wife to visit the quarters of a bachelor unchaperoned.

'No,' she said, smiling. 'Professional. That is why I am on my own.'

'You're not ill, I hope, Anna?'

'Far from it. I have never felt better, but I must

admit to symptoms of an event many married women seek, but not all find.'

'You mean you are expecting a baby?'

She nodded. 'Yes. I have missed two courses. I've also been sick these last three mornings.'

'Sit down,' I told her.

I would have liked to examine her but something made me hold back. I have examined many women, young and old, as every doctor must, but have never felt desire towards them or indeed any sexual interest in their naked bodies. Now I *wanted* to see Anna naked; I *wanted* to stroke and caress her, and I knew I could not trust myself to see her unclothed. I contented Anna by giving her vague advice about resting after meals and not taking undue exercise.

'Can I still go riding?' she asked me.

'Many women in your condition do ride side-saddle for a month or two,' I told her. 'But I would be very careful, especially here, with the extremes of climate.'

'I'd miss riding,' she admitted, with a faraway look in her eyes.

'You'll miss the flowers, I suppose?'

'The flowers?' Anna looked at me for a moment, as though not quite understanding what I meant, and then she nodded vigorously. 'Of course. The flowers. Yes, if I give up riding I'll miss so many things.'

I wanted her to stay, and yet I wanted her to go. My feelings were so complex, so strong, I feared I might do something I had never done before any woman. I might have wept, because the woman I loved was bearing another man's child.

Weeks, months passed. General Elphinstone's health worsened steadily. Not only was he unfit to command an army, he could not control the natural functions of his own body. He was unable to stagger from his bed unless supported by two orderlies, and

21

then he would need at least half an hour to gather his thoughts and his energies sufficiently to hold a conversation on even the most superficial level.

To deal with political matters he had two subordinate colleagues. Sir William McNaghten, the senior, had the title of Envoy. He had joined the East India Company in his teens as a cadet, and was remarkably fluent in several Indian languages. He became a judge and passed examinations in both Hindu and Mohammedan law. In my view, he was more Indian than any real Indian. Like many Europeans who became so closely immersed in native matters and customs, he could see no evil whatever in anyone with a dark skin. The rest of us might consider that some of them, especially Bengalis, were of a devious turn of mind, but not MacNaghten. Indians – or Afghans – could do no wrong.

MacNaghten's deputy was Sir Alexander Burnes who had been knighted at the age of thirty and promoted to colonel as a mark of the Government's approval of his abilities. He was a Scot who, like MacNaghten, had mastered several local languages early on and was so efficient that by the age of eighteen he had become his regiment's adjutant.

Burnes had undertaken several secret spying trips for the Company in the Punjab and Afghanistan. Now, above all else, he wanted to succeed MacNaghten as Envoy. This seemed certain, because MacNaghten was suddenly appointed Governor of Bombay and planned to leave within the next few weeks.

Meanwhile, Dost Mohammed removed himself from our very lax custody and, to everyone's surprise, arrived in Kabul to see MacNaghten, who took this as a mark of friendship and good faith. He did not appear to realise that a popular ex-king in Kabul, alongside an unpopular king on the throne, could prove dangerous to British policy. But because Elphinstone was too enfeebled to raise the point with MacNaghten, no one else did.

Now reports began to arrive of our soldiers on detachment having their throats cut, their rifles seized, their tents burned down, and beasts of burden stolen. Because of the siting of our commissariat, we were all totally dependent on the good will of local Afghans for access to food, water and ammunition. We were reluctant to antagonise them by dealing severely with the perpetrators of these crimes, even if we could catch them. Often we could not, because witnesses were afraid to talk.

Burnes lived in a large house known as the Residency, outside the cantonment wall. His servants and several Afghan friends all warned him that revolution was imminent, and, in view of his importance, he would be one of the first to be killed. But like the Envoy, Burnes could not believe these reports. He was vain and a philanderer. He had seduced literally dozens of Afghan women. Husbands, brothers and fathers now began to learn of his affairs – how, I know not – and announced they were prepared to kill him for dishonouring their womenfolk. He refused to believe this; like MacNaghten, he was blinkered to reality.

Then, one November morning, he saw a crowd of forty armed men gathered outside his gates. He sent a message to Elphinstone asking for urgent reinforcements to help the Residency guard which consisted of only a handful of men. Elphinstone ignored his request, not out of malice but simply because he could never make up his mind on any matter that required a quick decision. His attitude was always to do nothing precipitate, to let events run their course in the hope that then someone else would decide what to do.

Soon the forty men had increased to a thousand. They claimed they were there on a matter of honour. Actually, they wanted money stored in the Residency cellars; they also wanted blood, and Burnes dead.

When British troops did not arrive to send them on their way, they set fire to Burnes's stables, killed the guards and all the European officers, except for Burnes and his younger brother. One of the Afghans came into the Residency through a back door and swore by the Koran that if Burnes would only come out with him into the garden, they would all disperse. Burnes was foolish enough to believe this and, dressed in native clothes, as was his habit, he went down to meet them.

As soon as the mob saw him, they rushed forward and cut him and his brother to pieces within seconds. Burnes covered his eyes with a cloth so he would not see who struck the first blow.

Now, thousands more poured out from the hills and surrounded our cantonment. Instead of turning out the troops or even sending urgently for MacNaghten, who lived only a few hundred yards away, to seek his opinion as to the best way of dealing with this very dangerous situation, Elphinstone sat down and dictated a letter to him which he had delivered by hand.

'We must see what the morning brings,' Elphinstone wrote with characteristic procrastination. 'Then we can think what can be done.'

Morning brought much worse news. The rebels easily overran the fort that contained our provisions and ammunition. We now had three days' food left in the cantonment, and very little ammunition. Worse, we had no plan, but literally stood and watched impotently as the Afghans looted everything the fort contained.

MacNaghten now suggested we should retreat from

Kabul to Jalalabad. He said that if we withdrew he could persuade the rebels not to attack us.

A far better plan would have been to leave the cantonment, which was totally indefensible, and move to Bala Hissar, the fort on the hill, and hold out there until reinforcements came. But to do this would have meant abandoning buildings that had been expensive to construct. MacNaghten said that this was unthinkable, although under his proposal we would abandon everything, including our credibility.

Elphinstone neither agreed nor disagreed. His deputy, Brigadier Shelton, held him in such contempt that at the meetings Elphinstone called every day – with nothing decided at any of them – Shelton would have his orderly bring in his bedding roll and lie down on it on the ground. If the general asked his opinion, Shelton's only reply would be a snore, pretending he was asleep.

Shelton's contempt for Elphinstone was only equalled by his hatred of MacNaghten. These three men, locked in mutual dislike, controlled the destiny of forty thousand men, women and children. Bannerman and I were disgusted at this behaviour and exasperated by Elphinstone's weakness. A stronger man would have sent Shelton on his way immediately; but then a stronger character would never have allowed the military situation to deteriorate so dangerously.

We were soon so short of meat that we had to shoot ponies and camels and cut the carcasses into steaks. Our horses had no fodder at all: they survived by eating bark from trees and twigs, even gnawing wooden tent pegs.

Finally, after many inconclusive meetings, MacNaghten decided he must commence negotiations for our safe passage out to Jalalabad or we would starve to death where we were. The man he believed could arrange this retreat was Akbar Khan, Dost Moham-med's son.

Akbar Khan proposed another scheme. The British should remain in the country for nearly a year, and then leave in good order, instead of retreating now in humiliation and disorder. In return, he asked for a British Government pension of 400,000 rupees a year for life for himself, and a cash sum of 3,000,000 rupees. Shoojah would stay on the throne, but Akbar would be his vizier or chief minister. Other Afghan chieftains with whom MacNaghten had already signed agree-ments of friendship and co-operation would be deposed or abandoned.

If he agreed to this, MacNaghten knew he would break faith with them. If he did not agree, the whole garrison would literally starve to death. MacNaghten felt he had no option but to fall in with Akbar Khan's proposal and signed a memorandum in Persian to this effect.

Next day, he rode out with two colleagues to meet Akbar Khan and sign the formal agreement. Elphin-stone had promised him an escort but typically had neglected to give the necessary orders and so the troops were not ready. They therefore rode alone.

About 350 yards from the cantonment I saw that the Afghans had spread out carpets on the ground for the meeting. Akbar was already there. Suddenly a crowd of Afghans, armed with pistols and swords, encircled them.

I heard a cry, '*Begeer*! Seize!'

Immediately, Akbar shot MacNaghten. His body was carried away, dismembered and mutilated and then dragged through the streets of Kabul at the end of a rope. His companions were seized and imprisoned.

Akbar informed General Elphinstone that his orig-inal conditions for giving the British force safe conduct to India had changed. He demanded that all the money in the cantonment treasury should be handed over to him personally, that we abandon Shoojah, and march out, leaving behind our big guns. Weakly, Elphinstone agreed to these ruinous proposals.

I immediately started to pack up my medical equipment on the five camels, which had survived. Subalterns who had ridden north with as many as forty servants each – cooks, bearers, sweepers, *dhobis* or washermen, grass-cutters, cobblers, tailors, blacksmiths, boys to work the bellows for the blacksmiths, even fiddlers to keep the camp followers amused after hours – now wished they had obeyed orders and travelled light.

Fortunes in mess silver, crystal glasses and decanters, ornamental silver candlesticks and carpets had to be abandoned. Rather than leave everything to the looters, we burned as much as we could: chests of drawers, cupboards, sideboards, easy chairs. I saw Anna burning books and magazines and the wind blew a few charred pages towards me. I picked up one from *Pilgrim's Progress*. It described the death of Mr Valiant-for-Truth as he crosses the river of death: 'And so he passed over, and all the trumpets sounded for him on the other side.'

I handed the page to Anna.

'I love those words,' she said.

'I'd rather stay on this side of the river,' I replied, trying to make light of the moment. It seemed to me to be disturbingly prophetic; I threw the leaf on the fire, wishing I had never seen it.

Flames fuelled by so much oiled and wax-polished wood and books rose to prodigious heights, but they generated little warmth. The cold season was upon us. Within days, the land would be in the iron grip of winter. The thermometer outside my quarters already registered thirty-eight degrees of frost, and this was only the beginning. We might escape starvation if we left, but we would risk freezing to death on our journey. The Afghans had easily and totally outmanoeuvred us.

Our uniforms, while far too thick for a hot climate, were equally unsuited for the cold we would have to endure. Afghans who had thrown in their lot with us early on and guessed they would now suffer painful deaths if they stayed behind, ripped into strips horse blankets or clothes torn from dead men and wrapped them round their legs and feet to prevent frostbite. This seemed wise, but senior officers to whom I suggested it were contemptuous.

'We're soldiers,' one replied shortly. 'We will march in boots, not in rags.'

So they did, and within a day nearly every soldier suffered from severe frostbite. The Indian troops and camp followers had come from the hot plains; cold like this was beyond their comprehension. Their feet froze in their army boots, and their toes dropped off their feet. So intense was the cold that at the time they did not feel any pain. That came later. Unable to march, even to hobble, they had to be left at the roadside to freeze to death.

Each doctor took control of a number of ill and wounded. Some of the pregnant women came under my care. I was relieved at this because Anna Bannerman was very near her time.

For the week before we left, food was so short that soldiers were limited to one meal a day: half a cup of flour, moistened with liquid *ghee*, a native rancid butter, or *dhal*, a pulse of vegetables. Noncombatants had to make do with much less. Starving camels bellowed with fury at being both heavily laden and unfed. Horses and mules became frantic with hunger.

28

Grooms had to scoop up droppings and feed them to the pack animals.

We should have left Kabul at sunrise, but even on this vital point General Elphinstone could not make up his mind. Should we go then, or should we wait a little longer? Brigadier Shelton had been told late on the previous evening that we would march at dawn, and given orders to load our two thousand remaining camels by moonrise. But such was his sloth and the gross indiscipline of subordinates, who took their cue from his behaviour, that nothing was done. By ten o'clock in the morning, when we should have been miles on our way, General Elphinstone was still taking breakfast.

Finally, we set off, but so long was our column, with its train of mules and camels, that by late afternoon, when the advance guard was several miles out in the snow, the body of our army still lingered in Kabul. Now came an unexpected obstacle: a river, swollen with snow.

'It's fordable,' a subaltern pointed out, and rode through the icy water to prove it. But General Elphinstone, who was not on horseback but being conveyed on a litter, or *doolie*, decided this was impractical. Instead, he ordered gun limbers to be brought up and used them to build a crude bridge across the river. While this was underway, thousands of us waited in freezing snow already two feet deep.

When the bridge was ready, camp followers, mad with cold and terror, surged forward, fighting to use it ahead of the troops. Men clubbed each other to death for the privilege of crossing the stream on a mass of limbers already sinking into the river bed.

Now, General Elphinstone issued other orders: the march should be postponed. He explained that Afghan soldiers had been promised as our escort, but they had not arrived. We must await their arrival. So some began to march back into the cantonment while others, impatient to be away, marched on defiantly. I was with these columns; so was the general, despite his own orders.

Buglers blew 'Advance' and 'Retire' alternately. Against these contradictory calls came a crackle of fire from the long-barrelled rifles, known as *juzails*, in the hands of Afghan robbers. They thought it unlikely they would ever again have such an opportunity for plunder. They were determined not to let it pass them by. Behind us, our cantonment, constructed at such cost to the Company and the government, was already ablaze.

The general had most unwisely ordered that, as a gesture of good faith, our horse artillery guns, as well as the cannon Akbar had demanded, should be left behind. Now the Afghans wheeled them out and prepared to fire upon us with our own ammunition. We would have been annihilated had not Providence come to our aid.

While one group of Afghans struggled to load the guns, others lit fires under the freezing barrels. These burned through the wooden spokes of the wheels. So before the guns could be fired, they collapsed uselessly.

In the darkening hills all around, we saw little flickers of flame from rifle muzzles: skilled Afghan marksmen were picking off our soldiers, one by one. Our troops seemed too bemused to fire back. They trudged on, heads down, as though they neither saw nor heard. Cold had numbed their minds as well as their muscles. Speech became painful. As they formed words, their lips cracked and split and bled. Within seconds their lifeblood froze on their flesh like scarlet ice.

I ordered that fat should be cut from the flanks of dead ponies and rubbed into their lips and faces to stop these cracks, but this was only partly successful.

Soon, I counted more than one hundred dead soldiers in the snow, either shot by the snipers or frozen. I rode up to the *doolie* where General Elphinstone lay beneath layers of rugs and furs. In the normal course of events, I, as a junior surgeon, would never have access to an officer of his seniority. But nothing about our situation was normal. I saluted him.

'With respect, sir,' I said, 'we are being attacked on both sides in the rear. Can we not halt, form a square and return their fire before it is too late?'

He looked at me, his face yellow, lined with pain. He was beyond all comprehension of our plight.

'See the brigadier,' he replied weakly. 'I am too ill to take command.'

I rode forward along the column, and then back, but I could not find Shelton. Indeed, I never saw him again.

Snow was falling more thickly now, and gradually the whole column slowed, then stopped. A further braying of bugles sounded contrary calls. The troops paid no attention. Hundreds simply lay down where they stood, and I saw from the way they threw themselves on the snow, careless of the cold, they were at the point of death. No danger, no discomfort, could affect them now. They had lost their spirit. That night they lost their lives.

I rode back along the column. A few of the men were erecting tents, working slowly, like sleepwalkers. Barely were the canvas sides and roofs in place than many collapsed. The ground was frozen too hard for the pegs to hold the guy ropes. There was no attempt to site the tents neatly in rows, or to light fires to cook a meal. There was no firewood, no kindling, no leadership, nothing but snow.

So much frozen snow had clung to the horses' hooves that the grooms had to hack it away with hammers and chisels. Breath froze in our mouths and nostrils; we had icicles in our moustaches and beards. More snow began to fall, not gentle flakes like I remembered from Scottish winters, but flakes hard and sharp like chips of broken glass. Each breath was painful; the tiny hairs in our nostrils turned to icy needles.

And all the while, as this listless, defeated column crouched in the gathering dusk, Afghans rode past, firing at us from the saddle. A number of our camp followers abandoned their loads and melted away to join the Afghans, relying for safety on their dark skins and their Muslim faith. It did not matter to them on whose side they fought, or under whose flag, as long as they survived.

I helped some private soldiers set up a crude shelter, made of strips of canvas, for the wounded and the women. I had some lucifers with me, and an orderly produced a few sticks he had packed in a pouch and a copy of a newspaper, six months old. This gave us a fire which we kept going by burning the packs thrown to one side by men too exhausted or too ill to carry them further.

On the march next day, hundreds more soldiers, camp followers, wives and families, trudging through snow up to their knees, collapsed and fell from hunger and weariness or victims of Afghan bullets. Some lay still, shot through the head; others writhed, kicking legs and arms in the terrible extremity of death.

Snow which moments before had been white and virgin was now red with blood, dotted by fallen bodies. A fearful barking came from hundreds of wild pariah dogs. These had lived for months on dung and ordure in the city and they surged past us in packs, teeth bared, desperate for a feast of meat. They set upon the dead and dying, tearing mouthfuls of flesh from their bodies and made off, snarling, with chunks of human bodies dripping blood in their jaws.

We moved on. I wanted to be as certain as I could that nothing went wrong at the birth of Anna Bannerman's baby, so I rode on the left of the *doolie* on which she lay. Ben, her husband, rode on her right. She wore her warmest clothes and bore the constant jogging of the bearers without complaint.

A breeze began to blow, gently at first and then with an insane, immeasurable ferocity. We could not see anything more than a few feet from us: the driven snow felt hard and thick as a wall. We felt lost in a world of ice and despair.

Chapter Two

Chapter Two

On the fourth day out, the snow stopped falling for upwards of an hour. A few trees, wild almonds and junipers, stood out proudly from the sunlit white wastes. For a moment our predicament was forgotten in our awe at the majestic beauty of the scene. The only sounds were the crunch of thousands of marching feet and the blowing of camels, the whinnying of mules.

Then, under the wide, curving blueness of the sky, we saw fifty horsemen coming towards us. They must have been following us, unseen because of the blizzard. Now their time had come: our wretched, dispirited column lay at their mercy. They held their rifles high in their left hands and white spumes of frozen snow trailed from the hooves of their horses. One senior officer belatedly realised the danger. He halted the troops nearest to him and ordered them to take up positions of defence. A handful of soldiers reluctantly unslung their rifles and went down on one knee in the snow to take better aim. A corporal shouted: 'Fire!'

Two horsemen fell with a great clatter of accoutrements. Their horses rolled over, kicking their legs in the air. The rest galloped on, aiming straight for us – for the sick and wounded.

Many in the *doolies* would die within days in any case; I could not understand why the Afghans would wish to waste bullets killing them now. Shots crackled all around like dry twigs breaking. The soldier next to me dropped, blood pouring from his mouth. Ben Bannerman drew his pistol from his saddle holster and began to fire over the top of Anna's *doolie*. Then he reloaded and rode out to meet them, armed only with a pistol that in these circumstances we both knew was little better than a ceremonial toy.

I seized the dead soldier's rifle, fired it wildly at the nearest horseman. They were all firing at us now, taking aim as they rode. Bannerman suddenly threw up his hands. His pistol dropped in the snow as his horse reared up and fell back on him. I guessed horse and rider were both dead.

I heard Anna scream. From the *doolie* she had seen her husband die. Five Afghans now separated from the main body and rode towards us. I had no means of protecting her. Without ammunition, my rifle was only useful as a club. I grabbed it by the muzzle.

And then the riders paused. The leader wore a leather coat, a mail breastplate, and a leather helmet with a metal visor which had a horizontal slit cut for his eyes to serve as protection against snow blindness as much as against the enemy.

He reined in his animal and pushed the visor up on his forehead. Akyab Khan, who had so often been a guest of the Bannermans and with whom I had enjoyed so many evenings of chess and conversation, sat looking down at us. All Bannerman's early warnings about the cruelty and treachery of Afghans surged though my mind. So this was how Akyab Khan was repaying hospitality and friendship – by murdering his former host.

Hatred consumed me like fire.

'Kill that traitor!' I shouted. '*Kill him!*'

I looked at Anna and saw amazement, horror, disbelief – and something else in her expression: a yearning, as if she actually wanted to speak to this murderer. Grief had unhinged her mind. She was half sitting up in the *doolie*.

'Get down!' I shouted at her. 'Get down!'

I threw the rifle at Akyab Khan's horse. The animal whinnied and reared up and backed away.

'Give yourselves up!' he shouted to me. 'I will offer you both safe conduct.'

'Safe conduct to the grave!' I shouted back furiously. 'You have just shot a man who looked on you as a friend. Better to die of cold than by your torturers!'

Had I possessed even one bullet I could have killed him, and would have done, regardless of the armed men who rode with him. But I was powerless, and he knew it.

At that moment one of our soldiers fired at him. The bullet hit him in his right arm. For a moment he paused, as though he would repeat his insulting offer, and then he turned and rode back to the main body, not apparently in any hurry, not galloping or even trotting, simply walking his horse. He might have been on parade. I hated him, but I had to admire him. He had courage, he had style. With a leader like him, we would not have been in this total and humiliating disarray.

Then he and all his horsemen took off and rode away up the hill, vanishing in a white mist of snow kicked up by the hooves. The whole episode had lasted only a few minutes.

I walked over to Ben Bannerman's body. He had been shot through the head. His horse had rolled on him and crushed his chest. He would have died even if the rifleman had missed. I bent down, took his pistol from the snow and searched through his jacket pockets for anything of value or sentiment his widow might treasure.

37

He was carrying very little: a silver pocket watch, a lawn handkerchief, a few rupee notes in a metal clip. I stood bareheaded by his body for a moment, praying as I had not prayed since I left the manse. I followed no formal set of words, only a request for mercy on the soul of my good friend, on the widow he had left behind, and on his child, as yet unborn.

I prayed that the little boy or girl would have a different life than their father, who had known many disappointments and whose talents had never had the chance to flower.

As I stood in the snow, and behind me the column started to march again, I little guessed how my prayer would be answered.

I brought the handkerchief, the rupees and the watch to Anna Bannerman. She was lying back now, eyes closed. I saw she had been weeping. I placed the items under her pillow.

'Was it quick?' she asked softly, not opening her eyes.

'He died like a soldier,' I said. 'Yes.'

'Thank God. And Akyab Khan? Is he also dead?'

'No,' I said shortly. 'He has only a flesh wound. After those evenings we all used to spend together so enjoyably, he shows his real nature. I cannot understand such behaviour. It is unbelievable.'

Anna nodded weakly. 'Yes,' she agreed. 'It is all unbelievable. But then in life so many things are.'

I sensed she wanted to say more, but then she simply shook her head. Tears coursed down her cheeks. I closed the curtains of her *doolie* so that no one could intrude on her grief, and rode on, consumed by my thoughts.

By the eighth day of our journey we had less than a hundred camels left. Men, women and children, hungry and ill-attired for a journey in thick snow, were dying even more quickly. As we came through defiles, the bodies of the advance guard, humans and animals, lay where they had fallen, unburied, frozen stiff in attitudes of the march. Dead men held up their arms as though warding off a last attack. Camels and ponies lay frozen in groups, half buried in snow. A trail of looted belongings led up the hills on either side. Greedy robbers had seized more than they could carry and dropped half their pillage as they ran.

Sometimes, dying men screamed at us, beseeching us to kill them and put them out of their misery. But we looked the other way, and marched on, leaving them to be castrated and dismembered. We knew this would be their fate, and so did they, but we could not commit murder. There was always the hope they might survive. Death, like birth, we had to leave to the will of the Almighty.

Anna Bannerman had spoken little since Ben's death. Now and then she would raise herself on an elbow and scan the frozen expanse on both sides of the track as though somehow miraculously she would see Ben riding towards her. Then she would sink back and close her eyes. Often I saw tears trickle down her face unchecked. On the ninth day she called out to me.

'Douglas,' she said in an urgent whisper. 'My pains have started.'

It was late afternoon. I glanced at my watch; we would be halting within the hour. I soothed her as best I could, and when the column stopped I had a tent pitched immediately and brought her into it. She lay down thankfully on a small carpet I had unrolled across the snow. I called to a captain's wife to come and help me with the birth. About two hours later, as the regimental buglers sounded 'Lights out', with our only light a candle, and wiping our hands on snow because we had no water to wash, we delivered Anna of a male child.

'What does he look like?' Anna asked me weakly.

'Handsome,' I assured her, as doctors always tell new mothers. 'He'll be the best-looking man in England when he grows up.'

'We're not in England,' she said flatly. 'And I don't think I'll ever see England again.'

'Of course you will. Now, have a look at him for yourself.'

The captain's wife and I supported Anna as she peered at the baby.

'He's dark,' she said.

'Nonsense,' I said. 'It's dark in here, that's all. Look.'

I held a candle near the baby's face. His skin glowed in the gentle light.

'You're right,' she agreed happily. 'He will be handsome, I'm sure.'

'Takes after his father,' the captain's wife declared. 'And you.'

Anna smiled happily. 'Thank you,' she said. 'I only wish his father was here to see him.'

She sat up, looking at the child, while my helper wrapped the baby up against the cold as best she could in strips torn from one of Bannerman's linen shirts. Then Anna lay back satisfied, her eyes closed.

'I'm not well,' she said after a few minutes, in a very quiet, still voice.

'You'll feel better directly,' I assured her with a confidence I did not altogether feel. I had nothing nourishing to give her, not a sip of beef tea, or even a teaspoonful of calves' foot jelly to restore lost strength. However, I did have a quarter pint of rum, and I poured out a measure in a metal mug and gave this to her, neat. Anna drank greedily, seemingly not noticing its strength.

'I'm bleeding,' she explained as she put down the empty mug.

'That will stop,' I assured her.

She shook her head. 'No. Not this.'

I picked up the candle and raised the rug we had stretched over her to try and keep her warm. She had suffered a severe haemorrhage. Blood was pumping down her thighs, soaking the carpet. An artery had been ruptured; her life was draining away in front of us.

I tried to plug the wound with cotton wool and pieces of gauze, but it was useless. In the dim light I could not see exactly where the fissure was. My hands were bloodied; I felt like a butcher.

Anna sat up again, slowly, weakly. Her face was very pale in the candlelight, almost as white as the moonlit snow beyond the tent.

'I'm not going to recover,' she said flatly.

'You will,' I told her earnestly, trying to will her better. 'Of course you will. You must. For the boy's sake.'

'The boy,' she said, as though somehow she had forgotten all about him. 'What shall we call him?'

'Why not after your husband? Benjamin. Ben Bannerman the second.'

She nodded. 'A good name,' she agreed. 'Ben was a good man. He was kind to me. I want a second name for him. Something special to him. Not John or Paul or anything Biblical like that.' She paused; the effort of speech had tired her.

Again, in the silence, the bugles blew.

'Another fanfare,' I said, more for something to say to bridge the chasm of silence.

'Fanfare,' Anna repeated. 'They were sounding

bugles when he was born. I kept thinking of those words in *Pilgrim's Progress* you read to me, when Mr Valiant-for-Truth is dying: "And all the trumpets sounded for him on the other side." '

'Right,' I told her with a briskness I did not feel. 'Fanfare it is. Fanfare he is. But, one thing – *you're* not dying. You're going to get well directly and see him grow up. Ben's boy. Your son.'

I paused, then decided to say what was in my heart.

'Also, there's another reason for you to get well. I could never speak like this when Ben was here, but now I can and I will. I love you. I've loved you from the moment I first saw you in your house. Remember that time?'

She smiled. 'I remember. But, Douglas, I don't want to hurt you, but I must be honest, as you have been. I like you very much. But liking is not love.'

'It could turn to love,' I assured her earnestly in the way men try to delude themselves in these matters of the heart.

'Yes,' she agreed. 'It could. But . . .' She paused and then she turned and looked at me in the eyes. 'We're talking round the subject,' she said. 'I'm dying. You know that as a doctor. I know it as your patient.'

I could not deny it, although I tried. Anna shook her head, dismissing my assurances.

'It's an odd thing to have come this far, to have endured all this, and then to die out here in this empty land,' she said. 'And yet, you know, Douglas, despite everything, I have enjoyed my time here. I wouldn't have missed any of it. Not one moment. I've had my eyes opened. I have seen a strange part of the world that not many Englishwomen have even heard of. And I have met some good people here.'

'Even Afghans?' I asked her, trying to make a light remark.

'Yes. Even Afghans. There's good in everyone, you know. No one's wholly bad.'

'Agreed. But some seem to have a stab at it.' I was thinking particularly of Akyab Khan.

The candle guttered slightly. The captain's wife lit a fresh one from the dying flame. The action seemed symbolic; an older life going out, a new one beginning.

'Have you a piece of paper and some writing instrument?' Anna asked me.

I had a small pad on which I had noted some of the injuries I had treated, what medicines I had given to patients and the dates, and whether the patients had lived or died. The paper was damp with melted snow. I handed this to her and a stub of pencil; I had long since lost my pen.

Anna began to write very slowly and deliberately, as though the effort was almost too much for her. Now and then she paused and lay back, eyes closed. Then she forced herself upright again. She covered one sheet and signed her name. Beneath this she made a cross, as I have seen soldiers do, to mark a kiss.

'An envelope,' she said. 'It's a private letter.'

I found an envelope in my pannier, put the letter in this, licked it, and she addressed it to 'Ben'. That was all she could manage, before her hand fell away.

'When my son is old enough to understand, give him this letter from his mother.'

'I will,' I promised her, my voice thin and strained.

The envelope was smudged with blood. As I put it in my pocket I wondered whether the boy would ever know that this was his mother's blood, and whether he would ever hear how she died and learn the full, needless horror of this retreat.

'There is something else I'd like him to have,' she said. 'There's no money. My husband had nothing to leave him. But I have a ring I've never had the chance

43

to wear. Tell him I've kept it for him, from his father. When he wears the ring, I hope he'll think of the mother he's never known. Perhaps in some other world I'll be looking down, watching him, protecting him. Tell him I'll recognise him by the ring.'

She smiled at this idea, and scratched about feebly in a bag at the side of the bed, until she found a small white cardboard box and a plain gold ring set with a single polished ruby. The stone was cut in the shape of a triangle, each side straight as a knife blade.

'It reminds me of India, a country of two sea coasts, one land frontier,' Anna explained. 'But it's really been cut in the shape of some island off Burma where all the best rubics come from. I like the three sides. I think they stand for father, mother – and my son.'

The stone winked in the candlelight, red for blood, red for danger.

'I'll see he gets this,' I assured her, buttoning the box in my pouch.

'Thank you. I am sorry to cause you this trouble.'

'No trouble,' I said, trying to bite back my tears.

I had hoped that when Anna was well, when we both survived the march, as I had earlier convinced myself we must, she might come to love me, whatever she might say now. But as I watched her I knew that this was only a dream.

Anna Bannerman died at half past ten exactly by my watch; I made a note on my pad of the time and the date and where on the map I thought we were, so that I could tell her son when he was old enough to ask about these things – if I survived myself.

I closed Anna's eyes gently, and, on the impulse, cut a lock of her red hair and put this in another envelope. I wanted something I could remember her by; I had no portrait, no sketch, only the imprint of her beauty in my mind, and this was not enough. Then

44

I went out of the tent and stood for a moment in the snow.

Beasts of burden stood about wretchedly, heads down. Ponies neighed and stamped their hobbled feet, and camels blew and grumbled as camels always do. In the distance, somewhere along the white slopes of the hills, I could hear the angry crack of *juzails*; Afghan robbers were still out there, taking pot shots. Men and women and children were still being robbed out there, still being killed.

I hoped we had guards out there, too, but I doubted it. We were defeated, a rout, all discipline eroded. Our troops were too hungry, too tired, too dispirited to fight back. Most had not even bothered to pitch a tent, but lay like animals in the snow. In the morning hundreds would never wake up.

Snow began to fall. Clouds slid from the face of the moon and the whole vast, white, empty expanse was momentarily lit with a pale ethereal glow. I felt like a traveller in a lost and unknown world, and in a sense I was. I had never seen such emptiness, or been so keenly aware of the puny, solitary state of human beings against the might of nature. Did it matter when or where or how any of us were born and died? I liked to think it did, but somehow I could not be certain. I went back into the tent. The captain's wife was still there, kneeling by Anna's side.

'We'll bury her now,' I said.

She nodded. We had both become so used to death by starvation, wounds, or disease that we were numbed by the magnitude of catastrophe all around us.

I went out of the tent again and found two orderlies crouching from the snow in the shelter of an overhanging rock, smoking *bidi* cigarettes of rolled-up dried leaves. I told them what they had to do. Reluctantly, they got off their haunches, picked up shovels and

45

started to dig in the snow. It was impossible to make a proper grave, for the ground beneath was rock, but at least the snow would shelter Anna's body. I did not even have a marker for her grave.

Back in the tent, I rolled up the rug soaked in her blood, took it out and threw it to one side. I did not want to keep it and be reminded how she died, but I was almost immediately, because the baby started to cry.

Momentarily, I had forgotten all about young Ben. I had no food for the child, but the captain's wife knew that the wife of a sergeant was feeding a baby.

'She has enough milk for two,' she said. 'She's a strong woman.'

'If she'll take him, put him to her breast,' I told her. 'Otherwise, he'll die.'

She kept Ben away from me all night. When dawn came up, we found that the bearers who had carried Anna's *doolie* had deserted. My horse had died in the night, frozen to death, so I took the horse of a badly wounded major who had also died, and rode with the baby. Someone fashioned a sling out of old puttees and strips of cloth and I carried Ben on my back, as I had seen native women carry their children.

We rode on, hungry, cold, wretched, filthy. General Elphinstone died on the way; so did nearly everyone else. Most of our native troops deserted, going over to the other side. Many of them were probably joining their own relatives.

Now it was everyone for themselves. Life's most powerful force is not sex but simple survival. Courage and honour are soon forgotten.

One by one, British soldiers dropped out and were left behind in the snow. Looking back at them, I could sometimes see figures, clearly at first, then fading into a blur of white flakes. I told myself they had simply stopped to make water, to tighten a girth, or maybe a horse had gone lame; any sort of comforting explanation to ease my conscience. Deep down, I knew the truth was different. They had fallen back because they could not go on; their time was upon them. And the living were distancing themselves from the dying without offering them any help, not even a word of comfort or of farewell.

I was thinking about this when suddenly my own borrowed horse faltered, paused and fell forwards, dead under me. Fortunately, I was thrown sideways out of the saddle, otherwise the animal could have rolled on me, and Ben would have been killed.

I picked myself up, swung the baby's little hammock round to my chest and brushed snow off his face. I started to march, amazed that Ben was still asleep. A child is much stronger in many ways than a mature adult, and he was not old enough to realise his danger. Innocence and sleep shielded him from reality.

I paused, sweating from the effort of ploughing on through snow up to my thighs, and a baby on my back. In an automatic reaction, I checked my pouch and my pocket to make sure the ruby and Anna's letter were still safe. The ruby was in its little box and the pouch carefully buttoned. But my pocket was empty.

I tore off my glove and felt in the pocket with my bare, freezing fingers. It was empty. The note had disappeared.

I searched in all my other pockets in case I had put it in one of them for some reason, now forgotten, but it was not there. Perhaps when my horse died under me and I had been thrown the paper had fallen out. I stared back with raw, red-rimmed eyes at the footsteps I had left behind me, hoping that I might see it, that I had only lost it a few paces ago. But I could see nothing but snow and the remains of our tattered army passing me on weary horses. It had gone and I would never know what Anna had written for her only son. I had failed her and I had failed him; I had fallen down on a simple promise to give him a mother's last message, her final blessing. Standing there miserably, I wept tears of bitterness and failure.

Others were riding past us, as only moments before I had ridden past men in similar plight to me. At first, I nodded or even waved to people I knew. Then, gradually fear gripped me. I was waving goodbye to them all; they were leaving me, as I had left so many others on this march of the doomed and the dying. I was being abandoned with a baby boy.

The thought was so monstrous that I could not accept that this could be happening to me, of all people. Was it for this that I had studied medicine, that my father had scrimped and saved so that I could qualify as a doctor, simply to die out here in this frozen wasteland?

I stared with mounting horror as the column thinned. Soon only a handful of men on foot or horseback were left to pass me by. One of them paused, rode on, and then turned and rode back to me.

He was an Indian *subahdar*, a native officer, badly wounded in the shoulder. I had dressed his wound as best I could two days before, and had not seen him since. But then I had dressed the wounds of so many I could not remember every one. His face was shining with fever; his wound must have become poisoned. But he recognised me.

'You have no horse, sahib?' he asked me.

'No,' I said. 'None.'

'And you hold a newborn babe. A man child?'

'Yes.'

He swung down off his horse and leaned against the animal's steaming shuddering flank. He was too weak

48

from pain and fever to stand upright on his own.

'I have a horse, sahib, and a life that has not long to run. You are young and you also hold a life that is just beginning. It is a fair exchange. Take my horse. Allah the ever merciful will recompense in Paradise all sacrifice I make here on earth.'

'You need that horse,' I told him. 'You can make Jalalabad on it. We must be nearly there.'

'No, sahib, your need is greater than mine. I have eaten the Queen's salt. I have fought in many battles and always I have kept the faith. Now there is an end to fighting. It is written, he who helpeth his fellow creature in the hour of need, him will God help in the day of travail. My time is almost upon me. My horse is yours.'

He turned away into the snow, stumbling as he walked.

I called after him, 'Come back! Come back!'

Either he did not hear me or he would not listen. The horse blew wearily and stamped its feet. I waited for a few moments in case the *subahdar* returned. He did not. I climbed up into the saddle, Ben on my back, adjusted the stirrups, and rode on.

I rode through that day and then the night. The little boy began to cry, but I had nothing to give him to ease his hunger. I thought of pressing some snow into his mouth, but felt that this might do more harm than good. I suppose I slept in the saddle, for my next recollection is that the snow had stopped falling and I was entering a long defile. Rocks on either side towered vertically like two black cliffs facing each other only feet apart.

Ahead of me, I saw six horsemen standing across the way. Each man held a large stone in his hand. As I approached, one threw a stone at me. My horse shied, stumbled. I dug in my spurs, pulled the reins with one hand, and instinctively felt down for a sword with the other.

The *subahdar*'s sword was in its scabbard on the right. I whipped this out, waved it above my head and charged, shouting angrily, blade pointing forward. The men had not expected this sudden reaction and scattered in surprise. I cut one to the left, another to the right, and then I was through.

But beyond them, twenty yards ahead of me, three more Afghans sat on their horses and gave an ironic cheer as they saw me. I had escaped one danger only to face another.

My horse and I were exhausted. They and their mounts were fresh. This was simply sport to them, a game. To me it was life or death. I paused, not quite sure what I should do. As they saw me hesitate, they drew their swords. One man charged me.

I heaved my sword clumsily at him. The blade clashed with the tongue that Afghan swordsmiths fit to their hilts. He twisted his wrist expertly and my blade snapped off. I flung the hilt at the second man, and in doing so dropped the reins. With Ben on my back screaming in my ears, I bent down to retrieve them – and the third man fled.

At the time, I did not know why. Afterwards, I realised he must have thought I was about to draw a pistol from a saddle holster, and knew that at such close range I could not miss.

Then I was through the defile. On the far side I saw a track, trodden down with the hooves of many horses. And in the distance I saw the long wall of a mud fort and the Union flag flying from a turret. Jalalabad.

As I rode nearer, I heard a bugle call Reveille. Another fanfare for Fanfare, I thought lightheartedly. I knew then that at least I was safe, and so was Anna's son. I paused and looked behind me. The mouth of the defile was dark and empty. No one was following us. We had come through: two out of forty thousand.

I could not believe then that this could be so, but later I did believe. The terrible equation was true. We had survived. Everyone else had died.

Several cavalrymen rode out to meet me. They surrounded my drooping horse, plied me with questions I could not answer.

'Who are you? What is your unit? Who's the baby on your back? What happened? Where are the others?'

Where indeed? Dead of wounds or disease, frozen corpses in the snow. Perhaps some were prisoners in a remote Afghan fort. I could not begin to explain all this; I was too weary. I found I could not even speak my name. All manner of answers ran through my brain, but I lacked the ability to translate thoughts into words.

Someone caught me as I fell in a faint from the horse. I was carried in, laid on a trestle in the guardroom until my identity could be established. The child was taken from my back. I heard later that the regimental medical officer ordered milk to be warmed and mixed with sugar, and an orderly fed Ben with a spoon.

I regained consciousness to find that my clothes had been removed. My body had been sponged and I lay under a familiar grey army blanket in an officer's quarter. I knew I was suffering from some ague; my flesh felt dry and scaly, like a lizard's skin. The surgeon major was standing by my bed, looking at me.

'I am Dr Douglas Kintyre,' I explained. 'Surgeon with the Bengal Army. I think the little boy and I are the only survivors. There may be more. I just don't know.'

'Can you tell us what happened?'

'Willingly,' I assured him.

The surgeon major went out and returned with the

commanding officer, the adjutant, and a uniformed clerk who would make a note of what I had to say.

I told them everything, leaving out no detail of Elphinstone's wrong decisions, indecisions, no decisions, and MacNaghten's terrible miscalculation. I was frank in my account, because I felt most keenly that an entire army had been wantonly decimated, and whatever good to our country the march to Kabul might have achieved had been totally destroyed. I believed that a vastly different outcome would have resulted if we had enjoyed military and political leadership even half worthy of that name.

I explained about the perfidy of the Afghans, especially the prince who had enjoyed the Bannermans' hospitality so often and had then deliberately led a group of horsemen determined to single out the weak, the ill, the wounded, and kill them. I told them how young Ben's parents had died, and as many others whose names I could remember.

It seemed that we possessed an inordinately large number of poor commanders, and that the Afghans' attitude was engendered by our pointless incursion into the country. I gave instances of this, but as I did so I saw the colonel's face harden, and he and the adjutant exchanged glances as if they both disagreed with me.

I stayed in Jalalabad for several weeks. My fever left me, and gradually I began to feel fit and ready for whatever action might be proposed. There were no women in the fort, but orderlies looked after Ben and he became something of a mascot; he was a cheerful little fellow.

I made various enquiries as to where and when I could expect to be posted, but always received vague, almost evasive replies. Then one day I was ordered to report to the colonel in his office. This was a large whitewashed room with small unglazed windows. Birds flew in and out and perched on tarred beams beneath the high ceiling.

A guard, rifle loaded, stood outside the door, smart in red tunic, blue trousers and pipeclayed belt. Regimental colours had been tacked up on one wall facing a gaudily coloured portrait of Queen Victoria of the kind found in illustrated magazines.

'Take a seat,' said the colonel, when I had saluted him.

He was sitting behind a table with several papers on it, a pot of ink, two pens in a china holder. I sat down on a hard wooden seat opposite him. Above my head, birds nervously fluttered their wings.

'Glad to see you're in better shape than when you arrived,' the colonel said.

'Thank you, sir. I think I'm fully restored to health.'

'So the surgeon major tells me. Apparently the little baby's doing well, too. I don't know quite what we're going to do with him, or with you for that matter. The army to which you were attached is no more and we have our full establishment of surgeons here. I therefore propose to post you back to Calcutta, where you originally joined the Company's army.'

'And the little boy, sir? Mr Bannerman's son?'

'Ah, yes. Well, that's more difficult. I suggest you take the boy back to Calcutta where a more normal atmosphere of peacetime soldiering exists. Then you will be able to contact Bannerman's relations in England. No doubt one of them will wish to take charge of him.'

'When do you suggest I go?'

'A number of officers and men are moving to Ferozepore within the next few days. I suggest you join them.'

'And how will the boy get there?'

'Some sick and wounded are going out on *doolies*.

We'll put him in one of those. He's not a very heavy extra weight to carry. Anyhow, the bearers are strong.'

'Right, sir. I must thank you and your staff for your kindness in looking after me here.'

'We were pleased to do so. And if you really mean what you say, you can show your gratitude in a positive way.'

'If I can, sir, I'd be pleased to do so. In what way?'

The colonel leaned on the table and looked at me. I had never seen him so close. His face was not handsome. It was pitted with open pores, with blemishes and scars left by boils. He had cut himself shaving; a dab of white cotton wool stained with blood stuck on his chin.

I had not realised before how close together were his eyes, nor how large his nose. If I had met him in the normal course of my duties I would instinctively have mistrusted him. But I had only spoken to him a few times since my arrival, and he had always seemed civil. I also knew he was very rich. A passed-over lieutenant had told me without rancour that he had paid five thousand pounds for his command.

'When you arrived here,' he said, 'no doubt under the influences of severe fever and exhaustion and your harrowing experiences, you made a number of very serious criticisms of senior officers.' He paused.

'I did not criticise, sir. I simply reported what had happened. Had any others survived, I have no doubt they would have agreed with me.'

'That may be so. On the other hand, the gentlemen you castigated so severely are dead. They cannot defend themselves or their reputations. I would therefore ask you to keep your critical opinions to yourself when you leave here.'

'I am not likely to broadcast them, sir. But if I am asked to make a report, as you asked me, I feel I must say what happened, otherwise the report is useless. If I am asked for a medical opinion on someone, I have to tell the truth, otherwise my opinion would be without value.'

'I suggest that a critical report by a young surgeon on a matter of high military strategy would be no more valuable than the opinion of a regimental officer on a soldier's health,' the colonel replied coldly. 'These are difficult times for soldiers, Kintyre. Too many people are all too willing to criticise without knowing the facts. Damned penpushers and penny-a-line hacks are eager for any military disaster with which they can regale their readers in the public prints. Obviously, mistakes have been made. Everyone makes mistakes. But possibly the Afghans have made the greatest mistake of all in underestimating our will and purpose to return.'

'Possibly, sir. But if we do plan to return, it might be to our advantage to know why the earlier march on Kabul failed so disastrously.'

'The march was not in any way a failure. It was totally satisfactory. We reached Kabul. The enemy, if we may call them that, fled, and later accepted our suzerainty.'

'Agreed, sir, we reached Kabul. But at a cost of something like twenty thousand camels.'

'*Camels?*' He smiled contemptuously. 'If camels were our only casualties we did well, Kintyre.'

'They weren't, sir. We lost hundreds of men on the way north, most of them needlessly, and a great deal of equipment. We were grossly overcharged for food on the route. I heard the quartermaster estimate that the whole enterprise cost the enormous sum of two million pounds. And on the retreat we lost everyone and everything, possibly forty thousand people.'

'We did not lose you, Kintyre,' retorted the colonel sharply. 'And I do not accept quartermasters' opinions.

They always count in figures.'

'There was something else we lost, too, sir. Something more important, possibly priceless.'

'And what was that, pray?'

'Our good name.'

'I don't understand you, Kintyre. The Army of the Indus was ordered to march on Kabul to make the country safe for British subjects, to protect British interests in India and to counter serious threats of hostile Persian and Russian intrusion. The army marched on the direct orders of Lord Auckland, the Governor General. I cannot follow your argument.'

'Lord Auckland may have given the orders, sir, but he must have been wrongly informed. There was no threat to British interests. So we lost our army, and our good name with the Afghans.'

'What the devil do you mean, Kintyre? These damned savages who mutilate prisoners and live like wild animals in the mountains? How can we possibly have lost our good name with them?'

'Our defeat will become part of their folklore. And it was all so utterly unnecessary.'

I knew that what I said was true, but even as I spoke I realised I was doing my own reputation untold damage. The colonel leaned across the desk again. His eyes were red with anger now, like the eyes of a cornered cat. I knew I would be well-advised to watch what I said to him. I could back out now if I chose, apologise and claim that I was not myself after my experiences. He would have accepted any excuse that would enable him to pretend I was not criticising the army or its commanders, of whom, of course, he was one.

Instead, I looked straight at him. I met his eyes. And as I did so I realised that not only did I dislike him, I disliked the whole military hierarchy.

'Your whole future career can hinge on your

attitude,' he said, speaking slowly so that I would understand the gravity of his words. 'I feel the views you have just expressed are not ones you genuinely hold. Your mind has become deranged by your experiences. I will therefore put this conversation from my mind, and forget we ever had it. You understand me?'

'Perfectly, sir. But I am certain it is only by discussing what went wrong, by admitting that almost everything did go terribly wrong – and quite unnecessarily so – that we can avoid another similar catastrophe.'

'I am beholden to you for your thoughts. But doubtless the general staff will already have made their plans. Now, I bid you goodbye.'

We both stood up, shook hands formally, coldly. I saluted him. We both knew that he had no intention of forgetting the conversation. I guessed that not only would he remember it, but he would pass it on to his superiors. So far, my career in the East India Company's army had been brief and undistinguished. Now I did not think it would be of very much greater duration or distinction.

So indeed it proved. I joined the column with young Ben, who showed himself a trooper, although only a few weeks old. I knew nothing about children except what I had learned in my short time as a doctor, and that concerned their ailments rather than bringing them up. Some of the men in the column who were fathers told me he was a very good baby. He didn't cry at night. It shows how little I knew about babies when I admit I assumed that this was very normal behaviour.

In Calcutta, I soon fell into the routine of peacetime soldiering. Then something happened which made me realise that the colonel in Jalalabad had not kept his word.

Three old soldiers of the Company's army came forward for medical examinations. They were private soldiers, all bachelors although living with Indian women who had followed them loyally. One man had fathered three half-caste children. The others had one child each.

Their stories were remarkably similar and probably typical of recruits of those days. One of the soldiers had run away from home in his teens. Employment was impossible to find. He could neither read nor write, and since even labouring jobs were filled, he had 'gone for a soldier', as the saying was.

The second had fallen to the lures of a recruiting sergeant, and was then found to be too short in stature for the regular army. He had been pushed into the Company's army, where physical standards were less demanding. The third was a simple fellow who liked the thought of wearing a uniform and marching behind a band. He had never considered that soldiering could have a more serious, and dangerous, side.

I saw them one after the other. They had all served in India for more than thirteen years and were not in good physical condition. But very few Europeans of any class could claim to be fit after living in India for so long, without home leave. Most would never have survived, so these men's basic constitutions must clearly be sound.

One had lost his teeth, another was deaf from firing muskets close to his right ear, the third had developed a fever that seemed to defy all specifics. They might not be fit for front-line duty, but then, if one was being honest, nor were more than half the Company's troops.

At first, I could not understand why these three men had been sent to me. Then I realised the reason. If they served out their time of fourteen years in the Company's army, the Company would have to pay them a pension. This would be small enough, but it would be better than having to beg for bread at street corners, which was the fate of so many old soldiers and sailors. These men had only months to serve until they were due to receive their pensions. But if they could be discharged now on medical grounds, the Company would save a few pounds a year.

I felt that this would be both heartless and unwise. If word of the Company's parsimony spread, it could do a great deal of harm at a time when many in England were already questioning the wisdom of the Company's policies and authority in India.

These old soldiers could easily be given some undemanding job, such as sweeping a barrack square, or polishing brasswork. And then, in a matter of months, they could be discharged and thereafter draw their pensions. I therefore passed them as fit for work of this kind.

The CO, Colonel Deakin, called me into his office that same morning.

'I have discussed your report with the surgeon major, Kintyre,' he said brusquely. 'He is of the opinion that they should be discharged forthwith as being totally unfit for further military service.'

'Sir,' I replied, 'they have only a few months to serve to earn their modest pensions. They can fill in the time very adequately doing jobs which perhaps more able-bodied men are doing now, who would then be free for more active service.'

'We are not a philanthropic organisation, Kintyre. Nor are we a charity. I intend to follow the surgeon major's opinion and be rid of them now. I may tell you, by the way, that I have received a very poor confidential report from your previous colonel in Jalalabad. Your views contradicting those of a far more experienced officer give rise to grave concern in my mind that you are not fit to continue in the employment you hold.

'It seems strange to me, as it did to the previous colonel in Jalalabad, although perhaps he did not mention it to you, that you should be the only person to escape from Afghanistan – one out of forty thousand, not counting the child, of course. I had always assumed that the profession of medicine calls on its practitioners to help others, not to help themselves. Yet thousands died while you alone survived.'

'Thousands more would have lived but for the incompetence of our commanders.'

'The colonel also refers in his report to your harsh and uncorroborated criticism of superior officers, which, like him, I find distasteful. These gallant officers are not alive to refute your allegations.'

'Nor are thousands who would bear me out, sir.'

'Frankly, Kintyre, I find your opinions intolerable, coming from an officer who took another man's horse to enable him to escape. You cannot deny that you did. The saddle and the reins were stamped with the regimental number of a native officer.'

'I did not take his horse. He gave it to me.'

'*Gave* you his horse? In a retreat? Laid down his life for you – is that what you're telling me?'

'I'm telling you what happened, sir. He was severely wounded. I know just how severely, because I had attended him a few days previously. He did not believe he could survive to reach Jalalabad. He passed me as I was walking along with the boy, since my own horse had died under me. He heard the child cry and turned back and gave me his horse.'

'I find that difficult to believe.'

'Some people, sir, once found it difficult to believe that the world was round.'

'Are you being insolent, Kintyre?'

'No, sir. Just stating a fact.'

'I find yours a strange story, Kintyre. And I must

tell you bluntly, I do not altogether believe it. The gross, disrespectful, one might almost say anarchic, criticisms of superior officers, and this wish to pretend that obviously unfit soldiers are fit for service – all this leaves a nasty taste in my mouth. It is not the behaviour of an officer I can trust, nor of a gentleman in whom I can confide.'

I said nothing. I knew what was coming. They were going to get rid of me. For a moment, I felt a wave of dismay, almost horror. How could I make a living in this strange country if I were not in the Company's army? But almost immediately my own pride told me I could make a living, and a good one; and I would.

The colonel drummed his fingers on the desk. 'I think it would be in both our interests if you resigned your commission as surgeon lieutenant.'

'I will not resign, sir. If you have no faith in my abilities or my character, then I will ask for a court martial to answer your allegations.'

'That would not help you to gain civilian employment.'

'It would, however, be the more honourable course. In, as you say, both our interests.'

'I will not court-martial you, as clearly you wish me to do. Instead, I will have you dismissed on the grounds that your experiences in Afghanistan have turned your mind. I have two surgeon majors. They will examine you and issue a report to that effect.'

'If what you wish, sir, is to make them produce a false report, I have not the authority to do other than accept your judgment. But I must say, sir, I will not forget this. Nor will I keep silent about the matter.'

'And I'm damned if I'll forget you and your revolutionary views. If it were not so difficult to recruit surgeons, I doubt you'd ever have been here at all.

61

You may go to your quarters. You will receive a letter in due course. In the meantime, it might save embarrassment if you do not eat in the mess or use the anteroom. Arrangements will be made for your meals to be served in your room.'

'Is that an order, sir?'

'It is my wish as your colonel. That, to any subordinate officer, is better than any direct order. Perhaps you didn't realise this, Kintyre?'

'I didn't, sir,' I agreed. 'I am in your debt for informing me.'

By early evening every officer knew I was in disgrace. I kept out of the mess as the colonel suggested, partly because I did not want to provoke a scene by others who might wish to ingratiate themselves with the colonel, partly because I felt sick in the stomach with the army.

Colonel Deakin was a bully, I knew, but like all bullies, he was cautious. He wanted rid of me, but he did not wish to initiate any unpleasantness that might conceivably involve him. He assumed I was an insignificant surgeon, with no means beyond my pay, but he did not know this for certain. I just might have private means far greater than his, and influence with all manner of powerful political friends who could damage him if they wished. So he did not dismiss me. Instead, I relinquished my commission by mutual consent, and received 5,000 rupees as an honorarium.

By the end of that week I had set up in practice on my own, taking rooms off Chowringhee, the main street of Calcutta. I had no shortage of patients. For some, the fact that I had served as a medical officer in John Company's army was sufficient testimonial. For others, the fact that I had left the Company's service voluntarily was proof that I had confidence in my own abilities. Therefore, for quite different reasons, they considered I must be outstanding in my profession. So I prospered.

I engaged an *ayah*, a Muslim nurse, to look after young Ben. She brought along a buxom woman who was suckling her own child and was willing to hire herself out as a wet nurse. I was now clear about my future, but not certain about Ben's. I had not adopted him, but I liked the little fellow. He had an engaging grin; he seemed cheerful. And I believed, as all men closely involved with children tend to assure themselves, that he liked me.

A retired Company officer told me that my friend Ben Bannerman had an elder sister, living in England. She was married to a landowner, Sir Frank Beaumont. They had no children, so it seemed possible they might wish to adopt her nephew. I therefore felt it was my duty to write to her, explaining how I had been with her brother when he and his wife had died, and how I was bringing up their son.

I could find out nothing about Anna's background, and for some reason, which I could not explain, I did not wish to discover too much. Simply to remember her hurt me almost physically.

So my life went on in a not disagreeable way. I was earning a large income. I lived in a fine house with many servants; I owned a grand carriage. But, most important of all, I enjoyed the company, if only for a limited time, of a small boy whose appearance constantly reminded me of the only woman I had ever wanted to marry.

I therefore set myself to work hard and to be thankful, counting my blessings which were so many. My father had often recommended his congregation to do this, but I doubt he ever thought his only son would also benefit from his sound advice.

Chapter Three

Lady Victoria Beaumont stood at her bedroom window, looking out across the home park. Rain had been falling for several days, and bedraggled and wretched sheep stood in the fields beyond wrought-iron fences on either side of the long drive. She felt how they looked, she thought wryly: miserable, without hope.

Victoria was a slim, slightly built woman in her forties, but catching sight of her face in the cheval glass on the dressing-table she was surprised and alarmed to see how old and depressed she appeared. She was married to an irascible and impotent man in his sixties. Perpetually attempting to forestall his angry moods, always watching his face for any telltale tightening of his mouth, a narrowing of his eyes, so that she could steer the conversation into some calmer direction, had etched lines of worry on her face.

She remembered how her contemporaries had envied her marriage to Sir Frank Beaumont ten years earlier. She hoped that none of them had since realised just what an unhappy sham their marriage had been from the beginning.

Once, walking along on the shingle beach of the Sussex coast near her house, Victoria had picked up an unusually shaped shell. She had never seen one quite like this on that stretch of beach: huge, pink-tinted, curled whorls formed the shape of an angel's trumpet. She held the mouth to her ear and listened to the roar of unseen, unimagined oceans, as she and her brother Ben used to do long ago when they were children. The shell was gorgeously coloured outside, richly coated with mother-of-pearl, but inside was all drab and dull and empty. Just like my life, she thought sadly; all show outside, nothing within. With a sudden revulsion for the shell's cruel symbolism, she threw it away. The delicate colours shattered on a rock. Victoria walked on hurriedly, wishing she could as easily walk out of the life which once, from a distance, had seemed to be so infinitely more alluring than simply being young Miss Bannerman, who helped her father in his shops.

Her father was very proud of the way he had built up one small drapery store, selling yards of ribbon and reels of cotton, into three larger shops that dealt in rolls of cloth, curtains, carpets. He had never been able to appreciate that what he considered success was, to others born to greater wealth and privilege, simply something demeaning, lower class. Mr Bannerman wasn't a gentleman; how could a draper possibly claim gentility?

After her marriage, Victoria soon learned not to mention to people she met through her husband exactly how her father earned his living. Many of these new acquaintances lived on money inherited from rich fathers, grandparents, uncles. These initial providers might also have been milliners or speculative house builders or coal merchants, but years of affluence had successfully obliterated all trace of such humble origins. Time and two generations sanctified every kind of unmentionable beginning.

Victoria had helped her father in the main shop; another facet of her life which, after marriage, her husband was at continual pains to conceal. Yet that was how they had first met. His sister had bought some material; there had been a mistake about the order, and Victoria had gone to the big house, the Hall, calling, of course, at the back door, to apologise to Miss Beaumont for the error. The order was large, and her father was anxious not to lose it or offend such a wealthy customer.

By some further misunderstanding, the housekeeper had brought her into the house because the sister was not at home. Sir Frank was. Although he knew that the caller was in trade, he found himself attracted by her cheerful countenance. He was already old in appearance, with a plump, coarse face, mean eyes, a thick fleshy nose overrun by blue veins, reminding Victoria of rivers marked in her school atlas.

She had been amazed and flattered when Sir Frank had asked her to take tea with him, and then to stay and meet his sister on her return. She was even more astonished when, after a brief courtship, amounting to no more than half a dozen meetings – all chaperoned by his sister – he had proposed marriage.

Such a prospect had never entered Victoria's mind. She was certainly not in love with him. She did not really like him, but she felt flattered, and perhaps love would grow and flower, simply by proximity. She did not make up her mind at once, but discussed the offer with her father – her mother had been dead for years. He took a down-to-earth view of the matter.

'There's no doubt about it, Victoria, he's very rich. He's got a title. You'll be a Lady. In a single step you will go from one side of the counter to the other, for ever. I can't imagine that any other knight will ever offer you marriage, although you're as good as they are, in many ways far better. It's no use their going on about their long pedigrees. If, as the Good Book says,

67

we are all descended from Adam, ours must be just as long.'

'So you think I should marry him, Father?'

She knew this genealogical hobby-horse of her father and wanted to keep his mind on her problem, not on abstract issues of ancestors and their relative importance.

'I am surprised at his proposal, Victoria,' he admitted. 'I hoped you would eventually marry someone younger, nearer your own age, perhaps of our class, whose ways would be your ways, our ways. If you marry, you'll have a lot of money, but you will have to pay a high price for it. You will need to adapt. It'll be like walking a long way in shoes that don't quite fit – until you get used to them.

'But it's your future, child. If your mother were alive, she could guide you better than I can. I leave the decision to you.'

Finally, after weighing in her mind points for and against, Victoria decided to turn down Sir Frank's proposal. She was preparing to go back to the Hall to tell him, when, through the stained-glass window of the front door, she saw a carriage-and-four arrive. Sir Frank stepped down, walked smartly and purposefully up their narrow garden path – how different from the two-mile drive that led from the double iron gates through pastures to the Hall!

'I could not wait another moment for you to come to me,' he told her. 'I felt I had to have your answer now.'

Victoria was so flattered, so astonished, that her resolution vanished. Stammeringly, she accepted his proposal. They were married that summer.

How long ago it seemed now; far longer than ten years. It felt like a lifetime of bad temper, arguments, reconciliations and emptiness where there could have been fun and laughter, and something else, that had completely eluded her: love.

Her father died and she sold the shops, but for rather less than she hoped. By then she was accustomed to money being spent on a prodigal scale when her husband wished to do so. The two thousand pounds the three shops fetched would, before her marriage, have seemed a fortune. Now the sum was reduced to the status of petty cash. But although Sir Frank spent what to her seemed huge sums of money, it was always spent on things he wanted, never on her. As with many rich men, he was generous to himself, never to others.

As she stood now, staring at the rainy scene, pondering on the difference between the reality of her life and how outsiders might imagine it to be, she noticed a figure walking from the servants' entrance, down across the fields. He wore a blue uniform, a strange hat like an inverted coal scuttle, a cloak shining with rain. She took several minutes to realise he was the postman. She was seldom up so early and had never seen him wearing his cloak. She slept badly and, waking in the night, would frequently take a sleeping draught. Then she would sleep heavily until nine or ten in the morning and awake, heavy-headed, dry-mouthed, long after the postman had called.

She and her husband slept in separate bedrooms on opposite sides of the house. They had never occupied the same room, and never the same bed. They never would now, of course, but this did not concern her any longer. She and her husband had nothing whatever in common; every day, even every hour spent apart she secretly regarded as a bonus.

Victoria dressed quickly and went downstairs for breakfast. With luck, she might finish before Frank arrived; he was rarely an early riser. Two places were set in the morning room, a fire burned in the burnished grate. Sir Frank was a heavy eater. On the sideboard, silver chafing dishes contained devilled kidneys, scrambled eggs, strips of grilled bacon.

Her husband's letters were all delivered to him in his study, a room lined with books he never read, where he would retire for much of each morning to skip through some shooting magazine, or sip Madeira and eat seed cake with a handful of cronies whose lives were as empty and selfish as his.

As Victoria sat down, the butler came in carrying a silver salver, bowed as he presented it. On the salver lay a letter addressed to her, and an ivory paperknife. The butler bowed again and left her on her own. She glanced at the stamp before she opened the envelope.

The letter had come from India. At this, she felt uneasy. The last letter from Calcutta had been an official note of condolence from the Governor General on the death of her brother, Lieutenant Bannerman, in Afghanistan. She remembered that morning so clearly. It had been raining then, just as it was raining now. She had not seen her brother for many years, and they were both indifferent correspondents, but he was the only one left of her blood. Now she was on her own, the last of her line.

News of his death had depressed her greatly. She at once wrote to the Governor General asking for any more details about it, but not surprisingly had still not received a reply. Mails were slow; sometimes a letter could take six months to reach Calcutta, and a reply home perhaps longer.

She sat holding the envelope for several minutes before she opened it. She feared it might contain more bad news, although what exactly this could be now that Ben was dead she could not imagine. She unfolded the single sheet, glanced first at the sender's name and address: 'Douglas Kintyre, Physician and Surgeon,

Blairgowrie House, Chowringhee, Calcutta, India'.

Dear Lady Beaumont,

I expect that by now you will have heard the sad news of the death of your brother, Lieutenant Bannerman. I was present when he died by enemy fire, bravely attempting to drive off a party of marauding Afghans. He died as he had lived, a man of honour and courage.

He and I had served together in Afghanistan for some months. Hence this letter to you now, to offer my deepest sympathy in your great loss.

I have another reason for writing, of which I believe you may not yet be aware. Before your brother set off for Kabul from India he married a charming lady, Anna Greenway. Within days of her husband's death, she bore a male child, who has been christened Ben, after him, and Fanfare, after a passage in *Pilgrim's Progress* by John Bunyan. This describes the passing of Mr Valiant-for-Truth, for whom it was said that all the trumpets sounded for him – a fanfare of trumpets. This somehow seemed apt in view of your brother's bravery and his general character. He shared many of the noble qualities of Mr Valiant-for-Truth.

As you may imagine, in the grim conditions of an army retreating across snowy wastes, constantly under attack by armed tribesmen, your sister-in-law did not have an easy birth. Complications set in and despite all efforts to save her life, she succumbed. Your brother's son, I am pleased to say, survived. He is a healthy and most cheerful child.

I am a surgeon, lately in the employment of the East India Company's army, and now in private civilian practice in Calcutta at the above address. I care for him, but of course I have no legal authority whatever for his well-being. I am therefore writing to you, since I understand you are his father's only relative. I have no name or address for any relative of the boy's mother, so I seek your views on his future.

If you would care to adopt young Ben, it might be possible for me to place him in the care of an English couple returning home from India, and they could look after him on the voyage.

If you decide to do this, I would, as a physician, advise you not to seek the child's repatriation immediately, because the voyage is long, and conditions aboard ship can be harsh, and the older he is the better would be his chances of survival.

Doubtless you will convey your wishes to me when you have had time to consider the matter.

I look forward to hearing your decision, and, in the meantime, I have the honour to remain, at your command,
Douglas Kintyre.

Victoria read and re-read the letter, then folded it up, replaced it in its envelope. Her heart was beating like a drum. She had no idea that her brother had married. The news he had left a son and heir was equally unexpected. She must adopt the boy, of course; this was the least she could do. After all, he was her only blood relative; now the name would not die out. But she was not the only one involved in making a decision to adopt him; there was her husband to consider.

Sir Frank came into the room, nodded a brusque greeting to his wife, piled his plate with kidneys and scrambled egg from the sideboard, and sat down at the other end of the table. The butler poured a beaker of black coffee. Sir Frank began to eat and drink noisily, now and then picking his teeth with his thumbnail. He watched Victoria carefully.

'You have had a letter, I am told,' he said at last.

'Yes. From India.'

Victoria knew that the butler kept her husband informed about any correspondence or visits she received. In return for being his personal spy, Sir Frank overlooked the man's habit of drinking whisky neat from the mouth of the bottle and watering what was left. Sir Frank did not drink whisky himself. Victoria thought he might have taken a less lenient view if the butler had stolen his brandy; he drank a bottle a day.

'About your brother?' he asked his wife.

'Yes. From a friend who was with him when he was killed. He says my brother married before he went to Kabul. His wife also died on the retreat, giving birth to a son. I had no idea of this, none at all.'

Sir Frank said nothing. He speared some kidney slices from the side of his plate, swallowed them, belched, wiped his mouth with a napkin.

'What does he want, this friend? Who is he?'

'A physician. He was in the Company's army with Ben. Now he is practising in Calcutta in a private capacity. He asks whether I would like to adopt the child.'

'*You* adopt him? You mean *we*.'

'Well, yes,' said Victoria meekly. 'We should.'

'Why? Who did your brother marry?'

'He only gives her name. He does not know whether she has any relatives.'

'Then she would not be anyone of consequence. Your brother was repeatedly passed over for promotion because he could not afford to buy a captaincy. I would not think he would be in a position to meet anyone very special, let alone marry them.'

'He could not help not being rich,' said Victoria defensively. 'He was a very good soldier.'

'If he was, he would still be alive. He was foolhardy.'

'You know nothing about him. You never even met him.'

'He was a lieutenant for years. Even without private means, many officers are promoted on their own merits and talents. He wasn't. That, to my mind, speaks for itself. And there's another thing. I don't want to be encumbered by his son. You have no idea of his wife's background. We could be fostering a boy of most dubious and quite unsuitable ancestry. The boy is no relation of mine.'

'He is my nephew. My only close relative, Frank.'

'That's of no consequence in this situation. You write back to this physician friend, whoever he is, and tell him my decision.'

'I don't want you to make up your mind so quickly, Frank. Please read the letter. We cannot turn the boy away like this.'

'*We* cannot? *I* can and I will. I do not wish to read your correspondence. That is the end of the matter. Write to the sawbones and tell him so.'

'I intend to adopt my brother's son,' Victoria replied determinedly.

'If you do so, my dear, then you must make your own arrangements. I will not have the boy in my house. Nor will I be responsible in any way for his food, his clothes, or his upbringing and education. If you feel so generously disposed to him, then these matters are for you to deal with. That is my last word on the matter. Pray do not mention this subject again. It displeases me.'

Victoria stood up. A footman pulled back her chair. She had forgotten she and her husband were not alone. They had so many servants, indoor and outdoor, that she found herself increasingly following her husband's habit and ignoring them, as though they were not people with minds of their own. They didn't listen, he had so often assured her; they could not pass on to others discussions which they had not heard. This was not true, of course. And not for the first time, Victoria felt embarrassed arguing over private, personal matters in front of the staff. What would they think of Sir Frank's selfish, and, to her mind, most unreasonable attitude?

She had lost all appetite; she could not bear to spend another moment in her husband's company. She hurried from the room, turning her head away from the butler who opened the door, so that he might not see the tears in her eyes.

The carriage went through the archway into Gray's Inn and stopped opposite Raymond Buildings. A footman escorted Victoria across the cobbles, up white-stoned steps into the anteroom of the solicitor's office.

The head clerk bowed, led her up more stairs, past black varnished doors bearing the names of solicitors picked out in gold leaf, into the presence of Jonah Edwards, the firm's senior partner. Mr Edwards was a tall, thin man, wearing a black suit and a high winged collar. In the open triangle of the wing, his Adam's apple moved up and down uneasily, as though a marble was imprisoned within his throat. They shook hands. His clasp felt cold and bloodless as a fish; not the grip of a lively, vigorous man. He indicated a seat. Victoria sat down, trying to conceal her uneasiness.

'And how can I help you, Lady Beaumont?'

'By giving me some legal advice, Mr Edwards.'

'If I can, I will be most pleased to do so.'

'I know that you are my husband's solicitor, but in this case I would like to engage you on my own behalf.'

'But not against Sir Frank, I trust, dear lady?' Mr Edwards allowed himself a smile at such a ridiculous possibility. Would any wife be so ill-advised as to take action against a husband worth so much?

'I think not, Mr Edwards,' Victoria replied, taking the question seriously. 'But I would like this meeting to be confidential between us. I will settle up your costs before I leave.'

'I wouldn't dream of that,' said Mr Edwards immediately. The woman must be naive. He would treble what he might charge her, add a few more petty cash disbursements, and put it down to her husband's account. He had Sir Frank's measure; he never looked through his bills closely. He felt it was beneath his dignity to involve himself in such petty, sordid transactions. He invariably instructed his agent to pay them. Would that more clients adopted the same attitude!

'This week I received a letter from India,' Victoria said, 'from a Scottish doctor who was serving in the army with my late brother, Lieutenant Bannerman. He was killed on the retreat from Kabul which received so much mention in the newspapers last year. Unknown to me, my brother, whom I had not seen for several years, married in India. After his death, his widow gave birth to an heir, and in so doing she expired herself.

'The doctor has written to ask whether I would care to adopt my nephew. I would, naturally. As you know, my own marriage is childless. I would dearly like to bring up the boy as my own.' She paused, uncertain how to continue.

'But perhaps your husband has other ideas, Lady Beaumont?' the solicitor prompted gently.

'Precisely, Mr Edwards. He says he will not have anything to do with the boy. He says that I can do what I like, but my means are very limited. What would you advise in this situation?'

Mr Edwards stood up, paced the room, his hands

clasped behind his back beneath his jacket. From time to time he paused, looking out over the lawns. Beneath ancient elms, gardeners in green baize aprons were sweeping up the leaves. Almost as fast as they swept, the wind blew them across the grass. There seemed some symbolism in the sight. As fast as troubles seemed solved, new problems appeared. He turned to face Victoria.

'I have to tell you, Lady Beaumont, that your house, in the eyes of the law, is entirely your husband's property. He can, if he so wishes, say who lives there permanently, or even who stays under his roof on a temporary basis. A wife, under the strict interpretation of the law, is also held to be the property of her husband. So legally – and presumably you wish to know the position in law, which is why you have consulted me – if Sir Frank does not wish this child to be reared under his roof, there is nothing you can do about that except to persuade him to change his mind.'

'He will never do that. He is stubborn, obstinate.'

'It would be improper for me to comment on that observation, Your Ladyship. But, according to the law, he is entirely within his rights. If you, on the other hand, have private means, you can pay for this child's upbringing and his education, and keep him as and how and where you wish, but not in your husband's home. Unless he agrees.'

'My means are very limited,' Victoria explained. 'But my husband, on our marriage, did transfer to me ownership of some paintings.'

'You would not think of selling those, surely?'

'Of course I would not sell them – yet. But perhaps I could draw up a will and leave them to this boy should I die? Or could I borrow against them from a bank or a loan accommodation agent? He is the son of my dear brother, my only close relative by blood. I cannot stand by idly and not help him.'

'I quite understand your feelings, and sympathise with them. If you will give me the boy's name and present address, my learned clerk will draw up a will for your consideration. I will also seek to discover what monies could be advanced against the security of the paintings. Do you wish me to send this, and your will, to you?'

'No,' she said firmly; she knew her husband would somehow discover the contents of any letters, and this could only provoke further argument. 'I will come to your office one week from today at this same time.'

'Very good. I am sorry to be able to give so little for your comfort, Lady Beaumont. But I can only explain the law to you. I do not make it.'

'I quite understand, and I am indebted to you for giving me such a clear statement of the facts.'

She stood up. Mr Edwards bowed, pressed a hand-bell for a servant to open the door. Victoria went downstairs. The footman opened the door of her carriage and she climbed inside.

Upstairs, Mr Edwards stood looking across the lawns. He was sorry for the woman, but of course she was a nobody, a former shop girl or some such, so he had heard. Sir Frank had picked her up somewhere. Her brother had probably also been a person of little account; certainly not a man of means or else he would have bought himself promotion. Mr Edwards could quite understand that a gentleman would not want some upstart's son to be brought up virtually as his own. And yet, and yet . . .

Mr Edwards had no children of his own. His wife claimed to suffer from an almost perpetual migraine, spending days in a darkened room, surrounded by Siamese cats. Just for a moment he thought how pleasant it would be to hear young voices and to see young people and have sunshine and laughter in his tall and sombre house. Then he banished the absurd notion from his mind. He had more important matters to consider. He sensed big fees here. He would make much more from Sir Frank than he could ever expect from Lady Victoria. He must not allow his heart to influence his head.

Mr Edwards put out his hand to press the brass bell on his desk to summon his clerk. He would apprise Sir Frank of his wife's intentions. A man surely must be master in his own house, or he was not a man at all. Also, it could be unethical for a lawyer to be found advising a husband and also his wife, without the husband's knowledge.

Ethical. The word had a dull, muted ring about it, like a funeral bell muffled in crepe. It seemed to symbolise so much in his life – too much. He stood for a moment, recalling unethical deeds he had done in this office, all without the slightest concern as to the rights and wrongs of the matter. He had drawn up contracts between two parties who both trusted him and deliberately biased the documents in favour of the one who could offer him the most lucrative work in the future. He had carefully and cunningly rephrased agreements and then persuaded his client, ignorant of the labyrinthine legal complexities he had introduced, that it was in his best interests to sign as though nothing whatever had been changed. He had done so many other acts of like kind – legally, of course, for the law was his life as well as his profession.

As Mr Edwards stood in his darkening room, he felt a sudden revulsion for this chicanery. Why should not this unhappy woman, Victoria Beaumont, give to her nephew pictures her husband had given to her? Sir Frank had inherited them. They had not cost him anything. He had never in all his life earned a penny by

79

his own exertions. He was a parasite; even his title was inherited and earned by others. He had given the paintings to his wife because to make such a gift sounded generous, with the added bonus to him that he had not needed to part with any money. Viewed in any rational way, it was monstrous that an aunt could not give her own possessions to her only relative, an orphan boy.

Mr Edwards pressed the bell. The clerk appeared at the doorway, thin, cadaverous as a radish. He raised his eyebrows questioningly.

'I want you to draw up a will for Lady Victoria Beaumont,' Mr Edwards told him briskly. 'This is a confidential matter, and will not be included in Sir Frank's papers on any account. You understand that?'

'Perfectly, sir.'

'I want it phrased so that if anyone, on any pretext, should ever contest it, their case will fail. There must be no equivocal wording that could in any way be misconstrued. It must be absolutely clear that everything Lady Beaumont owns – in specie, notes of hand, pictures, ornaments, even clothes, *everything* – she gives and bequeaths to her nephew Benjamin Fanfare Bannerman.'

When the clerk withdrew, Mr Edwards walked across the room to a wall safe, opened it with keys he kept on a chain at his waist. Inside, on a green baize shelf, stood a single glass and a bottle of The MacAllan whisky.

He poured himself a small measure, paused, then doubled it. He felt he had something to celebrate. Indeed, he felt unusually cheerful, and he could not imagine why. Then, as the spirit moved like fire in his blood, he realised the reason. Without thought for any fee, and for the first time in years, he had done someone a good turn. Not a friend, not a client, but a stranger, a child he did not know, might never even meet. The thought cheered him. To mark his mood, he poured himself another drink.

One of Ben's earliest memories was of seeing the River Ganges near the house Dr Kintyre bought in Barrackpore, sixteen miles out of Calcutta. Here, they would go for weekends and sometimes for longer visits. Someone owned an elephant – Ben had forgotten who this could be – and often he rode in its howdah along the bank of the slow-flowing river. A *mahout* led the elephant, and they would walk as far as a mosque or a Hindu shrine and then turn back. Once, on the way home, Ben saw a human body being burned; the memory stayed with him, undimmed, all his life. So did the *mahout*'s remarks about it. The *mahout*, unusually for one of his caste, spoke English and was impressed by the boy's interest in the spectacle.

'The Ganges is more than a river,' he explained. 'We call it Mother Ganges because, like a mother, it is always ready to forgive its children. To bathe in the Ganges brings purification from all sin – as you Christians make confession or take holy Communion which you believe washes away your sins. To die on its banks is blessed. To be cast into the river after death ensures eternal peace. This person being burned now is fortunate indeed.'

The *mahout* said that the dead man must have been rich because, instead of being put on a pile of cheap green wood, his body, closely bound with white bandages and tapes, lay on a pyramid of sandalwood.

Someone applied a taper as they passed, and flames suddenly crackled and roared. The heat tightened the muscles of the corpse and it made as though to sit up in one last act of salutation, facing the holy river. Scented smoke from the sandalwood logs hung in the air like incense. Beyond the funeral pyre the evening sky glowed bright as polished copper. Against this curious metallic light, quickly fading, bats spread tiny wings like parentheses.

In the distance, Ben heard the sound of drums, and strange shrill flutes. People were honouring some religious festival, and merged with the sound of distant music he heard the cries of jackals and the despairing groans of water buffalo. He was moved by a trinity of sensations, sight and sound and the smell of burning. At the heart of a brief tropical twilight, the fire blazed furiously as the body of an unknown man surrendered its spirit to the heavens. This was all part of India; and India was all Ben's boyhood.

The house in Barrackpore was rambling and inconvenient. But Dr Kintyre employed so many servants that inconvenience was relative and minimised. In this bungalow, as in the far more splendid house in which they lived during the week in Calcutta, the doctor maintained full indoor and outdoor staffs. The butler wore livery of white pantaloon trousers, white starched coat down to his knees, a dark red turban and a wide belt of the same colour with a giant brass buckle. The doctor employed a valet; several cooks; a *bhisti* to carry water in shining hogskins to fill the sink and enamelled baths, each fitted, for reasons of modesty, with a hinged lid that only left room for the occupant's head to be visible outside. There was a sweeper to empty latrine buckets through a small trap door in the rear of each lavatory; gardeners, grooms and others who seemed to have no set job at all, but who waited patiently for any errand, squatting on their haunches outside the back door, or on the verandah outside bedroom doors.

The house in Barrackpore also possessed a menagerie. Here, in wooden cages, lived such curious, disparate creatures as black pheasants, porcupines, cheetahs and monkeys. Ben would stand for half an hour at a time watching them. One of his earliest recollections, after riding on the elephant, was of the sadness he felt that such wild birds and beasts should be confined and kept prisoner in such small cages. He felt an instant affinity with them. He knew and sensed how they yearned to be free, to run, to fly. Maybe they would face attack by predators and traditional enemies, and very possibly by man, but at least they would know the exuberance of spreading wings, or stretching their leg muscles. Instead, the animals padded up and down their cages, the birds fluttered here and there feebly, automatically going through the motions of semi-flight.

Years later, Ben would date his first realisation of the importance of freedom from watching the birds and animals in this menagerie.

In the heat of the day, lizards would run silently up and down the whitewashed walls of the house or across the bare boards of the verandah, dried and cracked and shrunk under the pitiless sun, pausing at any strange sound or movement. Once, Ben tried to catch one, and actually gripped its tail. But the reptile simply shed the end of the tail and fled without it.

Ben liked the evenings, and the sudden Indian dusks, with a constant twittering of unseen insects, a gentle whirring as night moths flew against oil lamps, attracted by the warmth and light, beating wings against the globes. There was something mysterious about them. Where did they go by day, these gentle creatures of the dark? No one could tell him: the answer was another secret in a land of secrets, where he felt totally at home.

In Calcutta, insects, bats, birds and heat were all kept at bay, outside the house, not allowed inside, as happened at Barrackpore. Every room there had a punkah, a carpet strip about a yard wide hanging from the centre of the ceiling and extending from one side of the room to the other. From the punkahs a rope extended over a pulley outside the room. Here an old man, a punkah-wallah, lay with the end of the rope tied round his leg. He moved it mechanically, sometimes awake, sometimes asleep. The pulleys creaked continually; even in his slumber the punkah stirred hot and humid air and made it bearable.

Outside the windows hung screens of dried grass known as *tatties*. Throughout the hot season, when wind blew in from the plains, drying the inside of Ben's mouth and nostrils, sand-papering his skin with heat and dust, relays of coolies outside would carry hogskins of cold water from the nearest well and fling the contents on the screens to cool the air.

Inside the bedrooms, beds were carefully protected from insects by screens of tight mesh. The legs of sideboards and cupboards stood in cups of water to keep white ants from boring their way into the woodwork. Humidity in Calcutta was so high that overnight a pair of brightly polished leather boots could be covered by soft green mould.

Beyond the end of the doctor's garden in Calcutta swamps ran down to the river. Vultures crouched on the white brittle limbs of long-dead trees, waiting to pick with their terrible beaks the eyes from dead bodies washed up by the tide. Sometimes, alligators thrust their impatient way through the rushes and the reeds to feast on rotting corpses, and the stench of death seeped into the house through the damp *tatties*.

In India, Ben soon realised, death and danger were never far away: they waited patiently out there in the darkness. The jungle was biding its time to move in on Calcutta's grand houses and wide streets and pillared buildings. In only one season the heat, the damp, the unhealthy lushness of the swamps could easily cover them all. Within two, it could be as though they had never existed. There was something timeless about India in its hugeness; the word for yesterday, *kal*, could also mean tomorrow.

Dr Kintyre employed more servants in Calcutta than in Barrackpore. Some carried messages, others saw that lamps were kept filled with oil and their wicks trimmed. Ben grew used to the company of coachmen, cowmen, grooms, blacksmiths, watchmen, gatekeepers and under-gardeners who dug a shallow trench round each plant in every flowerbed for the *bhisti* to fill with water.

The heat, allied to the lack of any need, or wish, for effort, the enervating humidity, and the boredom of meeting the same people day after day, produced an atmosphere of torpor among British residents. Social life resembled a living repertory theatre: the plays and the backgrounds might change; the cast was always the same.

Ben found a special affinity with the servants which the doctor noted but did not remark on. They did not live inside either of the houses, but behind them, in squat mud huts. Here, on open wood fires, they cooked rice, vegetable curry, with *dhal* in metal bowls. Sometimes, if they were lucky, there would be mutton curry or prawn curry, and Ben would squat with them, eating when they ate, without spoon or fork or knife, but rolling up a piece of chapatti and using this as a spoon. He liked to watch strolling jugglers and illusionists who could make an egg or a guava disappear, apparently in the air, and then produce it triumphantly from the turban of one of their audience. They would sit down with them for a meal and then be on their way, perhaps producing a chicken from someone's *dhoti* as a parting trick.

He learned the language quickly. The doctor engaged a *munshi*, an Indian teacher, to teach him. The *munshi* was an old man, toothless, his mouth sunk in on his gums, but still with a sparkle in his eye. He had the gift of teaching, and Ben learned to speak Hindustani as well as he spoke English.

A year after I wrote to Lady Beaumont about the possibility of her adopting Ben, I received a reply from her. It was the custom for people writing from England to put their name and address on the back of the envelope, and when I received the letter I could not understand who Mrs Gebbie of Brighton might be; I knew no one of that name. Then I opened the envelope and found the answer.

Dear Dr Kintyre,

I have received your communication regarding my brother's son, Ben Fanfare Bannerman. I am much in your debt for your kindness in informing me of my brother's marriage, his son's birth, and the death of his wife. This was indeed the first intimation I had that he was married, and my sorrow at the death of his widow was lessened by my pleasure at the news she left an heir to carry on the family name.

I would dearly like to adopt my nephew and bring him up as my own son because my marriage is childless, and likely to remain so. My husband, Sir Frank Beaumont, however, refuses to counten-ance this proposition. He will not even discuss the matter. He does not care for children, and he has refused to help in any way regarding my brother's son's upbringing or education.

My most earnest appeals to him have proved fruitless, and therefore I am asking you, as a medical man, who must be the safe repository of many secrets, to keep secret the fact that I have written to you. I very much hope, however, that you will keep me informed should you think I may be able to help in any way as my nephew grows up.

Please do not communicate with me at my home or by name, but write to me, if you will, as Mrs Gebbie, Poste Restante, Brighton Post Office, Sussex. I will call at the Post Office or send someone from time to time to see whether there are any letters from you. I deeply regret that I cannot help my nephew financially, as I have very little money of my own, indeed my sole personal means are what my father's three drapery shops realised when they were sold on his death.

In confidence, I must admit that my relations with my husband are not as cordial as one might wish between man and wife, but, as you know, a husband has a right over his wife's property as well as her person, and indeed her whole individuality.

I am sorry to write like this, but I felt I must apprise you of my situation so that you will appreciate – and, I hope, understand – the reason why I can, at this time, do little more than wish my nephew well. I look forward to having reports on the boy's progress in due course. Believe me, etc.

I believed her. As a physician I had attended the wives of several rich men in Scotland as well as in India, and I knew how often inadequacies in a man's character show themselves in harshness to a wife who cannot strike back. Husbands might be failures at different levels – financially, socially, sexually; they might be a laughing stock to other men in their club or regiment or profession, but as far as their wives were concerned they were paramount masters.

I understood Lady Beaumont's predicament, and I felt sorry for her and yet, in a perverse way, pleased for myself. I would bring up the boy – Anna's boy. How odd, I never thought of him, even at that date, as Ben's son. To me, he was simply the son of the woman I had loved, or thought I had loved, which can often be much the same thing.

I put Lady Beaumont's letter with the ring Anna had given to me, and locked them away in the safe. One day, I would write to Mrs Gebbie. One day, I would show Ben her letter and the ring. But not yet; not for a long time yet.

I watched Ben grow up. He ran about barefoot, though I was told this was bad for his feet and he could get ticks in the soles, which would bore their way right into his body. But somehow he didn't. His feet hardened, and he hardened. He was like an animal, I felt, but a friendly animal, with a kind nature. He liked Indians, and they liked him. He listened to the *munshi*'s stories of rajahs and warrior demons and sultans, of times long past; of battles, when elephants carried cannon and men wore all their treasure on their bodies in the form of golden armour.

Indians accepted him. In their relationship, there was no question of who was the master, who was the man; they were on an equal footing. I envied Ben his gift of getting on with people. I would like to have lived that way myself when I was his age, but I suppose that my upbringing, the austere background from which I had come, stifled any outgoing spirit such as Ben possessed. After all, he had never known the restrictions of a cold climate and a harsh religion.

One day I went to my safe to collect medicines. I kept

the dangerous drugs locked there: It was impossible to explain to Indians how deadly some European poisons could be; I could not make them understand that they could kill within minutes, and in the most agonising way. It was therefore better and safer to lock everything out of their sight and out of their reach.

I had to move the little box containing the ruby ring to find the medicines, and, on the impulse, I took the box out of the safe, carried it to the window and opened it.

The huge ruby glowed like a red and angry three-cornered eye. It seemed somehow much richer and larger than it had appeared in the tent on the road from Kabul. I had no doubt that it was extremely valuable. I had meant to have it properly valued, but I could not trust anyone in Calcutta with the task. If the stone was worth a great deal, they would give me a false price. They might even substitute a false stone – I had heard of these practices among jewellers – and I did not want to risk losing it. This ruby was not mine to put at risk in any way. I was holding it in trust for Ben.

As I examined it, I noticed the *munshi* watching me from the doorway, or rather not watching me but watching the stone. There was a look on his face that I had never seen before, as though he was somehow in awe of it, as though this single glowing ruby possessed some strange power about which I knew nothing. He was afraid of it, or what it represented. But what could that possibly be? It was only a jewel, valuable and rare without doubt, but nothing more.

I put the stone back in its box, locked it away quickly. He stood staring at the safe as though he could see through the metal door to what lay within.

'Very lovely ring,' he said slowly.

'Yes,' I agreed. 'His mother gave it to me for Ben.

It is a ruby. Do you know anything about stones?'

'That is a pigeon's blood ruby, sahib. The very best and the rarest. Its colour is carmine, like the blood of a bird, not the dark red of most rubies. But that is all I am knowing about it.'

I looked at him sharply. Something in his tone of voice made me think he knew a lot more, but for reasons of his own was indisposed to tell me. These old Indians could be very stubborn; if he wasn't going to tell me of his own accord, he would not do so if I asked him directly. And I saw with surprise that he was so frightened that he had momentarily lost his ability to speak good English, but had briefly lapsed into the sing-song idiom of the bazaar.

He went away quickly. Later that evening I saw other servants in the house glancing surreptitiously towards the safe. Clearly the *munshi* had told them about it, and they also knew something about the stone that I did not. But what this could be I had no idea, and no means whatever of discovering, for I knew they would never tell me.

Time passed quickly, as it does when you are doing a job you like, and especially when you are helping other people rather than simply helping yourself. Over the years I built up a large and lucrative practice. I was well paid by the richer nabobs, both British and Indian, but I also treated many poor people without any charge at all. This seemed to me a fair exchange, to help to balance the huge sums I took from my wealthy patients.

I could say that time passed without my noticing it, but that was not quite true. Bachelor friends of mine, who had arrived in India when I did, were now married with growing families of their own. I was still unmarried. I had not found anyone I wanted to marry, and I suppose in a kind of quixotic, dreamlike way I judged women I met by totally imaginary standards, against Anna's memory. In any case, European women in Calcutta seemed to me to be shallow and vapid. This was not their fault, of course. They had so little to occupy their time that their minds soon atrophied. With so many servants, they had only to clap their hands and someone would run to do their bidding. If they were married, their husbands might start work at six in the morning, before the heat became intolerable, or they might be sent up-country for weeks. If they worked locally, they would often come home for lunch and then spend the afternoon in bed, or reading papers months old. They would return to their office, the *daftar*, in the cool of early evening.

Single women led even duller lives. There weren't so many of them, of course. Usually, they had come out to India with the sole intention of marrying, and hence were known derogatorily as the 'fishing fleet' because they were fishing for husbands. Even the plainest, dullest ones married in the end, because European men outnumbered European women at least twelve to one. Frequently, they married two or three times in short order, one husband after another.

Many husbands, dressed in unsuitable serge suits during the heat, drinking a pint of claret a day, enjoying huge meals of mutton and potatoes and rice, with port, cigars and brandy to follow, did not live to grow old. They caught some fever or simply had an apoplexy and died. Their wives led more sheltered and abstemious lives and outlived them time and time again. I had grown accustomed to sitting at a patient's bedside to tell them, as gently as possible, just how serious their illness really was, that their time on earth was shrinking; the sand had all but emptied in the glass.

When the patient is himself a doctor, these roles are cruelly reversed, but he still snatches at whatever grains of comfort he can find. He assures himself that incurable cancer, which all his medical training tells him is eating away his insides, is really nothing more serious than indigestion. A pinch of bicarbonate of soda in half a glass of warm water will soon deal with that. Breathlessness accompanying a climb of even half a dozen steps is never a warning of heart or artery trouble, only a reminder that he had a little too much to drink last night, and is not quite as young as he was.

For some months, I had been suffering from a fever which no treatment seemed capable of curing. I had the familiar symptoms, so commonplace in India: sore throat, dry mouth, and a fluctuating temperature. Having failed to treat myself successfully, I called upon the senior surgeon of the Bengal Army for his advice. He was a man in his fifties, grey-haired, tough, wiry, no nonsense about him.

He examined me, listened to my list of symptoms, then sat me down in a chair opposite his desk in his surgery and looked me sternly in the eye.

'I have to be frank with you, Kintyre,' he said bluntly. 'We're both medical men, so I needn't pretend I know what's the matter with you. I don't. But it's clearly a most serious fever. The fact that you've suffered from it for so long and tried all manner of medicaments yourself without any success shows just how virulent it is.

'The trouble with this damned country is that the very air is poisoned. I had a patient – a sergeant – cut himself on a penknife, not more than a scratch. But a speck of dirt got into the cut, and he was dead within the week. The earth here is poisoned with the dust of thousands, maybe millions of bodies over the centuries. Plus all the dung and detritus of generations.

'Since I don't know what your fever is, I can't prescribe anything for it, except one course I most strongly advise you to take. Go home. Get out of these swamps, this pestilence, these monsoon rains followed by baking and sweating heat. Go back to a cooler climate.'

'How do I know the fever will die if I leave?' I asked him.

'You don't know. Nor do I. No one does. But I'll tell you this. You will die if you stay. Three months ago, I had a patient here, sitting exactly where you are sitting, suffering from similar symptoms of unknown fever, what to the layman I call NYD fever – not yet diagnosed. For three months he refused to leave. I attended his funeral at St John's last Thursday.'

'You have kept free of all these problems yourself?' I asked him.

'I have,' he said. 'But I don't know how. Fevers seem to be selective. I am fortunate that none of them have selected me – so far. When people express surprise that I have not been cut down by some infernal fever, I am reminded of the comment of the Abbé Sieyès. When asked what he had done during the French Revolution, he replied: "I survived." So take my advice and go, while you can, and survive.'

'Oddly enough, I like it here in Calcutta.'

'But maybe it doesn't like you. Anyhow, that is my diagnosis. Go and see anyone else you like, and I think they'll give you the same advice.'

'You may be right,' I said, and in my heart I knew he was. I had been in India before the present custom of going to the coolness of the hills every summer to escape from the pitiless heat of the plains. Transport was more primitive then. A journey by train now takes a couple of days, while in my time it could take as many weeks by bullock cart. I had seen too many of my contemporaries die after two monsoons. I did not want to die. I decided to go home and see whether a cold climate could cure where physic had failed.

That afternoon the mail boat docked, and I received a letter from my father's housekeeper, Bertha. It had been posted in Perth sixteen weeks earlier. She wrote to say that my father had caught a chill in a very bad winter they had experienced. Some complication set in – I suppose pneumonia, although the local doctor had not told her so specifically – and now he was dead. There was a further problem. The manse was needed for the next Presbyterian minister. She had been given three months to leave. Could I help her?

I wrote back right away, because the ship was leaving the following morning, and told her to take what accommodation she could, storing my father's furniture, because I was coming home. I would be responsible for whatever the rent and storage might cost.

I then sent by the same ship a letter to the manager of the British Linen Bank in Perth, which held my account. I asked him to make sure that Bertha had sufficient to live on and to pay any bills she presented until I returned. And if he knew of any house suitable for a doctor in the area, I was in the market to buy.

Now that I had reached this decision, I felt a curious sense of relief mixed with sadness. I had come out to India to find a better way of life. This, in a material sense, I had achieved. I had also briefly found a woman I felt I could love, and had lost her before I even knew her well. But I had grown fond of her young son.

And now this period of my life was over. The fever somehow marked its end, as asterisks can mark the finish of a chapter in a book. I was going home, and I believed I would not come East again. In life, one can sometimes stop and pause and think and look back, but one must then go on. The way always lies ahead. One must never go back.

When I told Ben we were going home, he looked at me surprised, not quite comprehending. Then I

94

realised that to him India was home. He had never left home. Now he was about to do so. He was going somewhere totally new, to a country that would be as strange to him as India had been to me when I first arrived.

'My father has died,' I explained. 'He was a very old man, very kind. I wish I had seen more of him, but that is too late to think about now. I've had a fever for some time, and I cannot be cured in this climate. These two circumstances have made me decide that I – we – should go back to Scotland. I can settle my father's affairs and you can go to school, a proper school.'

'I've learned a lot here, Uncle,' he replied, 'with the *munshi* sahib and the major's wife.'

She had been a governess before she sailed East in search of a husband. She was a good teacher and from her Ben had learned reading, writing, arithmetic, even history. She would be sorry to lose her only pupil. In helping Ben, she had also helped herself, by giving herself an interest and a goal: to teach him as much as she possibly could. She had no children of her own, and I guessed that she regarded Ben as a surrogate son.

'You will be able to take your place in a Scottish school without any problems. You'll have a few points up on them, too, because you speak Hindustani and you've lived out here.'

'*Must* we go?' he asked me, searching my face for an answer he guessed I could not give.

'I know how you feel,' I told him. 'Every departure hurts when you've been living in a place for some time. Especially when, like you, you've been living here all your life.'

'The *munshi* told me that every time one says good-bye, some part of you dies. Do you think that is so,

Uncle?' he asked me earnestly.

'I think it is so if you liked the people or the place you are leaving. But you can either say we're saying goodbye, or saying hello to something quite different. Always look on the positive side.'

'I will try,' he assured me, but not very confidently.

That night Ben lay awake long after the doctor was asleep, listening to the sounds of darkness. They frightened some other little boys, but to him they were all friendly; they never frightened him. He heard the cries of jackals along the banks of the river, the sudden shriek of horror and realisation of some little animal caught by a predator. He smelt wood smoke blown into his room through the filtered mesh of the mosquito net over his bed. He heard distant drums beyond the rim of firelight in the servants' quarters and the wail of Indian music.

The notes seemed to repeat themselves indefinitely and yet, when he listened carefully, they did not quite repeat themselves. They were a mass of minute variations; none ever jarred on his ears, though they jarred on the ears of the Europeans.

'Can't stand that bloody row,' they would say irritably. 'Gets on my nerves, all that wailing and caterwauling.'

Ben was always surprised at this attitude. To him it was not a row, it was the voice of a great country speaking through music.

He liked the early mornings, too, when mist lay over the *maidan* towards the river. Through this mist he could see white egrets and the shiny flanks of water buffaloes as they stood motionless, except for slowly champing jaws. On their backs little birds, white-winged, long-beaked, would peck away busily at the ticks buried deep in the animal's hide. There was a communion here which Ben understood and liked and felt comforted by. Here, he felt he belonged.

What would England – Scotland – be like? Could he adapt to life there after India? Sometimes in Calcutta he would be invited to tea with other little boys and girls. Like their mothers, they were pale-faced, perspiring, wan and weary, energy eroded or evaporated in the humid heat. He did not feel like this at all, and he knew he did not look as pasty as they did. The hotter it was, the more cheerful he felt. He simply could not understand how for them the heat was not a friend but an enemy. The basic difference was that he liked Calcutta and Barrackpore, and they did not. Their parents counted years, months, days, sometimes even hours, until they could embark for England, and so the children counted with them.

Ben only knew about England and Scotland from pictures in books the doctor had shown him: stone buildings, snow, fog, carriages on wide streets, people wearing tall hats and black coats. Everything seemed very impressive, but the sun could not bring out the colours, the life, the throbbing intensity of everyday living as it did in India because these qualities were not there. The northern sun gave light but little heat.

He had learned quickly with the major's wife, but he was just as happy, probably more so, in his daily sessions in the late afternoon after siesta with the *munshi*. Best of all he liked the stories the *munshi* told him.

'You were born in Afghanistan, yes?' the *munshi* asked him once.

'Yes, *munshi* sahib,' Ben agreed.

The *munshi* was to be addressed as sahib like a European; he was a learned man who spoke English and many other tongues. His abilities assured him of this courtesy title.

'I saw the doctor sahib with a very splendid ruby in a ring. He said it is yours.'

'Yes. My father gave it to my mother. He was a soldier. He was killed before I was born.'

'So I heard. I think he was a brave man. The bravest always die first because they are in the front of the battle. Cowards skulk away and so die a hundred deaths. Not the brave. They live every moment of their lives until the end. Have you heard of Alexander the Great, the conqueror?'

'I have,' said Ben.

'Did you know he marched the same route as your father?'

'No, I did not know that, *munshi* sahib.'

'He must have passed the very spot where you were born. But that is not what I tell you of Alexander now, my boy. I will tell you two stories, which are about other precious stones. Diamonds.

'Alexander led his army across a ridge of hills and saw a valley completely covered with diamonds. They glittered in the sun's rays like a lake of blinding glass. And among the diamonds lay the bleached skeletons of men who had tried to seize them. But all had failed.

'The diamonds were guarded by great birds with cruel beaks and long curved claws. They tore to pieces all who came near. Alexander wished to seize those diamonds, for a diamond the size of a tiny pebble can buy more than a bullock cart of gold, but he could not risk his soldiers' lives trying to climb down and fight off the birds while they collected the stones. Too many others had already tried and failed.

'So Alexander decided to use his brain instead of his men's muscles. He ordered them to kill several sheep grazing on the slopes nearby. Then they skinned them and hurled the carcasses down among the diamonds. Hundreds of diamonds stuck to the fat, and vultures swooped down and carried off to their nests in the mountain peaks the carcasses encrusted with diamonds. Alexander's soldiers followed them, killed the vultures, and dug out the diamonds.

'Near Golconda, where great diamonds have been found since time began, he travelled through another valley, again thick with diamonds, this time guarded by huge and poisonous serpents, thick as a man's body. Their forked tongues were a foot long, but most deadly were their eyes. If they looked into your eyes, you died.

'But again Alexander had a plan. He sent his men into the local bazaars to buy every mirror they could find. Then, keeping their own eyes shielded, they directed the mirrors at the serpents.

'The serpents saw their own reflections – and died instantly. So Alexander's soldiers could collect the diamonds safely. What do those two stories tell you? As a soldier's son, you should know the lesson.'

'That Alexander was a very clever man, *munshi* sahib.'

'True. But more than that, it tells you how his mind worked. Always he made plans before he went into action. Then he turned his enemy's strength against them.

'When you grow up, my boy, you may be a soldier, like your father. You may be in a war and have to fight when you are totally outnumbered. Fighting man to man, you would be defeated. But if you use your brains, you can win.

'Your holy book, the Bible, tells the story of the boy David going out to meet the giant Goliath. Now Goliath could kill him with one blow of his hand, and tear him apart with his little fingers. He had the strength, but David had the plan.

'He took three pebbles and his sling, and before Goliath could come to grips with him, David fired a stone at the giant's forehead and stunned him. Goliath dropped like a dead ox, and lay at David's mercy.

'Think of these stories, my boy. When you are older, you may be in a situation where everyone around you is in fear and turmoil and terror. Keep your head. *Think*. Remember the old *munshi* sahib. Remember his stories.'

'I will remember,' Ben promised him.

But he could not imagine how these legends of the past might ever help him in the future.

Chapter Four

They were hanging the man on Monday morning at nine, sharp. On Sunday, warders marched all the other prisoners in Newgate Prison into the prison chapel to hear what was called the condemned sermon.

The smell of their unwashed bodies, wearing rotting, ragged clothes clotted with faeces and dirt from the cells, was so overpowering that the clergyman, known as the Ordinary, for he was an ordinary clergyman not a deacon or a canon, insisted on entering the chapel in advance of his congregation. If he did not, he protested he could not bring himself to enter such a foul and stinking place.

The prisoners in the pews were serving sentences for crimes that ranged from attempted murder to owing trivial sums of money, as little as three or four shillings.

Those debtors who might originally have been imprisoned for small sums found that within a few weeks they owed twice or three times as much because of various fees which the turnkeys and other officials regularly extracted from them on various pretexts – for their food, or a place to sleep out of the dung and filth that coated the flagstoned floors. Lacking money to pay for such basic necessities, they could only run up a kind of terrible credit that increased daily, an ever-accumulating debt to be paid at some unspecified future time. If they did not pay, they would starve.

Many women had children with them, unwashed, uncared for, dressed in rags. How could they conceivably earn even pennies in this gaol? Their only way of paying their debt was by offering their bodies or those of their children to officials or richer prisoners serving sentences for other crimes.

In the chapel, two galleries faced each other above the heads of the felons. In one sat the plump City of London sheriffs, splendid in fur-edged robes, with gold chains of office round their necks. Facing them in the opposite gallery sat convicts originally sentenced to death but who, on the discovery of some further evidence or because of a political whim, had been reprieved to serve life sentences here or in Australia.

In the centre of the church, beneath the galleries, was a single raised pew, painted black. This was the condemned pew. Here sat whoever was due to die on Monday morning.

The condemned man was always the last to enter the chapel, walking slowly, in pace with the solemn pealing of the bell. The service was in fact a burial service, given in advance, so that the condemned prisoner could hear what, in other circumstances, would have been said above his new-dug grave. Sometimes ten or a dozen prisoners would sit here. On this particular Sunday, there was only one, a forger.

At sixteen, Mary Jane Green, watching with her mother Jane, only twice as old, was fascinated by the condemned man's face. It was not coarse and pitted with pockmarks, as were many of the convicts' faces, but grave, almost gentle. His suit, although threadbare, was as clean as he could keep it in his circumstances.

The Ordinary called out sonorously, 'The Service for the Dead.' Everyone shuffled to their feet. As he read the solemn words, 'The Lord giveth, the Lord taketh away, blessed be the name of the Lord', women prisoners began to keen, wailing with a strange, fearful sound that rose and fell and rose again like waves on some distant, terrible sea. Some screamed and fell to the ground in hysterics, urinating, defecating in their misery. Others fainted and lay where they fell.

The sheriffs, many of whom, but for natural cunning, good fortune, sharp lawyers or a combination of all three, might have been occupying the black pew themselves, blew their noses and looked anywhere but at the face of the man condemned to die.

The wailing continued for several minutes, and then, as it gradually died away, the prisoners filed back to their cells. As the condemned man passed within feet of Mary Jane, he turned and looked at her. Their eyes met briefly. He smiled wanly and then went on, a turnkey on either side, marching to his cell.

There were fifteen cells for the condemned in Newgate, all at present occupied. Each had a vaulted ceiling nine feet high formed in the shape of an arch. The stone walls were lined with planks studded with nails sticking out to a length of two or three inches to frustrate any desperate attempts by those under sentence of death to dig a way out though the stones with a knife or spoon smuggled in by a visitor.

Two sets of bars protected the only small window, high up in the wall. The door, four inches thick, had a circular hole cut into it to allow air from the corridor to circulate through the cell. The prisoner had the use of a metal bedstead without any bedding; a crazed or desperate man might cut bedding into strips and throttle or hang himself.

A turnkey had shown these cells to the women prisoners on the previous day. Mary Jane had tried not to imagine what it would be like for a prisoner to lie awake, waiting for the morning bell to toll. This would mark the moment when he would be led out and blindfolded on the scaffold platform.

'You're quiet, child,' said her mother.

'I'm thinking.'

'About what?'

'About that man. The forger. What did he forge?'

'Someone's signature.'

'For money?'

'Yes. For twenty pounds, I was told. Apparently he'd done it before, for a lesser sum, and got away with it.'

'A terrible thing to lose your life for twenty pounds.'

'It's the law,' her mother replied shortly. 'It's a terrible thing for us to be in here, owing only a few shillings. God knows when we'll ever get out, child.'

'What about Father?' asked Mary Jane.

Her mother shrugged. 'What about him?'

'Well, where is he? What's happened to him? Can't he pay the debt and get us out?'

'I don't know where he is, child. Men go their own way in this world. He went.'

'But *why*?'

Mary Jane had never asked this before, but somehow the thought of the man about to die, the fact that they were in this fearful place without any prospect of release, made her want to scream and shout, to stamp the floor in frustration and fear. What had they ever done to bring this on themselves?

She and her mother and father had been, as she imagined, a happy family; at least happier than they were now. But her father, in her mother's phrase, liked a drop, and often a drop too much. One day he walked out of their home and did not come back. He worked in a warehouse in Stepney, and they both went down to see the foreman in case he had been involved in an accident. The man looked at them both in amazement.

'You're Jack Green's missis, are you? And his daughter? Never even knew he was married.'

'Well, he is,' said her mother. 'And he hasn't been home for three days.'

'Sorry, but I don't know where he is.'

'But he works here.'

'Did.'

'What do you mean, did?'

'The boss sacked him six weeks ago.'

'Why?'

'Bad time-keeping. Skiving.'

'But he's left the house at six every morning since to go to work.'

'That's as maybe. But wherever he's working – if he is working – he's not working here.'

'Have you seen him recently?'

'No, mum. I haven't.'

'Do you think he's dead?' Mary Jane asked her mother as they walked back to their lodgings.

Her mother shrugged miserably. 'I just don't know.'

Her husband had been away several times before, but only for a couple of days. He had always come back, usually with a black eye and some loose teeth and a hangover, vomit and blood staining his shirt front. He'd go on a binge and get into a fight, but he hadn't lost his job.

Had he gone out each morning for these past six weeks to run errands, or sit in the back of a bar with a fourpenny rum and water, pretending he was working because he was too proud to tell his wife and daughter that he was unemployed? If so, how and where did he find fourpence a day to spend on drink? Had he been trudging round trying to find work? Or had he been run down by a tram, or even taken his own life? Had he gone off with a rich woman?

This last explanation was the most unlikely; there

105

was so little about him to attract a rich woman. He was an ordinary, dumpy man, so ordinary it would be difficult to describe him in detail. A moustache, a slightly bald head, weak eyes, a seemingly harmless disposition until he was in liquor. And even then he was not violent; well, not usually.

The news that he had not been at work for six weeks was the first shock. The second came when they returned to their rooms. The landlord was waiting for them in the doorway, with a uniformed constable.

'What's the matter?' Mary Jane's mother asked him. 'Has something happened?'

'Expecting something to happen, are you, then?' asked the constable, flexing his legs in their thick serge trousers.

'No. But why are you here? There must be a reason.'

'There is,' said the landlord grimly. 'I haven't seen your husband for the last few days. And he owes me three weeks' rent. I've spoken to him several times, but all I got were promises. I need the money to live on. Promises don't buy no food.'

'How much do we owe you?' Mary Jane's mother asked him. It was best to know the worst.

'Thirty-nine shillings,' he said. 'Exactly.'

'I can give you a pound,' she said. 'I've got that saved up.'

'I'll take that for the time being, then,' the landlord replied grudgingly.

She went into the room, lifted the mattress on the bed, pulled out a yellow oilskin pouch. She had left two pounds in it. Now it was empty.

'I had two pounds. They've gone,' she said flatly, unable to believe it. The landlord looked at her suspiciously, but she seemed honest enough. Not like her husband; a real fly one, he was.

'Perhaps your husband took them,' he suggested.

'I don't know. He's gone as well. I don't know where he is.'

'Done a moonlight flit, has he, then?' the constable asked, not unfriendly. Sometimes a man found he could take no more nagging from a wife or a mother-in-law, and just took off; he'd known this happen many times. But this woman didn't look the bitchy sort, and the girl was a real good looker. In fine clothes she could pass for a lady.

'His foreman says he's not been in to work for weeks. He could be dead for all I know.'

'I'm sorry, Mrs Green. But I've always had trouble with getting the rent off him, as you may know.'

'I didn't know.'

'It's always in arrears. Always has to be asked for. Several times. I've said nothing before because I was sorry for you and the girl. But I'll have to have you committed unless you can pay today. I'm a working man, too.'

'You're a rich working man,' said Mary Jane quickly.

'I wish I were, I tell you. But every room in my house has to pay, or I go under. The margin's very tight. And we're going through very hard times at the moment.'

He turned to the constable.

'Now you've seen Mrs Green, there's no need for you to stay.'

The policeman nodded, disappointed at not being able to take someone into custody. Such little triumphs helped promotion, which was slow enough.

When he had gone the landlord turned to Mary Jane.

'You cut along,' he said. 'I want to talk to your mother on her own.'

She went out of the house, but on an impulse came back and listened against the door. The landlord was speaking in a low, urgent voice.

'If we can come to some arrangement, Mrs Green, I can let this rent go. Not for ever, of course, because money's money. But say for a couple of weeks.'

'What sort of arrangement?'

'I'll be blunt. No good beating about the bush, is there? Fact is, I've fancied you from the first time I saw you come through the front door. You come to bed with me, that's what I'm saying.'

Mary Jane heard her mother take a deep breath.

'I can't,' she said. 'I'm loyal to my man.'

'He won't know, he's not here. Slice off a cut loaf's never missed.'

'The loaf misses it,' said her mother.

'Well, think about it till tonight. Otherwise I've got no option but to call the constable again. I don't want to do that, but it's the only way I'll ever get paid.'

Next morning, he called the constable. Mother and daughter appeared before a magistrate and were taken to Newgate.

'How can I ever get any money while I'm in here?' Mrs Green cried desperately.

The turnkey who showed them into the women's section shrugged his shoulders. 'Can't help you, mum,' he said. 'Wish I could. Every debtor who comes in here says much the same. But that's the law. Can't do nothing about it, can we?'

The women's section was beyond an area known as the Press Yard. It took this name from a punishment formerly given to male prisoners facing charges which could merit the death penalty, who refused 'to stand to the law'; that is, they would not plead guilty or not guilty. If they answered their charges and were found guilty, then, in addition to losing their lives, they would also lose all their possessions; this could leave wives and families destitute. If they kept silent, their goods would not be forfeit because they could not be tried.

To persuade them to change their minds they were marched to the Press Yard and stripped naked. A cloth was wrapped round their loins and they were ordered to lie down on their backs.

Iron weights so heavy that the prisoners could only just breathe were then placed on their bare chests. They were given three morsels of coarse bread one day; the next, three cups of stagnant water from any pool near the prison doors, not fresh water from a conduit. This treatment continued, with more weights being placed on their body, until either they decided to plead or they died. Usually, they died.

Sometimes, as an additional punishment, the prisoner was made to lie on a board with nails sticking up through it so that the weights forced his body down onto their points.

Prisoners would lie here for days and nights in agony, begging to be put to death, gradually losing their reason. If the prison authorities considered they would never plead, the weights on their bodies were increased to as much as three hundred and fifty pounds, and their arms and legs were strapped to stakes driven into the flagstones to keep them straight. Here they lay in their own dung and urine until death mercifully released them.

Three hundred women prisoners, with children of all ages, were crammed into nine small cells beyond this gloomy yard. Several women were pregnant, others had already given birth to crippled and blind babies, or idiots. There was no segregation according to crime. Debtors, some awaiting trial, shared cells with murderers. Most wore rags, some went almost naked. They seized the clothes of new and richer arrivals, literally tearing them from their backs. If newcomers objected, they were beaten about the face with fists or boots or pieces of wood. Some of the women were insane; they

109

would shout continually, tear off their clothes and run around naked, punching, kicking, spitting at any who stood in their way. The smell of blood and dung and sweat was chokingly strong. Surely *anything* would be preferable to this nightmare existence? Mary Jane could not understand why her mother had not agreed to the landlord's proposition. Now, it was all too late.

'Will we *ever* get out?' she asked despairingly.

'Only if someone will pay the debt.'

'But who? *Who?*'

Her mother shrugged. 'Maybe the good Lord will send someone our way.'

They slept close together on the stone floor. They would have had to pay the turnkey several shillings a week to share a straw palliasse with three other women. They did not have several shillings, not even several pence.

In the far corners of the cell, several pairs of women kissed and fondled each other. Some were wearing cast-off men's clothing, filthy shirts, trousers and jackets. They would lift the skirts of their companions, their hands continually probing, stroking, caressing.

A crowd of women arrived from Manchester to serve their sentence. They were all handcuffed. Round their bare ankles they had metal hoops, linked by chains. The metal was rusty and rough, and had eaten through their skin down to the bone. The wounds had swollen and festered. Others, facing longer sentences, were chained to each other in groups of four, in case any should attempt to escape.

'Who are they?' asked Mary Jane in horror.

'Gypsies. Travellers. Fairground people. The law doesn't like them. They're always on the move,' another woman explained.

Through that evening and far into the night, the sound of sobbing, crying, shrieks and yells, of fists and

110

feet beating on the floor in rage or despair or madness echoed through the cells as the hour of execution approached.

Usually, the gallows was kept dismantled inside the gaol. On the morning of any execution it was quickly assembled on a platform with iron wheels and pushed into the yard so that as many as possible could see the hanging, in an effort to impress on all the horror of such punishment. Male prisoners hammered metal stakes into the ground and lashed the wheels to them to hold steady the clumsy, top-heavy contrivance.

Visitors from all over London were now arriving to watch the spectacle. They were fashionably dressed. Many held perfumed silk handkerchiefs to their noses to filter the foul stench of the prison and its suppurating open sewers, buzzing with flies. The hangman Calcroft was already up on the platform, waving cheerfully at people he recognised in the crowd, shouting ribald replies to their questions and remarks as though this was a comic turn. He and the condemned prisoner were the stars, but only Calcroft would make a second appearance.

He was a kindly man, so the turnkeys assured Mary Jane. He had formerly been a ladies' shoemaker, then a watchman. By chance he had helped a stranger taken ill in the street. This man explained he was the public hangman and because of his indisposition would not be able to do his duty. Calcroft, on the impulse, offered to stand in for him, and was given the job permanently.

He was well known as an angler, fond of fishing on Saturdays in the New River. He also kept a number of tame white rabbits in hutches behind his house, and a pony that followed him about like a dog. His wage was one guinea a week throughout the year, with a second guinea for each hanging. Sometimes, when he came to

Newgate to claim his extra fee, he brought his grand-children with him.

Now he watched the condemned forger being led out of his cell. His hands were bound at the wrists, his arms pinioned to his sides. Round his eyes he wore a red and white dotted handkerchief. Two prison officers pulled a white cotton cloth like a nightcap over his head. It reached down to his chest. They guided him up onto the platform, positioned him above the concealed trap door.

At a given signal, Calcroft's assistant, crouched beneath the stage, would pull a bolt, the door would fall open, and the condemned man drop through at the end of a length of rope, decided by the hangman according to the condemned man's height and weight.

Calcroft was very casual about these calculations. Weights and measurements were quite beyond his limited intelligence. He relied on guesswork, favouring what he called a 'short drop'. If the victim did not die, he would jump on him and swing on his thighs to bring him down and break his neck. He called this 'steadying the legs a bit'.

Now he put the noose over the man's head, and adjusted it so that the knot in the rope was behind the forger's right ear. Suddenly, the victim leapt to one side so that both his feet were on the firm part of the stage. He bent forward slightly and the horrified watchers saw his shoulders heave and move, and within a moment, like a professional contortionist, he was free of his bonds. He ripped off the white death cap and the spotted handkerchief, shouting hoarsely, 'I'm innocent! I'm innocent! *Let me go!*'

Immediately, three turnkeys jumped on the platform and seized him. The Ordinary, who was standing nearby, turned away and made the sign of the cross. The prison governor gave a hasty signal, and the trap door dropped on its hinges. But the man was still standing on the platform, shouting, fighting, trying to knee or bite those who gripped him. The door swung open uselessly.

Calcroft saw his guinea fee in jeopardy. He rushed forward, pushed the turnkeys out of the way, flung his arms round the man and leaped with him over the gaping hole in the floor. For a second, the man's body twitched, his legs shot out spasmodically, and then he was silent, swinging slowly like a loose pendulum. Calcroft climbed up out of the hole. He wiped his hands on the sides of his trousers, spat on the dusty boards as though to show what he thought of this undignified performance.

The other prisoners turned away. The fashionable visitors also prepared to leave, comparing this hanging with others they had seen. Sometimes the rope broke. If this happened the man might go free, depending on who was conducting the hanging. Officials had been known to bring out two more ropes before the victim finally swung into the eternal mists.

A man in rough fustian clothes, with a large peaked cap, stepped from the crowd and pulled several short lengths of rope from his pocket.

'Buy it now!' he called. 'Same as the hangman's rope! Same as hanged the noted forger! You'll never buy better. Sixpence a turn. Half a bob for a bit of history!'

Several people paid willingly for this souvenir as Mary Jane and her mother walked back to the women's section. They sat down on a patch of straw spread in one corner. There were no seats, nowhere else to sit except the floor. Mrs Green broke the silence first.

'Well, you see what happens when you fall foul of the law,' she said sadly. 'Forging to get money to buy food – maybe he was married, and had children, and was desperate. It may be against the law, but he shouldn't have to pay for it with his life. And I don't want you to pay for mistakes your father made with *your* life.'

'But *I'm* not going to be hanged, surely?'

'Of course not. I mean wasting your life in here, measuring it away, hour by hour. I've been speaking to women who've been here for months, years in some cases. They owe so much money now that they can never hope to get out, unless a fairy godmother turns up, and that's not very likely.

'I'm going to get you out of here somehow, even if I can't do anything for myself. Then you can make your own way. So look upon our stay in here as a kind of education. You've already learned more about human nature and life's unfairness than most ever know in all their lives. And learn from my experience. I trusted your father. Now I've no idea what's happened to him. He's either lost his memory after being sacked, or he's taken his own life, or gone off, or something equally awful.'

'But I can't leave you here, even if I could get out.'

'You'll have to. Maybe you can find a rich friend, borrow some money, or make some money, and get me out, too. But stuck in here together, we've no hope.'

Mary Jane could not remember her mother ever being so gloomy or pessimistic. But then she could never remember a time in her life when she had been surrounded by so many terrible people in such squalor. In the far corner of the yard she noticed two women bent over a little boy, undressing him. This seemed an odd thing to do at that time in the morning. She looked more closely. The child was dead. They were stripping his body to give the clothes to some other child still alive.

She stared, so horrified yet fascinated at the sight, that she did not hear footsteps approaching. A turnkey tapped her sharply on the shoulder with his stick. She turned, forgetting for the moment where she was, who he was. Then she stood up hurriedly. These people did not like to be kept waiting, and she did not want a cuff round the ears to remind her of the fact.

By the man's side stood a middle-aged woman wearing a long black dress, black gloves, a black hat with a wide brim, a black, fine meshed veil. Through it Mary Jane could see her face, very pale, cold and hard as a waxwork image. Two angry spots on her left cheek had been almost, but not quite, concealed by powder and her dark veil.

'This is Mrs Mentmore,' the turnkey explained importantly. 'She's looking for a quiet girl to place in a good house. I told her you are well-behaved, and clean – when you have the chance. And you're not in any way responsible for being brought here. It would help you, help your mother, help everyone – give them more space – if she found you suitable.'

Mary Jane's mother stood up. 'My daughter doesn't want to go with you,' she told Mrs Mentmore bluntly.

'You know nothing about the appointment,' Mrs Mentmore replied.

Her voice had a West Country burr in it. She was not an aristocrat, although she dressed like one and Mary Jane guessed she hoped to be taken for one.

'I could offer your daughter a position that would pay considerably more than she could receive elsewhere.'

'How? Why? What has she got to do for that money?'

'She would have to take orders from people. Help to clean the house. Do whatever a girl in domestic service does.'

'And what would she be paid for that?'

'One pound a week. And a uniform. A clean bed to lie in and two meals a day.'

'First pound of her wages to me for introducing her,' said the turnkey quickly in case anyone should forget his commission.

'Where would she be working?' Mrs Green asked, ignoring the interruption.

'I can't give you exact details of the abode where she would be placed, but it would be in London. Perhaps Grosvenor Square or Berkeley Square, or in one of the new villas being built near Kensington village. I can assure you, she will be well taken care of.'

'We've often put girls with Mrs Mentmore,' said the turnkey. 'They never come back here. They all do well.'

'I don't want that life for my daughter,' said Mrs Green.

'Please,' said Mary Jane gently. 'It's a chance. I can save money and then pay off the debt. Then you will be released and we can be together.'

'You're a good girl,' said her mother, and Mary Jane saw she was crying. She looked suddenly very small and vulnerable, defeated. Mrs Green dabbed her tears with a handkerchief, and wiped away some of the dirt that covered her face like another skin.

'All right,' she said with resignation. 'I suppose anything is better than being here. How can I get in contact with you, Mrs Mentmore?'

'Through me,' said the turnkey quickly. 'Me and her have known each other for years.'

'When would you want my daughter for interviews?'

'Now,' said Mrs Mentmore. 'The sooner she gets out of Newgate the better. You don't want her to stay here, get corrupted, do you? The stench, the filthy people.'

'We're not all bad,' retorted Mrs Green. 'Not nearly as bad as lots outside with their big houses and carriages and pairs. Many of us are just unfortunate.'

'I know that well enough, Mrs Green. But I am sure you will agree that the sooner your daughter leaves Newgate the better for her. And if she saves money, the better for you.'

'I'll go now, if you'll have me,' said Mary Jane.

'Have you any other clothes?'

'Nothing, only what I'm wearing, and a bar of soap, a strip of towel.'

'Not a toothbrush? No scent? Powder?'

'No. Nothing else.'

'My dear, we'll have to change all that. You'll have a better life with me. That I can promise you.'

So, bewildered and puzzled by her mother's tears, and secretly concerned at her vehemence that she should not take this job, Mary Jane's departure from Newgate was tinged with wariness. As she walked behind Mrs Mentmore and the turnkey, prisoners on either side suddenly began to shout. As they passed the Press Yard, the uproar increased. Men and women were yelling abuse at them, stamping their feet, their faces contorted with hate, bitterness and loathing.

'What have we done to make them so angry?' she asked Mrs Mentmore nervously.

'You don't know much, child, do you? They're envious because you're going out and they're staying here – for weeks, months, years. Maybe for ever.'

'But won't they get out, too? I mean, some time?'

'If their debts are paid, yes. Or if they serve their time, and don't get more added for bad behaviour or such as that, yes. Otherwise, no. But don't worry your pretty head about that, child. You've got a good life ahead, I can tell you.'

They left the prison through a small wicket door let

into the main oak gate, dotted with black boltheads. Out on the cobbles, a carriage stood to one side, the coachman sitting high up, on the box. Two well-groomed matched horses tossed their heads impatiently and stamped their hooves on the cobbles. They did not like the smell of the gaol. Even out in the open air a sour miasma of stale sweat and clogged sewers drifted over the wall like poisoned fog.

Mrs Mentmore opened the door of the carriage. 'Get in,' she said brusquely.

Mary Jane put one foot on the step. Under her weight the vehicle dipped slightly on its springs. As she climbed in, Mrs Mentmore suddenly flicked up her skirt with an expert hand.

'So you've nothing on underneath,' she said. 'You don't wear drawers, then?

'No. None of us do.'

'Us? *I* do.'

'I mean the women inside don't. They haven't got any clothes except what's on their backs.'

'That's one big difference between them and you in future, then. We'll set you up in nice clothes. We've a lot to teach you, child.'

Mrs Mentmore sat down on the buttoned black leather seat, her back to the coachman, and closed the door. Mary Jane sat opposite her. For a moment, their knees touched. Mary Jane moved to one side. Mrs Mentmore's knees followed hers. She tapped sharply on the roof with a black umbrella. The coach gave a jerk forward. Iron tyres rumbled, striking sparks from the cobbles, and they were off.

'Have you got a place for me already, ma'am?' asked Mary Jane politely. She did not like Mrs Mentmore's knees pressing so hard, but when she moved again, Mrs Mentmore moved with her. The inside of the carriage seemed very small, very confined; the air hung heavy with the scents of camphor and waxed leather and Mrs Mentmore's lilac perfume.

'I'll find you something good,' Mrs Mentmore assured her. 'You're a pretty girl, you're willing to learn.'

'Learn what, exactly, ma'am?'

'How to behave, how to be pleasant to people – especially men. You know many men?'

'Only my father, and he's gone away. That's why we're in Newgate. My mother owed money to the landlord.'

'We all owe money to landlords,' said Mrs Mentmore philosophically. 'Depends who the landlord is, how he wants his payment. Cash or kind.'

'You mean in steaks or bottles of spirits or something like that?'

'Usually, something like that. Depends on what you have to offer. But my, you are an innocent one. Looking at you, I'd have thought you knew it all. You're like a fresh, blank page of paper. We'll have to write on it, learn you a lot of things. That's what one of my first clients told me, years ago, when I was your age. Like you, I was willing to learn, and I learned a lot.'

Mrs Mentmore lifted the veil. Mary Jane was surprised how hard her face appeared. How sharp and bright and discontented, almost feverish, her eyes were. The two spots which the veil had all but concealed now throbbed, pulsating as with a life of their own.

'What are you looking at?' Mrs Mentmore asked her sharply.

'Nothing, ma'am,' Mary Jane replied quickly. 'Just admiring your nice clothes.'

'Ah, they're all right, aren't they? They should be. Five guineas this dress, one guinea for the hat alone, specially made veil another guinea. Adds mystery, a veil, I think. So I'll give you your first lesson. If people – men, I mean – can see everything, they don't want it. They want what they can't see, what they can't get, what they can't have. So always keep something in reserve, child. Looks, money, anything. Never give everything away to anyone. Even if you think you're in love with someone and you want to, more than anything else. Especially then.'

Mary Jane was bewildered, and her unease increased; she did not like Mrs Mentmore, for reasons she could not explain. The woman seemed abrasive, like a piece of pumice stone, and hard enough to sharpen a knife against.

Mrs Mentmore turned and looked Mary Jane straight in the eyes. She had a quizzical, almost disbelieving smile on her face.

'I can't make up my mind about you,' she said at last.

'I don't understand, Mrs Mentmore. What do you mean?'

'You are so innocent, I can't believe you're not having me on. You do know who I am and what work you'll be doing, don't you?'

'Only what you've told me, Mrs Mentmore. That you'd place me somewhere nice in London.'

'That's true enough. But it's not a gentleman's residence, though every night it's packed with gentlemen, lords, dukes, knights. It's a whorehouse, Mary Jane, and I'm the madam.'

Mary Jane's eyes widened with shock. Her mother must have realised Mrs Mentmore's profession. No wonder she had not wanted her to take the offer of work.

The carriage bowled on steadily. Streets, at first narrow, crowded by shabbily dressed people, with stalls set up on pavements, their holders hoarsely crying their wares, gradually gave place to wider thoroughfares. Rows of yellow brick houses, blackened with soot and smoke, were left behind. Shops with shining plate-glass windows and scrubbed canvas awnings emblazoned with the shopkeepers' names now lined the pavements. Smart carriages, painted in their owner's livery, coachmen and footmen wearing uniforms to match, up on the box, took the place of horses and carts.

Their carriage trundled on along Fleet Street, up the Strand and finally into Leicester Square. Here the atmosphere was totally different, as though somehow they had left the working day behind them, and this was suddenly a Sunday morning in summer.

The square was built round a garden. In the middle stood a huge globe, sixty feet high, a model of the earth. It had been placed here after the Great Exhibition and showed the world's mountain ranges, oceans, rivers. They could be viewed from a series of platforms, four storeys high, now all empty. In fact, Mary Jane could not see anyone in the square and she could not understand why. Shutters closed like eyelids over the shop windows had a sleepy sabbatical appearance.

Two elegant foreign hotels, the Cavour and the Sablonière, appeared similarly deserted. A few omnibuses passed through the square, but no one left them or climbed on; they did not even stop. Charwomen with mops and pails of hot soapy water scrubbed front steps. In the neighbouring arcades and side streets, menservants swept the pavement outside front doors, yawning as they did so, as though only just aroused from sleep.

The carriage stopped at one such door, painted glowing maroon. It had a gold handle and a gold lion's head knocker.

'Follow me,' Mrs Mentmore told Mary Jane. She

opened the door with a key on a fine gold chain, closed it carefully behind them. They were standing in a wide long hall, walls dark with thick maroon flock wallpaper. In sconces, gilded lamps burned low as if their oil was almost exhausted. Candles had already died in branched candlesticks. A rich scent of cigars and beeswax polish hung in the air.

'I'll show you to your room,' said Mrs Mentmore briskly. She pressed a hidden button in what seemed a solid wall. Part of it opened on oiled hinges and closed silently on a spring behind them. They walked up a small staircase that smelt strongly of stale scent and powder. Several doors opened off a landing. Mrs Mentmore opened one of them. It led into a small room containing a single bed. Beneath a high, round window, propped open by a wooden wedge, was a marble-topped table with a ewer of water, a bottle of deep blue glass with a label on which was printed one word: POISON.

'Carbolic,' Mrs Mentmore explained. 'You only need a few drops in a bowl of water. Use it when you wash – now – all over your body. I will bring in some new clothes for you.'

When she had left, Mary Jane dipped her finger in the water and was pleasantly surprised to find that it was warm. She filled the bowl, poured in some carbolic, and washed herself thoroughly. Then she pulled back the quilt and lay on the bed. The linen sheets were coarse but clean; they smelled agreeably of soap. She must have slept, unused to such luxury, such warmth, because she suddenly realised that Mrs Mentmore was standing by her side, looking down at her.

'You know why you're here, I suppose?' she said, making the question sound like a statement of fact.

'To get a position, ma'am. Like you promised.'

122

'Yes. But the position in which you'll do best here is on your back with your legs apart. Unless someone has other suggestions, of course. Tell me, are you a virgin?'

'Yes.'

'Well then, your price must be adjusted accordingly. Virgins are rare round here, you know.'

'I didn't know.'

'Wait a minute, child. I'll be back directly.'

She came back carrying a silver tray. On this was a decanter of sherry and two large glasses.

'You drink?'

'Not alcohol. My mother saw what happened to my father when he drank. That put me against it, too.'

'Well, have one anyhow to mark the start of our relationship. Sherry wine is good for the blood.'

Mrs Mentmore poured out two glasses as she spoke. She handed one to Mary Jane, raised her own. They drank. Mary Jane coughed at first over the dryness of the drink, then swallowed it down gratefully.

'I can hardly believe you are as innocent as you appear,' said Mrs Mentmore. 'But you may just be – or else you're a very good actress. Let me tell you the sort of place I manage. This is a house of pleasure. We entertain men here. We sell them drinks, sherry, whisky, claret, but especially champagne, which costs as much as twenty-five shillings a bottle if it's vintage.'

'That's more than you said I'd be paid in a week.'

'Exactly. But our customers can afford it. They're rich. Your job is to make them want to spend money by being nice to them, by arousing them, by going to bed with them, letting them think they can arouse you. *Pretending*. Most of life, my dear, is pretence. Women pretend to love boring husbands because they provide for them. Husbands pretend to love plain, dull wives they secretly loathe but who have an income of five thousand sovereigns a year. I pretend to be Mrs Mentmore. You'll not find my marriage lines in Somerset House. I never was married. But in my time I've learned more about marriage than most wives. Marriage doesn't attract me. Nor do men. As a matter of fact, I prefer the girls. That's really why I lifted your skirt. I like you.'

As she spoke, Mary Jane remembered the women wearing men's clothes in the gaol, fondling each other; the look of revulsion, of horror in her mother's face.

'If you want to leave now, I'll have to charge you for a night's lodging, use of water, soap, a sherry. That will come to a pound.'

'But I haven't been here for a night, and I haven't a penny, as you know.'

'I do know. So you'd be out of here and back in Newgate in short order.'

'You tricked me.'

'Not tricked, persuaded. If I'd told you that I wanted you to work in a whorehouse, you might have said, no. You might have said, yes, of course, but I think not. But working in another sort of house, meanwhile possibly having to put up with the attentions of the father of the house or a son, is a different thing. You were willing to try that. But your mother guessed who I was.'

She put her finger up to her two spots. 'These give me away.'

'What are they, exactly?'

'Don't you know? They used to call it the King's disease. You'd never hear of the Queen's disease, though, would you? Not with Queen Victoria, God bless her. She'd never get the pox – not like me.'

'How did you get it?'

'Don't ask such a ridiculous question! Some damned fellow I knew years ago was diseased. We get them now and then. There's nothing anyone can do about it. We charge enough to keep the ruffians out. But the aristocracy are just as bad. Worse, in many cases.'

'Is there no cure?'

'Not yet. The doctors try all sorts – mercury, purges, blood-letting, standing in barrels full of hot salt – all kinds of treatment to kill the poison or sweat it out of the system.'

'But none of them work?'

'That's right. None. Some help a bit, and the spots may even disappear. But in a few months or so, back they come, worse than before. That's the risk you have to take to pay for fine clothes and good wines and living like a duchess. For remember this, girl, even if you forget everything else you'll ever learn. You have your pleasure, then you have to pay. There's nothing for nothing, for men as well as us.'

'I've never been with a man,' said Mary Jane. 'Not properly.' She had been kissed several times by the brothers of friends, but they had been passionless, inexpert pecks on her cheek. Once there had been a hurried forced kiss on her mouth while the boy's hands inexpertly explored her breasts beneath her shift, but that was all.

Mrs Mentmore shrugged her shoulders. 'That's as maybe. So what is her ladyship's decision? You stay, or you go back to Newgate?'

'I stay,' said Mary Jane slowly. 'But I'm sorry you deceived me like this.'

'If that's the only time you're deceived in life, child, you'll have got off very lightly. I'm glad you're staying. A pound a week isn't much, but you've got a lot to learn, and when you're ready, I'll increase it. Now you want something to eat, and you want some better clothes. But first come and meet some of the other girls, and see where you'll be working.'

'Working? That's what you call it?'

'That's what it is, child. And hard, labouring work it is with some of the men.'

Mrs Mentmore led Mary Jane across the landing, down a set of stairs and pushed open another door that locked behind her. They were in a large room without windows. Rows of oil lamps on wall sconces had polished mirrors behind them. Sharp-edged pieces of crystal dangled from candlesticks. Coloured prints hung on the walls between the lights. They showed men and women kissing, copulating, making water. They were lewd and terrible prints, yet they had been executed with such panache and lightness of touch that, after looking at two or three, they seemed no more shocking than watercolours of country churches viewed from water meadows. Around the walls red velvet divans were set out beside ashtrays on fluted silver stands.

'The girls sit here from nine o'clock on,' Mrs Mentmore explained. 'I bring in gentlemen. Some have their regulars. Others choose one here. Then they go up to the girl's room. We serve dinner, or a light supper – whatever they want. You must do your best to make the man buy a meal. You needn't eat anything. We'll give you something before you start. And if he orders champagne or whisky, the waiter will bring you your drink in a decanter – cold tea, or seltzer water with a little sugar. If the client wants to taste it, you say you're on a diet for two weeks or some excuse like that. He may suspect he's being rooked, but men don't care to think they've been made fools of. So he'll want to believe whatever you tell him. Now, come and meet the other girls.'

They were sitting at a long refectory table in an adjoining room. The windows had metal bars, as in a gaol. No one could get out and, perhaps more important, no one could get in.

'Here's Mary Jane,' said Mrs Mentmore. 'She's new. Never been on the game before, so treat her nice.'

She left Mary Jane with them. An older woman with a plump, hog-like face came up, looked her over critically.

'I'm Beatrice,' she announced. 'I've been here almost as long as Madam. You'll be all right. First of all, you want something hot inside you. I don't doubt you'll get something else hot inside you before the night's out, so have some food at the other end.' She laughed cheerfully. 'It's saveloys tonight, with mash and a cup of tea. The serving hatch is up there. I'll keep you a place on the bench.'

Mary Jane collected a meal on a thick plate, with a knife and fork, a mug of steaming tea with three spoonfuls of brown sugar, and sat down next to Beatrice.

'Now, listen to me, Mary Jane. You've got a pretty face and you'll learn. But don't trust any of the men. And don't criticise Madam to them. They'll tell her, bound to, and you'll get the sack. Then, the only way for you is down. This is the best night house there is. This is quality, I tell you. Where'd she find you?'

'Newgate. I was in with my mother. For debt.'

'Oh. Well, let me tell you something. You can get yourself a bit of money here, do yourself a bit of good, if you play it my way. Right?'

Mary Jane nodded, not really understanding what Beatrice meant, but not wishing to appear ignorant.

'Some of the men coming here are already drunk, or at least half seas over. They *think* they want a woman. But when they get you in a bed they can't do anything. It's all soft mick. So you butter them up, say you like them like that. Anything. You kiss 'em, do anything they want – or pretend to. They don't know, in that state, just what they want.

'Usually, they just fall asleep. Then get your hand

in their wallet or back pocket, and take some cash – not all of it, mind, because they know they've got some. But if you only take a few notes or coins, they'll think they've had their pocket picked in the street. That money's your bonus. Got your name on it, like. What's she paying you?'

'A pound a week.'

'There you are. She'll probably make fifty a week out of your tail for a slave's wage! A bloody pound! The sauce of it! You got to look after yourself in this world, dear. No one else will. Probably not in the next world, either.

'But don't keep the money here. There's an old, half-blind crone, riddled with pox, who used to be on the game. Her job's to clean out the rooms. She searches everywhere – under the bed, in the mattress, everywhere. Any money she finds she takes to Madam who pockets it and maybe gives her half a crown now and then. And the girl in whose room any money is found goes that day with only what she stands up in. She'll have burned your own clothes, what you're wearing now, because they're not suitable for this job. So you're wearing *her* clothes. She'll charge you for those, or put you out, Eve-naked.'

'She sounds a hard woman.'

'It's a hard life, girl. All I want to do is save enough to get out of here, start my own house.'

'Think you will?'

'Of course. In the end. Bound to. I've got some saved up, you know. But not here. Oh no, it's not here. Now, I've talked enough. I'm going to have another saveloy. Know what they remind me of, don't you?' Beatrice leered at Mary Jane and walked to the hatch.

When she was out of earshot, a woman across the table raised her eyebrows at Mary Jane.

'I heard what she said. All rubbish. She'll never get

out of here. She's made a few bob, right. So have we all. But the temptation is always to stay on. You get your own place and at once you've all sorts of problems. Rent, rates, paying the police to look the other way. Here we've only one problem – how to keep working and off the streets. And out of the debtors' prison. I've been inside and I'm not going back.'

'Nor am I,' Mary Jane replied with feeling. 'Whatever else I have to do to make money, I'm never going back there.'

The girls were sitting on the plush divans, waiting hopefully for clients to arrive. Their faces were painted, powdered, wrinkles concealed or erased with alum. But despite their brightened eyes and set smiles, Mary Jane sensed despair in their chattering conversation. This was the ultimate saleroom; they were selling themselves. And so far no potential buyers had arrived.

Through stained wooden grilles cut skilfully in the shape of harps, Mary Jane heard the sound of violins. Three out-of-work fiddlers, from the pit orchestra of a musical comedy that had closed unexpectedly, were playing a waltz in a side room.

As the girls chatted to each other, their eyes kept flitting towards the double doors, eager not to miss the arrival of any clients. Mary Jane was surprised to see the costumes some girls wore. One was dressed in a harelequin outfit, left leg encased in a black stocking, right in one of brilliant yellow, and a chequered tunic. Another wore a ball gown; a third, with darkened face and hands, lips and nails reddened, eyelids dark purple, appeared like an Eastern princess.

'Why are they wearing these odd costumes?' she asked Beatrice. She was wearing a dark blue dress, simple, almost demure, that Mrs Mentmore had provided.

'It's what the men like. Fantasies. You'd be amazed. Some of them want a girl to wear a white wig to remind them of their old mothers. Others have fixations about daughters, sisters. They even bring in pictures so the girls can make up their faces to look as near like the original as possible.'

'I'd no idea,' said Mary Jane.

'From what you say, you've no idea of almost anything, child. But remember what I told you. Never take your eye off the main chance to get out of this place. Then instead of working for Madam, you'll be Madam, working for yourself. Don't turn up any opportunity – you may never have another.'

In the anteroom, Mrs Mentmore was pouring two glasses of champagne for a plump, soft-faced man in his late forties.

'I am so glad you're here, Sir Martyn,' she said, smiling coquettishly.

'I received your message this afternoon,' Sir Martyn replied. 'It intrigued me, so I put aside a most important political engagement to accept at once.'

'You will not be disappointed, sir. It's not often we have a girl so fresh, so unspoiled, so totally virginal. Look at her style in clothes. I can say in all honesty I cannot ever remember engaging a child like her before.'

'Where did you find her? In the country?'

'No. Oddly enough, through a friend here in London.'

'I'm amazed there are any girls like that left in London these days.'

'I would not disagree with that, sir. She is unusual, I cannot deny. For this reason I have most reluctantly to ask a larger sum for her favours than I would wish.'

'How much larger?' Sir Martyn's voice was suddenly hard. He was known as a mean man who would pay for his own pleasure but only grudgingly, and after much haggling. No notes of hand could be accepted from him either; only notes of the realm that could not be repudiated.

'Fifty guineas, sir.'

'*Fifty guineas? A fortune.* For one night?'

'For a whole night, sir.'

'I must say, Mrs Mentmore, the charge seems exorbitant.'

'As I have explained, sir, I am reluctant to ask it, but high as it is, the money will barely cover my outgoings. Every young girl puts a high price on her maidenhead these days, sir. As you said, I am, like you, amazed to find a girl of this quality in London now.

'For a gentleman of your distinction and your temperament and, if I may say, your skill and experience in the lists of love, I have no hesitation in saying she is unique. And for every pearl there must be a price.'

'I do not feel disposed to pay this sum, Mrs Mentmore.'

'That, sir, I deeply regret to hear, knowing your good taste and your generous nature. But I must accept your decision, although I cannot think of anyone I know who would appreciate the youth and freshness of such a lovely creature more than you. Of course, the Prince has asked me to let him know of any especially interesting new arrivals . . .'

Sir Martyn did not speak, but his eyes clouded, the muscles tightened round his mouth.

'However, sir, if that is your final word, perhaps you would like to meet someone else tonight? I have a new arrival from the West Country, a young, strapping lass.'

'I do not wish to be fobbed off with second best. I say what I think, as you know, and I think your price is outrageous, Mrs Mentmore. But I have known you for years, and you are always a woman of your word. Fifty guineas will not ruin me, although I must say it will stretch my personal exchequer.'

'She will stretch even more personal parts of your anatomy, Sir Martyn, of that I can assure you!'

'You have wit and humour, Mrs Mentmore, as well as a shrewd head for business. Fifty guineas, you say? How about fifty pounds?'

'Sir, we do not bargain at the gates of paradise.'

'Well put. Well put indeed. All right. Fifty guineas it is. Paid tomorrow?'

'If I controlled the finances of this house, it could be paid tomorrow, next week, next month, because I trust you as a gentleman and a friend. But my landlord only looks at the profit and loss account. I regret that the rules are always payment in advance, even for one as valued as you, Sir Martyn.'

He finished the champagne, banged his glass sharply on the table to show he wanted it refilled and quickly. Then he unbuttoned an inner pocket, took out a wallet, attached by a short silver chain to his jacket so it could not be completely removed. He counted out five £10 notes, rubbed each one carefully between forefinger and thumb in case, by accident, two notes had stuck together. He replaced the wallet and from a locked purse chained to his trousers he took two sovereigns and two crowns, put them on the table. Mrs Mentmore poured him another glass of champagne.

'To a night of love, Sir Martyn,' she said archly, raising her own glass in a toast.

'To many such,' he replied shortly and swallowed the champagne in a single gulp.

Mrs Mentmore opened the double doors with a

flourish, like a herald in a play, and entered the big room.

'Mary Jane,' she announced, 'I have someone who would like to meet you. A dear good friend of mine.'

Sir Martyn stood in the doorway, casting his eyes around the other girls. Mary Jane came out to meet him, bowed demurely.

'You are young,' he said.

'Yes, sir.'

'And in strange surroundings, yes?'

'That is so, sir,'

'Well, come upstairs and let us discuss the matter. Send a bottle of bubbly up, Mrs Mentmore, with two glasses.'

'It is already there, sir. I have given you a special room, since this is a very special occasion.'

The bedroom into which Mrs Mentmore showed them was delicately lit by candles in silver candlesticks. A cheval glass hung above a dressing-table. Much of the space was taken up with a huge four-poster bed. Its curtains had been drawn back to show white linen sheets neatly turned down. On a side table stood a silver bucket of ice containing a bottle of champagne.

Mrs Mentmore bowed and closed the door. Sir Martyn turned to Mary Jane.

'This is your first time, I understand?' No need to waste time on preliminaries; he was not paying fifty guineas to engage a little tart in conversation.

'Yes, sir.'

'You are being honest with me?'

'I am, sir.'

He looked at her closely for a moment. 'I think you are, child. I think you are. Now, don't be nervous. There's always a first time. First love, best love, last love of all. You believe that, do you?'

'I've heard that said, sir. I don't know whether it is true or not.'

'Nor do I. It's poet's talk, I think. Sounds good, but doesn't mean a lot, eh?'

Sir Martyn sat down on a gilded chair by the side of the bed and pushed off his elastic-sided boots. He was thankful to be sitting down; why, he could not say. He had not been exerting himself recently. Perhaps the champagne Madam had given him downstairs was of poor quality. He had heard that some vineyards added acid to give it more taste, or even sodium bicarbonate to make it fizz. You couldn't trust anyone or anything these days.

He put his hand across his forehead and was surprised that it came away damp with sweat. Perhaps he was sickening for something. The fact was, he had been feeling a bit below par for several weeks. So why had he come out in answer to Mrs Mentmore's invitation? He didn't really want a woman, not even this pretty young girl. He had paid fifty guineas because he could not bear it to be thought that, for any reason, he was unable to cope, not quite up to the mark. Some jumped-up, so-called foreign royalty, Russian or Polish, would be bound to hear he had been offered first chance and had declined. He and his foppish cronies would laugh at him behind his back.

All his life Sir Martyn had been able to buy who or what he wanted, when he wanted. He could not stand to one side now and let someone else have first choice. Perhaps he should see a leech, be bled, given some specific, spend a spell in Baden Baden drinking the waters. He'd be all right in a moment, quite all right.

He started to stand up, but just for a moment felt a slight spasm of dizziness and a hint of pain in his chest. It was like a stitch, the sort he used to get as a boy at school after he'd run too far and too fast in a race and he was breathless. In a short race he'd drop out altogether. It didn't matter so much when you were a boy, dropping out, admitting you're not quite *au point* that day. When you were getting older it mattered a hell of a lot; you had to prove you were as fit as you had always been, not growing old, getting a bit past it.

He'd have this girl and get out. His carriage was waiting outside. He'd go back to his chambers in Jermyn Street. In the morning, if he did not feel any better he'd send a servant out for the physician. He would have him right in no time. It was wonderful what these medical fellows could do these days.

He stood up, took a pace towards Mary Jane. She was a damned pretty girl, no doubt about it. She could be his daughter if he'd ever married. His *daughter*? What an extraordinary thought!

What would his brothers think of him, if they could see him now in an expensive whorehouse about to tup a little girl at a ridiculously exorbitant price! He must be mad. But to hell with his brothers, one running the family estate in Scotland, the other not quite right in the head with a commission in the army, of all things. He didn't give a fish's tit what they thought about him. He drove such rambling thoughts from his mind and looked more closely at Mary Jane.

He could see nervousness in her eyes. She feared him because he was rich and strong, because he was going to have his way with her, and possibly this was not as she had imagined the first time would be.

Mary Jane could see bristly black hairs growing out of his nostrils, small blackheads round his eyes, wrinkles on his neck. Close to, Sir Martyn seemed much older and seedier than he had appeared in the room downstairs. His teeth were sharp like a rodent's, yellow with nicotine, greenish at the gums.

'Well,' he said, grinning, trying to appear pleasant.

135

'A bit of fun first, eh? You undress me, I undress you, and then we'll see. I'll show you what to do.' He pulled Mary Jane closer to him.

Slowly, reluctantly, totally without enthusiasm, she began to undo the buttons on his jacket. He threw it away from him impatiently. Then she undid the buttons on his shirt, and finally those on his trousers. As he pulled his shirt over his head, she smelled the sourness of a sweating male body, and wrinkled her nose in distaste. The unexpected smell took her back instantly to Newgate; she swallowed quickly to stop herself being sick.

Sir Martyn shook himself out of his trousers and stood naked. Then he turned to one side, opened the champagne, poured himself a glass, drank it quickly, then another.

'Want one?' he asked her.

Mary Jane shook her head. She wanted nothing but to be out of here.

'Well, then. Make my worm stand to its duty.'

He busied himself with her buttons. Soon she was also naked. The room felt very small and hot. Mary Jane hated him, and she hated herself for being in this situation, for what they were doing and, worse, were about to do. Without love, it seemed horrible, something from which she longed to escape and forget.

'Come on, then,' he said sharply.

She put down her hand as he indicated and gripped him, pulled back the skin from his phallus.

'Hurry.'

As he spoke, he bent down beside the bed and picked up a whip, thin as a bootlace, with three oiled leather thongs. It had been concealed beneath a white sheepskin rug. He began to belabour her furiously, on her back, her buttocks, her breasts. She was astounded, terrified. Had he gone mad? Would he kill

136

her? Why hadn't Mrs Mentmore warned her he was vicious?

'Stop!' she screamed. 'Please stop! *Please!*'

'Fifty guineas I'm paying!' Sir Martyn shouted, his voice clotted with rage and lust. 'I'll have my money's worth if I have to flay the flesh off your bones, if it's the last thing I do!'

'No! *No!*'

Mary Jane shut her eyes, put up her hands to protect her face, elbows tucked in across her breasts. She was so shocked she did not think of running away, but just stood, screaming.

Then suddenly the whipping stopped. She heard a thud on the carpet, opened her eyes. Sir Martyn was lying on the ground on his back, writhing in a paroxysm. His face was contorted with pain; it did not seem the face of a man but of a gargoyle, a monster.

Mary Jane drew back and watched him with horror, her mind full of loathing for him, disbelief that this could actually be happening. In the mirror across the room, she saw the red, pulsing weals the whip had cut into her flesh.

His body was damp, shining with sweat as though it had been varnished. His back arched, his fingers clawed at the carpet. Then he relaxed, his hands dropped to his sides, his back collapsed. He might have been sleeping.

She swallowed very quickly to stop herself screaming in horror or vomiting over the naked, repulsive body. She dressed quickly. She must see Mrs Mentmore, must explain what had happened. Then she remembered Beatrice's advice. There was something more important she must do first.

She picked up Sir Martyn's jacket, unbuttoned the inner pocket, pulled out the wallet on its chain. She counted fifty £10 notes; £500 – ten times her wages for a whole year. She must not be greedy, she told herself firmly; she must be careful. She took out three £10 notes, put these in her bodice, then replaced the wallet.

She looked down at him without any feelings whatever. Then she went out of the room, down the stairs. Mrs Mentmore was in her small anteroom, finishing the champagne. Her face flushed.

'That's quick,' she said, surprised at seeing Mary Jane.

'He's dead, that's why.'

'*Dead?* What happened?'

'He produced a whip and started to beat me. Suddenly he fell back, and that was it.'

'He was a swine, that one, dearie. He smoked opium and had his way with more women than I've had hot dinners. And always cruelly, always the bully. He was impotent, you see. Couldn't do anything else but bluster and beat you up. But the bastard was worth a fortune. There's no fairness in life, dearie.'

'I'm beginning to realise that.'

'Let's have a look at him,' said Mrs Mentmore. 'Then I'll call the doctor. We have one we pay well for emergencies.'

'What will he say?'

'What does that matter? It's his living to write Latin words no one can read. He'll see us right.'

'Had Sir Martyn any relatives?'

'Two brothers. One up north somewhere, the other down in Brighton. He's in the army, I believe, but that means nothing. He's got a screw loose, if you understand me. Should be put away, but they don't do that when you're rich. They buy commissions, you know, just as they buy titles. Captain this, Major the other, Colonel whatshisname, who cares?'

Mrs Mentmore went up to the bedroom; Mary Jane followed her. Sir Martyn lay on the floor, but not as

Mary Jane had left him. He had moved. And as the two women watched, he moved again.

'He's not dead!' Mrs Mentmore cried. 'I'll wait with him. You go downstairs. See Beatrice. She knows what to do, where the doctor lives. Hurry!'

Mary Jane ran out of the room, but not downstairs. She went up to her own bedroom, wondering how many notes Mrs Mentmore would remove from Sir Martyn's wallet. Never mind that; this was her chance to go. She must take it for she might never have another.

She packed up her old clothes, pulled a sheet from the bed, wrapped them in it. She did not want to steal the clothes Mrs Mentmore had given to her, but she felt she had no alternative.

She opened the door carefully and stood, listening for footsteps on the stairs. The only sound came from the violins scraping a waltz. She walked quickly down the stairs. As she crossed the hall, a door opened. Beatrice stood looking at her.

'What's happening?' she asked. 'Where are you going?'

'To fetch the doctor,' Mary Jane told her. 'Sir Martyn's had a fit. Mrs Mentmore wants you upstairs. In the room I was using.'

Beatrice ran up the stairs, two at a time; Mrs Mentmore was not someone she ever kept waiting.

Mary Jane went out of the front door into Leicester Square.

It was now teeming with people: smartly dressed women wearing yards of watered silk, men in brushed top hats and frock coats. In contrast to this opulence and elegance, unshaven louts clustered in alleys, some carrying clubs. Near them stood women so disfigured by age and disease they did not dare to venture out even into the dim light of oil lamps on the pavements.

139

They stayed in the shadows, creatures of the dark, calling hopefully, sometimes desperately, to passersby: 'Hullo, darling. Looking for a naughty girl, are you? I can give you a good time.'

Mary Jane hurried past them all; she must be out of the area before Mrs Mentmore discovered she had gone. She walked west along Piccadilly, past the park, until she reached a new housing estate being built on the outskirts of Kensington village.

Here the road petered out into a muddy, rutted lane. Piles of bricks stood on either side. Shadowy figures waited in the shade of half-built houses; whores were also working out here, the cheapest end of town. She did not know where she was going; she had no plan, no aim, except to escape. And first, she needed a shelter for the night. She was so ignorant of London life, she did not pause to think that with £30 she could book a room in any hotel. She had never been into an hotel; she knew nothing about them. All she knew was that, like a hunted animal, she had to escape from the whorehouse. If Mrs Mentmore found her, the money would be discovered, because she had nowhere to hide it; then she could be back in Newgate as a thief.

She turned off the lane, along a mass of wooden duckboards, into an empty house. The rooms were half finished, without doors or windows. Floorboards had been fouled by animals, by tramps drunk on methylated spirits who now lay snoring and snorting in their stupor.

She came out, went into the next house. This was cleaner, with a new staircase that smelled strongly of raw, unseasoned wood. She went upstairs, found an empty bedroom and lay down on the floor. The windows were unglazed and the moon shone brightly on the rough, unstained planks. She felt free; she had escaped. Tomorrow, she would decide what to do, where to go. Tonight, she would rest and thank God for her deliverance. Soon, she slept.

The sun shining directly into her eyes woke her. The room now had two other women sleeping in a far corner and a small squalid child that had dirtied itself. The smell of its dung hung sharply in the morning air.

Mary Jane picked up her bundle and went downstairs. A water tap had been connected outside. She washed under this, drank the cold water gratefully, rinsed out her mouth. Then she wiped her face and hands on the sheet and set out back along the unmade road.

It had been raining in the night, and her shoes were soon clogged with reddish mud that oozed through their thin, cheap soles. Her feet felt cold, her bare legs were spattered with mud. But she had achieved two things in one night of horror: she was still unviolated, she kept telling herself, and she had made enough money to pay her mother's debts and buy her release.

She decided to go to Newgate at once and find out to whom she should repay the debt. There would be an official of some sort, she was certain. Of course she had stolen the money, but Sir Martyn was rich; he would never miss it. That did not diminish the gravity of her theft, but she rationalised what she had done by telling herself that he was lucky to be alive.

Within a few yards, a hansom cab, moving slowly, overtook her. She called to the driver.

'Newgate prison,' she told him.

The driver looked at her smart dress, now clotted with mud. She could be a tart, although she did not look like one. Or she could be a society girl, out on the loose.

'Got the money, have you?' he asked her.

'If you have change for a ten-pound note.'

'I can get it,' said the cabbie. 'Let's see it first.'

Mary Jane showed him a corner of one note, not letting him see it all in case he tried to seize it. He was a big man and a tenner was a fortune.

'Satisfied?' she asked him, putting it back in her bodice.

'I'll take you,' he said at once. 'A hanging, is there?'

'No. Someone I know is being released.'

She climbed inside, sat well back against the shabby, creased leather seat. She had not realised how hungry she was or how cold and miserable. She dozed and only woke up when the jogging of the cab ceased and the cabbie opened the door and stood peering at her.

'You're here,' he said shortly. 'Gimme the tenner.'

'I will do no such thing,' she retorted. 'You might go off with it. Wait here and I'll get some change.'

She walked up to the main gate of the prison, banged on it with her fist. A turnkey opened a small shutter behind a metal grille. He was drinking a mug of tea. The sight of steam rising from it made Mary Jane's mouth water.

'What do you want?'

'Two things,' she told him. 'Change for a ten-pound note. Then I have come to redeem a prisoner's debt.'

'How did you get a ten-pound note?'

'That's my affair. Have you change or not?'

The man went away and came back with nine sovereigns. 'It's all I've got,' he said.

'You're lying,' she told him.

'Take it or leave it,' he retorted.

She took the coins, paid off the cabbie.

'Who's the prisoner you want to see?' the turnkey asked her.

'Mrs Green.'

Another turnkey came up, the one who had introduced her to Mrs Mentmore.

'Hullo,' he said, recognising Mary Jane. 'You're back soon.'

'She's in the money,' the other man explained.

Mary Jane nodded. She did not want to become involved in explanations. He would almost certainly tell Mrs Mentmore she had returned to the gaol. She had to be away before he could get in touch with her.

'I've come to pay whatever my mother owes and get her released.'

'You're too late.'

'What do you mean, too late?'

Surely he could not mean that her mother had died? She had a sudden recollection of Sir Martyn's body, flaccid, naked, disgusting.

'What I mean is, her husband came and paid. She's gone.'

'My father?'

'I don't know whose father he is, dearie. But he is her husband. She's gone with him.'

'What did he say?'

'That he'd come for his wife. That's all. He paid up. Everything. Even gave me half a quid tip. A gent.'

'Where have they gone?'

'How do I know? They just went out and away.'

'I see. You on the level?'

'Course I'm on the level. Wouldn't be in the prison service if I weren't, would I, dearie, eh?' He grinned at her lewdly.

Mary Jane moved away and walked slowly up the street. She became suddenly aware how weary she was, not only in body but in mind. Her mother and father had gone, and she had no idea where they could be. They would not go back to their old lodgings, of that she felt certain. Pride would prevent them; after all, their landlord had gaoled her mother and her. They were probably still here in London, if only because they had not had time to go elsewhere. But how could she even begin to find them?

She felt misery and hysteria rising like a tide within her. She put up her hands, pressed the palms into her eyes to try and clear her mind. She must not give way to tears. She must keep cool, decide what she was to do next.

She took her hands away. A man was standing watching her. He was in his fifties, with a sad, spaniel face. He wore fustian trousers, hobnail boots, a peajacket, so called because its length and the number of buttons on its single-breasted lapels made it resemble a pod of peas.

'In trouble, miss?' he asked her.

Mary Jane shook her head. She did not want to become involved with a man now, not after Sir Martyn.

'I'll help you if you are,' he went on.

'I'm not,' she told him firmly. 'You can't.'

'How do you know?'

She did not bother to reply. He walked towards her.

'I saw you in there,' he said. 'At the hanging.'

'The forger?'

'Yes. He was my brother. I've just been back to collect a few things – not that there's much left. Not even his watch. The bastards had everything except the handkerchief he had round his face. That had his initials on it. Meant a lot to me.' From his jacket pocket he pulled the spotted handkerchief the forger had worn over his eyes as he ascended the scaffold.

She looked at the man more closely. She might have seen him there, she might not. Anyhow, what did that matter now? He seemed genuine.

'You look hungry,' he said. 'I'll buy you breakfast.'

Mary Jane did not refuse. She could not be bothered to explain that she could afford to buy her own. The offer seemed safe enough; it could be meant kindly and he was unlikely to try anything in an eating house.

He led the way up a side street into a shop doorway. Its big glass window was streaked with condensation, the atmosphere inside was hot and steamy. Old men sat on wooden benches at scrubbed tables; they had nowhere else to go. One had fallen asleep, head down on his elbow on the table. Several others were lingering over mugs of tea and slices of bread dipped in dripping, making them last as long as they could. They were grateful to take the weight off their legs in warmth, and not be told to move on.

'I fancy egg and bacon, fried bread,' the man said. 'Same for you?'

She nodded. She did not want to argue. She just wanted to sit, to collect her thoughts. The man ordered the meal, carried the plates across from the service counter. They ate in silence. As they finished, she offered to pay her share. He shook his head. 'I asked you here, I'm standing treat. Tell me, who were you seeing in there?'

'I'd been in with my mother. She owed the landlord. I managed to make enough money to pay off the debt. I came back, but she's gone. Must have missed her by only an hour or two.'

'Who took her out?'

'My father. He had disappeared before. That's why she was arrested. It was his debt, not hers. Now he's turned up again.'

'You know where they've gone?'

'No idea,' she admitted. 'That's the worry. No idea at all.'

'Anything in mind for yourself?'

She shook her head. 'No. I don't know what to do, or where to go.'

'I could give you a job,' he told her.

'Doing what?' Mary Jane asked warily. She could

not risk another misunderstanding, another deception.

'Helping me. Ivan is the name. My brother and I ran a stall together, a tog stall. Know anything about it?'

'No. Nothing.'

'Then I'll tell you. You have a board marked out in squares, each with a number on it. The punters buy tickets, togs, off you with numbers on them. You throw a dice. It lands on a number and the punters win or lose. Mostly, they lose. We were making quite a good living. Then my brother suddenly thought he could improve himself by forging a name to a note. He did it once, twice, nothing happened. He got caught the third time. He'd got a wife, you see, a sick child always needing medicine. I'm single. I've no ties like that.'

'I don't want to live with you,' said Mary Jane, 'if that's what you're hinting at. I don't want to be your woman.'

'I'm not asking you. I'm not interested in women, anyhow. I don't care for a bit of the other. I like a bit of the same, if you understand me. but that doesn't affect you. I can give you a job at the stall, teach you the patter. It's quite simple and there's no risk. You decide who wins and how much. *They* don't know that, of course. But you do. I can't run the stall on my own, and my brother's widow's got this sick kid to look after, so she can't help me.'

'Where would I live?' Mary Jane asked him.

'My caravan. You'll have your side. I'll have mine. I won't put a hand on you. As I said, I don't like girls.'

'What about food? How much money?'

'I'll pay you a pound a week and all you can eat, and you cook for both of us.'

The money was the same as Mrs Mentmore had offered, but the job was different. It did not attract her greatly, but she was not in any position to turn down work.

'I'll do it,' she said. 'And thanks. It's very kind of you.'

'Not really. I'm helping myself as much as you. As I say, I can't run it on my tod. If I don't have you I'll only have to get someone else.'

They shook hands.

'Right,' Ivan went on. 'Come back with me. The fair's been wintering on Hackney Marshes. I'll take you there now.'

Chapter Five

Bertha had spent much of the day running between her bedroom and the bathroom to look out of the front windows along the Perth road, hoping to see the carriage bringing Dr Kintyre home. She examined her face closely in the mirror and held a hand-mirror behind her head to make absolutely certain the tortoiseshell comb in her hair was in the right place. She wanted to look her best to greet the doctor.

Her heart beating nervously at the delay – he had been expected soon after breakfast – she went downstairs to the kitchen. The daily maid had helped her to prepare a special meal: haggis, neaps and an apple tart with a crisp, sugary covering. Bertha knew that this had been the doctor's favourite pudding, and she wanted everything to be exactly as he would wish on his return. For this reason she had placed furniture and ornaments in the new house as they had been in the manse.

When the old minister died and Bertha had to leave the manse, she took a lease on this house at the end of the village. It was built of grey stone, with big sash windows set in white frames, a small garden in front, a larger garden in the rear that led down to a stream, a burn as it was called. On the far bank – not really very far, because the stream was barely twelve feet wide – fields ran on into the foothills of the Grampians.

She had always thought of these hills as being

mountains rather than hills. But since the doctor had been away, she had read books about the Himalayas and realised that now he would be used to hills ten, even twenty times as high. Indeed, he would be used to so many new and different things, she thought. She wondered about him, not whether he had changed, but how much he had changed. And whether, more important, he would think she had changed.

Of course she was several years older than he was. Everyone knew that, but she dyed her hair carefully every week, rinsing it out in an enamel basin with dye from the local chemist until no grey strands remained. She was not young, but then she wasn't old. Mature was how she could best be described, she thought. And surely, if so many things were better when matured – whisky, wine, so she had read, and certainly grouse and venison, as she knew from personal experience – the same should hold true for people.

The fact that she was older than the doctor need not be a bar to marriage. Lots of wives in the village, well, several, were older than their husbands and no one remarked on it. Of course he had never intimated even in the broadest terms that he cared for her in the slightest degree, beyond the fact she was his father's housekeeper. Bertha kept herself to herself. She did not intrude, and she had often eaten her meals on her own in the kitchen while the minister and the doctor had taken theirs in the small dining room. When the doctor was away, she and the minister had shared their meals, and he had confided his worries about his health to her. She was pleased about this; it showed the old man felt he could trust her. Surely that augured well for her relationship with his son?

Now that the minister was gone, Bertha realised that her future was less secure. If the doctor married someone of his own age – worse, someone much prettier and younger – there might not be a place for her. Two women sharing a kitchen was not usually a recipe for happiness.

Bertha knew that her best hope for the future was somehow to persuade Dr Kintyre to propose marriage to her quickly, before he could meet any other younger women. She was not quite sure how she could achieve this. Her life so far had not given her many opportunities of mixing with men, young or old. But then she had not sought such meetings and involvements. Instinctively, she distrusted men because she knew so few. And this business of marriage, even with Dr Kintyre, would inevitably involve sleeping with a man in the same bed, touching him, being touched by him. This prospect was not at all attractive.

Bertha knew nothing about sex, and she had not wanted to discover anything since that Sunday afternoon years ago when she had been out walking in the woods by the side of a cornfield on a sunny day in late August. The corn had been set up in stooks, waiting to be collected, and the afternoon was warm. Although she could see out into the field, because of the trees no one in the field could see her.

There were two young people in the field beside one of the stooks, apparently sitting face to face. But their attitude, their positions, seemed so unusual that she moved forward silently for a better view, sensing she was looking at something very private she was not meant to see.

A man was sitting on the ground, legs outstretched, his back against the stook. She recognised him at once: a handsome, vigorous fellow, who worked for the blacksmith. And there was Jenny Muldoon facing him, sitting astride him and moving up and down. As she drew nearer, Bertha could see the man's trousers were down round his ankles and Jenny's skirt was up.

Suddenly Jenny's movements grew faster and faster, and she gave a cry and sank forward against him and he gripped her tightly in his muscular arms and kissed her.

They lay like this for a moment, and Bertha saw with surprise that his face was sweating in the heat. Surely that could not be from his exertions; he hadn't been exerting himself. And then Jenny slid off his body and she saw what she could only describe as his thing, all shining, still large, and she was amazed and disgusted at what she saw.

She had never imagined this could go on with unmarried couples – and on the Sabbath, with people she knew, who she would pass daily in the street on the way to the village shop. Why, she might even see them at evening service. No. She could not bear to do that. What she had seen, what she knew about them now, must show in her face.

Bertha walked back through the wood very quickly and quietly, and was silent for the rest of the day. Marriage to her would need to have as little of that sort of behaviour as possible; none, if it could be arranged. Much more important, marriage would be for her a mark of social acceptance. Mrs Kintyre would be some*one* in the village, not simply some*body*, the minister's housekeeper. No longer would she be just a cipher, an appendage, but equal with anyone. Even the laird was friendly with the doctor, and therefore he would be with the doctor's wife. And in local society no one was more exalted than the laird who owned thousands of acres and a mansion besides.

Bertha went upstairs yet again and leaned on the windowsill, looking down the street. This time she saw a carriage approaching, a hackney from Perth. The horse clopped along bravely, and she saw the doctor leaning out of a window, directing the driver where to stop. Bertha drew back quickly and stood behind the net curtain so that, as in the wood overlooking the sunlit field, she could see and not be seen.

She felt suddenly bashful. What would Dr Kintyre think of her? Would he think she was older than he remembered? Oh, dear God, she prayed, let him like me. Let him love me. Let him marry me.

She saw the doctor step down and give instructions to the coachman to bring in two cabin trunks which were up on the roof of the coach. Then he turned back towards the open carriage door. Was someone with him? He couldn't be married, surely, and not have told her?

Bertha felt her heart contract with horror at the thought. Was she still going to stay a housekeeper, but now working for a married couple? That would be worse than being a housekeeper to a widower, much worse. That would mean abandoning all hope of ever marrying the doctor. Hope deferred maketh the heart sick, Proverbs 13, verse 12.

Then she saw a boy step down from the coach and look up at the house and then up and down the street. He was tall and tanned, quite good-looking. She did not know him. She had never seen him before. Who on earth could he be? Someone from Perth to whom the doctor had given a lift?

But, no. He was coming up to the front door with the doctor. Could he be the doctor's illegitimate son, conceived in sin, born out of wedlock? Surely not. He would have told her, wouldn't he? But you never knew, not with men. Who would ever have imagined that the blacksmith's assistant would have behaved as he had in the cornfield with Jenny Muldoon? She did not for one moment consider that Jenny might have welcomed his attentions. Men were the trouble. She had so often heard they were lustful, disgusting beasts, all of them. Even Dr Kintyre?

Bertha turned away and for a moment felt quite faint and dizzy. Her mouth was suddenly dry. She closed her eyes. Bright lights danced against the lids, and then faded. She must take a grip on herself, she thought. She walked down the stairs slowly, holding on to the banister, rehearsing the speech she would make, and which she had now all but forgotten. She opened the front door.

'Welcome home,' she said, and immediately forgot everything else as she stared at the doctor.

He had changed, of course. His face was more adult; mature was the word that again came to Bertha's mind. He looked at her and then at the boy.

'I'd like to introduce the son of friends of mine,' he said, shaking her hand. 'They died in Afghanistan. Ben Fanfare Bannerman.'

'Fanfare. That's a strange name,' said Bertha, because she could think of nothing else to say.

'Yes,' Kintyre agreed. 'But then he was born at a strange time, in a strange place.'

'Why is he with you?' Bertha asked. 'Have you adopted him?'

'No. I've just been looking after him in India because he was on his own. I couldn't leave him there, so he's come here with me. He will be staying with us.'

'*Us!*'

'Well, me, here. I take it you're not giving up your job?'

'No,' Bertha said. 'Certainly not. Unless you want me to?'

'Of course not, Bertha. Of course not. You're like one of the family.'

'Thank you.' She couldn't tell him that she didn't just want to be like one of the family; she wanted to be part of his family, his wife. 'Supper is ready when you are,' she said flatly. She could not trust herself to say more, in case she burst into tears.

'I'll just pay the cabbie, and then please serve it.'

She went through the dining room into the kitchen. The maid was standing by the sink, wiping her hands on a towel.

'Serve it as soon as you like,' she told her.

Bertha came back into the dining room. She had laid two places, one for the doctor and one for her, but now this boy with the ridiculous name would have the second place. She did not like to suggest laying a third for herself. She would have to wait and see how events worked out. She heard the horse turn and the cab moved away. The doctor's trunks filled the little narrow hall under lithographs of Highland scenes, Highland cattle.

'Most of the other stuff is still in the docks,' Kintyre explained. 'It's coming here shortly.'

'Of course,' Bertha said. 'I'll make up another bed, put a hot water bottle in to air it. I didn't know you weren't on your own. You didn't say anything about the boy in your letters.'

'Well, I'm sure you'll do your best to look after him.'

'*Me?*'

'Well, both of us, I should say.'

'I've bought a bottle of sherry wine,' she said. This was a great treat. They never had any alcoholic drinks in the house when the minister was alive. He was teetotal. He believed the Devil lurked in spirits. Bertha had bought this bottle herself, out of her own money, to welcome home the doctor. Use a little wine for thy stomach's sake, First Epistle to Timothy, chapter 5, verse 23.

Like many unmarried women of her age, Bertha liked to equate her actions, even her thoughts, with Biblical texts the old minister had taught her. In their

155

familiarity she found comfort and reassurance.

Bertha brought the sherry in on a tray, with two glasses, filled them nervously to the brim. She was not used to this sort of thing. Should they be quite full, or only half full? She did not know what the etiquette was.

She handed one glass to him, raised the other. She had never drunk anything alcoholic and she watched him as he sipped the drink. She did the same, hoping he appreciated the significance of two glasses when three people were present. One of their party was being excluded. Bertha was starting as she meant to go on.

'To the future,' the doctor said.

'The future,' Bertha repeated, and raised her own glass.

But she was not drinking just to that. She was drinking to a time when she would be alone with the doctor, when the boy would have gone. She was drinking to being rid of him as soon as possible.

The school was a stone building at the far end of the village, with black-painted iron railings round its yard and a bell in a tower that tolled before lessons began each morning with prayers and then every hour, when lessons changed. The school had two teachers, known as dominies: an old grey-haired man with bad breath and a growth on his bald head the size of a golf ball, and a younger man, thin and stooped.

Ben found it difficult to settle in here. His clothes, made in India, were of different, lighter cloth to the rough tweeds and fustian the other boys wore. He had shoes and they wore boots, and carried a slate under one arm. He had brought an exercise book and pencil to make notes. He was different, and while he could try and adapt, his classmates saw no reason to allow him to do so, or to adapt to him. He was a stranger, he didn't belong.

Ben had heard much about England, or rather Scotland, from Dr Kintyre but he had not realised just how chill the weather could be, and how grey and cheerless the landscape was on all but the sunniest days. He missed India, missed its bright, garish colours, hot spicy food, the constant background sounds of birds and animals, drums, native flutes. Here all was silent, lifeless.

In India, Dr Kintyre had taken Ben up to the Hills on several occasions during the hot weather; Darjeeling and Murree had been pleasantly cool and dry after Bengal. Here, there was so much mist that smooth surfaces of metal and glass wore a constant coat of water. The weather seemed perpetually cold, even in the summer. Ben slept with his vest and socks and underpants in the bed beside him to keep them dry. He did not like putting them on damp in the morning.

The doctor seemed different here, too; more serious, graver. Ben had no *munshi* to teach him, no servants in the house except for Bertha (whom he regarded as a servant) and the daily maid.

A man came twice a week to potter about the garden, as the doctor described his work. He was a retired corporal who had served in India. He appeared mildly interested in Ben's background, but his Scots accent was so broad that Ben could not always understand what he said.

Ben did not make friends easily with the other boys. Again, it was difficult to understand their speech, and they all seemed carroty-haired, with light blue eyes, ready to pick a quarrel without any reason, it seemed to him. Ben could not understand why.

He didn't give himself airs, but they sensed his difference as jackdaws and sparrows sense and resent the

157

arrival of any strange bird with brighter plumage. They all wanted to conform, and they wanted him to conform, to be like them; otherwise he would stand out from the crowd, and the crowd can never abide individuals. He did not fight by butting his head into an opponent's stomach, or on his nose. They could not understand why he did not want to join in when they caught some stray cat, tied a tin can to its tail and threw stones as it ran about wildly, trying to escape its tormentors. They could not understand, as Ben understood, how animals should be treated as friends, not as creatures to be deliberately abused and baited.

When he tried to explain this, and told them about birds and monkeys in the menagerie at Barrackpore, they hit him.

'You're making this all up,' they said. 'You're showing off because you're English. You're not Scots.'

'What's the difference?' he asked, for he did not know the difference.

'I'll show you the difference,' they would retort and hit him, two or three at a time.

He could deal with one, but not two, because the second boy would attack him from behind when he was fighting the first face to face. And why was he fighting at all? He didn't want to fight. He did not dislike these other bullet-headed boys. He had little in common with them, but he still wanted to belong, to be accepted by them. He thought that this crude butting and shouting and kicking in the playground was pointless. He began to dread the morning break when for fifteen minutes the boys ran about shouting and fighting, and always ready to pick on him.

Ben tried to explain his unhappiness to the doctor, but whereas in India Dr Kintyre had been expansive, cheerful, always ready for a talk, not as man to boy but as man to man, treating Ben as an equal, here his spirit seemed to have shrunk. His outlook had closed in, almost closed up, like these narrow streets with the grey stone houses, where empty windows looked at each other across the way, looking but not seeing. People stood behind curtains watching, wanting to see but not to be seen, not to be part of events outside, only uninvolved spectators who could comment on what they saw, and criticise.

Ben thought that this grey atmosphere, plus the chilly climate, must have affected the doctor's temperament. And also he was much busier here; he rode out on horseback to see patients who could not come to his surgery, often in the middle of the night. Ben knew that many of them never paid their medical bills, but he realised this was probably because they could not afford to do so.

There had been no trouble like that in Calcutta. Dr Kintyre had ridden in his carriage then, with a driver and groom on the box. Now his only vehicle was a go-cart which he sometimes took into Perth with Bertha when she did shopping for the week.

At first, Ben had gone with them. Then one morning Bertha came up to his room, pursing her lips, fidgeting with keys at her waist. She said there just wasn't room for him. They needed all the space in the cart for the groceries they brought back.

'So you'll have to stay behind, Ben,' the doctor told him, not realising how much the boy had enjoyed the trips.

Ben nodded. He knew that there wasn't room for him, not only in the cart, but in the house. Bertha didn't like him, that was obvious. But why? She was not someone he would have chosen as a companion, but he did his best to like her. Yet she repeatedly showed her dislike.

'You're eating us out of house and home,' she told

him once. 'I simply can't manage on the money the doctor gives me.'

'Perhaps he'll give you more money then,' Ben suggested; this seemed a reasonable response.

'How dare you say that?' Bertha asked him furiously. 'You're living on his charity as it is. You should be glad of what you've got. Most boys and girls in Scotland, without mothers and fathers, go into a home to be looked after. They have to work for their food.'

'I work at school,' he replied, not understanding her.

'I mean *proper* work, cleaning floors, digging the garden. The girls do needlework.'

'I am willing to help if you tell me what you want doing,' he assured her. 'Just let me know.'

'In the time I tell you, I could have done it myself. And probably twice as much.'

'I'm sorry,' said Ben. He could not comprehend the reasoning, any more than he could understand why this cold woman, with her lined face, pursed lips and dull hair drawn into a tight bun behind her head, resented him so strongly. How different was this chill, locked-in, lonely life, grey as the houses, oppressive as the pewter-coloured sky, compared with the freedom and the sunshine he remembered in India! Here there were no birds with bright plumage, no tigers, no excitement.

He had not met people like Bertha in Calcutta or Barrackpore. Perhaps people changed, became more relaxed in a warm climate. Or perhaps they were a different sort of people. He did not know. He tried, again and again, to tell the doctor how unhappy he was, but Dr Kintyre did not seem to understand. He simply replied that he knew this life must be a great change for him, but he'd get used to it. People in Scotland were very warm-hearted really, although they mightn't always wear their hearts on their sleeves.

So years passed, summer to winter and summer

again, and nothing changed in Ben's mind or in Bertha's. Increasingly, he felt trapped, like the creatures in the menagerie at Barrackpore. Outside, just beyond the bars, lay freedom, decisions he could make on his own, a whole world to discover, perhaps to conquer. But here he was only marking time, just staying alive.

The village school had no organised games. It did not possess a gymnasium, only two classrooms and about thirty pupils, boys in one part, girls in another. After school, Ben liked to go off on his own into the hills, to climb the Grampians and stand as near to the peaks as he could and look down on the valley and the villages beneath. The hillsides were littered with rabbit skulls, bleached by wind and weather and the acid in the heather.

Dr Kintyre had often told him of the retreat from Kabul, and up on the Scottish hills Ben wondered whether skulls of the dead British soldiers, their wives, children, and the camp followers and their wives and children, were also bleached like this. Perhaps, out there, in the snow, lay the skulls and skeletons of his parents, but where? Would he ever know and find them? And even if he did, what good would that be? They were dead and gone and that was the end of the matter. Or was it? Some day, somehow, he would go back to India and on into Afghanistan and see for himself where they had lived and died.

When Ben returned from these walks, on which he usually took a piece of cheese and a slice of bread, maybe an apple or a pear to eat on the way, Bertha always found fault.

'Your clothes are filthy,' she would say. 'Your shoes are all scuffed. The uppers are cut to pieces, and you've gone right through the soles. Look at them, boy. Have you been deliberately rubbing them on rocks?'

'No,' he would reply. 'Maybe I slipped. But I can polish them. They'll come up very well.'

'They'll never come up. They're ruined. You don't think about the money the doctor will have to pay for a new pair. And that fruit you took, I was saving that to put in a pudding. Now I'll have to buy more. That means another trip into Perth and more money spent. You're just an expense to him, a great worry, I'm sure, although he's far too kind a man to tell you so. You do nothing to help. Everything must go one way as far as you're concerned – *your* way.'

'That's not fair, Auntie Bertha. I'm willing to do anything to help. You've only got to tell me.'

'As I've already explained to you so many times, if I have to tell you, it's no good. You should know instinctively. And I am not your aunt, so don't call me Auntie. We're not related. Now, get those filthy things off. I don't know how I'm going to cope with the cost of everything these days. Your pullover is worn through at the elbows, your shirts are frayed, your socks full of holes. I've enough work to do without all this extra, I can tell you. I'll have to speak to the doctor about it. I really will.'

And she did.

I remember Bertha frequently telling me how busy she was now, what a lot of extra work Ben caused; how he ate so much that she had been forced to double her orders for food; how he grew out of his clothes so quickly and was so rough on them. She was working her fingers to the bone, she said, doing more than could be expected of any one person.

I did not pay a great deal of attention to this. I sensed she was on edge, and put it down to her age; she must be well into her forties. I should have put it down to something else: the fact that now there were three of us when she had hoped there would only be two.

I realised this later, but not then, for she had never attracted me in any way. Indeed, I had never considered Bertha in terms of attraction, only as someone who had worked for my father and who was now working for me. It never entered my head she could wish to change this situation. But, looking back, I wonder how many lives would have been affected, perhaps for the better, in any case out of all recognition, if I had thought more seriously about her attitude and reached a different conclusion.

Ben decided that as soon as he was old enough he would leave Bertha and the doctor. The house was not a home, although he called it by that name. He kept out of Bertha's way as much as possible and would walk into the hills whenever he could, even go without supper when she was sitting at the table with them. He spent more and more time in his own room. Cold and lonely though this often was, at least he was on his own, not the butt of her barbed remarks, the focus of her animosity.

He had no idea what his future held if he left, but he did not want to endure this existence – he could hardly call it a life – any longer than he had to. He had never discussed with the doctor what he might do for a living. Once or twice medicine had been proposed, but never seriously, for he had no real enthusiasm for the profession. He did not want to be called out at night for trivial complaints; to have to work hard attempting to help people who could, in his view, so easily have helped themselves. He wanted to be out of doors, his own man, in a wide and warm land, not here in the mists and chills of a small northern country.

Ben knew little of other people's careers and so did

not know what careers could be open to him. He realised it would be much easier if he had some professional qualification, but the village school did not provide a grounding for their examinations.

He stayed at school until he was in his late teens, which Bertha frequently told him was very late. Most pupils left when they were twelve or thirteen. Fathers wanted sons to go to work, to bring some money in to help run their cottage homes. They would become labourers, or if they had any aptitude with their hands they might be apprenticed to a carpenter, or work in the local sawmill or with the blacksmith. Girls went into domestic service.

Dr Kintyre sometimes asked Ben where he felt his inclination lay, but Ben knew so little of opportunities available that he found it impossible to answer specifically. All he would say was, 'I'd like something out of doors.'

'It's very hard, working out of doors,' Kintyre told him. 'You're labouring in the fields in the summer when it's hot, and in the winter when it's freezing and the ground's like iron. If you work in the sawmill or in the woods, cutting down trees, that's just repetition, every day the same, using your strength until you're too old to wield an axe.'

'But then every job is repetitious, surely?'

'Agreed. But on a different level, if you're using your mind as well as your muscles. If it's just your muscles, only one part of the body is in action. Similarly, if you're just pushing a pen at a desk, your muscles grow flabby, for you're only using your mind. You want something that combines mind and body. I don't know what that will be in your case, but we'll find it.'

One afternoon, when Ben came home from a long and solitary walk on the Grampians, he heard Bertha and the doctor arguing. Bertha's voice was shrill, high-pitched, as though it had been squeezed up a couple of octaves by the strength of her feelings.

'I don't like saying this, Doctor, but things have come to a head as regards Ben and me. I cannot be doing with him here any longer. I must be quite frank with you. I served your father for many years, and I would enjoy serving you. But not with him. On your own.'

'Why not, Bertha? I'm surprised to hear you talk like this.'

'I'm surprised myself, Doctor. But he and I don't mix. It's oil and water. Having a grown lad like him in the house makes a lot more work. And there's something about him, I can't put it into words. He picks me up on things when I ask for help.'

'Like what things, Bertha?'

'Oh, it's difficult to give examples just like that, Doctor. But I have often said to him that he should help a bit more. And he only says, well, tell me what you want doing and I will do it to help you.'

'That's surely not picking you up on anything, Bertha?'

'It's the way he says it. How *can* I tell him? He should keep his eyes about him, see what needs to be done – wood to be brought in, chopped up for the fire, all kinds of things. And then there's endless work I do on his clothes, and never so much as a thank you. He wears out the seat of his trousers and I have to sew on a new patch, or his socks have holes in them. I don't know – I really can't cope.' She paused. 'Perhaps I'm not as young as I was,' she added, hoping to be contradicted.

'None of us are. But you're not old, Bertha.'

'Well, I didn't feel old, but I do now. I've a little money saved up, Doctor, and I'm going to seek another position. I thought I had better tell you, so

165

you can make other arrangements. I've been here a long time and look on this house, as I looked on the manse, as my home. I have no other, and it hurts me to speak like this, but I felt I had to. I can't go on any longer. You know what they say, two's company, three's none.'

'Your mind is made up?'

'Well, I don't *want* to go, naturally. I used to feel more one of the family here, as you said, than a paid employee. But if he stays, I'll have to go. Things aren't like they were. And as far as I'm concerned, he's the reason. This house is just not big enough for both of us.'

'And if he goes, you stay?'

'Where *could* he go, Doctor? Out of the goodness of your Christian heart, you're bringing him up. But he's not trained for anything, seems to have no idea what he wants to do with his life, which is a pity, because there's lots of other people who have had all sorts of ideas, but never chances like he has.'

'He'll train up very well for something, Bertha.'

'Maybe, Doctor. But I have to consider my own future.'

'So what do you want me to do? You surely don't expect me simply to put him out?'

'I want you to do, Doctor, what you feel is best. In your own interests. Not in his. Not in mine. In yours.'

'Then I suggest we wait and see, Bertha. Please do not make any hasty decisions. I'll have a talk with him.'

Bertha went away then up the stairs. Ben flattened himself behind a curtain until he heard her bedroom door close. Then he went up to his room, walking on his toes not to make a noise, carefully avoiding the stairs that creaked.

He did not want to disrupt Bertha's life. The doctor had been very good to him. They had been close in

India, but now, in this remote, withdrawn country, they were not. He felt he must be interfering in the doctor's life as well as in Bertha's. The doctor relied on Bertha; she knew his ways. If she left, he would have a difficult task to find another housekeeper who would be discreet, not discuss his patients with people in the village and keep his house as he liked it.

Ben looked at himself in the mirror. He was tall, broad-shouldered, he could speak Hindustani, and even read and write the script. He must leave and find a job; he did not know how or what the job might be, but almost anything would be better than to stay on here, unwelcome, unwanted, the cause of continuing dissent. Then, when he was earning his own living, he'd write and tell the doctor, who he felt certain would understand. He felt embarrassed at going, but more embarrassed at staying.

It would be best to make his decision and follow it quickly, get out of the way. This was a time for action, not for talk. After all, the doctor had set off for India when he was young. Ben was certain he would approve what he was going to do, once he had done it.

He went to bed early that night. Next morning, when the doctor was out on his rounds, he decided he would leave. Bertha was at the other end of the village on some business of her own. Ben packed a spare pair of socks, some underpants, a vest, a sweater, two pounds in money he had saved, a flannel cloth wrapped round a bar of soap, a toothbrush.

He went into the doctor's study, felt under the carpet where he knew the doctor kept the key to his safe, opened it. He took out the small box that contained his mother's ruby ring. This was the only thing of value he owned. He did not consider what it might be worth to sell or to use as security for a loan. Its value to him was that his father had given it to his mother. Ben felt that somehow it bound him to them both; indeed it was his only link with them.

He wrote a note to the doctor and put it in the safe:

Dear Uncle,

I am going away. I do not want to cause hurt to Bertha by staying, for that would also mean hurt to you. She would leave you, and you might not find another housekeeper. I will be back, though, when I have found work. I am not leaving you for ever.

I have taken my mother's ring. I will keep it safe. Do not worry about me, or for me.

Yours in gratitude and love,

Ben

Then he locked the safe, replaced the key under the carpet and went out into the village street. It was empty at that time of the morning, except for a dog sleeping in the centre of the road. Little traffic passed through the village and what did come was slow, mostly riders on horseback or bullock carts from the farms.

Ben felt certain no one would see him go. He walked quickly along the main street, round the corner at the end. He did not look back, in case he saw the doctor and his resolve withered. He knew he had to go on. If he did not go now, he might never go, and the doctor had always told him, go on, never go back. Look what happened at Kabul when the Army of the Indus had turned back.

Ben took a deep breath, eased the bundle on his shoulder to a more comfortable position, and set out as though he was also a soldier starting on the first stage of a long march to an unknown destination.

The wooden signpost, white paint peeling after

unnumbered seasons of Scottish rain, pointed to Perth, ten miles in one direction, and to Blairgowrie, sixteen miles away in the other. Ben stopped, swung the bundle thankfully off his shoulder and flexed his muscles.

It was that special hour of evening, before darkness crept down slowly from the hills, which he still found so strange after the swift, dramatic dusk of India.

He decided to take the Perth road. Perth was the larger town; he should have a better chance of finding work there, or at least someone or something to give him a sign as to what he should do, where his future lay. The road stretched away, bleak and empty, growing darker as he stood; he had a long way to walk. Perhaps he should look for a farmhouse or a labourer's cottage where he could spend the night and continue his journey in the morning.

So far he had passed only two other solitary travellers, both on horseback. They had nodded brusquely to him, not wanting to be drawn into conversation with a stranger carrying a bundle. He could be harmless enough or he might be a decoy for armed companions hiding behind the hedge. Then, as soon as they stopped, the ruffians could leap out on them, cut the horses' reins and rob them.

Once or twice, looking behind him, Ben had seen a cart in the distance going in his direction, but it did not overtake him; it was probably only a tinker stopping at houses, hoping for pots and pans to mend.

Wind blew down the valley, rustling dry heather, bringing with it the bitter acidic scent of peat. He could never settle in this country, or this climate, he thought. Everything here was too rigid, too harsh and cold. Even in summer there was so little warmth. But if he could not live here permanently, then where?

For the first time since he had left home that morning, he wondered whether he had been wise to go. At the time it had seemed a good idea, an escape from an unhappy house he could not call a home. But what was he going to do now he was on his own? How was he going to keep himself alive?

Well, he would never find answers standing at a crossroads, he told himself. He heaved the bundle up on his shoulder again, feeling perspiration damp on his back under its weight. And then, as the wind changed, he heard a sound he had not heard for years, and had all but forgotten – elephants trumpeting.

He turned his head towards the noise, and heard it again more clearly; it was not imagination. But elephants in a Scottish glen by the roadside? The idea seemed absurd. He walked on, frowning with concentration, as he strained his ears to catch the sound. It did not come, but instead he smelled the unmistakable scent of curry cooking. The warm, spicy fragrance made his mouth water, bringing back evenings when the doctor's *khansama* had given him a bowl of curry and rice and a warm chapatti to eat, squatting with the other servants, outside their quarters.

How good those simple meals had tasted! How totally different from the boiled potatoes and greens, and cold mutton slices that Bertha would so often place before the doctor and himself as their main evening meal, and wait, her head bowed reverently, hands folded, eyes apparently closed but actually watching him, as the doctor repeated the grace his father had said before each meal: 'For what we are about to receive, may the Lord make us truly thankful.' Ben repeated the words silently to himself. Just what was he about to receive?

He rounded a bend in the road. Hedges on either side were now only visible as a deeper darkness against

170

the sunset sky, and then he saw the source of the sounds and the smells. A fair, or perhaps a circus, was camped in a field to the left of the road.

Flares, soaked in oil and tied to posts driven into the earth at intervals of several yards, cast a smoky, eerie light on caravans and wagons drawn up in neat rows. Some, the beast wagons, had one side removed to reveal vertical iron bars. Behind these, tigers and lions prowled, padding to and fro uneasily in their cramped wooden cages, yearning to be free. The elephants he had heard stood nearby, tethered by chains round their legs to iron stakes hammered into the ground.

They were eating hay, but all tossed up their heads, flapping their huge ears as they heard the cautious approach of a stranger. These sights and sounds brought back memories of the menagerie at Barrackpore. Who was living in that house now? Ben wondered. Who was looking after the animals in their cages – and who was the *munshi* sahib teaching?

Ben stood for a moment, surveying the scene through a gap in the hedge. Women wearing long dresses and blouses, with brightly coloured shawls round their shoulders, were cooking meals in pots over wood fires. A dog barked, and at once other dogs took up his warning chorus. This was no place to stop. Fairground folk – gypsies, Dr Kintyre called them – were well known for their dislike of strangers. He had no wish to be beaten up simply because they thought he was looking at them.

Ben walked on, and as he walked, the smell of curry grew stronger. At the far end of the encampment, away from the other vans, through a gap in the hedge, he saw a small cooking fire. Above this, a cauldron, blackened by soot, bubbled excitedly. A man was stirring the contents with a long-handled ladle. The sight was so evocative of childhood meals in India, that Ben paused.

In an instant, almost animal reaction, the man turned towards him, as though he knew he was being watched, although as yet he could not hear or see anyone. He stood up, holding the dripping ladle as a weapon.

'I am just now saying who is that?' he called.

It seemed a lifetime since Ben had heard that once familiar, Welsh-sounding sing-song accent of an Indian speaking in an alien tongue.

'I am just now looking,' Ben replied, instinctively falling into the idiom. 'Only looking. Not wishing anyone any harm. *Ham dhost wallah*. I am a friend.'

'*Idhar ao*. Come here,' the man commanded him.

Ben walked through the gap in the hedge. On the other side of the fire stood an Indian. He was about forty, well-built, wrapped up against the cold in an odd assortment of shirt, shawls and pantaloons.

'Who are you?' he asked, without any accent now.

'Ben Bannerman. I lived with Dr Kintyre, some miles up the road, near Coupar Angus.'

'And now?'

'I have left him.'

'How do you speak Hindustani? You have learned one or two words to make fun of an Indian? Is that it? Yes?'

'No. That's not it,' Ben replied. 'I was born in Afghanistan, and brought up in Calcutta. As I came along the road, I smelled curry and I heard elephants. I could not pass by these sounds and scents of India. I had to stand and watch.'

'Only hungry men, and cooks, stop to see a meal being cooked. Are you hungry, boy?' the man asked him, more kindly.

'Yes,' Ben admitted. It did not cross his mind to follow Bertha's teaching, that good manners meant one never admitted to being hungry or thirsty.

'I have enough rabbit curry for two,' said the Indian, 'and some rice. Not what I would wish to offer a guest. Not lamb or chicken or prawn. But to the hungry, even rice on its own can taste like a feast.'

'Thank you very much,' said Ben gratefully; he had only realised how hungry he was when he smelt cooking. If he did not accept this invitation, he faced a long walk and no meal that night. Also, the fact that the man was Indian, cooking Indian food, had brought back so many happy memories of life in that country, he wanted to talk to him.

'I can pay,' said Ben. 'I am not begging for food.'

'Of course not. Whoever heard of a poor sahib? Although there are some in your country, if not in mine. It would be my pleasure if you ate with me as my guest.' The man smiled. His teeth gleamed white in the firelight. 'It is not good to eat alone. A meal shared gives double pleasure. And it is written that we should all help a stranger. In your holy book, the Bible, it says how one might even entertain an angel unawares.'

'But not, I think, in this case,' said Ben. Instinctively, he squatted down Indian fashion, near the fire. The Indian handed him a metal plate and a copper bowl of water.

'To wash your hands,' he explained. 'We have no spoons. You told me your name. Mine is Karim Khan.'

He dug his long ladle into the cauldron and pushed the handle towards Ben, who scooped up a spoonful of steaming rabbit flesh onto his plate, then a pile of rice and a warm, dry chapatti. Karim Khan watched him closely as he tore the chapatti into four pieces, folded one and used this to scoop up the rice and meat. The boy knew how to eat without a spoon or a fork; he was not lying, he had indeed lived in India. No one would eat like that so naturally if they had not.

'And now?' asked Karim Khan, tearing up a chapatti himself. 'How long are you living here?'

'The doctor came home from India some years ago and brought me with him. He has a woman who looks after his house, for he is not married. This woman does not like me. Our feelings for each other are cold. Everything here is cold.'

'It is a cold country,' Karim agreed. 'My joints ache here even in summer. They are like rusty hinges. But curry helps to keep out the cold. It oils the hinges, yes? Have you a place to sleep tonight, boy?'

'No,' Ben admitted. 'Nowhere.'

'I have a small caravan with two bunks. You are welcome to one if you wish.'

'I can pay,' said Ben again.

'I don't want money,' said Karim Khan. 'I offer you shelter, because I am thinking perhaps you can help me tomorrow.'

'In what way?'

'I had a young man like you working for me. He left me last week in Blairgowrie. He did not like the travelling life. I also think he had got a girl into trouble on our last visit. He said he was going to marry her, or some such madness.'

'What work did he do for you?'

'I have a sideshow,' Karim Khan explained. 'I am practising magic. Or what local people think is magic, and not something worked out very carefully, like a military operation. I am telling you, most people who come to the fair or a circus have never seen an Indian, so from the start I am a mystery man to them. They are half afraid I will put them in a pot and eat them! My skin is dark. I cook strange food. I speak a different language. I worship a different god, or maybe the same god but under a different name. They have never travelled more than a few miles from where they are born, while I have travelled thousands of miles.

'So they are ready to suspect me of all manner of evil, foreign habits. I play on this, of course. They pay to watch my tricks. And I heal them when they are ill – or so they imagine. I need someone to help me.'

'I know nothing of tricks,' said Ben. 'In India I saw men with flutes charm snakes so that they come out of sacks and I used to watch illusionists pluck hens from people's hats. But I don't know how they do these things.'

'It is well you do not. The secrets are often simple and once you learn them, the magic goes. As with everything in life, do not probe too closely. That way lies disappointment and disillusion. But your mind may be open to learning some of the secrets of my tricks, if you so wish. Not for your amusement or entertainment, I am telling you, but to baffle those who will pay to see me perform them.

'Now, my friend, I have travelled a long way today and I shall retire early. There is no performance tonight. We start tomorrow. I have told you, stay, if you wish. Go if you wish. But you must decide. Now.'

'I will stay,' said Ben slowly. He held out his hand. The Indian shook it; his clasp was firm and warm and dry.

'No one has ever shaken my hand in this country before,' said Karim Khan slowly. 'I am thinking we will work well together. Yes?'

'Yes.'

The next day, Ben helped Karim Khan to set up his booth. It consisted of a small stage, about twelve feet square, with a wooden pelmet across the front and two red curtains that could be drawn by ropes on one side to close in the centre. The pelmet was decorated with fanciful paintings: Indian dancers, rajahs in turbans, bejewelled elephants and snakes curled like coils of rope on carpets; men sitting cross-legged played flutes. To one side of the stage, behind the curtains, stood a small metal table with a number of holes bored in it.

'For joss sticks,' Karim Khan explained. 'The scent adds to the mystery. Except for one or two old soldiers, no one has ever been to India. And those old soldiers probably never left the cantonment in all their service. I am telling you, I have known British soldiers to be in India for ten years or more and never once even visit the local bazaar! So they all expect mystery from me in this cold country.'

'What mystery do you give them?'

'I can make my helper disappear – and then reappear. I can run him through with a sword so that the blade goes into his chest and out of his back. And I tell them I can heal people. Maybe they laugh at me. I let them laugh. Then my helper comes through from the back of the crowd on crutches. He trips and falls and some of the audience pick him up and help him up on stage and then I am curing him.'

'But he isn't crippled?'

'Of course not. He is as fit as you or me. He then throws away his crutches. This always impresses the crowd. Afterwards, I will see people in my tent, tell their future, and maybe cure them.'

'Of what?'

'Sometimes of nothing, my friend, because most are not ill with any physical disease. They are depressed, worried, frightened. I am telling you, fashionable doctors have barrels of different coloured pills, all harmless, made of bread. They tell patients: "Take this pink pill at nine o'clock *exactly* every morning. And this green one at five *exactly* each afternoon. It must not be a minute earlier or later, or it cannot cure you." The patients believe this, and it works. Because they

176

have faith. In your holy book it says that faith can remove mountains. It can also cure.'

'I know,' said Ben. 'I have seen Dr Kintyre treat people in this way and even cure them. Amazing, it seems.'

'Not so. Not at all amazing. There are far more illnesses of the mind than of the body. And if the pill doesn't work, the doctor can always excuse himself by saying they must have taken it too late or too early.'

'I don't like the idea of deceiving people,' said Ben uneasily.

'All life is deceit of one kind or another,' replied Karim Khan grandly. 'Perhaps death, also. Who can say? How many religions promise paradise everlasting to true believers? All. Yet not one of the priests or mullahs or rabbis has any personal experience of what they promise. And no one ever comes back from the dead to tell us whether what they were told is true or false. But people believe because it is in our nature to believe in something.

'For twenty minutes every evening a handful of people outside my booth are believing what I tell them. And they feel better for it, and go away and another lot take their place. I have had people come up to me weeks later when the fair is in another town, and tell me I cured them. Maybe I did. Maybe they cured themselves, because for a few moments I directed their thoughts away from their problems. And in those moments they are free of worry, concern, even physical pain for the first time in years, because for once they are not thinking about themselves. But you can judge for yourself.'

That evening, the field became alive with flames from tarred torches round its perimeter. Hesitant yokels, accompanied by their wives and children, all awkward in their best clothes, usually only worn on

Sundays, came to see strange sideshows: a woman with a beard a foot long, a man so emaciated he was billed as the Living Skeleton, an apparently disembodied head lying on a stall counter.

Karim Khan handed a folded bandage to Ben, told him to wrap it round his left leg, and gave him a wooden crutch. Keeping well out of sight, and holding his crutch like a rifle in the crook of his arm, Ben made his way to the back of the crowd. Karim Khan had deliberately set up his booth slightly apart from the other stalls. The less light he had, the less chance that any of the audience would see how his illusions worked.

He stood now at the front of the stage, the red lenses of the oil lamps casting an eerie, satanic glow on his dark face. It glittered on imitation glass jewels sewn into his purple turban and the lapels of his silk costume. The burning joss sticks produced a sweet-smelling smoke.

He juggled three balls, and then four, threw them all up together, caught them expertly one by one, bowed to the crowd in front of him.

'Now,' he said, in a deep, resonant voice, 'I sense that some among you may be in pain. Some have fears of illness, but lack money to buy physic from the doctor.

'I sense this, my friends, because, as one from the East – and remember how in the holy scriptures the three wise men came from the East – I know what it is to suffer secretly and in silence. I believe I can help anyone who is afflicted in this way. I ask any of you, who suffer whatever tribulation, to step forward and feel healing hands upon your head.'

He stood for a moment, his arms stretched out in invitation. No one moved, for no one wanted to be first. They were afraid of looking foolish, of being laughed at. What would their neighbours say if they heard they'd asked an Indian at a fair to cure them? And how could this odd man wearing robes and a turban possibly help them? They glanced at each other, wondering who would be first. Yokels puffed on clay pipes; a woman coughed nervously; a child began to cry. Karim recognised the signs. He pointed above their heads, looking beyond them all, into the darkness.

'I see behind you a youth, crippled and forced to limp through life when he should be able to dance and sing.'

He nodded almost imperceptibly. Ben began to walk forward clumsily on his crutch. People moved aside to let him have a path between them. They could not see his face until, laboriously, he managed to climb onto the platform and stood, swaying slightly on his crutch, looking at Karim Khan.

'What is the nature of your affliction?' Karim asked him.

'A break below my knee that has not healed,' Ben replied quickly.

Karim Khan nodded, stroked his chin gravely, took several paces to one side of the stage. He paused as though to consider the matter. An oil lamp with a green lens bathed him in an eerie, ethereal glow. The crowd stared in silence. Even the baby stopped crying.

'Walk towards me,' Karim commanded Ben.

Ben took a hesitant step and paused.

'Throw away your crutch,' ordered Karim.

'I cannot,' Ben replied, entering into the spirit of the charade.

'I repeat, throw it away! Then walk towards me!'

Ben let the crutch drop onto the stage, took a tentative step forward, stretching up to his full height.

'I can walk!' he cried. 'I am cured! I am cured!'

Karim Khan bent down, undid the bandage and threw it to one side. The crowd stared at Ben in amazement. Could this be possible – a cripple healed so soon? And yet they had seen it happen right in front of them. That was proof, surely. Now, several people started to walk up to the stage, all self-consciousness forgotten. If this Indian could cure a cripple so quickly, then their coughs and backaches and stiff joints should not present any problems to his skill.

At that moment, a woman at the back, beyond the reach of the lights, shouted in a shrill and accusing voice. 'You are *frauds*! *Charlatans!*'

The crowd turned in surprise. Ben peered through the hot oily smoke from the lamps as the woman marched resolutely towards the stage.

'What is the nature of your complaint, madam?' Karim Khan asked her politely. 'Do you object to making a cripple walk?'

'I object to this ridiculous play-acting,' she replied sharply. 'I object to these totally false claims.'

She climbed up the steps onto the stage, and Ben saw, to his horror, Bertha's face only feet away, smiling at him in triumph.

'This young man is not a cripple!' she shouted to the crowd. 'I know him well. Dr Kintyre in Coupar saved his life as a baby and brought him up as his own son, may God bless him. This young man has returned this Christian kindness by running away from home. He and this Indian are meet companions for each other. Do not believe them.'

'You followed me here,' said Ben dully. As he spoke, he remembered the cart he had glimpsed on the road, always a long way behind him. Bertha must have seen him leave and followed him.

'Yes,' retorted Bertha. 'I did. I always knew you

180

were bad. All smiles outside, rotten and corrupted within.'

'You have come here to take me back?'

'I don't want you back. The doctor is better rid of you. I will not tell him of your new job. But I will see that you and the Indian do not go unpunished. The false prophet who wrought miracles was cast alive into a lake of fire burning with brimstone! Revelation, chapter 19, verse 20.'

At that moment, a sudden, brilliant explosion of light engulfed the stage, bright as an incandescent blaze. People cried out in fright and shielded their eyes. Karim Khan pulled Ben to one side of the stage. Ben, still partially blinded by the power of the flash, had not seen two constables waiting in the wings. Karim Khan had, but too late. They seized his arms, marched him down the steps, through the crowd and away into the darkness.

Through the hedge, in the lane beyond the flares, a two-horse police wagon waited. They bundled Karim Khan inside, padlocked the doors. Then the constables climbed up on the box beside the driver. The conveyance began to move forward slowly.

Ben ran alongside. 'Where are you taking him?'

No one replied. The driver cracked a whip, and the heavy old horses lumbered into a trot.

Ben walked back towards the caravan. He paused before going through the hole in the hedge. People were shouting, cursing, on the far side. He could see them smashing up the stage, tearing down the painted screens, overturning lights, breaking the coloured lenses. Above their angry cries, he heard Bertha shouting, urging them to destroy everything in Karim Khan's booth.

'Burn it to the ground! Purge the earth of these evil-doers!'

181

Kerosene spilled from the lamps burned away quickly and the flames went out, one by one. Gradually, the crowd drifted away. The incident had provided a welcome break from routine; it would be a talking point for weeks ahead.

When they had all gone, Ben stamped out the embers in case they caught fire again and went into Karim's caravan. He closed the door behind him, lit a candle, and sat down on his bunk, wondering what to do.

He had not wanted to take part in Karim's deception; he should have followed his own inclination, and refused. But in agreeing he had learned a valuable lesson he would now only forget at his peril. He must never again be persuaded to follow any course against his conscience, his own feelings of what was right and what was wrong. Even so, no one had been harmed. It was also just possible that someone might have been helped – if Bertha had not destroyed the opportunity.

Would she tell Dr Kintyre she had seen him, despite her assurance that she would not? Ben thought she would, and he did not want to hurt the doctor who had been so kind to him. What should he do? Go back like the Prodigal Son returning, or go on to make his own life?

As he pondered the problem, he heard a tapping on the door and opened it. A middle-aged man, with fustian trousers, waistcoat and a coloured silk scarf tucked into the collarless neck of his shirt, stood on the caravan step.

'You are with Karim?' he asked Ben.

'Yes. Who are you?'

'King Drummond,' the man replied. 'King George Drummond. I own the circus. You've heard of me, surely?' he appeared surprised that Ben had not instantly recognised him.

'I'm sorry, no. I only joined up with Mr Khan yesterday.'

'It looks like your association is going to be brief.
He's in the lock-up at Ardrey.'

'What will happen to him?'

'Depends who's on the Bench. If you get a landowner who has had trouble with gypsies or poachers,
he'll get a whipping at the least, and maybe six months
inside. He'll probably get one or the other in any case.
Lucky if he doesn't get both.'

'That seems very harsh.'

'Life is harsh, son, as you're about to find out. For
if he goes inside, your job goes, too. When you travel
like we do, you learn to accept there's more rough
than smooth. So, never explain, never complain, and
accept what luck you get, good or bad.'

'Where exactly is this lock-up? I'll go and see him.'

'You're wasting your time. But then you're young.
You've still got time to waste. Walk into town, take
the first right and it's fifty yards up on your left. You'll
see it easily. Ardrey's small and the lock-up's large –
probably the biggest building in the place. He'd be glad
to see you, if the constables permit it, for not too many
people ever want to help you when you're down. But
I'll give you some advice, son, which many people
don't know about. Never hit a man when he's down.
He may get up!'

Ben locked the caravan, and set out along the road
to Ardrey. He found the lock-up easily enough, pulled
a polished brass bell handle outside the front door. An
elderly constable opened the door cautiously. His tunic
was unbuttoned, the waxed ends of his moustache
sagged above the corners of his mouth.

'Who are you? What d'you want?' he asked.

'I have come to see a prisoner. Karim Khan.'

'The Indian, eh? You know him?'

'Yes. He helped me.'

'Then it's a pity you can't help him in return. He's up before the Provost tomorrow and the Provost hates fairground travellers. So I don't reckon anyone can help him now, except the Almighty.'

The constable led the way down the corridor, which smelt of urine and stale cabbage water. Oil lamps burned smokily in wall sconces. He stopped outside a metal door. It was like one of the doors to the wild animal cages in the fair: its frame held thick bars about three inches apart, extending from top to bottom. The door was secured by an old-fashioned heavy padlock. Inside, some sour straw had been scattered thinly on the cold stone floor. Karim Khan crouched in a corner, like a beaten animal.

'There he is. Your Indian Miracle Man. Let him work a bloody miracle now, if he can, and get himself out of here!' The constable roared with laughter at his wit; Ben smelled whisky on his breath.

At the sound of his voice, Karim Khan stood up, came slowly towards the bars, gripped them in his hands.

'No touching,' warned the constable. 'No shaking hands. You might pass him a knife or a file. Can't have that.'

'I have nothing to give him,' said Ben, holding out his hands, palms uppermost. 'Only my hope he will not be here for long.'

'He'll be here till tomorrow, then I'd say for six months more, if the Provost's on form.'

'Do you want me to bring you any clothes, or anything else from the caravan?' Ben asked the Indian.

Karim Khan bowed. 'How kind of you to call on a prisoner. I am telling you, blessed indeed is he who helpeth the unfortunate, the poor and the needy. He

184

will have a special place in Paradise. He will walk with the faithful in the glorious garden of Allah.'

'We don't want no heathen talk here,' said the constable sharply. He turned to Ben. 'There. You've seen him. Now you'd better go.'

'My shoelaces, look,' said Karim Khan, his voice suddenly urgent. He bent down, pulled a length of lace from his right shoe. 'They are worn through. The fear of tripping myself up is ever with me. In my caravan, my friend, in the drawer beneath my bunk, you will see two new pairs, one black, one brown. Please, if you are allowed, bring me the black laces. They will match my boots.'

'Trying to look smart, are you?' asked the constable, amused at the thought that this Indian pedlar, wearing his extraordinary native costume, could even imagine that a new pair of shoe laces would smarten his appearance. He was having a shock coming to him all right in the morning. The Provost would give him what for then, no doubt about that. None at all.

'Yes, sir,' Karim Khan replied meekly. 'I have to appear before the Provost tomorrow, so I would like to march in like the military man I once was, and not shuffle about as a beggar. Will you allow this young man, the only one of all my colleagues who has shown the Christian virtue of charity and has visited me, to bring these laces to me?'

'If he is back within half an hour, before I go off,' said the constable. He turned to Ben. 'But remember one thing, son. I smoke. I like Walnut Plug. It's sixpence an ounce. And I'd like two ounces.'

Karim Khan turned to Ben. 'In the same drawer, my friend, you will be finding a small bag with some silver coins. Bring the officer a shilling.'

Ben ran back to the field. The fair had been dismantled; the caravans and beast wagons had already gone. Karim Khan's caravan seemed to be the only one left.

Ben climbed up the steps, went inside. He locked the door behind him, lit a candle and opened the drawer. Two pairs of black laces and two of brown lay on a sheet of newspaper. He ran them through his fingers. They seemed stronger than their appearance suggested; they would not break easily. He put one set in his pocket, opened a small leather bag in a corner of the drawer, took out one shilling. Then he blew out the candle, locked up the caravan and ran back to the lock-up.

The constable was waiting for him, and held out his hand. Ben put the shilling on his palm. The constable bit the coin between his teeth.

'If this is counterfeit,' he began menacingly. Then he nodded approvingly and put the shilling in his pocket.

He led the way down the corridor. Karim Khan was standing close to the bars, looking out at the dingy corridor.

'Let's see those laces first,' said the constable. Ben handed them to him. He tugged at their metal ends.

'No harm in it, I s'pose,' he said and pushed them through the bars, deliberately missing Karim's outstretched hands. The Indian had to bend down to pick them up from the straw.

'Now get out!' the constable told Ben crossly. 'I'm off duty. Should have gone ten minutes ago. Hope the laces impress the Provost tomorrow because the Indian won't.'

'What is the charge?'

'Several. All serious. Causing an affray. False pretences. Claiming to have the ability to heal without any medical training. No settled abode, and so could be a charge on the parish. That do for a start?'

Ben was silent; there seemed nothing to say. If Karim

Khan escaped one charge, he could be sentenced for another.

Ben walked back slowly along the empty lane, climbed thankfully up the steps into the caravan. He would sleep here, and see what happened to Karim Khan in court next morning before he made any plans.

He checked that the old horse had water and a bale of hay, then undressed to his shirt and underpants, and lay down on the bunk where he had slept the previous night. He felt tired and hungry and worried. He had started the day in high spirits, beginning a job with a man he felt he could like. He was ending it with the knowledge that this man would almost certainly go to gaol, and after exactly one day as his employee he would be out of work. Who would look after the horse then, and the caravan?

Pondering these problems, Ben fell asleep.

Suddenly he was awake, sitting up. The moon shone through net curtains and the caravan felt very cold. He heard the horse blow outside and stamp its feet, and then realised what had awoken him – a faint and urgent tapping on the door.

Who could it be at such an hour – one o'clock in the morning?

Ben swung himself off the bunk, looked around for a possible weapon. He found a carved walking stick with an ivory head and opened the door cautiously. Karim Khan came in swiftly, locked the door behind him.

'How did you get out?' Ben asked him in amazement. 'Did they drop the case and let you go?'

'No. I decided to leave on my own.'

'But the cell door was padlocked.'

'For every lock, my friend, there is a key.'

'But you hadn't got a key.'

'Not in the accepted sense, agreed. But a key can

have many shapes. And I had this.'

He took from his pocket a fine flexible saw blade with a loop at each end, the sort of blade Ben had seen craftsmen use in Calcutta to cut delicate fretwork patterns.

'But how did you get that?' he asked. 'You didn't take it in with you. You would be searched, surely?'

'I was searched, but I didn't have it then, so they couldn't find it. You brought two in for me, inside those black laces. Remember?'

'You keep blades inside shoelaces? What on earth for?'

'Questions, questions, my friend. Do you never cease to ask them? They are part of my equipment for one of my magical tricks. I am bound in chains, but I can escape by sawing my way out, just as I cut the padlock.'

'They'll be after you tomorrow.'

'Not tomorrow, my friend, *today*. So we are just now putting the wagon to the horse, and we leave.'

'They will still find you.'

'Is one Indian in a travelling fair worth spending parish money to find when he may be twenty miles away in any direction? I think not, and I have had experience of these people. I know how their minds work. They will deal harshly with someone they think cannot strike back, but grovel to the rich and powerful. Since we are neither, we must always be using whatever small advantages we possess over them. In one word, brains, my friend.'

'In India, a *munshi* told me about Alexander the Great. How he used his brains to overcome what seemed impossible odds.'

'Of course. You must learn to do the same, Ben. I will not be returning here for a few months – not that the fair is intending to in any case. We will not be back here until the spring.'

'The flash that dazzled all of us just before you were arrested,' said Ben, suddenly remembering the moment before the constables arrested Karim Khan. 'What caused that?'

'I caused it. If I see that one of my tricks is not going to work, I light a packet of magnesium that I keep in my pocket and make a great blaze. The light is so bright and unexpected that it blinds people temporarily and conceals the fact that something has gone wrong. I used it this evening to divert attention – and look what happened.

'Now, to remind you of events this day, I have two presents for you. First, a pair of these most useful laces. Second, this belt.'

Karim Khan opened a drawer, took out a belt made of soft black leather, with a large German silver buckle. He handed it to Ben.

'Thank you,' said Ben. 'But why would the belt remind me?'

'Because, as in life, there is more to it than seems at first. The leather is actually in two parts. They are held together by a very few stitches. In between them is a deposit of magnesium and a dusting of chemicals. If you hold the belt at each end and pull sharply the chemicals will ignite, and so will the magnesium. This makes a great flash just as you saw.'

'Your stage and everything is ruined,' said Ben. 'You won't have an act.'

'Maybe that is so. But I have you, my friend. You stood by me when others melted away. You and I will build a new stage, and a new act. Together.'

I was sitting reading by the fire, with my dog asleep

on the carpet at my feet, when I heard the click of the back door latch.

I thought it must be Ben, coming in too late for my preference and so trying to make as little noise as possible. I remembered how I used to do this myself when I was his age, tiptoeing past my father's study door and up the stairs to my bedroom. I would know when my father was still at work, usually writing next Sunday's sermon, because I could see a faint strip of light under the door. I would walk upstairs with special care, treading on one side of the stairs only, never in the centre, because there was less chance of a board creaking.

But my father had been dead long since; and it was strange to realise that to Ben I must be as senior a figure as he had been to me. We all know how others grow old, but we are surprised at any evidence that we are also ageing. I had not seen Ben all that day or the previous day, either. I opened the library door and called out to him.

'Ben! I'm in here.'

'It's not Ben, Doctor. It's me.'

'You?'

I recognised Bertha's voice and glanced at my pocket watch. It was just after midnight, late for her; she was a creature of habit, who liked to keep early hours.

'You're out late,' I said, surprised. 'Is all well?'

Bertha was about four steps up and stood looking down on me. In the dim light of the oil lamp in the hall, her face looked lined and old, as though carved from stone, not a face of flesh and blood. I saw how harsh and stern she appeared. From my own boyhood, when my father was alive, I had grown used to Bertha in the house, cooking, making beds, ordering the maid about, so I had long since ceased to regard her as a person, with feelings, thoughts, hopes of her own, if indeed I ever had done so. She had threatened to leave, but she had stayed. Had she now decided to go?

I would have noticed the harshness of her face earlier if I had been more observant. I wondered whether she had been too hard on Ben, taking out on him her own frustrations and disappointments. He had attempted to explain his unhappiness and I had not bothered to listen.

'I cannot utter a lie, Doctor. You ask me if all is well. As far as the boy Ben is concerned, it is far from well. The Lord knoweth I lie not – Second Corinthians, chapter 11, verse 31. I had not wished to tell you, but as you ask, I must.'

'What are you talking about, Bertha?'

'The boy, Benjamin.'

'What has happened to him? What is not well with him?'

'He has sinned and come short of the glory of God, Romans, chapter 3, verse 23. I found him tonight with an Indian in a travelling fair on the Perth road.'

'With an *Indian*? In a fair? Doing what?'

'Helping in this man's sideshow. The Indian claimed he could heal people – a total lie, of course. I saw the Indian's fraudulent claim as a blasphemy on our Lord. Ben was dressed up to appear as if he was a cripple. He had a bandage on one leg and walked with a crutch. Then, when the Indian told him he was cured, he threw away the crutch to walk unaided. I denounced them both.'

'What happened?' I stood staring at the woman, wondering whether this could possibly be true.

'There was a sudden, blinding flash of light, Doctor, so bright it seemed to come from Heaven itself. A mark of divine displeasure, or some machination of the Evil One through the black heart of the Indian. For a moment, everyone was blinded. People started to shout and scream in terror. But I had previously warned the police that I believed some mischief was likely. Constables were there and they arrested the Indian and took him to Ardrey lock-up.'

'All because of your actions?'

'In no spirit of pride, I have to admit it was, yes.'

'How did you come to be at the fair?'

'I saw Ben leave this house carrying a bundle on his back. I guessed he was running away, and I followed him.'

'You did not tell me.'

'I did not want to alarm you.'

'Well, you have. Where is Ben now?'

'I have no idea. I told him you would not want to see him.'

'Not want to see him? But how did you get that idea? I brought him into the world. His parents were my dear friends. I saved his life. I have brought him up. I intend to pay his fees at university when he is old enough if he wishes to take a degree. What right have you to tell him that I do not want to see him?'

'He has an evil heart, Doctor. He has taken advantage of you ever since he and you arrived here.'

'Who says so? I know he has not been as happy here as when we were together in India. But never once has he taken advantage of me. Everything I have given him I have given willingly. Do you not understand that, Bertha?'

'I think you refuse to believe how wicked and self-willed he is, Doctor.'

'Rubbish! Ben is young. And like all young creatures, he wants to be off on his own, to make his own way. Birds do not linger in the nest when they are old enough to fly. The spread their wings and go. As he will, one day.'

'He has gone now, Doctor. He will not be coming back.'

'How do you know?'

'I told him to stay away.'

'*You?* By what right?'

'By the right of not wishing to see your generosity abused.'

I turned away in anger and disgust. I tried to tell myself that Bertha meant well, but I recognised the signs of bitter feminine jealousy. I wished then, as I wished so often, that Anna had lived. If only . . .

I took down my coat from the peg behind the door, put on my hat, and took a heavy oak walking stick from the rack. Then, on the impulse, I paused. If Ben had genuinely planned to leave me permanently, I could not believe he would do so without any farewell. Since he had not told me of his plans, he would probably have left me a note. Where could it be?

I reasoned he would almost certainly have taken Anna's ruby; that was virtually his only possession. I opened the safe. The jewel box had gone and in its place was a single sheet of paper. I recognised Ben's handwriting and read his letter.

I put the letter back in the safe, locked it.

'I am going out,' I told Bertha briefly.

'At this hour, Doctor?'

'At this hour. I am going to find Ben and bring him home.'

'He has gone with the Indian,' she replied. 'Let him go. He will not come back here. This is not his home.'

'If this isn't, Bertha, then he has no home anywhere.'

My dog followed me out of the house, through the sleeping village, along the main road. I found where the fair had been easily enough. The field was trodden flat by hundreds of feet and animal hooves, and rutted by caravan wheels. These people did not care for houses or for a settled world; they were nomads, creatures of the road, born under wandering stars. One night could be long enough for them to stay anywhere. They had packed and gone as they always did, quickly, quietly.

Here and there in the field piles of rubbish still smoked and smouldered. To one side I saw splintered pieces of wood bearing traces of Indian paintings: a man with a delicately curled black moustache wielded a curved sword, a girl with slanting almond eyes held a zither. Clearly, there had been a disturbance of some kind. The booth bearing these decorations had been badly damaged. Because of the nature of the designs, this would almost certainly have been the Indian's sideshow. Where was he? And where was Ben?

I had no idea where the fair was going or where it might be; the boy could be almost impossible to find. It is very easy for a wild animal – or a young person of wild spirit – to cover all tracks and traces if they do not want to be hunted or followed. And, clearly, Ben did not.

I stood for a moment, irresolute, looking up at the hills, bright under the moon. In their chill austerity and remoteness they reminded me, as always, of the hills and passes in Afghanistan. I could almost hear wheels creaking on dry axles, the blowing of camels, the whinny of a horse, and the muffled tread of marching feet as our column trudged on to suffer and to die.

I thought of Anna Bannerman and the baby I had carried on my back – to what? To allow him to go on his way without a single goodbye when he should be studying for a profession or, if that was not to his taste, for a trade or craft?

I felt I had failed him, and yet, while part of me wanted to go after Ben and find him and bring him back, the other part of me counselled, 'No. Let him go. He is not a boy any longer. He is a man.'

Like the Prodigal Son, about whom my father had so often preached sermons, I realised that Ben must find his own way, make his own mistakes and finally reach his own destiny, under whatever star he chose. When he was ready he would come back as he had said in his letter – if he still wanted to do so.

I had foolishly allowed Bertha to have far too large a say in his upbringing, but in those days the life of a country practitioner was hard, far more demanding than it had ever been in India. I had little spare time to spend with a growing boy; I knew then I should have made time, but the knowledge came too late.

Ben Fanfare should have been more important than curing the aches and pains of people I hardly knew. Ben was the son of the woman I had loved once, my only living remembrance of her. And now he had gone, and so had my chance to help him.

I walked home slowly, borne down by thoughts and regrets. I had missed one opportunity with him. Would I ever have the chance of another?

Chapter Six

When Ben came out of the caravan early to open up the front of the booth, a girl wearing a white blouse and a long white dress that touched the grass was standing, arms folded, watching him. She did not look like a potential customer – indeed, it was far too early for visitors; nor did she appear to be a fairground woman. Her dark hair was drawn neatly into a bun at the back of her head. Small gold earrings shone in her ears. She wore no other jewellery, whereas most fairground girls liked huge golden bangles on their wrists, and earrings the size of key rings. She regarded him with a quizzical, questioning expression, as though she had never seen anyone quite like him and was not sure whether she approved of him or not. He grinned at her.

'Who are you?' she asked.

'Ben Fanfare Bannerman is the name.'

'A big name for a young fellow.'

'Maybe. But then I'm a big young fellow,' retorted Ben.

'Big-headed, perhaps.'

'Why do you say that? Who are you?'

'Mary Jane Green,' she said. 'I'm with Ivan here on his tog stall. You're with Karim Khan? I've not seen you before.'

'I only joined him a couple of days ago. And we've had some bad luck since.'

'So I heard. You're not a showman, really, are you?'

'No. And you're not a showgirl.'

'I am for the moment.'

'Well, I'm a showman for the moment, too. You watch me in operation tonight and you'll see what I do. Have you worked long with the fair?'

'No,' she admitted. 'Just a bit longer than you.' She smiled.

She had an engaging smile, Ben thought, and an easy, engaging style about her.

'This isn't my life,' she went on.

'So what is your life?'

She shrugged. 'I don't know really. My mother's living away. My father—' she paused, shrugged again. 'I don't know. I'm saving up money. I want to get out of here one day.'

'What's he like to work for, Ivan?'

'He's kind and he works hard.'

'Then why do you want to get out?'

'I'm guessing, but probably for the same reason as you. There's no future here.'

'Is there a future in any job unless you're trained?' Ben asked her.

'Maybe not much,' Mary Jane agreed. 'But here we set out the stall the night or the morning we arrive. Then we have a few hours trying to make money out of people who've got very little to spend. And late that night or early the next day we pack up everything and move on to the next pitch. And this goes on day after day all through every summer. We're lucky if we have two days in the same place.'

'What happens in the winter?'

'The caravans are parked behind pubs, in farmyards. All the equipment is mended and painted. In the circus, they keep the animals as fit as they can, maybe try to teach them new tricks.'

'What will you do next winter?'

'Whatever comes along. Make or mend clothes for the circus people, trapeze artistes and so on. Dye heather white and sell bunches in pubs. Good-luck charms. And you?'

'I don't know,' admitted Ben. 'I hadn't thought of it.' He had, but the future seemed so indeterminate and unpromising, he preferred to put all consideration of it out of his mind.

'What did you do before you came here?'

'I ran away from home. My parents are both dead. They were killed in Afghanistan.'

'Where's that?'

'A country next to India. All mountains and snow. My father was in the army. A friend of his is a doctor. He brought me back here. I like him. But I couldn't get on with the woman he had in the house.'

'His doxy?'

'What's that?'

'Woman he sleeps with, lives with, his wife in everything but name. You don't know much, do you?'

'No,' Ben agreed. 'But I'm willing to learn.'

Mary Jane smiled. 'Maybe I could teach you. Now, watch what I do for a living tonight and you'll see why there's no more future for me than there is for you. If you're taking the place of the other man who helped Karim, you'll disappear two or three times a night, maybe breathe fire, that sort of thing.'

'It's a living,' said Ben defensively.

'I know it's a living. But that's all it is. And I want more. Now I make just enough money to buy food, so I can go on and work another day to make enough money again to buy food for that day. It's like running on the spot. I want to get rich, then I can watch others run, making money for me.'

'You're quite a philosopher,' said Ben.

Mary Jane frowned. 'What's that?' she asked him suspiciously.

'Someone who thinks things out.'

'You ought to think things out yourself. No one else is ever going to think anything out for you.'

'True enough. Well, I'd better get on.'

Ben busied himself with his brush, sweeping the dust and wisps of straw that had collected on the stage. Mary Jane went into her tent.

That night, when all the lights were lit, while Karim Khan endeavoured to drum up people for his illusions, Ben walked across to her stand and stood at the back of the crowd where he hoped she would not see him.

Mary Jane now wore very large, bright earrings, a gold-edged blouse, several necklaces, and rings on all her fingers. Her face was rouged, lips reddened, eyelids darkened. She looked mysterious, romantic, foreign, immensely attractive. And to his surprise and admiration, she seemed totally in command of the stall, and the audience.

Under four of the new naphtha lights that hissed and fumed, a table about fifteen feet square had been set up with a strong rope barrier round it so that neither the audience nor the players could come too close. The table was printed in squares, each painted a different colour with a sum of money marked on the background: white for one pound, blue for ten, red for fifty, gold for a hundred.

Behind the table, in the booth, where no one could grab them, two net bags hung from a supporting pole. One was full of polished silver coins, shillings, half-crowns; the other contained equally highly polished golden sovereigns. The coins glittered and gleamed and glowed bewitchingly in the bright unwinking light. The crowd stood staring at the money, mesmerised by the sight, more than they earned in a whole year and just out of their reach. Now some could possibly be theirs for the modest outlay of sixpence or a shilling at the most.

Mary Jane picked up half a dozen polished ivory dice with black markings, dropped them in a bowl and began to shake it as she spoke.

'Here we are, gents all,' she said brightly. 'Let's see the sportsmen. Who's going to be lucky today? Count the numbers, shall I? One and three are four. Four and seven make eleven. Twice eleven is twenty-two. Add on eight, and you're thirty, which is a good age for a man to marry.

'Add five and you're half your lifespan, which is three score years and ten, seventy. Add one, seventy-one. Add ten, eighty-one. Add five, eighty-six and four is ninety.'

As she was speaking, she shook the dice and threw them on the board. Then with a long stick with a metal hook on the end she gathered them up into one corner and threw them again.

'Ninety. Take away five is eighty-five. Eight and five is thirteen. Thirteen is unlucky, but who's it going to be lucky for tonight? Someone, I can see it. Thirteen. One and three makes four. Add six and you've got ten. Is that *your* lucky number?'

She looked at the board.

'Yes, sir. Someone *is* lucky.'

She lifted one of the dice. It had landed on a blue square marked ten pounds.

'Ten gold sovereigns to you, sir. All for one shilling. Not a bad return in anyone's language. That's how the great fortunes are made, gents. Now, who's the winner?'

A man stepped forward. He stretched out his hand.

Slowly, deliberately, so that nothing was lost of the glitter of the coins in the blaze of lights, Mary Jane counted out ten sovereigns. The man touched his cap to her, slipped them in his pocket and vanished in the darkness, but not before Ben recognised him. He had seen him earlier that day leading a circus elephant. He was not a genuine punter, just one of the fair employees. The turn had been staged, but staged to good effect. Immediately, money poured on the board: sixpences, shillings, pennies, ha'pennies.

Every time Mary Jane threw the dice it just missed the number that she called.

'Very bad luck, sir. *Very* bad luck. That was fifty-one and you were fifty-two. You're next to it, and you would have won a *hundred* golden sovereigns. My goodness, sir. Just one out. One away from a fortune. Have another go, I beg of you, sir.'

The show went on. One or two other men who Ben recognised as workmen came up and won sums ranging from one pound to ten. Then the crowd seemed to lose interest. When only half a dozen were round the board she threw the dice, and turned to one man.

'I think, sir, you are the lucky number. I will give you five pounds now for your number. Five pounds, sir. Now. For your hand. Before I begin to throw.' Just for a second, Mary Jane paused, then Ben heard a man shout from the back of the crowd.

'Wait a minute! I called first!'

'I didn't hear you, sir,' she said.

The man pushed his way through to the front. Again Ben recognised him; he was a carpenter in the circus.

'I have the call,' he announced.

'You damn' well don't,' said the man who had shouted first.

They began to yell at each other; a fight threatened.

Mary Jane waited until the two men were actually squaring up to each other for a sum which represented a month's wages. Then she intervened.

'No, gents, we can't have any trouble. Fair's fair. No quarrelling. Everything's above board here. I'll give you both a free throw, *and* the same number, a free throw it is to you, sir.'

She threw the dice; the carpenter won. The first man went away, grumbling. It was a swindle, of course; Ben saw that. But then wasn't Karim Khan's show also a swindle, if of a different kind? Nothing for nothing was the rule in life. These simple folk thought they could break this universal law.

Later, when the visitors had gone and stallholders were packing up to move on to the next site, Ben sought out Mary Jane.

'You were very good,' he said, and meant it.

'Good?' she replied, surprised but pleased.

'Well, all that bamboozling people.'

'They're fools,' she said simply. 'They're all men, and men are fools. They want to be bamboozled. Women don't waste their money like that.'

'They haven't got any money, that's why.'

'We're more cautious. We know there must be a catch somewhere. It's obvious there is. Otherwise how could Ivan make a living by taking in pennies and giving away pounds? But men's minds don't work like that. They want to believe they can turn common sense upside down.'

'I said you were a philosopher.'

'I remember. I just wish I could win some of that money I pretend to give away, and get out.'

'Perhaps you will one day.'

'Which? Get out or win?'

'Whatever you want to do most.'

'Are you a philosopher? Like you said I was?'

203

'No. An optimist. Where's your sideshow stopping next?'

'Ten miles up the road. A big show, I'm told.'

'See you there, then.'

But Ben didn't, and he missed her. Someone told him that Ivan's caravan had shed a wheel and had been delayed for a day, and that was the day of the fair.

He was surprised he missed her; without realising it he had been looking forward to seeing her there.

The Provost was overweight, red-faced and irascible. On this particular Monday he had three reasons for feeling more irascible than usual.

First, he suffered from boils and was in discomfort from two eruptions at different extremities of his person. One was beneath his right buttock, which scored him like a knife blade every time he eased his heavy body in his chair. The second boil was a hard, inflamed lump the size of a pea on his left nostril. The Provost also suffered from a cold, and each time he wiped his nose the boil throbbed and pulsated with pain.

As if this was not sufficient torture for a wet Monday morning, the sight of Sergeant Macduff of the Ardrey force standing rigidly in front of him, his homely face creased with worry, provided a third cause of irritation. The Provost dabbed his nose carefully.

'I see you have chosen to give me a verbal account rather than a written report of this extraordinary happening at the lock-up?' he said grimly.

'I thought that best, sir.'

'Best from whose point of view, Sergeant?'

'In the general interest of the force, sir.'

'I can quite understand why you would wish to keep this humiliation quiet. Should anyone connected with the Press hear about it, the police would lose all credibility.

'Here we have a black vagrant, alleged to be an Indian, a known faker – although doubtless he would describe himself more elegantly as a *fakir*. He is arrested for fomenting a serious and riotous disturbance among labourers and ne'er-do-wells outside his fairground booth, and incarcerated in your lock-up.

'A young white man, apparently his assistant, visits him and, at his request, brings him a pair of bootlaces. The duty constable examines these and swears that they are ordinary laces, of a type sold to labourers.

'That is at the least arguable, because within an hour, the so-called Indian has fled, leaving a padlock cut through. Presumably he had a saw or a file concealed about his person – or in one of the laces. I don't know. What I do know is that we must find this man and charge him, and also the youth, his accomplice, who doubtless is of an equally devious nature. What did you put in the charge book about this Karim Khan?'

The sergeant coughed, stalling for time. This could be the most delicate part of the interview.

'As a matter of fact, sir, we had not made an entry.'

'Not made an entry by Monday morning about a prisoner taken in charge on Saturday night? A travelling man of no fixed abode, the most elusive sort of vagrant? Why not, pray?'

'We are making other enquiries, sir.'

'That is no excuse whatever,' retorted the Provost angrily. 'You, as Sergeant, were in charge of the lock-up. It was your duty to make a proper entry *at once*. If this man is of a litigious nature – although I doubt whether he can even read or write – he might prefer charges against the force for wrongful arrest and detention. Whether they succeeded or not, that would still attract a lot of unwelcome publicity.

'This is a very serious matter, Sergeant. I regret to have to remind you that it is not the only example of slackness involving you. Only last week, a minister of the kirk, visiting the lock-up for Christian reasons to preach the Gospel to prisoners, found you, if not actually drunk, in a state which he has charitably described as having taken drink.'

'I was suffering from a severe chill, sir. I only took a wee dram.'

'And you are now fully recovered, I trust?'

'Yes, sir.'

'Good. Then your indisposition will not present any impediment to your discovering the whereabouts of this Indian and charging him with breaking gaol – at once. In case of any questions about not having made an entry about him in the book, has anything else been put in the book since Saturday?'

'No, sir.'

'Then record his arrest in the book forthwith and date it Saturday.'

'That is not in accordance with orders, sir. Nothing can be backdated.'

'This can and will. It is in accordance with common sense, Sergeant, which must sometimes come before strict adherence to procedure. Now, have you any idea where the Indian is?'

'I understand, from my enquiries, that the fair and sideshows are in a field ten miles away. He is most likely to be there, sir.'

'Who owns this travelling fair?'

'A showman known as King George Drummond.'

'King George, eh? A fine, high-falutin name for a vagabond,' replied the Provost shortly, easing his weight to a less painful position. 'I leave the matter to you. And inform me as soon as this man and his accomplice are in custody.'

Karim Khan faced Ben across a fire lit outside his

caravan. They sat on two boxes, frying eggs and mushrooms and Scottish oatmeal puddings. A kettle of tea swung on a tripod over a second, smaller fire. The autumn air felt crisp, and clear as glass. When the wind changed, Ben smelled the raw animal scents of caged monkeys, tigers, lions, which always reminded him of the menagerie at Barrackpore. He had often thought about India since he arrived in Scotland, but always with sadness, as though he had said goodbye to that world for ever. Now, for almost the first time since he had left India, he felt content, relaxed, free. Maybe he was born to be a travelling man?

'I owe you a lot for getting me out of the lock-up,' said Karim Khan, stirring the mushrooms. 'As I told you, my assistant left last week. If you are still willing to learn how to help me with my art, my offer of a job at one pound a week and all your food stands. Not a permanent position, for nothing is permanent for fairground folk. But it could help you for the moment.'

'Thank you,' said Ben gratefully. 'That will help me a lot.'

'Good. Then it is agreed. Tonight we will not attempt any faith-healing. It seemed to arouse harsh feelings, and that we must avoid. People in Scotland are very narrow-minded. It is very easy to offend them.

'You may not realise the dangers we run with sideshows here. The customers all believe in Satan, or the Devil, as they call him. He is as real to them as their neighbour next door. Anything they cannot understand frightens them, so they think magicians must be in league with Satan. Sometimes they become so agitated they attack us and break up our booths, as you have seen. And since the ministers often preach in the kirk on Sundays on wickedness among fairground folk and the theatre – people with painted faces – they actually think they are doing God's work when they destroy our livelihood.'

'So why do you take this risk, night after night?'

'What else can I do to make a living? I have no other skills.'

'Why did you come here from India in the first place?'

'I was in the Bengal Army, a *havildar*, a sergeant. The East India Company thought we might impress possible investors in Britain with our discipline, our shows of marching and counter-marching. So they taught us English and brought us here. We stayed for several months and gave drill displays and such things, marching to fifes and drums, and then the Company disbanded us. Some went back to India. Some stayed. We found odd jobs here and there. I come from a family of jugglers, so I followed that calling.

'Now, tonight, I will do three tricks I hope will interest the audience. First, you and I will appear to have a sword fight. You will run me through. The audience will see your blade pass right into my chest through my body and out again from my back. But without harming me in the slightest! Then I will lock you in a wooden trunk, bind it with ropes, and when I open it you will have disappeared. Then, miraculously, you will come back.

'Lastly, I will destroy you by fire and explosion. All that is left will be your skull and some bones. But then I will call you back from the dead and you will walk up to the stage from the back of the audience and reassure them all.'

'Can you really do these things?' asked Ben, impressed.

'Of course,' Karim answered him. 'And now I will tell you how . . .'

* * *

Sergeant Macduff and Constable Keiller did not often have the opportunity of wearing civilian clothes when on duty. In dark fustian suits and collarless shirts like labourers, they both thought that their regulation boots must seem unnecessarily large and over-polished. They had therefore smeared the toecaps with horse droppings on the way to the fair. Now, clay pipes aglow, they stood at the back of the small crowd watching Karim Khan on the stage.

Half a dozen oil lamps with polished silver reflectors shaped like scallop shells cast a blaze of smoky light on him as he juggled with four white balls. The lamp wicks were all linked by metal rods, connected to a lever at the side of the stage. By moving the lever, Karim Khan could turn all the wicks up or down, instantly increasing or decreasing the light.

He threw the balls up in the air behind the canopy. They vanished. He then drew a posy of flowers from his right sleeve, a white dove from his left and bowed to a thin scattering of applause. Ben stood behind a screen to the left of the stage. The screen was decorated with painted dragons and serpents. One of the dragons had a small hole cut into its right eye. Through it he counted the audience: thirty-two men and women and a handful of children, who were allowed in free. They helped to fill the booth; Karim Khan had explained how people always prefer to join a crowd instead of being the first to form one.

At the back, Ben saw two men standing close together, not applauding; just watching impassively. He sensed they had not come to enjoy themselves. He did not know why, but somehow their presence seemed menacing. Then one of them struck a match against the sole of his boot to relight his pipe and Ben recognised the policeman he had seen at the lock-up on Saturday.

As Karim Khan collected the dove, put it back carefully in its wicker cage, Ben told him about the two men.

'One is the constable on duty when I brought you the bootlaces.'

'Did they recognise you – and me?'

'They'd have to be blind not to.'

Karim Khan shrugged. 'Then there's nothing we can do but wait.'

He nodded to Ben to raise the curtains and stepped up to the lights.

'Now, ladies and gentlemen,' Karim Khan announced briskly, 'I have to tell you that my young assistant, Prince Amin Khan, whom I regard as my closest friend, has, in the manner of so many young men today, picked a quarrel with me. I will try to reason with him, but he has a sword, and, as you see, I only have my tongue to persuade him how wrong he is.'

At this, Ben stamped out on stage. He had darkened his hands and face with walnut juice and put on a large purple turban, studded with brilliants, so that in the uncertain light he could pass for an Indian. He carried a sword. Its unusually long blade glittered in the glow of the footlights.

'I do not seek a quarrel with Karim Khan,' he declared. 'I only seek my rights. He has deliberately offended me and refuses to honour my ancient title. Accordingly, under the rigid code of honour of the East, he must die!'

Ben flicked the sword through the air, so that none could doubt that he intended to carry out his threat.

A gasp arose from the crowd as he approached Karim Khan, who immediately held up his hands in an attitude of total surrender. People stood transfixed with amazement and disbelief as Ben prodded the point of his sword at the centre of Karim Khan's stomach.

Karim Khan seized the blade between his hands in what appeared to be a desperate attempt to keep its deadly point away from his body.

'No!' he cried. 'I beg of you, no! *Mercy*, I pray you!'

He went down on one knee. At this, Ben gave a great cry of triumph and lunged forward, sword arm outstretched. The long shimmering blade forced itself between Karim Khan's hands, into his chest. The crowd gasped in horror. Several women screamed. Murder was being done before their eyes.

Karim Khan turned slowly, as though in an almost unbearable extremity of agony. As he moved, the audience saw that eight inches of steel stuck out from the back of his jacket. The sword had gone right through his body. Karim Khan paused for a moment, threw up both hands in a last appeal for mercy, and collapsed on his face on the stage. The sword blade trembled in the lamplight. Down came the curtain.

Ben instantly pulled out the sword, threw it to one side before the curtain went up. Karim Khan bowed to the audience, who stared at him in silent amazement, unable to comprehend how a man they had just seen run through by a sword now appeared totally unhurt. Perhaps what others had said was true. The Indian and his companion must be in league with the Devil. This could not be a simple conjuring trick, this was black magic. How else could it possibly be explained?

Constable Keiller turned uneasily to the sergeant. 'What did you make of that, Sarge?' he asked hoarsely. 'Does it come under the heading of gross and unwarranted attack, grievous bodily harm to the person?'

'No,' Sergeant Macduff replied. 'It's obviously a trick of some kind. But this crowd of yokels will start to get excited soon. They can't see how it was done – nor can I. Some of them will think it really is black

211

magic, and then there'll be trouble. Remember what happened when that other magician, Professor Anderson, who calls himself the Wizard of the North, appeared before Queen Victoria at Balmoral?'

'I've heard of it, but that was before my time, Sergeant,' Keiller replied tactfully.

'It wasn't before mine. I was on duty there. Anyway, this fellow arrived at the local inn with all his boxes marked in big letters "The Wizard of the North". The landlord was a stupid man. He thought a wizard was a man possessing real powers of evil, and that Anderson was blatantly advertising that he was the Devil's own emissary.

'The landlord made such a fuss that he roused his customers and they set about poor Anderson with pitchforks and brooms. Others fetched pistols and rifles, meaning to shoot him. He would have been killed if a steward hadn't arrived from Balmoral at that moment to make sure he was being well looked after. He explained that Anderson was an important man, due to give a special performance before the Queen that evening.'

'So it ended happily, Sergeant?'

'Eventually. But the innkeeper was still not entirely convinced. When Anderson came back that night he accused him of stealing a pillowcase in which he had sewn some sovereigns. Then at sword-point he locked the Wizard of the North in an outhouse, telling him he would appear before the magistrate in the morning on a charge of theft.

'Luckily for Anderson, the landlord discovered that a maid had used the pillowcase to make up an extra bed for an unexpected guest. So he had to make a very handsome apology to Mr Anderson. People round here don't like magicians. Never have done, never will. They smack of the Devil. Give the Indian ten minutes more, and we'll have him.'

'You think so, Sarge?'

'I know so.'

'Here, he's calling to us.'

'You, sirs, you two gentlemen in the back!' shouted Karim Khan. 'I would like the benefit of your knowledge up here on stage.'

'To do what?'

'Please come up, gentlemen, and I will tell you.'

Everyone was looking at the two policemen now. The last thing they wanted was to be picked out in this way, but to refuse would only result in argument and then someone might recognise them. It was easier to go forward as though they were genuinely members of the audience.

They pushed their way sheepishly through the crowd, climbed up onto the stage. Karim Khan and Ben had brought out a solid wooden cabin trunk, of the sort used by travellers undertaking a long sea voyage. The sight of its black metal bands, the brass catches and locks reminded Ben of the trunks in which Dr Kintyre had brought his belongings back from Calcutta.

'I want you gentlemen to examine this trunk and then tell these people what you find,' Karim Khan explained to the policemen. 'Is there anyone hidden inside, for example?'

Karim Khan unlocked the trunk as he spoke, swung open the lid. The sides and bottom were covered in pale green pleated cloth. The two policemen prodded at the pleats, then shook their heads.

'It's empty,' Sergeant Macduff announced.

'Then, gentlemen, as a punishment for his extraordinary attack on me only moments ago, I will – before your very eyes – make Prince Amin Khan disappear.' He motioned to Ben to climb inside the trunk, then

213

shut down the lid and handed a key to the sergeant.

'Please lock all three locks,' he told him. Macduff did so.

'Now be so good as to help me bind up the trunk, in case, by some potent and secret Eastern magic, Prince Amin attempts to spirit himself through the pores of the woodwork.'

Karim Khan produced a long hemp rope and wound it round the box in one direction and then at right angles, as though tying up a parcel. He sealed the knot with a stick of red sealing wax. Then he picked up a canvas sack and, with the help of the two policemen, lifted the heavy trunk, slid the sack over it, and tied the sack's mouth with another rope.

Karim Khan now brought two trestles out on the stage and the three men lifted up the trunk and placed it on them.

Karim Khan came forward and addressed the audience.

'You saw the Prince go inside, ladies and gentlemen. Do you believe he is still there?'

The yokels nodded dubiously. How could he be elsewhere?

'Of course he's still there!' one man shouted angrily.

'So, ladies and gentlemen,' said Karim Khan. 'We will see how he is faring.'

The policemen helped him strip off the sack, untie the ropes. Karim Khan unlocked the lid, swung it open, and turned the box on its side towards the audience.

It was empty.

'So,' he said, addressing himself as much to the policemen as to the audience, 'you see what happens to people who offend me. They simply *disappear*.'

As he spoke, he heard a rustle of dismay. The audience was uneasy now, genuinely worried. This man *must* be in league with Satan to do such a thing in front of them. But they did not wish to voice their doubts and fears – yet. The brightly lit empty trunk which should have contained a young man held a fearful magnetic fascination for them. They could not take their eyes from it. Darkness outside pressed in on them, somehow deeper and more sinister than the night had appeared only moments before. Karim gauged their mood. It was time to relieve the tension.

'Your help for a last time, gentlemen,' he told the policemen. 'We will put this trunk back on the stage.'

Again they lifted it and set it down behind the foot-lights. He turned away for a moment and immediately everyone heard a tapping from inside it. Karim Khan looked at the trunk in amazement – could it also be in fear? Then he shrugged his shoulders at the policemen, at the audience. The tapping increased. He flung open the lid.

Out stepped Ben and bowed. The audience's relief was almost tangible. So this was only a trick, after all, not the work of the Devil! They started to clap, stamp their feet. Some of the men whistled.

Karim Khan bowed, pleased at the reaction. Everyone seemed in a good mood; there should be no trouble tonight. The policemen were wasting their time, he thought, conveniently forgetting his departure from the lock-up.

'He has beaten me – or so he thinks,' he told the audience. 'But I cannot have him make a mock of me like this. I will destroy him once and for all. I will burn him to a cinder.' He turned to the policemen. 'Thank you for your help, gentlemen.'

They climbed down from the stage into the audience, took up their previous positions at the back, on the fringe of darkness, while Ben and Karim Khan man-handled the trunk to one side.

Ben now pulled a rope that rolled up the painted

backcloth of the stage like a blind. Behind this stood a small circular table painted white, with elegant gilded legs. Beneath it, the gentle flames of four candles trembled in the evening breeze. Eight feet above the table top a circular curtain threaded on a hoop hung from a rope over a pulley.

Ben climbed up on the table and stood, hands clasped in front of him, facing the audience. Karim Khan slowly lowered the tubular curtain until it totally concealed him. Then he turned to the audience.

'Now, ladies and gentlemen, for my last exhibition, I make him disappear for ever.'

As he spoke, he drew a pistol from the folds of his cloak, pointed it towards the centre of the curtain, and fired.

Immediately a far louder explosion came from inside the curtain. A brilliant flash blazed through the curtain, clouds of white smoke billowed out from the top. At this totally unexpected sound and sight, some of the audience cried out in alarm. A woman screamed. But no one could take their eyes from the table as the curtain rose slowly.

Just as the Indian had promised, Ben had disappeared. On the table lay a pile of smoking grey ash. And on top of the ash were two crossed bones and a skull that grinned emptily at the spectators' surprise and horror.

'You've killed him!' shouted someone. 'You're a murderer!'

Immediately the crowd's unease returned, and now it erupted in shouts and screams. Their first impression had been right. The minister had often warned them about the evil ways of these foreign wanderers. Fear gripped them with iron claws. The night beyond the smoking flares suddenly came alive with unknown terrors and dangers.

One man, fuming with drink, rushed up to the stage, shouting incoherent abuse. Karim Khan pushed him back. He fell – and at that moment Sergeant Macduff blew his whistle.

Instantly, Karim Khan kicked the lever connected to the footlights. All the wicks dropped as one. Every lamp went out. In the sudden, unexpected darkness, with the night air still sharp with sulphurous smoke from the explosion, the audience panicked.

As Karim brought down the curtain, desperate to save the equipment on the stage, Ben stared in horror at the faces of the crowd, distorted by rage, fiery red in the light of the flickering torches. They tore up stakes and planks from other sideshows and waved them triumphantly.

Three whistle blasts sounded shrilly above the angry shouts and screams. The two policemen produced truncheons. Behind them, other policemen came in at a run, carrying truncheons and bull's-eye lanterns. In the centre stood a man wearing a dark suit and a dress hat. He kept dabbing his handkerchief at a boil on his nose.

'He is the ringleader!' the Provost called, pointing to Karim Khan. 'Arrest him! And his accomplice!'

One policeman swung a truncheon at Karim Khan. He dodged the blow to his head, but it hit him on the shoulder. He went down in a mass of flailing bodies.

Ben felt a sudden jerk at the back of his jacket as he was lifted off his feet. He sensed rather than saw a truncheon swing up in the air, then a brief burst of pain, a blaze of light. He fell.

The shouting and the crash of splintering woodwork awoke Mary Jane in her caravan. She had gone to bed early because business had been poor and they had an early start to make in the morning.

She ran to the door, opened the top half to see what

217

was happening outside, keeping the bottom half bolted in case anyone tried to force their way inside.

A crowd was milling around Karim Khan's booth and caravan next door, shouting furiously and waving their fists. Mary Jane closed the door, stood with her back against it for a moment, heart thumping. She slept naked. Now she hurriedly pulled on a dress, then a shawl round her shoulders, boots on her feet and came out of the caravan. She locked the door carefully behind her, tied the key to a tassel on the end of her shawl so it would not get lost, and stood in the darkness, listening.

Rough hands heaved Ben upright. He stood, still dizzy, his head beating like a drum. He was handcuffed to a constable. Six feet away stood Karim Khan, also handcuffed, his robes torn, his face bleeding. The crowd had melted away. No one wished to become involved with the constabulary. Names could be taken, and reports made to employers who might be friends of the Provost. The end result could too easily mean dismissal and then eviction from their cottage homes.

The Provost was addressing Karim Khan. Ben heard his voice vaguely and faintly, as though from a great distance. He squinted at him, because he found difficulty in focusing his eyes.

'I arrest you in the name of the law, in pursuance of the powers granted to me by Act of Parliament under the authority of Her Majesty the Queen. Karim Khan, you are charged with breaking out of Ardrey lock-up while awaiting trial, maliciously damaging a padlock, the property of the Perthshire Constabulary, by sawing through it with a saw or other sharp instrument concealed about your person, and with causing an affray through making false claims to people with the intention of swindling them. And now with causing a second affray.

'The youth here, called Ben, surname as yet unknown, will be charged with you when we ascertain his identity. Have you anything to say?'

Ben straightened up, shook his head to try and clear his mind. Half a dozen constables surrounded Karim Khan, holding truncheons and lanterns. Ben had no idea what the punishment would be, but clearly for both of them it must be severe. Karim Khan had escaped from custody and he had helped him, if unknowingly.

'Do either of you have anything to say?' repeated the Provost. He wanted to get both men away from the fairground as quickly as possible. There had been severe fights in the past between vagrants and constables. On the last occasion, only weeks earlier, when the police had attempted to arrest a pickpocket, stallholders and fairground labourers had come out with picks and shovels and knotted ropes, and a pitched battle had followed. In the confusion, the pickpocket had escaped.

'Nothing to say, then?' he asked.

'Nothing,' Karim Khan admitted dejectedly.

'But I have,' said a quiet, cultured voice behind the row of policemen. They turned in surprise, shone their lights on the face of a new arrival. He was a man in his forties, well-dressed in tweeds, wearing a floppy tweed hat. He stood taller than them all, arms folded, surveying the scene with a sardonic expression on his face.

He had about him an aura of power and authority. His suit alone must have cost more than the total annual wages of all the constables. The Provost held authority by reason of his office. This man's authority stemmed from something deeper and older. He did not owe his confidence to any official position; he had been born with it.

219

'Who are you, sir?' The Provost's unease showed in his voice. He had never seen this man before, but he instantly recognised the signs of great wealth and social superiority.

'My name is Grimsdyke. I am the new laird of Long Glen. I have recently moved here, so we have not met. I own this field. And I have been enjoying this Indian's remarkable sleight of hand. He has been conducting himself in a totally proper manner. The fact that a member of the audience appeared drunk and obstreperous is not his fault. So why have your constables assaulted him and his colleague as if they were felons? Tell me that, pray.'

The Provost cleared his throat. He had heard there was a new laird of Long Glen. He had inherited a hundred thousand acres and, it was said, half of Perth, much of Blairgowrie and nearly all of Ardrey – in addition, of course, to enormous properties in London. He must be one of the richest men in Scotland.

'I have arrested this itinerant stallholder on a charge, as you may have heard, sir, of breaking out of a lock-up on Saturday and causing an affray.'

'On what charge was he arrested on Saturday, pray?'

'He was due to appear before the Bench following complaints that, with this healthy young man, who pretended to be a cripple, he claimed he could heal the sick. Dangerous play-acting, deliberately deceiving people, claiming to have medical powers when he has none.'

'Dangerous? Play-acting? Was anybody actually deceived to the extent of losing money, or put to any embarrassment or inconvenience as a result of his alleged claim?'

'We have no evidence yet of that, sir, but the matter is being looked into. People are sometimes reluctant to come forward and admit these things.'

220

'But less reluctant to invent them. Who made the complaints to which you refer?'

'That will be revealed in due time, Mr Grimsdyke.'

'So, doubtless, will be the secrets of the pyramids,' retorted the laird drily. 'I must tell you that I saw that performance also and I can bear witness to the fact that it was totally harmless entertainment. Was he charged formally when he was in the lock-up?'

The Provost paused for a second. 'He was about to be.'

'But before he was, he escaped by cutting through a padlock while under your guard? Not a very good testimonial to the security in your lock-up, eh?'

The Provost did not reply. People were drifting back now to see what was happening. A few sniggered at the laird's remark.

'What has caused you to arrest these two men now, beating them about the head quite unnecessarily, as I can testify?'

'There was trouble in the crowd. They thought this young man had been burned to death.'

'Clearly they were under a misapprehension. The only injury he has suffered has come from the rough handling of your constables.'

'That is your opinion, sir,' said the Provost. 'Now, we have work to do.' He turned to Sergeant Macduff. 'Take them away,' he ordered curtly.

The constables began to move towards a gap in the hedge. On the other side, a two-horse police wagon was waiting with its driver.

'Just one moment,' the laird said sharply. 'You have a warrant for the arrest of these men?'

'A warrant is not necessary, sir, as you must know, in the execution of our duty in a public place.'

'Agreed. But since you quote the law, I must remind you that a warrant is necessary when you come on private land without permission, and when without obvious cause you attack people who are attempting to make an honest and harmless living in a peaceful way.'

'It is not necessary to have a warrant to arrest anyone causing a breach of the peace.'

'In that case all your men should be arrested,' said the laird. 'They have fomented this incident, as these men with me will all bear witness.'

The policemen shone their bull's-eye lanterns on half a dozen grooms, ostlers and farm labourers who had arrived silently and unnoticed, and who now stood in a row behind the laird, faces grim, arms folded.

'They will say what they saw,' continued the laird. 'They are unbiased witnesses, unlike you and your constables. I therefore suggest you drop these ludicrous charges and remove your men immediately from my property. If you do so, I will let the matter rest – providing, of course, that Mr Khan and his colleague are willing to do so. Otherwise, you will hear more of this, to your detriment.'

'There is the matter of breaking out of the lock-up.'

'But you have just admitted that he was not charged with anything. He could claim that there is also the matter of apprehending him without any charge being made. A serious matter, sir.'

The Provost stood for a moment, watching the crowd gather around them. If he argued, he would most likely make a fool of himself. On top of the humiliation of having a prisoner release himself from his cell, this was unthinkable. His boils throbbed like captive hearts with the anger he could scarcely contain.

He turned to Karim Khan. 'On this occasion I will not press charges,' he said gruffly. 'But I have to tell you both that if either of you come up before me in the future, I will remember your behaviour.'

'And so will I, sir,' said the laird. 'With total clarity. Now, release these men at once.'

Sergeant Macduff glanced uneasily at the Provost, who nodded. The sergeant took a key from a length of chain in his pocket, unlocked both sets of handcuffs, put them in his jacket pocket.

The constables marched away, their lanterns throwing a flickering path of light ahead of them. The laird's men followed them out, to make sure they did not re-enter the field at some other point.

Karim Khan turned to the laird. 'I don't know how to thank you, sir. I cannot imagine why you should help us in this way.'

'Because once, Mr Khan, you helped me.'

'But, to my knowledge, sir, I have never met you before.'

'Possibly not. But you have met my wife.'

'Your *wife*, sir? When?'

'At one of your healing sessions some months ago. She was suffering from nervous depression, long periods of unhappiness, even despair. She had visited all manner of physicians and specialists who prescribed pills and potions at great expense, but to no avail. Then you spoke to her, Mr Khan. And in her own words to me that night, she felt as though an evil spirit was leaving her. She regained her strength, and her previous cheerful disposition. So I owe you more than you know.

'When my land agent hired out this field to the fair people, I looked through the list of stallholders and saw your name. I enjoyed your performance tonight with your young helper. I am glad I have been of some help to you, as you have been of such great assistance to my dear wife.

'Now, gentlemen, it occurs to me that after the unpleasantness you may not wish to continue with your performances tonight. In that case, I would be pleased if you would give me the pleasure of your company for a glass of port – and possibly a private explanation of how you perform these remarkable tricks with such dexterity.'

Mary Jane followed the three men across the trodden grass towards a big house. Something about the face of the man in the tweed suit seemed familiar.

She watched them go inside, saw a light come on in a downstairs room. Then she approached the building carefully, like an animal, wary in case a guard dog might hear her and raise the alarm.

A magnolia tree near the window had several branches sticking out at right angles under the window. Other branches were pinioned tightly against the wall. She climbed the tree and perched on the branch nearest to the window. From this viewpoint, she could see through a gap in thick curtains into the room.

Its far wall was covered with books on white shelves. Red and green and brown leather bindings bright with gold lettering reflected the flickering flames of a dying fire. This was not a crude fire, the kind to which she was accustomed outside the caravan, with a soot-blackened pot suspended above it from a tripod, but a fire that burned neatly in a burnished metal grate. On the marble mantelpiece above it stood porcelain urns and silver candlesticks. A polished brass pendulum swung to and fro behind the crystal window of a clock case.

On either side of the fire, in leather chairs of a sumptuousness Mary Jane had never imagined, sat Karim Khan and Ben Bannerman sipping glasses of port. Between them, sprawled on a settee, feet up with the casualness born of privilege and great possessions, was the man in the tweed suit. He appeared to be listening intently to Karim Khan. By pressing an ear closely against the window, Mary Jane could hear the conversation.

'It is all a matter of illusion, sir,' Karim Khan said. 'The people want magic. They don't want an easy, rational explanation for the illusions they see, although there usually is one. The secret is to get the audience on our side – not very easy, especially up here in Scotland where the ministers preach sermons against us in the kirk on Sundays. To try and keep tempers down, I do tricks that appeal to young and old alike.

'You saw Ben here run me through with a sword just now. Youngsters think that's what they'd like to do to crabby old folk who're always telling them, don't do this, don't do that. And the old people think that is how youth behaves today, no respect for their elders.'

'I can understand that,' agreed the man on the settee. 'But how can he run you through and not shed a drop of blood, eh?'

'Teamwork, sir. Teamwork. When he presents his sword to me, I seize the blade and appear to push it away from my body with all my strength. In fact, I am pulling it towards me and guiding the tip so that it enters a small hole made for its insertion in my shirt, and concealed under my cummerbund.'

'And then?'

'Under my shirt I wear, strapped to a belt, a hollow tube in the form of a half circle. The blade goes into the opening in front of me, travels round the tube and comes out of another hole through my shirt in the small of my back. The sword's flexible, you see, sir, not solid, it's made to bend. But the audience don't know that. They assume it has gone right through me – as it appears to do.'

'How simple!' exclaimed the man in surprise. 'And the trunk? How does Ben escape from that?'

'The trunk, sir, has a full-length lid that the audience

see, and which we lock. But there's another lid they don't see, in the bottom of the trunk. This is very much smaller. Ben climbs into the trunk, which is securely locked, no mistake about that. The trunk is on the stage, placed so that the small door is directly above a trap door in the floor. Ben immediately opens both doors and drops down beneath the stage. The door in the bottom of the trunk has a spring catch so that it closes as soon as he leaves.

'We then bind the empty trunk with ropes, seal the knots, pull a huge bag over it and place it on two chairs. Now when I open the trunk, there's no one inside. So we put it back on the floor, above the trap door, and open it a second time. By then, Ben has climbed back inside. Of course, the trunk contains lead weights, so if we ask members of the audience to help us move it, as we did tonight, it feels heavy, as though someone was inside all the time.'

'Most ingenious,' said the tall man, pouring more port, and passing the decanter round. 'And the fire?'

'Ben stands on what appears to be a table with four legs. Four candles burn underneath it. In point of fact, sir, there are only two legs and two candles, for this table is not at all that it seems. Underneath it, from the centre, are two vertical boards, set at an angle, the apex pointing to the audience. Each board is covered by a mirror which reflects the candles under the table and the legs, so that the audience sees four candles and four legs – two real and two reflections. When the curtain is lowered to cover Ben, he immediately opens a trap door in the centre of the table and drops under the stage. Before he closes the door he sets out two crossed bones and a skull. As I fire my pistol, he sets light to a firework, which causes the explosion and the smoke.

'Sometimes, after I have shown that he is no longer

226

there, I lower the curtain for a second time and he appears exactly where he was. But tonight, sir, the crowd did not allow me the opportunity.'

'Most ingenious, Mr Khan. I am in your debt for telling me these secrets of your strange and magical trade. I wish you every success, and I look forward to seeing more illusions from you on your next visit – and to hearing how you manage to create them.'

He turned to Ben.

'And you, young fellow. Will you continue to follow this trade?'

'I don't know, sir. I have only recently met Karim Khan, who has been kind to me.'

'You do not speak like a fairground person. You have had a good education?'

'My father was an officer in the East India Company's army in India. He was killed in the retreat from Kabul.'

'And your mother?'

'She died giving birth to me out there. I was brought up by Dr Kintyre.'

'I have heard of him. Was he not the only man to escape that terrible massacre?'

'Yes, sir. He carried me out on his horse.'

'So why have you left him?'

Ben shrugged; he did not want to go into a detailed explanation. 'I suppose I wanted to be on my own, sir. Make my own way.'

'A capital idea. My younger brother, Francis, is an officer in the Ninety-first of Foot, stationed in Brighton at the present time. Our elder brother, Sir Martyn, has most unhappily been struck down with an incapacitating illness. A heart attack, or something of that kind.'

'Does your brother like the military life?' Karim Khan asked solicitously.

'Tolerably. To be frank, he is "not quite right", to

use the homely Scottish phrase. He is, as you say in the vernacular, eleven pence in the shilling, or nineteen shillings in the pound. I make myself clear, I trust?'

'Perfectly clear, sir.'

'He is at present a lieutenant, but I had a letter from him only this week to say that he expects to be posted to India. He cannot stand heat, never has been able to endure even a summer day, poor fellow, so this has caused him great concern. However, he is not due to leave for several months. This should give him time to find a brother officer to take his place, or someone else who does not mind heat and who could buy a commission. More likely he'll find someone who needs money – or to leave the country for some reason – and my brother will pay him to accept the posting in his place. Hindustan is not a very popular place for the military with means. Apart from the heat, there are too many fevers, too many pestilences. Few British officers out in India live long enough to make old bones.'

He passed the decanter round again.

'As a Mussulman, it is forbidden for me to drink alcohol,' said Karim Khan. 'But I have read in your holy book how your Lord Jesus changed water into wine. If I am rebuked for drinking wine, I say I conduct this miracle in reverse. I turn wine into water – as soon as it touches my lips!'

Mary Jane held tightly to the branch to prevent herself falling. No wonder the face of this man in the tweed suit seemed familiar. He was Sir Martyn's brother. Mrs Mentmore had told her he had one brother in the north, and another not quite right living in Brighton. She must climb down and be away immediately before a watchman making his rounds discovered her. With her background in Newgate and then in Mrs Mentmore's house, she could not expect any mercy from the law.

Mary Jane slipped down silently, walked back across the damp grass towards the field and the fair. A pale mist shrouded the tents and caravans. As she walked, an idea grew in her mind until it assumed the proportions of a plan. If she followed it closely, she believed she might escape for ever from poverty and loneliness and fear.

Then, she thought, smiling to herself at the prospect, she might never have to stand behind a fairground stall or hide outside a great house, looking in. Then she would be inside, rich and successful, looking out.

The housekeeper at the laird's house looked quizzically at the girl standing in the back porch. She had never seen her before; she did not welcome casual callers.

'You want to see me?' she asked.

'Yes, ma'am,' the girl replied politely. 'I've found something which I think belongs to the laird.'

'And what's that?'

The girl produced from under her shawl a heavy metal ashtray decorated with a regimental crest, handed it to the housekeeper. She recognised it instantly, turned it over in her hands. This ashtray was usually on the table in the conservatory behind the house.

'Where did you find this, child?' she asked, more friendly now. The girl might not appear particularly prepossessing, but at least she was being helpful – and apparently honest. She could have kept the ashtray, or tried to make a few shillings on it from a pawnbroker. So many young people would, these days.

'Half a mile up the road, ma'am,' the girl explained. 'In the hedge. This is the only big house nearby, and so I thought it might belong to you. If it doesn't, I'd like it back. I can make a few pennies on it.'

'A few pennies? It's worth shillings,' said the housekeeper. 'Maybe even a pound. It was good of you, bringing it back. Did you see any suspicious people hanging about, who might have stolen it? Fairground people, perhaps?'

'No one, ma'am. No one at all.'

'I see. Well, you've been honest. And honesty is all too rare these days. Mr Grimsdyke will be pleased to have it back – if he's even noticed it's gone. What's your name, child?'

'That doesn't matter, ma'am. I'll be on my way now.'

'You live round here?'

'No. I'm just staying with people who do.' She made to move away.

'Wait,' the housekeeper told her. 'You look as if you could do with a square meal.'

The girl said nothing.

'Just wait there for a moment. I'll bring you a haggis.'

'You're very kind, ma'am.'

'Well, honesty pays, and should be seen to pay. Wait until I come back. Don't come in.' She didn't want a stranger in the house; they might see something they liked, and even if they didn't take it themselves, they might tell someone who would. This girl seemed to be honest, but it was foolish to put temptation in the way of people.

The housekeeper walked up the long corridor into the kitchen. As soon as she closed the kitchen door behind her, Mary Jane moved quickly and did what she had to do. She was standing just as she had been, eyes demurely on the floor, when the housekeeper returned.

'Here's a haggis,' she said. 'Not a very big one, but

it's the only one I could find. Thank you again. The laird will be pleased.'

'Thank you, ma'am.' Mary Jane dropped a curtsy and walked away down the path out of the tradesmen's entrance into the road. She did not look back.

The young assistant in the ironmonger's shop eyed the girl lasciviously. Through the thin stuff of her blouse he eyed the points of her nipples and saw, or imagined he half-saw, the dark spreading aureoles. He licked his dry lips. She was a very attractive girl, but she did not appear to realise it, which considerably increased her appeal.

'What do you want, love?' he asked her, and was surprised that his voice was suddenly hoarse.

'A key to be made from a pattern.'

'That will cost you.'

'How much?'

'Two shillings. Cash or—' The young man paused.

'Or what?'

'Kind. A bit of a kiss, a feel, say.'

The girl smiled. Her eyes were dark, mysterious. She might have been looking at him from a different world. In a sense, she was.

'Which would you rather have?' she asked the young man, moving towards him.

'The second,' he replied instantly.

'Let's have the key,' she said. 'And you will.'

'Where's your pattern?' he asked her briskly. Business was business; he had to do his part before she would do hers.

She took out a piece of soap. It bore the impression of a key.

'How did you get this?' he asked.

'Off a key I want copied,' she explained.

'Never done this before, made a key from a mould.'

'Maybe we could do other things you've never done before.' She smiled again.

The shop felt very dark and hot. The front window was almost obscured by spades and shovels hanging in rows, by sets of overalls and metal buckets piled one inside another. She drew the young man towards her, kissed him lightly on the mouth, let her right hand move slowly, casually, gentle as a butterfly's wing, down the outside of his trousers. His body tensed and then relaxed. She felt him grow beneath her touch.

'How long will it take for that key?' she asked him, pressing her hand slightly against him.

'Come back at five,' he said hoarsely. 'It will be ready then.'

'Will you be alone?'

'Yes. The master's going out at four.'

'Then I'll be here at a quarter past,' she promised. She smiled, kissed him again, and then was gone. He turned the bar of soap over in his hands, went into the workshop. But it was some time before he could give his full attention to cutting a new key.

Under the moon, the big house lay dark and empty. Its blank windows reflected the pale moonlight. A few bats fluttered from the eaves on silent, nervous wings. Mary Jane paused near the hedge. This was going to be the difficult part, getting inside. If she was caught, it would mean gaol. And that was unthinkable. She must not get caught. She wasn't sure whether she would find what she was looking for, whether it was even in the house, waiting to be discovered, but she assumed that it must be. She could only hope. She had to pull herself together, she told herself sharply. There could be no backsliding, no going back.

She watched the silent house, pulled on a pair of cotton gloves to protect her fingers. She had read that policemen now could trace people through their fingerprints: every set of prints was unique, millions and millions of them. Amazing things were happening all over the world, and she wanted to be part of these exciting changes, not out here, on the periphery, looking in when she should be on the inside of events, looking out.

She crossed the lawn, keeping close to a small ornamental hedge. Suddenly, right in front of her, a woman held up her arms, white in the moonlight. She almost screamed in fear. Then she realised it was not a ghost, only a life-sized marble statue. She had never seen things like that outside a cemetery. She paused for a few minutes until her racing heart slowed. Then she went on.

She had checked earlier, when she had removed the ashtray from the conservatory, that no dogs were kept in the house. It was strange that the laird did not own a guard dog or even a lapdog. Most men in the country kept a dog. But what was his loss must be her gain. She would not have risked what she was about to do if he kept a dog. They sensed strangers. Even if they couldn't see them, they smelt them out.

She was very near the house now, carefully keeping in the shelter of the hedge, pausing to listen, ear turned towards the house to catch any faint noise or movement. Perhaps there was a dog somewhere? But if there was, it wasn't barking tonight. She came up to the back door, paused for a moment, adjusting her eyes to the gloom of the porch after the brightness of the moon. Then she put the new key in the door and turned it.

Just for a moment, the key stuck and she thought it would not turn. She felt sweat bead her shoulders like drops of rain. If it did not open the lock, everything would be lost; all had been in vain. She pressed more strongly, and suddenly the key turned. She took it out of the lock, turned the doorknob and pushed the door.

The door might be bolted on the other side. But it wasn't. She had examined the bolts on the previous visit and they were rusty, hadn't been used for years. If she had thought they were in use, she would have wedged them open with split matchsticks.

Inside the corridor, she closed the door behind her, stood for a moment, listening. The only sound was the dripping of a scullery tap into a basin. She walked forward slowly, hands outstretched on either side of her, tips of her fingers touching each wall.

The corridor was empty, with a door at the far end. Now she was in the main hall. It smelt pleasantly of beeswax polish and cigar smoke. A clock was ticking somewhere heavily, slowly, regularly. The sound had a soothing, almost soporific effect upon her. Curtains across the hall windows had not been drawn and moonlight streamed in through leaded windows with crests let into the top panes. The moon shone through red and blue and yellow heraldic beasts that supported coats of arms of daggers, fish, birds' beaks. It would be wonderful to live like this, she thought; to know who your ancestors were, to have the confidence security brings; never to be concerned about money, or where you would find your next meal.

She opened the nearest door. She was in a large room, with scented logs on a dying fire. What she was seeking would not be here. It was more likely to be somewhere in a smaller room, a study or a library.

She found the study beyond the third door she opened, went into it, closed the door silently behind her.

She struck a lucifer, shielded the flame carefully, then lit a shaded candle on the desk. This had a green leather top, edged with gold; sheets of unmarked green blotting paper were in a leather folder near pens in holders and a polished wooden box with partitions for notepaper, envelopes, postcards. By the side of this, under a glass paperweight, she saw a pile of letters and picked them up. She had to start somewhere in her search; this was as good as anywhere else. Several bills were clipped together, then an estimate of repairs to the conservatory roof, an invitation to a political meeting – and then the letter she wanted.

She read it carefully. Taking out a stub of pencil from a pocket in her skirt and a small square of paper, she wrote down the name of the man who had signed it, his address at the top of the page, and put the letter back under the weight. She nipped the candle flame between a thumb and forefinger. This left no smell; if she had blown out the candle, it could have left a smell of burning and whoever came into the study next morning would know someone had lit a candle during the night. Enquiries might be made; she could be discovered.

She went out of the room, paused in the hall, listening to the clock, smelling the furniture polish. The clock began to whir like someone drawing breath before speaking, and then it struck the hour. Two o'clock in the morning. She opened the door into the corridor, closed it behind her. In the back porch, she locked the door, put her key in her pocket.

For a moment she paused again, listening, but there was no sound save the hooting of a solitary owl. She crossed to the safety and shadow of the hedge, and within minutes was down the garden. Near the statue she looked back towards the house.

A light had come on in an upper room. Was someone going downstairs? Had she set off some alarm about which she knew nothing? She could not stop to discover. She had found what she had sought. She could have stolen all manner of things in that house, but she had not taken one. She had no quarrel with anyone. Not now.

Within half an hour she was back in her bed, the piece of paper torn up and burned by her bedside candle. She had memorised the name of the sender and his address. She would not forget them; too much depended on her remembering them. Mary Jane closed her eyes contentedly; soon, she slept.

One by one, the flares along the edges of the fairground burned out as the customers drifted away. The smell of oily smoke hung heavily on the night air. Ivan pulled down the sliding shutter on the front of his stall, beckoned Mary Jane into his caravan. He struck a match, pumped up a naphtha lamp he had bought secondhand. The mantle burst into hissing brilliance. Mary Jane sat down wearily in the chair. It had been a hard day; she had been on her feet since early morning, and her throat was sore from constant talk to customers, cajoling, sympathising, assuring.

'You're tired,' said Ivan. 'A drink?'

She shook her head. 'No, thank you.' She still remembered her father drunk, and what had happened as a result. A feeling of loneliness and desolation engulfed her.

'Well, I'm having one,' said Ivan.

He took the cork out of a blue medicine bottle with the label POISON on it, poured a measure of raw gin into a glass and drank greedily, thankfully.

'There's something on your mind,' he said as he refilled the glass.

'Yes,' she admitted.

'Not in trouble, are you?'

'No, no. Nothing like that.'

'So what's wrong? Can I help you?'

236

'I just want to try and sort out my life, where I'm going, what I'm going to do,' she said. 'I'm very grateful to you for helping me, but how long will this job last?'

'As long as you like it to, love. It's doing well. You've got a feel for it. We took seven pounds and ten shillings today.'

Ivan put his hand in his pocket, took out a five-pound note.

'You have that.'

'But why? That's five weeks' wages for me.'

'Never look a gift horse in the mouth, love. Or in any other part of its anatomy. Take it. You've worked hard. Maybe if things keep going as well we can start another stall. The Learned Pig is always a draw. You could run that on your own. A nice pleasant job for a girl.'

Mary Jane nodded, but not enthusiastically. A gypsy with a fat, well-washed pig ran the stall next to theirs. Above it was a large sign that read: 'The only pig in the world that can answer your questions.' To prove this claim, the gypsy would put down on the floor of her booth a set of cards, face down, arranged in a circle. The pig stood in the centre. The gypsy would appeal to the audience to select a card they wished the pig to identify. Someone would call out, 'Ace of spades', or 'Three of diamonds', and the card would be replaced, face down. The pig would then walk round the cards. As he reached the named card, he would stop and nuzzle the card with his nose.

Then the pig would stop opposite a man in the audience who liked red-haired girls, or a woman out without her husband. The permutations were almost endless and no one seemed able to understand how the pig could possibly be so clever.

In fact, a pig could be trained to perform this trick

in a few days. The owner put a collar round its neck and tied the collar by a long string to a large nail in the floor of the booth. Then, with a tap on the pig's backside, or holding a slice of apple in front of him, the owner would persuade the animal to walk round in a circle. Every so often, the owner would click his fingers and then give the pig a piece of apple. They would keep up this routine morning and evening for several days, then remove the collar.

When the pig saw the owner holding a slice of apple, he would at once begin to walk round and round in a circle, as though he still wore his collar. The owner could make him stop at any card, or in front of anyone in the audience, simply by clicking his fingers.

Ivan was right; it was an easy way for a girl to make a living in a fair, but it led nowhere.

'It's good of you to think of it,' Mary Jane told him, 'but I'd still be travelling all the time. A day here, two days there, then off again miles away. I want something where I don't have to keep moving. I want to belong somewhere, maybe to someone. Not be a vagrant – and treated like one.'

'I agree. Every girl wants to marry, have children, make a home. It's natural. But unless you have some money of your own, or a generous husband, you can be a hundred times worse off than if you're single. Got anyone or anything in mind?'

Mary Jane shook her head. 'No,' she admitted. 'Only an idea.'

She took out of her pocket half a page from a newspaper, handed this to Ivan. He read it carefully, puzzling over some of the words.

'I found it thrown away the other day when I was clearing around our stall. The article interested me. I've learned a bit about people since I've been with you. What you can make them believe. This article tells how a young woman, like me, made a lot of money by fastening on to gullible people with more money than sense. She persuaded them to believe what she wanted them to believe. Just like I persuade them that on the tog stall they're going to win huge prizes. If she could do it, so can I. After all, I've served a good apprenticeship with you, Ivan.'

Ivan handed the piece of paper back to her. He shook his head doubtfully. 'Interesting,' he agreed. 'But it says it took place years ago. Things have changed since then.'

'People haven't,' Mary Jane answered him. 'They still believe what they want to believe. If God hadn't intended them to be fleeced, he wouldn't have made them sheep.'

'It'll never work,' Ivan said. 'You won't be dealing with yokels and labourers who can barely read and write. You'll be hoping to take money off the gentry, rich people. They didn't get where they are by being idiots.'

'Most of them didn't get their money by their own efforts. They got it because they were lucky enough to be the son or grandson of someone who had already made it. I'm not going after them, but after those who've inherited it – if I can find the right ones. Anyhow, that's my plan.'

'Got anyone special in mind?' Ivan asked her.

Mary Jane nodded. 'A possibility, yes,' she admitted.

'Well, good luck, girl.'

'Thanks. But tell me, Ivan, how did you start?'

'Through a kidsman, when I was ten or thereabouts. Me and my brother.'

'What's a kidsman?'

'Fellow who trains kids to pick pockets. My father disappeared, just like yours. My mother was on the

239

game. No time for us, and no place. The kidsman picked us up because he saw we were quick on our feet and we had small hands.' He held them out. 'See? So he started me off tailing – picking wallets out of the tailcoats of swells and toffs. Strange place to keep your wallet, but they do. Me and my brother would work together. He'd bump into the man and apologise, take his hat off, almost go down on his hands and knees saying how sorry he was, and meanwhile I'd have his wallet.

'We'd work St Paul's churchyard. There are some very fine shops down there, and we'd wear sober clothes as though we'd been to a funeral, and so wouldn't attract any attention.

'We'd also go to theatre matinées. When mothers have taken their kids to a pantomime and the kids are crying because they don't want to go home, or because they do, one or the other, and the mothers are worried, you're into their pockets like a flash.'

'Don't they feel you going in?'

'No. They wear stays like armour, starched petticoats, crinolines. Bloody elephant could put his trunk in and they'd never feel it. But the police got on to us. They remembered our faces and picked us both up. I reckon that's why they got my brother for forging. He'd done nothing bad, really, but they knew him, he had a record, so give a dog a bad name and hang him. And that's just what they did, the bastards.

'Then I got into this business. It's legitimate and the pickings are not too bad. I'm sorry you're going, kid. I've liked having you here. As I told you, I don't like girls, not for what you mean. I got into those ways with the kidsman. He was that way. But your cheerful face brings in the punters. Now I'll be on my own again until I can find someone else. When do you want to leave?'

'When can you best spare me?'

'Stay over next weekend, at least. We should have a good deal then. The fair's going to Bostal Heath, near Woolwich. Lot of money there. All the dockers and workers in the arsenal.'

'I'll go after that, then.'

'Sure you won't have a drink now?'

'Well, a small one,' Mary Jane agreed. 'Seeing as how I'm saying goodbye.'

'Yes, it is goodbye, isn't it? Odd the people one works with, me and my brother, for instance. Now I've just got used to you, and you're off.'

'What about his widow? Would she work for you?'

'No, can't stand her. Cow. I told you she'd got an ill son, didn't I? Don't want to be lumbered with him. You're different. But like all the women I've ever known, you want to marry. Children, a nice house, servants. Well, that's how it is. I'll find someone else, I suppose. Save some money. Then maybe I'll buy my own fair. Let others work then while I walk round keeping an eye on them.' Ivan smiled wryly.

As he spoke, Mary Jane remembered Beatrice in Mrs Mentmore's house. How many employees yearned to be free to run their own lives – and how many ever achieved this aim?

She was going to be one who did.

Chapter Seven

From where Ben stood, the heath spread wide and empty almost as far as he could see. In the far distance towards the west it vanished beneath a smoky pall which hung over the arsenal and dockyard of Woolwich on the south bank of the Thames, eight miles from London.

Farther south, the heath stretched to marshes and then the river. He could see the distinctive Thames barges, with tarred hulls and dull red sails, each barge pulling a small dinghy, going upriver, low in the water with full loads of coal and hay. Tracks led over rough ground past several large houses and inns towards Plumstead in the west, the villages of Belvedere and Erith in the east.

The fair had camped on Bostal Heath for Whitsun Saturday, a one-day event. They would move on to Essex to open there on the Monday. Because this journey would take only three hours at the most, they would have little to do on the Sunday except strike the tents.

This would be a welcome change from some of the sites they occupied when, as soon as the last customers had left, stallholders had to work through Saturday night so that they could be away before sun-up. The alternative was to pay extra fees for renting the ground for another day, and if business was poor many could not afford this. But since Bostal Heath was common land, there were no fees to pay and consequently no hurry to leave.

Ben stood, arms folded, surveying the wide circle of caravans, tents and booths. Outside many of them owners or their wives were already cooking breakfast. The World's Strongest Man, wearing black trousers and a shabby cotton vest, was exercising with dumbbells. The Bearded Lady was filling a teapot with boiling water. A smell of fried bacon, sausages and mushrooms, picked only moments earlier from the heath, rose like a benediction.

Karim Khan came towards him, and shook his head sadly as though he had grave news to tell. 'There is evil in the air,' he declared solemnly.

'Evil? What sort of evil?'

'Violence. I smell it like a sailor at sea can taste the wind and know a storm's coming up although the glass may still be steady.'

'And there's trouble brewing here?'

'Yes. There often is on this site. Pickings are good, but the risks are high. Most of the day, nothing happens. Families come out, for it's a holiday. They spend their money, buy gingerbread, ginger beer, try their luck on the coconut shies, visit the stalls. Their children go on the roundabouts and then they all go home. And that's when the trouble starts.'

He nodded towards the smoke cloud above Woolwich.

'From there. There's a mass of slums down by the docks. Thieving from ships that come in to be unloaded and those that go out loaded is enormous. Watchmen on the docks are corrupt, and frightened, and the dockers run their own gangs. They come out here just to make trouble, break things up. That's their idea of enjoyment.'

'What can we do?'

'Nothing, except batten down everything that's movable as soon as the punters leave.'

It seemed difficult to believe this on such a warm, sunny morning, and as the day went on Ben felt convinced his employer was being needlessly pessimistic.

Families in their best clothes arrived on foot, by horse bus, in gigs, on farm carts. By evening they started to drift away. Mothers carried tired children, fathers puffed at clay pipes; it had been a great day out.

As dusk fell, the fairground became alive with lights. Flickering flames from what were known as dips, candlewax or beeswax in metal pots with a thick wick, lit up every stall and booth. Round the perimeter blazed flares of rolled-up rags soaked in oil. Some of the richer sideshows had naphtha lamps that hissed and roared, and cast a greenish glow for yards around on the trodden grass.

Behind the lights the sky lay dark, pricked by stars. The air was heavy with the smell of burning oil and hot ash from fires and the sweat of performing animals, now out of the big top and back in their cages.

The lights attracted moths and fluttering winged insects and, like a magnet, they were also drawing out unwelcome visitors of the night: men from the stews and congeries of Woolwich.

Stallholders on the edge of the fair were the first to see them appear. Ben heard the Fire-Eater, Mr Salamander, shout in a hoarse voice: 'Lock up! They're here!' He saw the woman with the Learned Pig quickly push the beast to the safety of its sty behind her booth and drop a wooden shop front across the opening where, only moments before, she had been giving her cheerful patter about the pig's remarkable talents. Men were hurriedly throwing huge canvas tarpaulins over the tops of their booths, roping them round at the bottom to preserve the contents from direct assault. Others ran with the horses, leading them away from the lights, out into the relative safety of the dark beyond the ring of flares.

Karim Khan came up to Ben. 'Give me a hand with the front,' he said. 'They'll smash it up otherwise.'

They bolted wooden screens in front of the stage. What they could not pack quickly into crates they stowed in the caravan or underneath it, and ran a long rope round the wheels.

Shouts and yells and screams and whistles began to pierce the night. A group of men pushed their way along the front of the booths, beating on the protective wooden screens with fists, hammers and axes. They swung them at the brightly painted pictures of kings, queens, castles that decorated many stalls. One man, apart from the rest, carried a huge metal rod with two prongs at one end, a sharpened chisel face at the other.

'That's the leader, Jed,' Karim Khan explained. 'I've suffered from him before. He's a docker. He uses that for opening crates, and he'll open our skulls if he has half a chance.'

Most of the men were converging on a booth about fifty yards away. This sold bottled beer, sarsaparilla, herbal wines and nips of rum and brandy. They beat on the counter with hammers and axes.

'Now then, gents all!' shouted the proprietor as calmly as he could. Behind him, his wife and son, who helped him run the bar, were frantically taking down full bottles and rows of glasses from shelves, stowing them in crates beneath the counter.

'One at a time, if you please! Let's have your orders! Last orders!'

'My orders are, I take what I want!' shouted Jed, and smashed his metal pole on the counter. Glasses jingled like sleigh bells. He swept the pole along the counter top; glasses shattered by the dozen. Then he poked the pole roughly into the stomach of the owner. The man fell back, gasping for breath, writhing in agony. As he collapsed, half a dozen men vaulted over the counter and seized the bottles the owner's wife and son had been attempting to save.

They did not bother to mix brandy or rum or gin with soda water or lime juice; they drank the neat spirits directly from the bottles, passing them hand to hand after half a dozen swallows. Within minutes the stall was drunk dry. The son tried to stop them. Jed hit him over the head with his iron rod; the youth dropped senseless to the ground. Another man broke a long stave over Mr Salamander's head as he attempted to remonstrate with him.

'Wreck the place!' shouted Jed, his voice thick with alcohol. 'Kill 'em all!'

'Kill! Kill! *Kill!*'

The word was taken up and repeated, and suddenly the whole area was filled with running men, faces contorted with drink, sweat and hatred. Half a dozen stallholders, brandishing shovels and pick handles, rushed at them, shouting, 'Get out! Get out! You're ruining us!'

A constable blew a whistle and was immediately seized from behind, tripped and trampled underfoot. New arrivals turned on the stallholders and beat them about their heads, legs, bodies with hammers and axes. As the World's Thinnest Man fell, they surrounded him, kicking him in the crotch and his face until he was just a long mass of bloodied pulp in a shabby suit. The mob heaved him to one side like an old sack, and raced on, shouting and cursing, to attack another stall selling drinks at the far side of the fair. For a moment, Karim Khan and Ben seemed on their own. Karim

Khan bent over the World's Thinnest Man.

'He's dead,' he said.

'Murdered,' said Ben.

'But who is going to say who started it or catch them? Those swine will all be off by dawn.'

'They'll stay that long?'

'If there's anything left to loot, yes.'

King George Drummond came running by. 'They're setting fire to the big top!' he cried. 'Everyone get a bucket and run! *Quick!*'

'There's a dead man here,' Ben told him.

'I heard. I've sent off two runners for the police in Plumstead. Two have more chance than one.'

'But there's only a small police station there,' Karim Khan pointed out. 'Probably no more than half a dozen men.'

'They can call the military out from Woolwich.'

'It's as bad as that?' Ben asked him.

'It will get worse. They've broken up one drinks booth. Now they're on the second. We have six here. It's going to be murder.'

'It is already,' said Ben.

'The northerners are here,' said Drummond grimly as half a dozen small men, wearing flat caps and greasy clothes, with metal-tipped clogs on their feet, came running between the stalls. Jed was leading them. He picked up a stone, smashed it through the glass front of a fortune-teller's booth.

The owner, a widow, with the pseudonym of Madam Zita, because it sounded more alluring than her real name, Nora Sidebottom, ran out from behind her tent, shouting: 'Why are you doing this to me? I'm a widow woman. Why are you doing this?'

'You old bitch,' shouted Jed in answer, and threw another stone. It hit her in the face. She fell back.

She was lucky if she made a couple of pounds a

week after all expenses, but she was grateful: she could provide for her deformed daughter. Now Madam Zita buried her face in her hands, weeping in pain and despair. If her booth was ruined, how could she earn a living?

A man ran out to seize Jed, his fists raised to fight. Jed kicked him hard, left and right foot on both his shins. Steel clogs bit to the bone. As he fell forward in agony, Jed bit off the end of his nose, spat it out.

'You see?' said Drummond. 'That's how the bastards fight. They'll kick or bite you to death.'

'And we're doing nothing.'

'What can we do?' asked Drummond. 'Be reasonable, boy. There are probably a hundred of these men here, and more to come. They're all raving drunk and they're out to hit, to hurt, to kill. You go in there, and maybe you hit one of them, even knock him down. But then ten others are on your back. You'll be dead in ten seconds. Look what happened to that poor devil already.'

'So we just stand here and do nothing?'

'We wait for the police and maybe the military.'

'I was here last year,' said Karim Khan. 'We had the same trouble. By the time the constables came everyone had gone.'

'I've got an idea,' said Ben. 'Get everyone out on the heath, in the dark, beyond the lights, with whistles. I'll lead riders west towards Woolwich. It's dark, we'll be on horses, we'll take sticks as weapons. The others blow their whistles – maybe we put up a firework as a signal. These roughs think the police are here in force and they run, right into us.'

'Can you deal with a hundred?'

'Probably not. But we'll get the ringleaders, teach them a lesson. Who's the worst?'

'Jed. He just attacks anyone he can literally get his

teeth into. He's mad, a killer.'

'What do you say, Mr Drummond?' Karim Khan asked.

'I say we go.' He dodged into a booth and came back with a rocket which he handed to Ben. 'Here's your signal. When you're in position, send it. I'll get everyone with a whistle, a drum, a trumpet, anything to make a noise, out on the heath. That'll make them think the military are here as well as the police.'

Ben ran behind the booth, untethered a horse. He picked up a spade in one hand and a coil of rope, swung himself up and rode bareback. He could hear Drummond shouting to other men. Soon he could sense rather than see other riders, and hear the blowing of their horses, the grunting of angry desperate men, lacking saddles or stirrups, holding on with one hand, wielding spades and pick handles with the other.

As his eyes grew more accustomed to the dark he could make out twenty in a line, Karim Khan among them. Ben led them over the soft springy turf for about forty yards, then turned to face the lights of the fair. After the smell of oil and sooty flames, the air felt fresh and cool.

'We stand here,' he said.

'We'd better,' said someone in the darkness. 'There's a river behind us. It runs down to the Thames. We don't want to get in there. We'll never get out.'

'How did the men get across it?'

'There's a ford just to our left.'

'Right,' said Ben. 'Let's wait for them coming back to cross it.'

He jumped down from his horse, stuck the stick of the rocket in a patch bare of heather and lit the fuse. The rocket soared up into the sky, exploded in a cataract of crimson and yellow stars. Horses whinnied and moved uneasily.

Then, in the darkness beyond the bright lights of the fair, above a cacophony of shouts, curses, snatches of drunken song, the splintering of glass and screams of pain, they all heard whistles, thinly at first like flutes. They blew, and stopped, and blew again. Now came a rumble of drums, a bray of trumpets and bugles. And then Ben heard the running of feet, clumping through the heather and cries and curses.

'Bloody fallen, twisted my ankle. Sod this.'

'Run, man, run! The constables are here, and the military. We'll do years if we're caught.'

Men were running blindly, heading towards the ford.

'*Now!*' shouted Ben, and kicked his heels in his horse's flanks. The animal charged forward.

He rode down one man, jumped off his horse, seized him by the right arm, flung him to the ground and bound his arms behind him with his own belt. Others were doing the same. Some of the stallholders, maddened with rage at the knowledge that their livelihoods were ruined, seized two or three. They dragged them all back to the camp, roped together like animals.

As Ben and the other riders shepherded them into the middle of the fair, everyone else crowded round them. Twenty-five men, now subdued, full of drink, some vomiting and retching or urinating in fear stood sullenly in a group.

'Right,' said Drummond. 'You've had your fun. Now you can pay the reckoning. Strap 'em to the wheels, boys!'

Men and women, even children, helped to drag the reluctant men to different caravans. Here, they ripped off their shirts, strapped the men spreadeagled to the wooden spokes of the wheels. Others ran forward with stock whips and whalebone riding whips.

'What's it to be, friends?' King Drummond asked the crowd.

'A dozen of the best!' shouted someone.

'And a dozen more for me!' shouted an old woman. 'You've ruined my caravan, tipped it over on its side. Everything inside is broke. Even my budgie is dead in its cage. Everything I had is gone.'

'Twenty-four it is,' agreed Drummond, and the whips went up.

No one spoke. The only sounds were the swish of the whips, the thwack as leather hit sweating naked flesh, the grunts and screams of the men on the wheels.

'Help me, I pray you!' one cried. 'Stop! You're killing me!'

Twenty-four times muscular right arms went up and came down. When they stopped, Drummond called everyone together.

'Bring lamps,' he said.

'You're not going to brand us now, are you?' gasped one of the men.

'Not this time. We just want a good look at you to remember you in case we meet again.'

The showmen and booth owners brought out naphtha lamps, smoking flares, bull's-eye lanterns and peered closely into the men's faces.

'Cut 'em down,' shouted Drummond.

Sharp knives snipped through the cords and ropes that bound them to the wheels. Two or three of the men, fuming with drink, immediately put up their fists and made to attack Drummond. He dodged out of the way.

'Catch 'em!' he shouted. 'They want cooling off!'

On went the ropes again.

'Take them all down to the river,' said Ben. 'Give them a cold bath. They can wash out their mouths at the same time.'

A great cry of agreement came up from the showmen and their families. Someone brought a long rope and willing hands tied the men to it about three feet apart. Then, like a chain gang of convicts, with showmen on either side holding lanterns and flares, they were marched over the heath to the river.

Two showmen waded across it, pulling one end of the rope with them. The others waited on the near side.

'Now,' said Ben. 'Pull them to and fro. Make sure they all get a good ducking. They'll feel better for it – in body and mind.'

'You'll drown us!' shouted someone hoarsely.

'You're too good to drown,' Drummond retorted.

Half a dozen more men jumped into the river and pulled the rope across.

'Now then, *heave!*'

Slowly, all the men were pulled into the river. The water came up to their chests, but a sudden jerk on the rope from the far bank made them lose their balance. They fell, and before they could stand up, were dragged to the opposite bank.

As soon as they reached it and regained their balance, choking, spluttering for air, crying out to be set free, another pull in the opposite direction made them fall. To and fro they went from one bank to another, until Drummond called a halt.

'That's enough, gentlemen!' he cried. 'Pull them out the far side and cut them free. They'll not trouble us again. If they show any disposition to do so, lather them with the end of a rope.'

The men showed no such wish. Shambling, cursing, groaning in pain, they slunk away towards Woolwich.

'We've missed one,' said Karim Khan. 'The worst of them all. Where's Jed?'

'I'll tell you where he is,' cried Madam Zita. 'He's hiding. I watched where the bastard went.'

'Can you lead us to him?'

'Willingly.'

They all went back now at a run, towards the ruined camp. Jed was cowering underneath a caravan.

'Don't hurt me,' he pleaded desperately. 'I don't mean no harm.'

'Nor do we,' they assured him. 'Only some correction. But what shall it be? What shall we do to a man who likes biting off people's noses?'

'I'll tell you what,' said Drummond. 'We'll take him over to the Pig and Whistle, Plumstead. I've got an idea to make the punishment fit. Let him do a bit more biting.'

'How?' asked Ben.

'You'll see, son. You'll see a sight there, I warrant, you've never seen before.'

Drummond bound Jed's arms behind his back and with twenty or thirty others led him at the end of a rope along the track to Plumstead.

The Pig and Whistle stood to one side, behind a low thorn hedge. A number of carriages were waiting outside, coachmen dozing on the boxes. They looked surprised at the size of the crowd arriving.

'What's on tonight?' Drummond asked one of them.

'A big match,' one of the men explained. 'For a wager of five golden sovereigns.'

'What sort of wager?' Ben asked Drummond.

'This landlord is of a sporting turn of mind,' Drummond explained. 'He organises rat fights. He has a big pit for them at the back of the bar. If you have a good ratting dog, you put him in there with twenty or thirty rats, or maybe a hundred, according to the dog's ability. He kills them as fast as he can. Landlord makes a note of the time this takes, then the challenger goes in and puts his dog in. The best one wins, picks up five sovereigns. There's a lot of money in it.'

254

The publican came to the front door, wiping his hands on a towel.

'Good evening, gents,' he said. 'Come to see the show, have you?'

'And to have one of our own.'

'You're fair people, aren't you?'

Drummond nodded. 'That's right. Do you object to that?'

'I don't want no trouble. I've got the gentry here. You see the carriages.'

'You'll have no trouble. We'll sit and watch your match. Then when the gentry go, we'll have ours.'

'What for?'

'A special wager,' said Drummond. 'You'll not be out of pocket, landlord, I assure you.'

'This man with his hands bound,' said the landlord sharply. 'I know him. He's tried to ruin my place many a time. I don't want him here.'

'We'll wait out here with him until your match is finished. Then we'll tell you why he's here. I give you my word, landlord, we won't let him cause you any trouble. He's caused us enough tonight already.'

There came a round of applause from the inn, faint cheering, sounds of laughter. 'Match is just finishing now,' the landlord said. 'Challenger's dog must have been a lot quicker than I thought.'

A crowd of men wearing smart breeches, coats, tall hats, came out. They ignored the fairground people. They'd had their match, they'd won or lost on the betting, and now it was back home. They didn't want to get involved with vagrants and travelling folk. They climbed into their carriages. Coachmen whipped up the horses. Gentle lights flickered on the roads, and away they went.

'Now,' said the landlord, 'you can come in. But no trouble, please.'

'I've given you my word,' Drummond replied shortly.

They came into the main bar. The floor was covered with fresh sawdust. A fire died in a black-leaded grate. Candles on the bar counter and oil lamps on the walls lit the room. Bottles and glasses reflected their trembling flames, blue, green, amber.

'Where's the pit?' Drummond asked.

'Through here.'

The landlord led them to a side door, into a square room with wooden seats arranged in rows round it, as at a boxing match. In the centre, instead of a ring, was a pit about twelve feet deep. The air smelt foul with the sharp stench of newly dropped dung. A boy was down in the pit, picking up dead rats, putting them in a sack.

'What's your pleasure, gentlemen?'

'A pint of porter each,' said Drummond and produced two sovereigns. 'Take it out of that. We'll probably have more later. A lot more. Depends how the betting goes.'

'Where's your ratter?'

'Here.'

'I don't see no dog.'

'This man Jed's the dog.'

'A *man*? How?'

'You'll see, landlord. Where are your rats?'

'In cages. We've got two sorts. Barn rats, sewer rats.'

'What's the difference?'

'Barn rats eat grain, straw, chaff. Sewer rats eat shit. Some people make pets of barn rats. They're plump, like little cats. But they don't fight so good.'

'And the sewer rats?'

'What would you imagine with a name like that? Their bite's poisonous.'

'How do you get them?'

256

'From rat-catchers, paid to kill rats in warehouses and so on. They get a ha'penny for every dead rat they can show. I give them tuppence, threepence, even sixpence a rat if they're really big 'uns. So they make a lot more money by bringing them live to me.

'When the harvest is in, out in the country, labourers got nothing much to do, so they go through barns, hedges, anywhere, catching rats. I've got whole families who live on it. I take roughly five hundred rats a week, every week of the year, sometimes more, sometimes less. And there are others like me.'

'You're well known for this round here, then?'

'The best matches in the area, gentlemen, though I say it as shouldn't. You've heard of me. So have others. It's all done fair and square. No fiddling. And I'll tell you this. I was in the boxing business before, so was my brother who's out in the back, the potman. He was heavyweight, I fought middleweight. Any trouble, we sort it out ourselves, as sportsmen should.'

'I've told you. There'll be no trouble. Let's see your rats. Sewer rats,' said Drummond.

'What's your wager?'

'How many rats can a dog kill in an hour?'

'Depends. Twenty, thirty. They run everywhere, the little bastards.'

'Right. I want twenty good sewer rats to start with. We put this man in, bind his hands behind him, and he can go at them like a dog, with his teeth.'

'I've seen that before,' said the landlord. 'But not with sewer rats. Their bite is poisonous, like I said. Barn rats is different. I've seen two men wager against each other with barn rats.'

'Any harm come to them?' Ben asked him.

'They got cut a bit about the mouth. A rat gives a three-cornered bite, like a leech. You put salt on it. It festers, and you may have to cut it out, but you'll live if it's a barn rat. Sewer rats is different, like I said. Their bite can be deadly.'

'That's why I want them,' said King Drummond grimly.

Jed stood, shoulders hunched, eyes glowering and glittering like angry sparks beneath his heavy brows. He grimaced and Ben saw sharp yellow teeth, stained with nicotine.

'Get his shirt off and drop him in,' said Drummond. Willing hands ripped off Jed's shirt. His pustuled, heavy body shone with sweat, pale as a bale of lard.

The landlord brought a wooden ladder and placed it against one side of the pit. Half a dozen men pushed Jed towards it.

'Climb down or we'll throw you in,' said Drummond tersely.

Jed climbed down unwillingly and stood in the centre of the pit, looking up at the others. No one spoke. The only sound in the room was the occasional guttering of wax from the candles. And then they heard a scratch and scrabble of tiny urgent claws. A sliding door no one had noticed low in the wall of the pit went up at the end of a rope. Rats poured in.

Some were sleek, some thin, all had ears well back, sharp teeth bared. They ran, one behind the other, following their leader round the base of the pit. Then the leader saw the man, raced across his boots. One rat attempted to run up his trouser leg. Jed cursed it, kicked it away.

'I'll give you three to start,' said Drummond and pulled out a German silver turnip watch.

'If you do it in ten minutes, you go free. You have my word. Now, ready to begin. One, two, *three*!'

Jed spat on the ground and waited, following the rats with his eyes. Round and round they ran until he felt dizzy. Then he dropped on his knees, faced them.

258

The rats swarmed away in panic at the movement. With his teeth, he gripped the nearest behind its head. The rat wriggled, squealed, waving its tiny pink paws frantically, mouth open. Jed shook it desperately like a terrier. Its head dropped. He spat out the loathsome body.

'One for the man. Rat for a rat,' said Drummond. 'Now get on.'

Jed killed fourteen and then lay down on the ground, in exhaustion, revulsion. He vomited. Rats ran up and over his head as he lay there. One nipped his ear, drawing blood.

'I can't go on,' he said weakly. 'I can't.'

'You will,' said an unexpected voice.

Everyone turned. Madam Zita was standing at the side of the pit. No one had heard her arrive.

'My daughter's dead as a result of your drunken bullying,' she said in a toneless voice. 'She's had a fit and she died, God rest her soul. My whole caravan is broken up. How am I going to make my living now, you swine? You go on, or I'll kill you myself.' She raised a hammer.

'Hey, now, mother,' said Drummond soothingly. 'We don't want that. We've given him our word. He kills 'em all in ten minutes and he goes free. He's only six to do now.'

'I've given him no word, the murdering bastard,' the old woman retorted. 'But I've given a sovereign to the landlord. Deeds is better than words.'

She suddenly put two fingers to her lips, blew a sharp whistle. At once the trap door whipped open for a second time. In rushed a horde of rats in a furry, black, stinking tide, bright eyes, sharp teeth, razor-edged claws. In an instant they swarmed over Jed's body, biting his ears, his lips, his eyelids. Then they were at his throat as he rolled about, screaming helplessly in

259

an agony of terror and despair. Rats ran up his trouser legs, nipped his soft, sweating flesh. He choked, screamed and suddenly his voice gurgled in his throat. He rolled to one side, alive with rats.

'Get them off him!' shouted the publican. 'He's had a fit. You'll give my house a bad name!'

He jumped down into the pit. Someone opened the trap door. The rats were gone as quickly as they had come, leaving only the dead, the dying and the droppings, and a man, marked on his face, his wrists, shoulders and chest with the three-cornered bite. The publican cut loose his bonds, rolled him on his back.

'He's gone,' he said in a horrified whisper.

'What d'you mean, gone?' said Drummond.

'He's dead. What are we going to do?'

'Get him out. Dump him in the river like the rest,' said Madam Zita. 'Only this time, leave him there.'

Everyone looked at her in surprise, turning over in their minds whether this was a feasible solution to their problem, or indeed any solution at all.

'When are you leaving the heath?' the publican asked nervously.

'Tomorrow.'

'Then if you're out of the area, no one's going to bother over this man much, so long as you keep your mouths shut.'

'The same goes for you, landlord.'

'I'll do that all right. I've got to live here.'

'That settles it, then,' said Drummond slowly. 'Give a hand now and we'll chuck him in the river, like Zita says.'

In nearly twenty-five years' service with the River Police on the stretch of Thames between Woolwich and Erith, Sergeant Robert Lowe had seen many sickening sights. Bloated bodies of suicides and other drowned men, women, even children, in various stages of decomposition, had been hauled aboard his fast sailing vessels and rowing boats which patrolled the river. Arms, legs, even heads, crawling with worms, had fallen back into the water. He thought he was beyond all feelings of shock and disgust. But the condition of the body he now examined on the marble slab in the River Police mortuary made him choke with revulsion.

The River Police had been formed as the Marine Police about sixty years earlier, the first organised police force in Britain. An enormous amount of pilfering, thieving and murders had accompanied the growth of the Port of London to the biggest port in the world. Two-thirds of all goods imported into Britain or sent out from the country passed through London docks. The congestion of vessels waiting to load or unload was so great that in the Upper Pool alone one thousand, seven hundred and seventy-five ships were regularly moored in a space originally designed to hold only five hundred and forty-five. As many as eight thousand other ships could be waiting in the river for a berth for as long as two months.

Most of the incoming ships were packed with valuable cargoes. Theft and smuggling were so blatant and profitable that it was estimated one out of every three men working in the port was either a thief or a receiver. The River Police, initially two hundred strong, had been formed in a desperate attempt to stop this haemorrhage of wealth into the underworld. The prospect of huge profits, the hatred of informers, the greed of everyone involved meant that murder was an everyday occurrence. Sometimes, bodies were concealed in a crate hidden in a warehouse or aboard an empty barge until putrefaction made their faces unrecognisable. Then they were tipped into the Thames at high tide to let fish do the rest.

At first, Lowe thought that this body was one of these, but the police surgeon had pointed out that from its condition, it had not been in the water for more than a few days, and indeed could have died only days, maybe even hours, before it entered the river.

One body was of little consequence to anyone except the immediate family. But local newspapers had been running a series of articles about the violence that seemed to be endemic on the docks and surrounding the visits of travelling fairs and circuses.

This man had been killed as a result of violence of some kind. The body was bruised and pummelled, and, oddly, he had been bitten by rats all over his face and hands before the corpse had been found face down in a river leading to the Thames, east of Woolwich. If it had been found in a field or at the roadside, the matter would not have involved the River Police. But because water was involved, so was Sergeant Lowe. The police surgeon stood on the other side of the marble slab, hands in his pockets, cigar alight against the foul smell of decomposition.

'Recognise him?' he asked.

Lowe shook his head. 'Not after what's he's been through. His face has been eaten away. Even his eyelids. He's probably got a record. Most of the corpses we see have.'

'Anyone come forward yet to say they've lost a husband or a father?'

'No. He probably lived with a woman. Maybe even more than one. You don't get the police called in by these people.'

'From his physical condition, he was a manual worker. A labourer. A docker, I think. There was a fight the other night on Bostal Heath, so I heard. A pitched battle, by some accounts. The Press, confound them, are bound to get wind of this and say Bostal Heath is not safe for ordinary people.'

'It isn't,' replied Lowe shortly. 'Not after dark.'

'We know that. Probably never has been, never will be, if they have fairs and so on there. But that's not the point. The point is, the mayor wants someone he can point to and say this man did it. And he also wants to be able to say how good the River Police are.'

'I know that,' said Lowe. People were always ready to accuse the police of slackness.

'I heard a lot of men came out from the docks and started the fight.'

'That's right,' Lowe nodded. 'How many fairground folk fought back?'

'Pretty well everyone able to do so.'

'Didn't anybody stand out? Someone we can go after? Even if they're not the man concerned, they could lead us to him. I'm only telling you what the mayor says.'

'There was an Indian. Middle-aged. He had a younger fellow with him. English. Only thing I know about him is that his first name is Ben. One of our informers told me that.'

'Where's the fair now?'

'They moved south to the coast. We can find it easily enough.'

'Where was it before this?' asked the surgeon. 'Maybe there's been trouble at other sites. If these men were ringleaders, or even just involved, that could be helpful.'

'It was up north. Across the border and over into Scotland.'

'I don't want to teach you your job, Sergeant, any more than you'd want to teach me mine. But with elections due and the newspapers always eager to criticise, it might be a good idea to get in touch with the local forces up there, find out if anything is known about these two people.'

'It might cause them to be hanged.'

'Not necessarily. They might lead us to the guilty party, if it's someone else. Didn't Dr Johnson say that the prospect of hanging concentrates a man's mind wonderfully? Put it to the test. Let's see for ourselves.'

The Provost sat back in his chair carefully. The boil on his buttock had not subsided. It was still painful, but not as painful as it had been. The letter he had just received from Woolwich, outside London, gave him cause for some quiet satisfaction. The Chief Superintendent of the River Police was asking if anything was known about an unnamed Indian and his assistant, both working for a travelling fair. There was the possibility they could help with a murder enquiry.

The Provost tapped the bell on his desk. A clerk came into the office.

'Get me Sergeant Macduff,' the Provost said.

Macduff marched in smartly, hoping the Provost had not found anything in his conduct that could call for criticism. The Provost pushed the letter across the desk. Macduff read it.

'Our two friends,' said the Provost genially. 'The leopard doesn't change its spots, nor the Ethiopian his skin. Nor this damned Indian. The superintendent doesn't go into details, as you can see, but some violence has resulted in death, and maybe these two are involved. I think this will show that we were right before in arresting them, and the laird of Long Glen was wrong.'

He touched the spring button on his bell. The clerk appeared.

'I want to send a letter. Please take a note.' The clerk

sat down and wrote rapidly as the Provost dictated his letter.

> These two characters you mention are almost certainly Karim Khan and his helper Ben Bannerman. They are most unfortunately known to us here. They were arrested as a result of an affray outside their booth. By some sleight of hand, Karim Khan, who is a conjurer and an illusionist, managed to escape. We later made arrangements to take him again into custody. However, the fair was appearing on private ground, not in a public place, and we were thus frustrated in our attempt.
>
> I feel that the most vigorous interrogation of these two characters could only be beneficial to you in your search for whoever was responsible for killing a man violently in a brawl on Bostal Heath. I would appreciate it if you could keep me informed as to the outcome. You will understand that this would be of great use to us here in keeping our records.

'That will do,' the Provost told the clerk. 'As quickly as you can.' The man nodded and left the room.

'You see,' the Provost told Macduff expansively. 'We're not always wrong up here. We Scots are not all fools. We still know a bad one when we see one. And in my view those two men are very bad characters indeed, and fully deserve whatever retribution should now shortly be coming to them – largely, you will note, from our information.'

For three days, the fair had been in a field adjoining a hop farm outside Rochester. Attendances were disappointing. It was best to play the hop fields during the summer when thousands of people from the East

265

End of London came down by horse and cart or on the new railways to pick hops for two or three weeks. This provided a welcome break from the filth and stench of the garrets and stews in which they lived for the rest of the year. The brewers paid their fares and a small wage, and the money they earned was spent in shops owned by the hop farmers. So, although families were paid for picking hops, most of the money went back directly or indirectly to the brewers.

Out of the hop season, attendances were obviously lower, and after three days of barely breaking even, the fair was moving on. Karim Khan sought out Ben on the morning of departure.

'I was in a local inn last night,' he said. 'A crowd of us went down there while you were packing up the gear. We spotted a couple of off-duty policemen, and so paid our dues in pints of porter. It's useful to know what the police have in mind before they pounce, such as, are they going to claim we've broken some ancient by-law about vagrants and arrest us?'

'Are they?' Ben asked him.

'No. But there's something much more dangerous that affects you and me alone. In Woolwich the police have somehow discovered our names. I'm the only Indian travelling with the fair, and you're my only assistant. We're going to be questioned over Jed's death. They think we may know who did it.'

'Well, it wasn't us, though we were there. Old Madam Zita arranged to put in more rats because she'd lost everything.'

'True. But she's no longer with this fair. She's gone west with another one, and the police don't know her. No one has mentioned her name. But they remember you and me. I stand out as an Indian, and you because you're my helper.'

'We can prove we didn't kill him, surely?' said Ben.

'How? Nobody's going to admit to being a witness
and risk implicating themselves. And the police aren't
really concerned about who had anything to do with
it. They just want to find someone who is recognised.
We could swing.'

'You mean *hang*?'

'Exactly.'

'Are you serious?'

'Never more so.'

'Didn't the police in the pub suspect you could be
the Indian?'

'Possibly. Probably. But they were drinking at our
expense, so they didn't say anything. But that won't
stop them coming round to pick us up now they know
we're here.'

'So what do you suggest?'

'That we disappear, now.'

'How can we disappear? Where to?'

'I've saved a little money. Rochester is a port. Ships
bound for India revictual there. I'm going back home.'

'To do what?'

'What I'm doing now, possibly. I told you, I come
from a family of jugglers. Better be a living juggler in
India than a dead conjurer here.'

'And me? What do you suggest I do?'

'Try your luck in India, too.'

'But as what? How? I was born out there, agreed,
and I love the country. But I've no trade. I'm not a
physician, not a merchant, not a missionary, not even
a soldier. I don't want to enlist as a private in the army.
If I did I'd be found in any case, and easily. Anyhow,
they may not be recruiting.'

'I wouldn't suggest you go as a private, but as an
officer. Then no one will check on you.'

'But how? I've no money. I'd need a thousand
pounds at least to buy a commission in the poorest

regiment of foot. Double or treble that if I went into
the cavalry. I know nothing about the military anyway,
except what little I picked up as a boy in Calcutta and
Barrackpore.'

'That's more than many officers know. They're not
a very intellectual group. I know. I served under them.
But the idea is worth following up.'

'How?'

'I'll tell you. You remember up in the north, the
laird of Long Glen, Mr Grimsdyke, said he had a
brother in Brighton who was in the army but who
didn't want to go to India?'

'Vaguely. What about it?'

'This. As Mr Grimsdyke mentioned, the custom
among rich officers who don't wish to sail East and risk
an early death from fever is to pay others to go in their
place.'

'But presumably such a man would already be a
serving officer?'

'That's not very difficult to become, my friend. The
laird's brother might pay you to go. Then out of that
money you could buy yourself a commission and go in
his place.'

'But my name would still be found. They'd know
who I was. I'd be arrested before I set foot on the
ship.'

'You have an unusually straightforward attitude to
life, Ben. I would have thought your brief sojourn with
me as an illusionist would have changed that. If not,
I'll change it for you now. Quite simply, you die and
your death is reported in the papers. You cease to
exist. And if you don't exist, your name is struck off
any list of suspects for Jed's death. Maybe you leave a
note that you've committed suicide, because you could
not bear to be questioned about the death on Bostal
Heath. That would strengthen your case.'

'But that is ridiculous.'

'Not so. Nothing is ridiculous, my friend, if it has a useful purpose. And as far as you are concerned, this could have the most useful purpose of all. It would ensure your survival. As I say, I have saved a little money. I can give you ten sovereigns to help you disappear. Who knows, perhaps in the East we might meet again. I hope so. One does not meet too many friendly companions on life's lonely road.'

'But I'd disappear under my own name?'

'Your name is B. F. Bannerman. B. F. can stand for Bloody Fool. It can stand for Ben Fanfare or Bruce Frank – anything. One B. F. Bannerman dies. Another of that name does not, but goes abroad to a new life.'

'You think this can work?'

'I don't see why not. It's simply a contest of wits. Ours against those of the constabulary. From what we have seen of their intelligence, at least in the person of the Provost in Scotland, I would not rate them very highly in any contest of the mind.'

'You really think this is possible?' responded Ben doubtfully.

Karim Khan shrugged. 'We can only try and see for ourselves. In your religion you believe in death and resurrection. Here is a chance to prove what you believe. And may we both meet again in your resurrected life.'

Karim Khan held out his hand. Ben shook it.

I was taking evening surgery when the last patient came in from the waiting room. He was a carpenter who had once done some small jobs for me: a set of shelves in my surgery, a small table in the kitchen. I had not seen him for many months. He had moved south because he unexpectedly came into money and a house in Kent through the death of a distant relative. He gave up his

269

job in Scotland and went to live in this house near Whitstable, the centre of oyster beds.

'Are you back here for good?' I asked him.

'Just visiting my sister,' he replied. 'But now I am here I wanted to see you, Doctor. Not about my health, about something else. It saves writing a letter, and I was never much of a hand with a pen.'

'You want my help over something?' I asked him.

'Not this time,' he replied. 'I have news that concerns you. Not very good news, I fear, but something you may not have heard up here, although I am sorry to be the bearer of such sad tidings.'

'About what?'

'About that young fellow you brought back from India. Ben Bannerman.'

'Yes?' I said eagerly, leaning forward. 'How is he? He went off, you know, ran away with a travelling fair. You have seen him?'

'No.' He hesitated, as though unwilling to continue. He put his hand in a pocket, opened his wallet and took out a folded newspaper cutting, which he handed to me. I read it.

Sad Discovery on Tankerton Beach

A correspondent informs us that a small pile of men's clothes, with a pair of neatly polished shoes, was found on the shingle beach of this watering place near Whitstable on Tuesday afternoon last.

Held down by a stone, was a note which read: 'To whoever finds this: I have reached the end of my life. I am only young in years, yet already I feel old in experience and ill fortune. I am sought by the police in connection with the death of a man on Bostal Heath, south-east of London. I am not guilty of his death, but I have already found how unfair the workings of the law can be when you cannot prove innocence by the testimony of many witnesses.

'I feel that I cannot go on with my life. I am therefore about to end it, and hope at last to find mercy at the hands of the Almighty. I deeply regret such sadness or distress I may cause by my action to my dear mentor and guardian in Scotland. I will not embarrass this kindly physician by mentioning his name, but I hope and pray he may understand the reasons for what I am about to do. I trust he will remember me kindly as I was, not as I am now. B. F. Bannerman.'

I read and re-read the report with increasing sadness. Could this really be so? Could Ben, the boy I had come to love as a son and in whose features I saw the dear face of the woman I had loved, take his own life in such a way?

He had been away for only a matter of months. Surely in this short time he could not have sunk so low amid evil companions as to be suspected of murder and so take his life? Why had he not appealed to me for help? I was not without funds. I would willingly have engaged the best lawyer in the land to state his case. But perhaps he was too proud to ask me. I had not heard from him since he had left. Perhaps he had wished to become settled in some steady employment before he told me where he was living and what he was doing. It seemed out of Ben's character simply to disappear, or so I kept telling myself. But now, I would never see him again; at least, not in this world.

For him to take his own life meant I had failed him on every level. I should have spent far more time with him. I should have supervised his studies. I should have told him of the pitfalls in life. If only I had known of his troubles, I would gladly have helped him.

But then I remembered how he had tried to tell me of his problems with Bertha and I had thought he was exaggerating petty differences, and fobbed him off with platitudes. I had forgotten the sharpness of one's feelings at his age. I had been too concerned with my own affairs and not with his. And now it was all too late. If only . . .

I closed my eyes and sat back in my chair, imagining Ben walking out into the sea, feeling cold water rise inexorably above his knees, his groin, his heart, until finally he cast himself upon the deep.

'May God rest your soul,' I said to myself. 'And may God have mercy upon me for my sins of omission.'

I opened my eyes.

'I can keep this?' I asked the carpenter.

'Of course. I brought it for you to keep. As I say, I am deeply sorry to be the bearer of such painful news.'

'I had not heard from him since he went away,' I explained. 'I knew he was with the fair, but by the time I reached the site they had moved on. I heard later there had been some trouble with the police here. I don't know what exactly. A fight or some such thing. Apparently he was working for an Indian stallkeeper, an illusionist of some kind.' I picked up the newspaper cutting again. 'Ben was a young man of immense promise, the son of a dear friend shot in the retreat from Kabul years ago.'

'I've heard of that,' he said.

I nodded. Many people had heard of it. I was now the only survivor who had taken part in it. History soon recedes into the past. People forget events, add to them, subtract from them; like the Indian in the fair, they substitute their own illusions.

'Tell me,' I said hesitantly, for I had difficulty in asking the question. 'Was his body found?'

The carpenter shook his head. 'No. There's a very

big tide there. The sea goes out a long way, possibly a mile, over sand. He was never found.'

'And the Indian he was with? What happened to him?'

'I know nothing about him. I've never been one to go to fairs. There seems always the risk of violence there. Pickpockets, people getting drunk and puking or quarrelling. I like a quiet life.'

I nodded. I could understand his wish. He stood up.

'Goodbye, Doctor. I probably won't be up north of the border again for some time. I wish you well. And once more, I'm sorry.'

We shook hands. He went out.

For a long time after the man had gone I sat in my chair. Through the windows I could see the hills, with cattle on the slopes, and clouds riding above the peaks. They were gentle peaks, these, compared with the hills in Afghanistan, but they continually reminded me of those other harsher mountains.

And in reminding me of those, they also recalled Ben Bannerman, the passed-over lieutenant, his lovely wife Anna, and their son. A whole family gone, I thought. I was the last survivor who had known them all. I sat until the shadows grew long, and finally veiled the hills from my sight.

When I was alone in the darkness, I stood up, locked the surgery and went upstairs to bed. But it was a long time before I fell asleep.

The blinds of Lady Beaumont's carriage were tightly drawn as it stopped outside the Old Galleon Hotel in Brighton. When she stepped down, she drew a dark veil over her face.

'I am Mrs Gebbie,' she told the clerk at the reception desk. 'I have an appointment with Dr Kintyre.'

'He is in his suite, madame,' the man replied. 'He

has asked that you should be shown upstairs as soon as you arrived.'

The man rang a handbell for a flunkey.

Lady Beaumont followed the servant up the wide, red-carpeted staircase. She felt thankful that the man was old and walked slowly. For some time she had been aware of a strange and unusual weariness; little things assumed ridiculous proportions and stairs seemed steeper than they had been only months previously. She rested for a moment on the first landing, leaning on the rail, then she went on even more slowly.

I did not know what to expect. Lady Beaumont must be middle-aged, I guessed, but was she good-looking, pleasant or disagreeable? I had no idea. When the flunkey tapped gently on the door and she stepped inside, I suppose I was really expecting to see Ben's features mirrored in her face. But to my surprise she did not resemble young Ben at all. He was tall and dark. She was small, fair-haired, much more like his father. I could see at once they were related: they had the same bone structure in their faces.

We shook hands. When the servant withdrew, I locked the door. I did not want anyone butting in while we talked, for I had no idea how Lady Beaumont would take the sad news I had come south to give her.

Some women, I knew from my practice, accepted the death of a dear one stoically. Others became hysterical, and threw themselves on the ground, screaming against God and what they considered injustice. Why should one be taken and another left? Or, to be more accurate, why should someone they loved die while someone else, perhaps much older and maybe much less worthy, even unloved, lived on in good health for many more years?

I had arranged for tea to be served, but Lady Beaumont shook her head.

'No, thank you,' she said. 'It's really too early for me, and unfortunately my time is limited. My husband does not know I have taken the carriage. But, tell me. Why did you write to me after so long without a word? You have news of my nephew Ben?'

'Yes,' I said, sitting down opposite her. 'But it is not news that gives me any pleasure to impart.'

She did not appear to hear, or if she did she ignored the remark. 'Where is he?' she asked me.

'I brought him back to Scotland some time ago,' I explained. 'I could not leave him in India on his own. He went to school here, and I intended he should go on to the university.' I paused, not quite certain how I should continue.

'And?' she asked impatiently.

'I am unmarried, Lady Beaumont. The housekeeper of my late father looked after me, and it appears that, quite unknown to me, she nurtured the hope that I would marry her. Such a thought never entered my head, but she formed the opinion that Ben was the reason why I did not seek her hand in marriage.'

'She was unkind to him?' Lady Beaumont asked, going instantly to the root of the matter. She was like her brother in possessing this gift, I thought.

'It would appear so, although I did not realise it at the time. She had a sharp, spinsterish nature to which I was so accustomed I tended to ignore it. Ben did not, or could not. I did not understand the extent of Ben's unhappiness, until he left home.'

'Left home? Where did he go?'

'He could speak Hindustani very well. He had been happy in India, and so had I. Here, he fell in with an Indian illusionist in a travelling fair. They got on well, apparently.' Again, I paused.

'And? What then?'

'Most unfortunately there was some violence at a fairground outside London. I don't know what exactly, but sometimes a very rough element patronises these places. I can't believe Ben was involved, or at least no more so than anyone else. The same is true, in my view, of the Indian. But with his dark skin and his turban, he was the only person witnesses remembered. And Ben was his companion. The police wished to interview them both.'

Lady Beaumont leaned forward in her chair, her face drawn with worry and concern. '*Wished?*' she repeated. The past tense had an ominous ring to it.

'I don't know what has happened to the Indian, but I have to tell you that Ben appears to have taken his own life.'

'Killed himself? Surely not. My brother's son. I cannot believe that, Dr Kintyre.'

I took the newspaper cutting from my pocket and handed it to her. She read it through, handed it back to me without any comment.

'We must assume, Lady Beaumont,' I said, 'that the poor fellow did what he describes he was about to do.'

Lady Beaumont did not reply. She walked across the room and stood, hands clasped behind her back, looking over the promenade and the white-painted railings and the shingle beach at the sea. I followed her to the window. We stood side by side for a moment in silence, each sharing the same thoughts. Somewhere beyond our sight, beneath a restless sea, where gulls swooped and cried, lay the body of a young man I had known and this woman had dearly wished to know.

'I can't believe he's dead,' she said softly, almost thinking aloud. I understood her optimism though I could not share it. So many times have mothers with dead children, wives with dead husbands told me this.

He could not be dead. He had simply gone away; he would come back. One of the comforts of the Christian religion is that death is not an end so much as a beginning; one day, we will all meet again. Comforting as this can be to those who mourn, I must confess I have sometimes felt that the belief is open to doubt. But this was not the moment to express my opinion.

Lady Beaumont walked back to her chair and sat down.

'I have changed my mind,' she said quietly. 'I will have a cup of tea after all.'

I poured her one, added two spoonfuls of sugar to help soothe her shock.

'I'm glad we have met,' she said, 'but very sorry about the circumstances. I had hoped to see my brother's son, even if my husband would not allow me to adopt him.'

'I should have been in touch before,' I admitted. 'But I came back to start a country practice in the Grampian hills of Scotland, about five hundred miles from here. After years in India, I had to adapt myself to so many new ways. I found it hard to do so. These are all excuses, I admit. I should have been in touch with you before. But there seemed to be no urgency, there was so much time. I do apologise most sincerely.'

She shook her head. 'There's nothing to apologise for, Doctor. But please give me your address. If, as I very much hope, Ben is not dead but has been picked up by some ship, perhaps taken on to a far country – you hear of all manner of shipwrecked people being rescued when you live on the coast – I can be in touch with you at once.'

I gave her my card. She put it in her handbag.

'I have some possessions of my own,' she said. 'Not many, mostly paintings. I made a will, leaving everything I own to Ben. I suppose I should change that, in view of what you tell me. But if I do that, I feel that it shows a lack of faith in what I believe . . .' She paused.

'And what do you believe, Lady Beaumont?' I asked her, as if I did not already guess.

'I believe he is alive and well somewhere. And that anything I can leave to him may some day help him.'

'I hope you are right,' I told her.

She stood up, glanced at her gold watch. 'I must go,' she said. 'I hope we will meet again, Doctor. And in happier circumstances. Perhaps our next meeting will be a reunion with Ben!'

'May that be true, Lady Beaumont.'

I escorted her downstairs to her carriage. As I watched it bowl sedately along the promenade, blinds still drawn, I did not think I would ever see her again. The unhappy woman carried the seeds of terminal illness in her face. Lady Beaumont was dying. Maybe, if she did not already know this, she suspected her health was failing.

I estimated that she had less than six months to live.

Chapter Eight

The vicar sat on one side of the white wrought-iron table on the terrace overlooking the sea on the cliffs near Brighton. He perched uncomfortably on the edge of the metal chair, which bit into his thin buttocks, sending his legs to sleep.

His host, Francis Grimsdyke, sat on the other chair, watching his unexpected visitor warily. Grimsdyke, probably the richest man on the south coast, was not a regular churchgoer but sometimes he gave modest amounts to good causes if they touched his heart. He would, however, never subscribe to any charity involving help to children. He did not like children any more than he liked flowers. When he visited one of his tenants, the mother was well advised to push her children out of the back door into the garden, or give them a ha'penny each and tell them to go to the village shop, buy sweets and stay out of sight until the landlord had left.

He was unpredictable and widely said to be difficult to know. He had few friends, and what in a poorer man would have been condemned as outrageously churlish and unforgivable behaviour was passed off as 'his way of doing things'. The possession of wealth invariably transmutes what would be a poor man's gross rudeness into a rich man's eccentricity. Sycophants called him a character. Others, more honest, declared (but never, of course, to his face) that he was mad and should be in an asylum for the insane. The vicar thought it doubtful whether Grimsdyke cared what anyone said to him or about him.

Grimsdyke assumed the vicar had come to seek a donation towards the church spire, or the organ fund, or whatever part of the church the vicar or churchwardens considered most in need of repair or renovation. He watched the clergyman carefully as he delicately chewed a finely sliced cucumber sandwich. The vicar did not seem in a hurry to raise the reason for his visit, so Grimsdyke decided to ask him outright.

'It is always a pleasure to see you,' he said insincerely. 'But to what do I owe your call today?'

'I came, sir,' the vicar replied, licking butter from the tips of his fingers, 'because, knowing your interest in people, something quite extraordinary happened to me last evening, and I felt I simply had to apprise you of it.'

'What could that be?' asked his host without interest.

'About eight of the clock I heard a knock on my front door. The maid opened it. I was not expecting a visitor, and so was surprised when she came to say that a young girl was standing outside.

' "Who is she?" I asked.

' "She cannot speak, sir," the maid replied. "She is dumb."

' "Dumb? Has she come from some asylum, a lazar house?"

' "I do not know, sir," the maid replied, obviously puzzled.

' "Does she want to see me? How can she ask for me if she is dumb?"

' "She's not asking to see you, sir. She seems of gentle birth, and I just thought you might wish to see her." '

'Come on with it, man,' said Grimsdyke irritably. 'Who was she? What did she want?'

'I have still no idea who she is, or what she wants. I invited her in, asked her name, her place of residence. She did not reply, but just stood and looked at me. Not in any way insolently. Quite the reverse. Rather pathetically.'

'Is she deaf as well as dumb?'

'Again, I simply do not know. It seemed to me that she didn't understand a word I was saying.'

'She is foreign, then?'

'It would seem so.'

'White? Coloured? A native?'

'Clearly a native of some place, but presumably not from anywhere in these islands. I called for some soup, which was left over from dinner. She looked at it, smelled it, and then put her mouth down to the plate, and drank it down like an animal, a beast of the field.'

'Didn't she use a spoon?'

'No. She picked up the spoon, looked at it and then put it down. She didn't know what it was for, or even what it was. I sent out my man to the Overseer of the Poor. He came back and offered her a sixpenny piece to be on her way. She turned the coin over in her hand and sniffed at it as though it might be food of some kind. Then she shook her head – very politely, I must say – and gave it back to him.'

'He didn't want her to be a charge on the parish, I suppose?' said Grimsdyke.

'Of course. We have enough people already on the parish.'

Grimsdyke nodded his understanding – not of the vicar's comment on the parish poor but of the reason for his visit. He had come to the point at last: he wanted money for this stray female.

'Anyhow,' the vicar went on, pressing home his case,

'we could not turn the woman away. Clearly, she had come to me because she felt I, as vicar, could help her.'

'Very likely. She's a grown woman then?'

'Well, yes. I would think in her late 'teens, perhaps very early twenties. Indeed, a very good-looking, comely young woman. So I had the maid make up a bed for her in the attic. But she didn't know what a bed was! She lay down on the floor, like an animal again, or a savage.

'The maid climbed into the bed and showed what was expected of her, but still she did not comprehend. She simply lay on the floor in her clothes. I got a change of linen for her the next morning, or rather my lady wife did. What she had been wearing was very threadbare and in need of a wash. She had a wash herself, but just sloshed water on her face and body. Cold water, too. She did not use soap. Again, she didn't seem to know what it was. She sniffed at it and licked it with her tongue, in case it could be food.

'I called in Dr Blake. He examined her, and pronounced her fit. He is a magistrate, and he spoke to her sternly and slowly and loudly, so that if she was simply hard of hearing she could hear him. He told her plainly, and in my presence, that if she was pretending to be dumb or someone who she wasn't, then he had the power to send her to prison with hard labour. But she just looked at him. She couldn't understand him any more than she understood me.'

'And then?'

'Well, sir, one of these foreign fellows selling onions and cloves came to the back door of the house, as is the custom, and he saw her. He was French, and he spoke to her in French. But she did not reply, only smiled at him. He had some Spanish and Portuguese, and spoke to her in these languages. She appeared to understand him to some extent but replied in a tongue that was not Portuguese or Spanish. He said he understood at least a little of what she said.'

'Did he know what language she spoke?'

'Apparently not. I asked him, but possibly he did not understand my question completely and he just shrugged his shoulders. He was not a man of great intellect. But apparently she told him she was a person of some consequence, from one of the Spice Islands. She had been brought here, apparently kidnapped or aboard a ship that was taken by pirates. He wasn't quite clear on all the facts. But how she reached this town, where she'd walked from, is still a total mystery.'

'Didn't you question him further?'

'That was all he could discover. At any rate, he left.'

'What an odd story, Vicar. And the strange girl – woman – where is she now?'

'My housekeeper is waiting with her at the servants' entrance here. I thought you might like to see her.'

'Me? Why? I know nothing of whatever language they speak in the Spice Islands.'

'Then, sir, I will have to send her on her way,' said the vicar stiffly. 'I am sorry to have taken up so much of your time.' He rose to leave.

'No, no, my dear fellow,' said Grimsdyke quickly. It wouldn't do to antagonise the vicar unduly. He might as well have a look at this curiosity and then pack them both off with a sovereign to ease the way. He smiled thinly at the vicar. 'It would be churlish of me not to meet such an unusual visitor when you have gone to the trouble of bringing her to my door. I will most certainly see her.'

He rang for his butler and gave him instructions. The vicar's housekeeper appeared at the door, curtsied, turned to one side and ushered in a young girl.

She was cleanly dressed in a maid's clothes. Her hair

was neatly brushed. Her face shone with scrubbing, her nails were closely trimmed. He noticed all these things. He hated slackness, dirt in any form. He asked her name in Spanish. He also had a smattering of German and French, but to all his questions in these languages she just stared at him. He noticed that as she looked, her eyes dropped so that they were fixed not on his face, but on his body, his lower abdomen. He found her attention somehow disconcerting. He was becoming aroused.

She had a certain spark about her, an animal sexuality he had not encountered before. Her breasts were full and firm, as were her buttocks. Her legs were strong, her shoulders broad, the face without blemish. Her lips were especially attractive, her mouth wide, the lips not thick but sensual and shining, as though painted with some kind of salve. She looked immensely attractive, and he lusted after her.

'What are your plans for this person?' he asked the vicar.

'I will give her a shilling and put her on her way.'

'I think that's rather harsh,' said Grimsdyke musingly. 'Give her a shilling, by all means, Vicar, but I have many rooms in my house, and friends who have travelled widely in foreign parts. Maybe they can place her country of origin and then we can find out her story. Perhaps that onion seller will turn up again at the door and we can question her through him. If she goes now, we will never discover who she is and how she has arrived here, obviously far from her native place.'

The vicar smiled with satisfaction. 'I think that is a very Christian act,' he said. 'And quite in keeping with your character, if I may say so.'

'You may,' said Grimsdyke magnanimously. 'We will put her up in a maid's room in the attic. I will discover what food she likes by trial and error, and make notes in a scientific manner. You're a busy man, Vicar, with the cure of many souls. I am not busy. It is one thing to have enough money not to need to work, but it can be boring. Did not Shakespeare say that if every day were making holiday, to sport would be as tedious as to work?'

'Very likely,' the vicar agreed. 'I am not as well versed on the works of the Bard as you, sir. But I cannot imagine you being bored. You hold the Queen's commission and I hear that soon you may be leaving for India to join your regiment out there.'

'That is where they wish me to go, yes. But I'm not at all keen. I like the climate here, I like my life here, although I say I'm bored. But in India there are far worse possibilities than boredom. You die very easily of distemper, fever, dysentery. It has a most unhealthy climate. In any case, whether I go or stay, I will be here for a while yet, and in that time I would like to learn what I can about this poor, unfortunate creature.'

When the vicar had left, Grimsdyke patted the brocaded cushion of a seat next to his. The girl smiled as though not quite understanding. Grimsdyke stood up, bowed to her, pointed to the chair, sat in it himself, stood up again and returned to his own chair. She smiled and sat down as he had directed. He felt absurdly pleased, as though he had taught an animal a new trick with unexpected ease. That's what she was, of course, a lovely, sexual animal.

He stood up, poured two glasses of sherry, and gave her one. She sniffed it, looked at him quizzically, shook her head.

'You don't want it?' he asked.

She smiled vacuously. He drank both glasses himself. Then he sent a messenger out to give his compliments to Mr Crosbie, a retired don from Cambridge who lived nearby. Crosbie was a fussy old man, with a few strands of black hair stuck by Macassar oil to his otherwise bald head, which glistened, pale as a giant billiard ball. Grimsdyke met him in the hall.

'You want to see me urgently?' Crosbie asked, as though this irritated him.

'Yes,' said Grimsdyke. He explained about the girl.

'I have a knowledge of some Eastern languages and I have travelled widely in those parts,' said Crosbie pompously. 'Perhaps I can help you.'

He came into the room, smiled at the girl. He addressed several questions to her in tongues Grimsdyke did not know. Each time, she bowed and smiled and looked charmingly at him.

'Does she understand anything?' Grimsdyke asked Crosbie.

'She doesn't appear to. Wait a minute, though. I have some books at home with pictures. I'll fetch those.'

He was back within half an hour with an armful of large, leatherbound books. He put them on the table, opened the first at an old map of Sumatra. She looked over his shoulder at it and smiled again. It meant nothing to her. He turned the pages. They contained coloured pictures of pineapples, palm trees, line drawings of strange animals and fish and birds. Now and then she smiled and pointed at some of them, nodding.

'You see?' he said triumphantly. 'Must be where she comes from. Sumatra. She knows what the pictures are of.'

'Are they peculiar to those parts?'

'Possibly not entirely restricted to Sumatra but certainly they indicate she has knowledge of the East. There must be someone here who speaks her language. A retired missionary from the South Seas is living in furnished rooms at Hove. I was introduced to him only the other day. He may be able to help. I'll fetch him along.'

Mr Crosbie did so. The missionary brought a Bible with coloured pictures of scripture lands. Men in white robes walked in the desert; Jesus Christ wore a halo; fishermen hauled in nets from an unnamed sea. She smiled at all these pictures politely, but they made no impact on her.

Grimsdyke sat the girl down at a table, showed her how to eat with a knife, a fork, a spoon, how to drink from a glass, holding it in one hand, how to wipe her lips with a starched table napkin. She seemed to learn easily enough, but without enthusiasm, without spirit or interest. Grimsdyke, watching her, decided that here was a woman he could mould to his own will, someone he could virtually create in his own image.

He was an inadequate man, fortunate in the accident of his birth. Otherwise, his talents would have limited him to serving behind the counter of a corner shop. He could barely add numbers, and this liability would have precluded him from even the lowly employment of a clerk in a counting house. But with his wealth he had no need of such abilities; they could easily be hired from those who did possess them.

Mr Crosbie returned with more picture books. These showed men and women wearing national costumes: robes, turbans, pantaloons, shoes with thongs that fitted over their big toes. Now the girl's face became animated. She picked up a piece of pencil and started to draw on the back of an envelope. She had some talent in that direction.

'Those are the clothes she should wear,' said Crosbie excitedly.

'Of course,' said Grimsdyke. 'I think we're on the brink of solving the riddle.'

'If you are, you must give her a name.'

'I say Miranda, Prospero's daughter. In *The Tempest*. You are familiar with the work?'

'From my schooldays. She was a sweet girl, ignorant of the world. Fell in love with a shipwrecked sailor. But until then, the only man she'd ever known was her father. You think this child is as innocent?'

'I don't know,' said Grimsdyke. 'But I intend to find out.'

The girl stayed with him for several days. Every morning and afternoon he would set her down in a chair opposite his. On his knees he held a board with some papers pinned to it. He would draw letters of the alphabet, and ask her to repeat them after him. Gradually, he made her repeat small sentences, if only parrot fashion, not really understanding their meaning: 'I live near the sea. My name is Miranda'.

'Are you happy?' he asked her.

'Happy,' she said. 'I am happy Miranda.'

One afternoon after his lesson with Miranda, Grimsdyke went out for a walk along the sea front. A wind was blowing and waves scattered spray against the long promenade. The beach was deserted. It had rained before lunch, and the fronts of all the houses shone with dampness. He started to walk towards the Downs, but the day seemed unusually cheerless, so he decided to go home. As he turned, he saw a young man coming towards him. He was soberly dressed, not in the height of fashion, but he appeared a clean, respectable person. To Grimsdyke's surprise, the young man stopped and took off his hat in polite greeting.

'Excuse me, sir. But am I right in thinking you are Mr Grimsdyke?'

'You are.'

'A brother of the laird of Long Glen in Scotland?'

'That is correct. And who are you?'

288

'I was done a great service by your brother, sir, and I bring you his fraternal greetings.'

'That's very civil of you. I haven't seen him for some time. What sort of service?'

'I was, sir, working briefly with a travelling fair and circus.'

'Oh,' said Grimsdyke, and wrinkled his nose in distaste. He did not like fairs; they were noisy, rough, with people shouting, getting drunk, enjoying themselves in a boisterous way. He liked a quiet life, with everything well-ordered, dignified, gracious.

'I see that work of that nature is not to your taste, sir. Or so it would seem by your tone of voice. But I was there with a former member of the East India Company's army.'

'Really?'

'My father was an officer in India, sir. I was brought up in Calcutta and Barrackpore. He was killed in the retreat from Kabul, in which my mother also died.'

'How very sad,' said Grimsdyke without feeling. Who the devil was this fellow?

'And what do you seek now?' he asked him.

'Maybe I can return the favour your brother paid me by helping you.'

'What favour did he do to you?'

'Some constables were under a misapprehension that I had been involved in an argument on his estate,' Ben replied, adapting truth to his needs. 'He spoke up for me. I was innocent, of course, and he knew that. But not everyone would have spoken so favourably on behalf of a stranger.'

'He has a nice nature, my brother,' Grimsdyke allowed. 'I often say he is the kind one of the family. But what could you do for me to repay this good deed?'

'I understand, sir, that you hold a commission in the Queen's army, or the army of John Company, and are

289

under orders for posting to India.'

'How do you understand that?' Grimsdyke asked him sharply. What was the fellow after?

'Your brother happened to mention it, sir.'

'Really? And what is that to you?'

'It may be that a gentleman in your position, with your wealth and wide cultural interests here in this country, might not wish to proceed to the East, where the expected lifespan of a European can be as low as two monsoons, just over twelve months.'

'That's if they're lucky,' replied Grimsdyke. 'I've known friends who haven't lasted anything like as long.'

'I would be willing to offer my services and go in your place.'

'You? Why?' Grimsdyke looked at the young man curiously. He was good-looking, tall, broad-shouldered, with a very tanned complexion. His eyes did not flinch from Grimsdyke's gaze. He could be honest, genuinely intending to pay back a favour done to him, small as it might actually have been.

'As I say, sir, my father died in the East. I spent the early years of my life there. I would like to return as a soldier.'

'Then why don't you?'

'I lack money to buy a commission.'

'So how would you procure a commission and take my place?'

'I understand, sir, the custom is that if an officer does not wish to accept a posting to India, he may pay for someone else to go in his place. If you paid me, I would purchase a commission.'

'A lieutenant's commission in a regiment of foot would cost around a thousand pounds.'

'Indeed, sir. But that is less than a quarter of what officers unwilling to take an Indian posting frequently pay to someone who does not share their reluctance.'

'You may be right,' said Grimsdyke shortly.

'I can assure you, sir, that if I went in your place, I would at all times act in the best traditions of the army.'

'So I would hope,' replied Grimsdyke. 'What's your name?'

'Benjamin Fanfare Bannerman.'

'A fine name.'

'I hope not to bring discredit on it, sir.'

'You speak very well. You have high aims?'

'It is written, sir, that someone who aims for the sun may hit the moon. Someone who aims for the moon may hit a star. But if the stars are your aim, you will probably hit nothing at all.'

'Very true. Who wrote that?'

'I did.'

'*You* did?' Grimsdyke's surprise showed in his voice. This fellow was an odd cove, but not unamusing. And he might be useful – if they could negotiate a price.

'Come back to my house,' he said. 'I would like to discuss this further with you.'

They walked back in silence and sat down in Grimsdyke's study.

'How do I know you are who you are?'

'I have this paper, sir.'

Ben took from his pocket a copy of a page from the *London Gazette* which Dr Kintyre had given to him years previously. It recorded the death of his father in action. He had also obtained a copy of a marriage certificate of the kind recently issued by Somerset House in London. It described his father as a lieutenant, his mother as a spinster of private means. Grimsdyke read the papers and handed them back to Ben.

'You will have a glass of Madeira?' he asked.

'I would be pleased to join you, sir.'

Grimsdyke poured two glasses, and made up his mind. He had no intention of going to India, which meant he would have to find a suitable officer or other person who was willing to go in his place. He would have to pay, and quite heavily, and also inconvenience himself arranging interviews. He might have to meet all manner of unprepossessing candidates, possibly embittered lieutenants, passed over many times for promotion, before he found one he could trust to go in his place, not just accept his money and then disappear. This had happened to others in his regiment. He might even have to advertise in the Press, or visit auction rooms where commissions were bought and sold, and deals were struck with impoverished officers to accept boring postings in unhealthy and unfashionable places. Those who were very rich, of course, never left London or whatever military headquarters where they wished to serve.

This young fellow Bannerman was of an army family; he appeared keen and honest. Possibly his brother had mentioned the idea to him; he was unlikely to have thought of it himself. He could not be bothered to write to the laird and find out. They were not on close terms. Grimsdyke knew the opinion the laird held of him, that he was mentally retarded, or even mad. Well, he would show them he was not as green as he was cabbage-looking. He'd pay this young fellow, not the going rate, but rather less. He'd do a deal.

'What is your price?' he asked him now.

'I leave that to you, sir,' said Ben.

'A thousand pounds.'

'On top of what I have to pay for a commission?'

Grimsdyke frowned. He had intended simply to pay for the young fellow's lieutenancy, no more. But now his bluff was being called.

'Of course,' he said unconvincingly.

292

'And that, I assume, sir, is on top of what I would need to pay for a uniform, accoutrements, and my passage to India?'

'Well, yes, I suppose so.'

'That is rather less than what I believe is called the going rate.'

'I'm helping you,' said Grimsdyke.

'I believe we are in fact helping each other, sir,' said Ben.

'Well, what *do* you want?' asked Grimsdyke, beginning to feel irritable. He hated anyone to cross him, to voice a contrary opinion. He could feel blood begin to surge more quickly through his veins; a pulse started to beat in his neck like the tap of a warning drum. He would have a bad headache within a few minutes, and then he would start to shout, and then this fellow might leave. He must not lose his temper.

'Wait here for a moment,' he said. 'Help yourself to more Madeira. I will return.'

Ben stood up as Grimsdyke left the room, then sat down again and poured himself a second glass. The sums of money were high to him, but he sensed that it would be unwise to accept the first offer. That way he could only diminish himself in his host's estimation. And if Grimsdyke suspected how desperate he was for money, any money, he wouldn't engage him at all. Ben sipped the drink as calmly as he could.

The door opened. A girl came in, looked at him in amazement and then horror. She closed the door quickly behind her.

'What are you doing here?' Mary Jane asked him.

Ben stood up, his mouth open in surprise. 'I might ask you the same question.'

'You followed me here,' she said quietly. 'You're going to expose me.'

'I don't know what you're talking about.'

293

'Then why are you here?'

'I heard from the laird of Long Glen, after our trouble with the constables, that our host was to be posted to India and didn't like the prospect. I made discreet enquiries and discovered where I might run into him. I have offered to go to India in his place – if he pays me enough. And you?'

'I left Ivan. There was no future there. Nothing. I did not want to trek about the country all my life with a fair.'

'What are you doing here? You are a servant?'

'No. I happened to read in an old newspaper an account of a girl who appeared in a village in Gloucester about forty years ago. She claimed she did not speak any language but let it be believed she was a victim of shipwreck, a princess from a far island. Rich people took her up, fed her, clothed her. They gave her a name – Princess Caraboo. She saved enough money to emigrate to America.'

'Is that a true story?'

'Totally.'

'And you thought you could do the same?'

'I didn't just think I could. I have done it.'

'And who was this girl?'

'Actually a servant girl who had run away to find a better life.'

'Like you.'

'Yes. I have my own room here. I've been bought clothes. I eat good food, have a bath every day. Think of that! It's better than being in Newgate prison or in Mrs Mentmore's night house, I can tell you. People come and stare at me, and they show me pictures of the South Sea Islands, hoping I will recognise one as the place where I was born. They've given me a name. Miranda. It was in a play. Some of them give me money. I save it all. Then I can go to America or

Australia, somewhere far away, and start a new life, like this other girl.'

'What happened to her?'

'She was found out. Just by bad luck. A woman heard about her from a friend and came to see her. She recognised her immediately. She'd actually been a maid in this woman's house. Princess Caraboo was exposed as a fake.'

'So you think I've come here to do the same to you?'

'Yes.'

'Well, I haven't. You keep your secrets and I will keep mine. But this seems a risky ploy to me. If you're found out, Grimsdyke might become very unpleasant. I've heard he is mad.'

'So have I.'

'Then be careful. If he realises you are just pretending, having him on . . .'

'I have to take the risk. It's the only way I can think of to make any money, even a little, except on my back. And I'm not going to do that – not yet, at least. You're taking a risk, too, in a way. Going to India, getting out of here.'

'It's different for a girl.'

'It is very different for a girl. But I'm determined to succeed, unless I find someone rich I could love, who would marry me and take me away as his wife.'

'Perhaps Grimsdyke will.'

She shrugged, wrinkled her face. 'No. Not him. He's kind enough, but he's not for me. I could not live with him.'

'When he comes back, do I say I know you?'

'Of course not. Speak to me in Hindustani.'

'But you don't know Hindustani.'

'I picked up a few words from Karim Khan. Enough to have a very simple conversation. But don't *know* me at all, I beg of you.'

At that moment they both heard footsteps in the corridor. Grimsdyke came into the room.

'Ah,' he said to Mary Jane. 'Have you introduced yourself?'

She smiled at him. He turned to Ben.

'This young lady is a complete mystery. I believe she comes from the East, possibly the Spice Islands. Sumatra. We call her Miranda after a character in one of Shakespeare's plays who lived on an island and knew no one except her father.'

'She seems a very charming person,' said Ben.

'She is.'

Grimsdyke opened the door for her, pointed the way out. 'We have business to discuss,' he explained.

She looked at him, her face empty of all understanding, and smiled vacantly.

'Thank you,' she said slowly, as though searching for words and not finding the ones she wanted. 'Miranda says thank you.'

'You see?' said Grimsdyke expansively. 'I'm teaching her how to speak English. I'll make a lady of her yet.'

'That would be a more worthwhile achievement, sir, than going out and dying in India.'

'Exactly. Exactly. Well, I will make you my offer. I pay for your uniform, your accoutrements, your passage to Calcutta. And in addition I buy your commission as a lieutenant, whatever that may cost, and I'll give you fifteen hundred pounds in sovereigns. In your hand. What do you say to that?'

'I say, sir, that is a most generous offer. I am honoured to accept.'

Chapter Nine

King George Drummond came out of the Cavalier Inn on the front at Brighton and stood for a moment, savouring the warmth of sunshine reflected from the sea.

He had just eaten an extremely agreeable lunch: two dozen oysters, a very fine chop, a pint of claret, then an apple pie with thick cream, and he felt totally at ease with the world. It was good to be alive, and tomorrow it could be even better. The caravans had halted up on the Downs and would be there for three days. This was an unusually long stay anywhere, but if the weather held, everyone should make a very good profit for this time of year. And the weather looked like holding.

King Drummond was not a king, of course, nor had he been christened with that name. But he had heard how the great showman George Sanger became Lord, and followed his example. Sanger had been involved in a court case with the American 'Buffalo Bill' Cody. During the hearing, Cody had been continually referred to as the Honourable William Cody, a title acquired when he became a member of the Nebraska legislature.

'If that Yankee can be an Honourable, then I shall be a Lord,' said Sanger, and this title appeared on all his advertisements and on the sides of his wagons, which would stretch for two miles when on the road from one site to the next.

Drummond had considered adding Duke or Earl to his name, but finally decided to take the most prestigious title he could imagine, and had chosen King. He might not be a monarch, but on a day like this he felt like one.

He took out his clay pipe and tobacco pouch, rammed tobacco into the bowl, lit it, and then, hands in his trouser pockets, sauntered happily along the promenade.

A heavy tide was running and waves thundered on the shining shingle. A few fishing boats had been drawn up well beyond the reach of the tide, and fishermen sat on stools or old lobster pots, checking their nets. Drummond wondered vaguely what it would be like to depend on the sea for a living. Probably no worse, he thought, perhaps better, than depending on punters who continually wanted to pit their wits against a stallholder's ingenuity; or whose lives were so drab they had to titillate their dull minds by paying to see unfortunate human freaks – a man born without legs or arms, a woman with a red beard or three eyes.

Suddenly, he paused. Across the road he saw a girl from one of the booths. She'd left to better herself, so Ivan had told him. And now, miles away, he had found her; why, he had literally almost run into her.

'Mary Jane!' King Drummond called out excitedly.

At the totally unexpected sound of her name, Mary Jane turned towards him. Drummond saw fear and then horror chase disbelief from her face. She made as though to run away, and then paused. She had been discovered; escape was useless. She had to stay and brazen it out.

'I didn't expect to see you here,' he said, crossing the road, offering her his hand.

'I could say the same, Mr Drummond.'

'Ivan told me you'd gone. He was sorry to lose you. What are you doing here? Working?'

'In a sense, yes. And you? Where is the fair?'

'Up on the Downs.'

'I didn't know you came down to this part of the world?'

'This is our first time. We got an offer of cheap rent. A weekend with weather like this and we should do well. And you?'

'I hope the same,' she said carefully.

He fell into step beside her. 'Why did you run away?'

'I didn't. I told Ivan. I was getting nowhere, Mr Drummond. It's one thing to work on a tog stall when I'm a girl, but not when I'm an old woman.'

'That's a long way ahead of you yet, lass,' Drummond replied drily. He saw she was obviously ill at ease, and wanted to get away.

'I won't detain you, then,' he said. 'But good luck to you. And if ever you want a job, I can tell you Ivan's always got a place for you on the tog stall. He told me so himself.'

'Thank you – and him. I'll remember that.'

He paused, as though making up his mind about something.

'There's something I should tell you,' he said hesitantly. 'We've had the police to see us.'

'About what?'

'That business at Bostal Heath. The man in the rat pit. There was a charge of murder out.'

'Who are they looking for?'

'Some witness they've got hold of says he remembers a black man being in the pub. No one else, thanks be. That can only be Karim Khan. He was the only Indian in the fair. And this witness says a young fellow was helping him, called Ben. That could only be our Ben.

I believe there was a warrant out for both of them.'

'They're no more guilty than the rest of us. A lot less so, in fact.'

'I know. But when your face is black in a white country, it's remembered. Just as, if we were in India, our white faces would stand out. The whole business preyed on Ben's mind dreadfully, poor fellow. Very sad what happened to him, rest his soul.'

Drummond paused.

'What do you mean? I don't understand you.'

A week had passed since Mary Jane had seen Ben in Grimsdyke's house. What could have befallen him in that short time? Had his plan to go to India fallen through? Was he dead? Surely not?

'You don't read the newspapers?'

'No, I never see them.'

'Then you wouldn't know that when the fair was in Rochester, he and Karim Khan left. A day or so later, Ben's clothes were found on the beach at Tankerton, a seaside resort some miles away. He left a note which the newspaper printed. I fear he took his own life, poor fellow, when he heard the police were after him.'

'You are *certain* of this?'

'I saw it in print, my dear girl.'

Mary Jane shook her head in bewilderment. How could Ben be dead – drowned – when she had seen him and spoken to him only days before? For a moment she thought she would tell Drummond of their meeting, then decided against it. She knew Ben was still alive, but perhaps it was best if she kept this knowledge to herself – at least for the time being.

Mary Jane walked back to Grimsdyke's house pondering what Drummond had told her.

It was a big enough strain pretending she did not understand what people were saying, that she was a total stranger in her own country, without knowing that the circus was encamped only a couple of miles away, and that everyone in it would recognise her. And now Ben was reported dead after being sought on a charge of murder. What was happening to her world? She felt caught up in a tightening net of make-believe and horror.

Mary Jane walked along the edge of the sea for longer than she had intended, pondering on the problem. Then she turned back towards Grimsdyke's house.

As she went up the garden path, the front door opened and Grimsdyke came out. To her dismay, she saw he was talking to King Drummond. What could this possibly mean? How could Drummond know him? Again, it was too late to run. Grimsdyke had seen her and waved, and Drummond also saw her and waved, smiling in a surprised way.

'I didn't know you lived here,' he said as she approached.

'You know this young lady?' Grimsdyke asked him in surprise.

'I should do. She worked in the fair for me.'

'In the *fair*? I think you are mistaken, Mr Drummond, sir. She is a high-born lady from Sumatra. A princess.'

'A *princess*? Who says so? Does she?'

'Well, not in so many words. She's dumb. Can't speak, you see.'

'Can't *speak*? I saw her twenty minutes ago walking along the front and we had a chat. We were surprised to see each other.'

Grimsdyke turned to Mary Jane. 'Is this true?' he asked her hoarsely.

For a moment she thought of continuing the absurd charade. Then slowly, reluctantly, she nodded.

'Yes,' she admitted. 'I'm sorry. It is true. I have deceived you.'

'You've deceived more than me,' he said bitterly. 'You have also deliberately deceived and made fools of a number of distinguished people here who were absolutely certain you were who you seemed to be, a princess from the South Seas. But what is the meaning of this wicked and ridiculous deception? Simply to make us all appear fools? Did someone put you up to this?' He glanced angrily from King Drummond to Mary Jane and back again.

'Have I said something I shouldn't have?' asked Drummond, bewildered.

Mary Jane nodded. 'But it would have come out in the end,' she said. 'I have deceived this very generous man, but not, I swear, from any ill intention.'

'From what then?' asked Grimsdyke. 'You can't claim it was a *good* intention. You've made me a laughing stock to everyone in Brighton, probably in all Sussex. Come inside.' He turned to Drummond. 'And you too, sir. We cannot discuss this out here where people may hear us.'

'I'll go away,' said Mary Jane.

'You damn well will, girl. And maybe you'll go with a constable on either side of you. Were you trying to get into my house to find out where I kept valuables? Then to leave the door on the latch and let a thief come in?'

'No!' she cried. 'Nothing like that. I swear it.'

'I would not put much weight on your word now, or your oath.'

Grimsdyke shut the front door carefully, took them into the study, closed that door and turned the key in the lock.

'Now,' he said, 'no one can hear us. Tell me the truth. No more fiction. No more make-believe, or I'll

302

call the beadle immediately, and you'll do hard labour. That I can promise you. Dr Blake, who you have also deceived, is a magistrate, as you may recall. False pretences, claiming to be someone you are not. That can carry a heavy sentence. Now, speak. What is this about?'

'I will tell you everything. The truth. You can check it for yourself if you don't trust me, and I can't blame you if you doubt me. But this *is* true.

'My father deserted my mother. Our landlord had her put into Newgate because she could not pay a few shillings owed on the rent. I got a job and saved enough money to pay the debt. But when I went to the gaol to do this, so she could be released, my father had already turned up and she'd gone back to him. I had no idea where they were. Then I met someone who had a booth in Mr Drummond's fair. He gave me a job. I worked there for some months.

'One day I found an old newspaper on the ground and read an article in it about a girl who, years ago, appeared on the doorstep of a house in Gloucester. She couldn't speak a word of English, so it seemed, and no one knew who she was. When they showed her pictures of the South Sea Islands she appeared very excited, so they assumed she was a princess from one of them. They called her Princess Caraboo. People paid to meet her. She'd been a housemaid before.

'I thought if she could do this, so could I. It was my only hope of making any money, of getting out of this country, starting a new life, in a new world. That is the truth, sir. I have nothing else to say, except I'm sorry to have deceived so kind and generous a gentleman as you. And also your friends and neighbours.'

'They'll laugh at me because of this,' said Grimsdyke slowly. 'They'll never forget it or, worse, let me forget it.'

'Not necessarily, sir,' said Drummond. 'Since I am the unwitting cause of this exposure, might I propose a solution which I feel could be satisfactory to you?'

'And what is that, pray?'

'Mary Jane packs whatever belongings she may have and leaves here for ever. You tell your friends that out of the kindness of your heart, because you were so struck with the plight of this unfortunate young girl, you gave her some money. She showed her true character by disappearing. Unknown and uninvited, she arrived. Unknown, without even a farewell, she departed into the darkness from whence she came.'

'You think they will believe that?'

'It will be the truth, sir. There is no other explanation.'

'Well, I'm damned,' said Grimsdyke slowly. 'You may be right. But if I heard of this happening to someone else, I'd never credit it for a moment.'

'Truth, sir, is often hard to accept. But that, I suggest, is a quick and practical solution to the problem.'

Grimsdyke stood for a moment, pulling on his lower lip as he did when perplexed. The fellow Drummond might only be a fairground person, but he had a clever brain. He was sharp. He was also right. Why, he might actually turn this incident to his own advantage. Make a bit more mystery about it. Who really was Miranda? What had happened to her? Was she alive or dead?

And if he didn't follow Drummond's suggestion, what could he do? Have the girl arrested, committed? He'd have to give evidence, and he'd look a fool to have to admit being taken in so easily by some little chit. The vicar wouldn't like it either, or Dr Blake, or Mr Crosbie, or the retired missionary and all the other people who had come and nodded sagely as this girl smiled and pointed at pictures of savages in books. They would all look stupid, and they'd blame it on him. That was unthinkable.

'I'll do it,' he said. 'I have to believe your story, girl, strange as it sounds to me. I'm sorry you have chosen to deceive me. I felt that, in time, I could mould you into a real English lady. Maybe I was just being foolish, but I felt that if I liked you, you might also grow to like me. However, all such feelings are now at an end. I will give you some money to help you on your way; twenty sovereigns on the understanding that you leave tonight, after dark, when no one can see you. And that you never come back. I don't want the neighbours saying they've seen you walking along the road. I want you to go as you came, as Mr Drummond said, from the dark to the dark. Do I make myself clear?'

'Abundantly, sir.'

'Then go and pack. You can take the clothes I have bought for you.'

He crossed to a wall safe, unlocked it and took out a japanned tin box. He opened it and counted out twenty sovereigns. He gave them to Mary Jane. Then he put the box back and relocked the safe.

Mary Jane packed her belongings, put them in a bundle over her shoulder. She waited until evening, then let herself out of the door. At the end of the road, King George Drummond was waiting. She saw the glow of his pipe in the darkness before she recognised his voice.

'I'm sorry for spoiling the illusion,' he said.

'You didn't know you were. I should never have attempted it in the first place. It was madness. But what took you to his house, out of every other house in Brighton?'

'A very simple reason. He owns the field where the fair is camping. His brother up in Scotland wrote to him about us, said we paid promptly and cleared up when we left. He was glad to take a few pounds' rent from us. The richer they are, my girl, the keener they become to make more. I paid him half on arrival, the other half just now.'

They walked slowly along the road. The tide had ebbed and the waves were small and weakly phosphorescent under a half moon. In one of the big houses a string orchestra was playing; they must be holding a ball or a musical evening. Mary Jane felt a sudden longing to be back in Grimsdyke's house, with all the trappings of luxury: thick carpets, brocaded curtains, a fire behind a burnished brass fender, afternoon tea on a tray with finely cut sandwiches at the ring of a handbell. Now she was on the outside again – but with twenty sovereigns in her purse.

'Sure you don't want to see Ivan about coming back?' asked Drummond gently.

Mary Jane shook her head. 'No. He was kind to me. But if I go back, I'll be tempted to stay, and I really must go on. But where, I don't know.'

'You'll find a job in a big house.'

'Doing what?' she said. 'A scullery maid? A tweeny? No.'

'Then what do you have in mind?'

'To get out of this country, to try somewhere else. I'll follow the advertisements for families going abroad who want someone to help with a child. They usually offer a free passage. Perhaps I could marry someone in the colonies or do some sort of job I can't find here.'

'Such as what?'

'I don't know,' she admitted. 'I'll think about that when the time comes. First, I have to get a job that takes me overseas.' And before I do that, she added to herself, I must try to find my mother, if only to say farewell.

Mary Jane walked up the scrubbed steps of the rooming

house and pulled the bell handle. At that moment, the landlord came out of the door. He double-locked it behind him, looked at her enquiringly, and then recognised her.

'You?' he said, surprised.

'Yes. Me. I've written to my mother several times here but I've not had any reply.'

'Not surprising. She's not living here any more. You didn't think I'd have her and your father back, did you?'

'Have you an address for them?'

'Oh, yes. When your mother got out of Newgate and found somewhere else to live, she gave me her new address in case you turned up looking for her. It's taken you a while, though, hasn't it? But I never forward letters to old lodgers. If I did, I'd need to hire a clerk, they get so many – unpaid bills, mostly. She's living with your father down south London way, near Erith, on the Thames. Number 14, Quendon Terrace, as far as I remember. Now, I'm in a hurry.'

He brushed past Mary Jane into the street. She stood for a moment, irresolute. She should have come here as soon as she heard her mother had left Newgate, but something had prevented her. Was it because she felt deeply hurt that her mother had gone without leaving any sort of message for her? She did not care to think ill of her mother. Perhaps she had been in touch with Mrs Mentmore who had no address to give her? This seemed a plausible explanation. She wanted to believe it; she could not bear to think that her mother simply did not care where she was, not after all they had been through together.

Mary Jane walked along the pavement until she came to a bus stop and waited for a horse bus to Charing Cross Station. Here she booked a return ticket to Erith and when the train came in, took a seat in a

'Ladies Only' compartment. She did not like the idea of sitting in the usual Third Class carriage. A man might accost her; she felt she could not cope with that.

The train ran between rows of sooty terraces where the children played with hoops in cobbled cul-de-sacs. Smoke rested like a physical weight on grimy slate roofs. Gradually these small houses fell away. Fields grew between streets. They passed heathland on one side, and flat marshes that led to the Thames on the other. The name of Plumstead on a station platform recalled the riot on Bostal Heath and the Pig and Whistle public house. The train passed smaller country stations, with white wooden palings, and polished oil lamps above black and white name-plates: Abbey Wood, Belvedere, Erith.

A porter directed her to Quendon Terrace, a row of houses, each with a bow front, a little privet hedge, a narrow gravel path from the gate to the front door. The paths wound and curved deliberately to give the impression of being much longer that they were. She walked past Number 14 without looking at it, paused at Number 18, and then retraced her steps, went up the path of Number 14 and pulled the bell chain.

Through multi-coloured glass panes on the door, she saw a figure move in the hall. The door opened. Mary Jane stood staring at her mother face to face. Her mother fell back against the wall in amazement.

'*You?*' she said in total disbelief.

'Me. I've found you,' Mary Jane replied delightedly.

'Why have you come here?'

'Because I had to see you. I've written letters to you at the old address, but I've never had a reply, so I called. The landlord told me you were living here. Is Father in?'

Her mother glanced quickly down the street. 'No,' she said nervously. 'But he'll be back any minute. He's just slipped out to the shops for an ounce of tobacco. I can't talk to you here.'

'Why not? What's the matter?'

'Go down the road,' her mother told her. 'On the left you'll see another smaller road. Wait round that corner. I'll join you. But go *now*. Quickly!'

Mary Jane saw fear in her mother's eyes. Dread of something, or someone, had sharpened her voice. She looked much older, tired and defeated, in a way she had not seemed even in Newgate. But now she was free, back with her husband. What could the matter be?

Mary Jane waited round the corner. Her mother, with a veil down over her face, joined her. They fell into step, walking away from the terrace.

'I made some money,' Mary Jane explained. 'I came back to the prison to pay the debt, but you'd gone.'

'He came back.'

'My father?'

'My husband.'

'The same.'

'No,' her mother replied. 'Not the same.'

'I don't understand you.'

Her mother stopped and looked at her. 'Listen, child,' she said. 'He's not your father. But he married me. He thought he was your father. I cheated him. And he found out. That's why he used to go off from time to time. He didn't mind so much when he was sober, but the drink acted on him, made him think he'd been cheated, cuckolded, and he'd clear off.'

'Then who is my father?'

'I worked as a maid in a big house in Kent, Beechwood Hall. Your father was the son of the house. You're quality, if you like, at least on his side. He had his way with me. I thought he was fond of me. He told me it would be all right, but it wasn't. I had to find a husband quickly. So I found a man and let him have his way, too. Then I told him I was expecting. He thought he was the father and married me. Not willingly, but I have to give him fair, he did bring you up. And then he found out. After that, nothing was the same.

'We might have stayed out of Newgate if I'd allowed the landlord some favours. But I couldn't. Not after all the trouble I'd had already.'

'You should have told me before.'

'About this?'

'About everything.'

'I know – now. But it was not an easy subject to raise. I kept meaning to, and then lost my nerve. Anyhow, he's come back again. And this time, so he says, for good. On conditions.' She paused, looked behind her nervously. The street was empty.

'What are they?'

'That he doesn't keep you. That he has nothing whatever to do with you. That you stay out of our lives.'

'I can't go out of your life. You're my mother.'

'You'll have to stay out of his. For my sake. He's kept us both. He's done all he felt he could in his own way. I understand his feelings. And if I leave him now, how do I live? On the streets? One of Mrs Mentmore's lot? I'm too old for that, and in any case, that's no life, none at all. Just a degradation. I could sew, but my eyes aren't what they were, and you're only paid pennies for what sells for pounds in the West End shops. I'm sorry, Mary Jane, but I have no alternative. I can't see you. At least, not if he knows.'

'I know where you live. We can meet. I can write to you.'

'Don't. I never get any letters, nor does he. Who is there to write to us? He'd only be curious and open them and then where would I be?'

'I could write to you care of the post office.'

'No. I'd have to go in there every week, just in case there was a letter. Someone would wonder who I was expecting to hear from. They might tell him. No. But I know you're alive and you know I'm alive, and we know we love each other, although what I'm telling you now may make you think mine is a funny sort of love. But believe me, dear child, it's not. It's a mother's love. But to love, a mother has to survive. I'm surviving the only way I know. Where are you now, anyhow?'

'In lodgings.'

'What happened at Mrs Mentmore's?'

'Nothing – at least in the way you mean. She introduced an old man and he had a fit or something.'

'*On* you? You were having congress?' Her mother's horror sounded in her voice.

'No, fortunately. Just the thought of it, I suppose.'

'So what did you do?'

'Took some banknotes out of his wallet, told Mrs Mentmore, and ran away.'

'Did she come after you?'

'Not that I know of, I left a lot more money than I took. She was probably content with that.'

'That was stealing, Mary Jane.'

'Yes. But he hadn't paid me, nor had Mrs Mentmore. And I wanted to get you out of prison. I guessed I'd never have another chance like it. So I took the money.'

'You became a thief for my sake?'

'I suppose so.'

'You make me feel even worse.'

'Then don't, Mother. I understand your situation.'

'You're very forgiving, child.'

'Not really. I've learned to accept things, I suppose, if I can't alter them. And I can't alter this. But really I came to see you to say goodbye. I'm going away.'

'Where to?'

'I'm not sure yet. It depends where I can get a free passage. Australia, America, India, anywhere.'

'To do what?'

'Seek my fortune, I'd say if I was a man. But mainly to leave all my troubles behind. I know I've no special gifts. I just want to get enough money – I don't care how – so that I can never be at other people's mercy again. Not ever. Then have a pleasant life, perhaps a man who likes me, loves me, maybe children.'

'That's a dream we all want, not the nightmare most of us have to put up with.'

'I'll make it come true. Then, Mother, I promise you this. I'll find you wherever you are. There'll always be room for you with me. I owe your husband something, too, for keeping me. I can understand how he feels. It's pride, and men are much prouder than women.'

'May God bless you and keep you,' said her mother. She began to cry. 'Please go now,' she said through her tears. 'Don't say any more. I can't stand it.'

Quickly she put up her veil and kissed Mary Jane on the lips. Mary Jane tasted the saltiness of her mother's tears.

'I will pray for you every day of my life. May God keep you.'

She dropped the veil and turned, walked back up the road. Mary Jane watched her mother out of sight. She waited for a moment, hoping that her mother might have second thoughts, that she would come running towards her, that they could go away together, start a new life together. But her mother did not come back; she did not even look back.

Mary Jane walked to the station and caught the next train to London. Although she sat demurely in the corner seat of a compartment looking out of the window, watching as fields gave way to houses, although she looked outwardly calm, her mind was in turmoil. She *must* get out of this country. She must start somewhere else. It was easy to say that, but could she do it? Then she remembered that Ben had called her a philosopher, someone who thought things out. That was what she must do – and now.

She left the train at Charing Cross and, as in a dream, walked past Nelson's column, up the Mall towards Buckingham Palace. The royal standard fluttered from its mast on the roof. A small crowd had gathered around the black lacquered iron railings.

'What's happening?' she asked a woman pushing a child in a perambulator.

'Don't you know? Her Majesty is expecting her seventh child,' the woman informed her.

'Oh. I didn't know.'

The woman pursed her lips disapprovingly; how could any loyal subject of the Queen not be aware of this important moment?

Mary Jane stood near one of the sentries, looking through the railings at the vast courtyard spread with washed sea sand.

'What's that for?' she asked.

'It's to stop any noise from the iron wheels of the carriages,' the woman explained importantly. Who *could* this ignorant creature be? 'When the Queen is in labour, the sound might offend Her Majesty, upset her, even.'

'I see.'

Mary Jane stood, irresolute, one of the crowd; with no idea where she should go, what she should do. As she watched, a coach, glittering in maroon paint lined with gold and black, bearing on its doors a splendid crest of a unicorn and a double-headed wyvern above the motto *Ora et Labora*, Pray and Work, turned in at

313

the main gate. Polished iron tyres struck sparks on the gravel. A footman in the royal livery, with a white powdered wig, came down the palace steps, bowed low and opened the silver-handled door.

As he did so, one of the two footmen who had travelled standing rigidly at attention on small metal rests at the rear of the coach jumped down and saluted. A very small man stepped out of the coach, ignored them all and walked up the steps. He was the size of a manikin or a monkey, in morning dress. His top hat caught the glint of the morning sun, bright as burnished black metal.

'Who's he?' Mary Jane asked.

'Don't you know *anything*?' asked the other woman in disgust. 'You up from the country or something, are you? That's Lord Dalhousie. He was Governor General in India. Now he's retired. There's a new one out there, Lord Canning.'

'Oh. You know these people?'

'They're *gentry*. Course I don't *know* them, but I read about them. Don't you read the papers?'

'No, I don't,' admitted Mary Jane.

She turned away and walked slowly down the Mall. India. She'd heard of people who went to India and made fortunes; nabobs, they called them. It was warm there, not cold like in England; not empty, vast and unpopulated like Canada; and not quite so far away, on the other side of the world, right down under everything, like Australia.

India. It seemed the perfect compromise. She made up her mind. That was where she would go, somehow, soon.

Lord Dalhousie stood for a moment in the sunshine outside the palace doors. He was unconsciously comparing the sun's weak London warmth with the hammering heat to which he had grown so accustomed in his years in India.

He knew about the preparations for the imminent birth of the Queen's seventh baby; even the so-called serious newspapers, like *The Times* and *The Enquirer*, had published articles on the subject. Some of his colleagues had expressed surprise, and a few were impressed, that at such a time the Queen had personally expressed a wish to see him. Some considered it an honour that while she awaited the birth of a child she should grant him an audience to discuss the condition of a country thousands of miles away, which she had never visited, and never would visit. Dalhousie, like many physically small men, had an immense awareness of his own importance. He found nothing unusual in this situation. Indeed, it was his due; no more than that.

The vast size of the palace appealed to him. A thousand windows reflected the sunshine like so many heliographs. They opened on to six hundred rooms in a tasteless building surrounded by forty-five acres of garden, with a lake, in the centre of the capital of Empire. This was indeed a palace on a maharajah's scale.

He remembered the disapproval at the cost of building it – upwards of a quarter of a million pounds – but then some people always found fault with the plans of the great. Dalhousie also knew that when Queen Victoria had been enthroned, extraordinary deficiencies in the palace had been discovered. Dozens of doors and windows would not open; as many others would not close. Lavatories lacked any ventilation; drains stank continually, and chambermaids found that the architects had neglected to fit sinks on the floors with bedrooms.

To Dalhousie, however, this obverse side of grandeur

was of no significance, any more than the views of old India hands, who had found fault with his policies. The only thing that mattered was the outward view, how everything appeared.

That morning, two nurses, Mrs Lilly and Mrs Innocenti, had installed themselves in the palace. They had taken over a room where the birth would take place. In this, behind a decorated Chinese screen, they had set up a table on which stood a remarkable contrivance of metal barrels connected through brass valves to red rubber tubes and bladders. This was Dr James Young Simpson's anaesthetic machine.

Four years earlier, a smaller version, also designed by this Scottish physician, had produced its soothing, sleep-inducing vapour to ease the birth pains of the Queen's sixth child. Royal acceptance of such advanced medical research had immediately resulted in requests for similar treatment from mothers all over the country. Overnight, James Simpson, a poor, hard-working doctor, became fashionable and rich.

Next door to this room, a sitting room was ready for ministers of the Crown who would wait within earshot, but naturally not within sight, to assure themselves that the child which would be presented to them had actually been born to the Queen.

This tradition began in the late seventeenth century, when the ailing wife of King James II, all of whose children had died in infancy, gave premature birth to a son who miraculously survived. Caricaturists and others claimed that, in fact, this baby had died like the others. In his place another baby of the same age had been smuggled into the palace, concealed in a copper warming pan.

Such irrelevances did not really concern Dalhousie as he handed his white gloves to the royal butler. Two more footmen appeared, bowed deeply and then marched in step ahead of him along a corridor lined with marble busts of former kings, queens, princes. They paused outside the door of an anteroom to the audience chamber. Dalhousie entered.

The Prime Minister, Lord Palmerston, was already there and grunted a greeting. As one vain man noting the vanity of another, Dalhousie saw that Palmerston had dyed his whiskers to conceal their whiteness. The Prime Minister was in cheerful mood, and with reason; he had just won a general election by seventy-nine seats, the largest Government majority since the Reform Bill, twenty-five years earlier. The two men exchanged courteous but cold greetings. Neither held a very high opinion of the other.

'Thought you were going to be late,' said the Prime Minister. His house was in Piccadilly, just across the park; he was a very punctual man and always allowed himself exactly six minutes to walk to the palace.

Dalhousie took out his gold pocket watch, examined the face closely as though he had difficulty in reading the figures.

'It is eleven eleven precisely, Prime Minister,' he said. 'My audience is at eleven fifteen.'

Double doors at the far end of the room opened. A senior footman in livery, his highly polished buttons embossed with the royal arms glowing like liquid gold, bowed deeply to them both.

'My Lord. Prime Minister,' he said, looking from one to the other. 'Her Majesty will see you.'

A Gentleman of the Household appeared and led them down another corridor to the audience chamber. At the far end of the room, at least forty feet from the door, Queen Victoria sat on a throne decorated with gilded lions' heads. She seemed smaller than Dalhousie remembered from his last audience before he sailed for India. At thirty-seven, her face was puffy and unhealthy, the flesh soft and dull as suet. From the ceiling, gilded cherubs, painted by Cellini, soared against a sky of Circassian blue and watched them all with innocent eyes. The curtains were drawn across the windows so that the sunshine was only visible through gaps where the edges did not quite meet. There seemed something remote, unreal, almost unhealthy about the dimness. Fresh air did not reach this room often enough; it had the stale, flat atmosphere of a museum. Queen Victoria might have been a statue like those in the corridor, dressed and placed on this magnificent throne, a waxwork manipulated by others. The Prime Minister and Dalhousie went down on their right knees. The Queen motioned them to stand.

'My Lord Dalhousie, pray come forward,' she said. Her voice sounded thin, like the voice of a petulant child. 'And how did you leave our Indian enterprises?' she asked him.

Dalhousie waited for a moment before he replied; he had not expected such a direct question or so soon. Also, he had hoped he might have had a private audience, without the Prime Minister listening. How should he reply?

He realised that his time was strictly limited. The Queen's mind was clearly preoccupied with the imminent birth of her baby, not with what some of her more commercially minded subjects might be doing in a country ten thousand miles away. This was not the moment to give any considered opinion about the Company's future in India. Nothing he might say now could alter anything in India, but it could affect the Queen's view of him. This, surely, was a time to be confident, to assure her that all was well in Hindustan. Bearers of unwelcome news were never highly regarded.

'Your Majesty,' he began ponderously, 'there are

many complexities in India, as there are many religions and castes among the people of that country. But, if I were asked to prophesy, I would say that this year will be a year of unparalleled peace, prosperity and good will to Your Majesty throughout the length and breadth of all India.'

The Queen inclined her head to show her approval. Palmerston nodded more vigorously. This little fellow Dalhousie might not be very impressive to look at, but he certainly had a clever head on his shoulders. He might not have been a great success as a Governor General either – some went so far as to say his policies were disruptive and ill-conceived. Even so, no one could deny the man's tact and his ability to give the sort of answer his sovereign wanted. Whatever else he lacked, Dalhousie did have the makings of a damned good courtier.

Chapter Ten

As Lord Dalhousie was giving Queen Victoria his optimistic and confident assessment of the future in India, two men in Peshawar, near the Indian frontier with Afghanistan, were taking a rather more sombre view.

One was John Nicholson, the Deputy Commissioner. The other was Gulab Singh, the Maharajah of Jammu, a part of Kashmir, an area of lakes and rivers and snow-capped mountains to the north of India. Both men were of heavy build, broad-shouldered, black-bearded, and in their early thirties.

They sat in cane chairs, feet stretched out on a thick, locally woven carpet. On a table, candles in hammered silver holders cast a mellow, flickering light on their grave faces. Outside the window, beyond the compound's whitewashed wall, mountains across the border loomed blue and empty under a half moon. The air in the room felt thick with wood smoke, for the fire had burned low. The only sounds were an occasional crackle as another log collapsed, and the whir of unseen crickets and cicadas. In the distance, somewhere out of sight, a chained guard dog barked a warning, and a child was crying in the direction of the bazaar.

Gulab Singh was a Sikh. The Sikhs were originally a minor religious sect whose founder, born a Hindu, had preached a faith drawn partly from Hinduism, partly from Islam. Soon they became one of India's most powerful and warlike communities. Every Sikh male child was trained to arms. When he grew to manhood he swore an oath never to shave, never to cut his hair, but to carry a comb in it, to wear a knife in his belt, and always to keep his body clean as a sword blade.

Twice the Sikhs had fought the British, and twice they had been defeated. In what was already called in school history books the Second Sikh War, Gulab Singh had led his people, while Nicholson had fought on the side of John Company. The war had ended without bitterness; it could almost have been a huge sporting contest waged by opposing armies in place of teams.

Sikhs and British admired the same manly virtues: courage, chivalry, honour. The Sikhs also admired Nicholson personally, because to them he embodied all these qualities, and another, rarer in Englishmen in India: a total indifference to acquiring wealth. Some even believed he must be a reincarnated Indian god, and formed their own small sect to worship him.

When Nicholson heard of this – which he regarded as blasphemy – he ordered the men concerned to be flogged, an instant and typical reaction which the Sikhs understood and which made them admire him all the more.

To Nicholson, evil was a potent force; the Devil was everywhere deliberately undoing the work of good men. As a boy, his mother came into the nursery one day and found him waving a knotted handkerchief, pretending that it was a sword.

'I'm trying to get a blow at the Devil,' he explained to her seriously. 'If I could get him down I would kill him.'

He hated inefficiency, corruption, unfairness, and

was ruthless in rooting out such practices and punishing those involved. As a result, in a corrupt and unfair world, where promotion went too often to the candidate with the deepest pocket, he had few close friends.

Nicholson had joined the Company army when he was seventeen, without private money and without any hope of family wealth or inheritance. He learned native dialects and studied Indian history, which seemed poor preparation for his first posting to Meerut, forty miles from Delhi, the site of the Company's biggest arsenal. Here, weapons of war, muskets and mortars, shells, grenades, rockets were stored by the thousand. And here the Company's officers enjoyed one of the most splendid messes in India.

Meerut was renowned for the excellence of its social life, with amateur dramatics and regular musical evenings, and balls to which hundreds of guests were invited. Meerut was not a posting sought by impecunious officers who could not afford to spend four or five times their army pay on horses or lose as much in a single game of cards. Unscrupulous and dishonest Indian servants, however, welcomed the constant opportunities of theft from officers so rich that they were careless of their possessions.

On Nicholson's first night in Meerut, a servant, realising he was new to the country, absconded with a set of silver spoons and forks and knives Nicholson had brought out from England. This was a serious loss to the young man, and worse was soon to come. When he was posted up-country, another thief with a sharp knife cut a hole in his tent and through it removed his dressing case, his pistols, and all the spare cash he possessed. Nicholson reported both incidents to his commanding officer who could not understand the newcomer's concern. Goods worth only a hundred pounds or so were at stake. What was such a petty sum among gentlemen?

'It means a great deal to me, sir,' Nicholson explained.

'In that case, I think you'd better go on detachment where you will be able to save some money and so recoup your losses,' the colonel told him shortly. Best be rid of the fellow.

Next day, Nicholson was posted off with a corporal and half a dozen *sowars*, cavalrymen, on a pointless political mission to the frontier. The colonel still felt irritated by his attitude, and did not give him provisions for his journey, as was the custom. Instead, Nicholson carried a letter from the British political agent to show to the head men of the villages through which he would pass. The letter asked them to provide Nicholson with food, and assured them this would be paid for on delivery.

The political agent was a weak, drunken old man whom the head men had held in contempt for years. The first head man read the letter, then spat on the ground contemptuously and laughed at the request it contained.

'I see nothing funny in this,' Nicholson told him in the man's own language. 'You provide the food and I will pay you a fair price at once. And you will bring it to me *now*.'

'And if I don't?' the head man asked him. 'What will you do to me?'

'I will flog you myself,' replied Nicholson quietly. 'And then I will personally flog every male in your household. In the meantime, I will count to three, so you have time to consider your decision. *One*.'

As he spoke, his *sowars* dismounted and stood by their horses. The head man looked at them, then back at Nicholson. He was a tall fellow, this one; he had

324

hard eyes. He also spoke his language, and he
just mean what he said. It could be humiliating if
put this possibility to the test and lost.

'*Two*.'

Nicholson held out his hand. His corporal passed
him a horsewhip. The oiled leather cracked in the air
like a pistol shot.

'I will bring you the food,' said the head man quickly.
'There is no need for us to fall out. I mean no disre-
spect. You understand me?'

'Perfectly,' Nicholson replied. 'I think that now you
also understand me.'

News of this spread from village to village; Nicholson
had no further trouble on his journey. By the time he
returned to his regiment the colonel had also heard of
the incident and used the knowledge as an excuse to be
rid of him; Nicholson was posted almost immediately to
political duties.

During the Second Sikh War, he fell ill with fever.
His colonel, coming into his tent, found him suffering
from a high temperature.

'Had you been fit, Nicholson,' the colonel said sor-
rowfully, 'I would have wished you to secure Attock.
But in your condition that is obviously quite out of the
question.'

Attock was a fortress fifty miles away, held by a
huge detachment of Sikhs. It was a staging post on the
immensely important Grand Trunk Road that linked
Peshawar to Ferozepore and Delhi, and on to the holy
city of Benares. With Attock in Sikh hands, the road
could be blocked indefinitely.

'I will go, sir,' Nicholson replied, and, in spite of his
fever, set off at once with sixty Pathan horsemen and
twice as many infantry sepoys. He realised that he must
take the fort before the Sikhs could reinforce their
garrison; then it would be impregnable.

He rode so quickly that thirty of his horsemen dropped out, their horses lame. By the time Nicholson, with thirty weary Pathans, crossed the Indus River, his infantry detachment had fallen so far behind him it was still sixteen hours' march away. Nicholson knew he could not wait for them to arrive; his approach had already been observed. He could not possibly go back, he must go forward.

He saw that the main gate of the fort was still open and led his men at a gallop to it before the Sikhs could close it. The defenders instantly capitulated. They imagined that this must be an advance part of a huge avenging army that would speedily overwhelm them and put them all to the sword. So Attock fell without a shot being fired, and without a single casualty on either side.

Nicholson, looking across the room at Gulab Singh, remembered that moment; so did the Maharajah.

'You have heard rumours?' Nicholson asked him.

'I have heard the British are out of touch with events.'

'What events, exactly?' Nicholson asked, although he knew quite well what his companion meant.

'There are many,' said Gulab Singh. 'First, there is the grave matter of the kingdom of Oudh.'

Nicholson nodded agreement. Lord Dalhousie, as Governor General, had annexed Oudh, a kingdom about the size of Scotland, between Nepal and the north-west frontier. Its ruler had been corrupt and a tyrant for years, but the East India Company recruited in Oudh for their Bengal and Bombay armies. As a result, sepoys' families in Oudh enjoyed important privileges. In any dispute, their status had assured them of justice, not biased judgments invariably favouring the litigant who had given the biggest bribe to the judge.

'Soothsayers foretell the future. They smell blood in the air.'

'Blood?'

'It is a symbol. From village to village, chapattis, dyed red to symbolise blood, have been passed from head man to head man. The sepoys seem on edge, as though they're waiting for a sign.'

'To do what?'

Gulab Singh shrugged. 'Make trouble. There's a rumour that the flour used in their food is mixed with the bones of unclean beasts. An attempt by the British, they say, to undermine the caste system. In Lucknow, apparently, the surgeon in a regiment tasted a bottle of medicine before he gave it to a Brahmin – another attempt to break down caste. So what did they do? They burned down the MO's bungalow. Lucky he wasn't in it.'

'I've just been reading an intelligence report from the artillery station in Dumdum, outside Calcutta,' said Nicholson. 'A *classie*, a low-caste workman, asked a high-caste sepoy in the Second Native Grenadiers to let him have a drink of water from his *lotah*, his drinking vessel. Of course the Brahmin refused. He would be defiled if such a low-caste man touched it. The *classie* got angry. "You're very particular about your caste today," he said. "But you don't mind biting cartridges greased with pig lard, cow fat, anything. Isn't that unclean, too?" '

'I have heard the same story, Nicholson sahib. And your regimental officers, they're not what they were. You know that. We both do.'

Nicholson nodded. The aim now of many young officers was to be posted to the staff. This might only put them in charge of a remount depot in some obscure station, but that was better than rising at dawn to inspect ammunition pouches, shakos and crossbelts of a new intake of recruits and then spending the rest of the day wondering how long this dull inertia would continue.

Most of the army's senior officers were very old. Many regimental officers were incapacitated by drink or gout or indolence. They had bought their commissions and their promotion to colonel, the highest rank that could be bought and sold. And now all that awaited them, day after day, year after year, was routine inspections until retirement and death brought final oblivion.

'In the background, sahib,' said the Maharajah, 'there has always been the feeling of Britain's great strength. The British were never heavyhanded, or only very rarely so, otherwise they could not have ruled this country. Forty-five thousand English troops here with possibly another two hundred and fifty thousand Indian sepoys controlling *millions* of Indians. There is only one soldier, either Indian or British, to every six hundred civilians. Not a very good ratio if there should be trouble.'

'But why should there be trouble?'

'A combination of all these reasons, sahib. Oudh is the largest surviving Muslim state in northern India, and they feel insulted. Britain has also offended the Hindus. Brahmins fear that their supremacy is threatened. The electric telegraph, the railways, steam ships all bring changes. And people do not like changes if their ancient privileges are threatened.

'The Company, doubtless with the best intentions, has outlawed two ancient Hindu practices: thuggee and suttee. They have also stopped parents killing unwanted baby girls. But this was intended to keep constant the number of boys to girls, a very important matter in an agricultural country like India.'

'I know,' agreed Nicholson. 'But what fair-minded

person could back such disgusting practices?'

The Thugs were fanatical Hindus who worshipped Kali, the goddess of death and destruction. They held it as their sacred duty, in honour of Kali, to strangle with a scarf travellers on lonely roads. Suttee was a custom by which Hindu widows were forced to throw themselves upon the funeral pyres of their dead husbands and perish in agony in the flames.

'I personally agree with you,' said Gulab Singh. 'But, to the mass of Hindus the customs are important – or their leaders say they are. In addition, your Christian missionaries arrive here in ever increasing numbers. People fear that their religions are under threat, that soon they will be forcibly converted to Christianity. British officers have marched Hindus and Muslims to their churches and compelled them to sit through Christian services. They may mean well. But it is said in your country, Nicholson, that the road to Hell is paved with good intentions. Not all your countrymen view our customs, our religious ordinances, with the sympathy you show, Nicholson.

'But the Indians are not against the British as people. We in India are volatile and quick to anger. But our temper cools as quickly as a horseshoe dipped in water by a blacksmith. Why, only the other week, one of my favourite cooks attempted to poison me. *Me!* His guru, his Maharajah!'

'What action did you take? A merciful one, I trust, in view of your comments?'

'There is a time for mercy, Nicholson, and a time to warn others not to overstep the limits of prudence. I had to make a public example of him, or else others might try to succeed where, fortunately for me, he failed. I ordered my guards to take him out instantly and separate his skin from his skull, all the hair from behind his neck to his throat.'

'I hope he died quickly.'

'Oh, my dear fellow, no. He lived for weeks.' Gulab Singh slapped his thighs and sat back in his chair, laughing at the memory.

'And I tell you this. No other cook of mine will ever try to poison me in future.

'This is a cruel country,' he went on more seriously. 'You know that, while others do not, or forget what they knew. Fierce heat burns the land like fire. Storms and rain wash away entire towns and villages. Pestilence and plague kill hundreds of thousands. This is not a small country, like yours. You look at me with disapproval, but I remember that you can also act with speed and fierceness. Remember the time when you were in your garden with only one sentry at the gate? Some madman came running in, waving a sword and shouting he would kill you. You seized the sentry's musket and presented it to the madman's chest and ordered him to drop his sword or die. He lunged at you, so you shot and killed him, point blank. Everyone on the frontier knows how you reported this to the Chief Commissioner. "Sir," you wrote. "I have the honour to inform you that I have just shot a man who came to kill me. Your obedient servant, John Nicholson." ' Again, Gulab Singh roared with laughter. 'As I say, there is a time for mercy and a time for action. This present time, my friend, is one when all of us who wish for peace in this land must act.'

'But how, when there are so many who do not understand this country?'

'That, my friend, is a question to which time will, I hope, provide the answer.' The Maharajah stood up. 'It is late,' he said. 'I will leave you.'

They shook hands. Gulab Singh went outside. An orderly, squatting out of the moonlight against a wall, stood up and brought him his horse.

Nicholson looked out at the mountains beyond the wall. As the Maharajah had said, it was late. Did he mean simply the hour, or did he mean that the time for action was also very limited?

A constant procession was passing by the house, shadowy, soundless: men carrying swords or rifles or staves, or large burdens of indefinite shape. Their feet made no sound as they moved through the dust. Nicholson wondered who they were, where they were going, and why. There seemed something ominous in their silent progress. But Peshawar was a frontier town in which it was unwise to ask direct questions of travellers about their destinations or their intentions.

Nicholson turned on his heel, walked into the house, blew out the candles and went into his bedroom. As always, he knelt down by his narrow bed and prayed. Tonight, he prayed that the catastrophe he felt looming over India could somehow be avoided. He prayed for understanding among Indians and British alike. He prayed for guidance should the worst befall, and courage to act even if others held back. Then he climbed into bed. Within minutes, he was asleep.

A hundred days out from England, Ben, standing on the upper deck in the morning sunshine, heard a faint flutter of wings above his head. A sailor nodded briefly at the birds alighting in the rigging.

'Swallows,' he explained. 'We're coming near land. Within a week we'll take the pilot aboard, and in another three days we'll be in Calcutta.'

'Its been a long voyage,' said Ben.

'It has that. But safe. Many's the time we've lost all our rigging in a storm, and half the passengers, too, when waves smashed the glass in the portholes and flooded their cabins. It's been very quiet, in my reckoning.'

Three months at sea, thought Ben, and not one day had been as he had imagined. He had bought cabin space for the voyage. When he reached Calcutta, he had to find someone who would buy the cabin from him for the homeward voyage.

Families coming out adapted their cabins to their own special needs. They installed cupboards, put up bookshelves, bolted tables and chairs to the floor to stop them moving with the roll of the ship. Many had brought with them pet dogs and cats, and cages of singing birds. A cavalry captain returning to his regiment brought eighty-four hounds for a pack he was establishing. On the afterdeck, cows gave milk for babies. Sheep, pigs, chickens, ducks, geese stood in pens waiting to be killed for food. To add to the noise of these imprisoned beasts and birds, there had been a constant cacophony of pianos. Twelve passengers had brought their own pianos and for several hours each day they practised scales. In the evening, they organised sing-songs in their cabins, with hymns on Sundays. Others with an interest in music joined in with guitars, violins, trumpets.

Food was dull and repetitious: salt beef, followed by suet puddings and custard, then dried fruit. Drinking water mixed with lime juice was stored in barrels lashed on deck. During the voyage two women gave birth; a young man was washed overboard in a storm off the Cape of Good Hope; a girl died of an unknown fever.

As the ship came slowly up the Hooghly River, past Garden Beach, Indians paddled alongside in canoes, shouting their wares, tamarinds, coconuts, eggs. Down in the holds sailors were making extra money by hammering together rough crates in which the more fragile belongings of the passengers – plates, glasses, china jugs – could be carried ashore.

Ben leaned on the wooden rail, warm through the

thin sleeves of his shirt, and watched the shoreline pass slowly by. At intervals, trees had been cut down and lawns planted around splendid houses with white pillars and porticoes. On the other bank of the river lay the Botanical Gardens and the Bishop's College and, ahead, the harbour and the white palaces of the nabobs. He had never seen such outward manifestations of great wealth. The hot, harsh sunshine made them stand out from the drab background of warehouses and godowns. It flashed a message from rows of glass windows. The message was always the same, repeated from house to house: I am rich, very, very rich.

Ben felt a thrill of pride that he should belong to the same country as these merchants who, only a few years earlier, unknown and often from poor backgrounds, had also sailed East, risked their lives in hazards of all kinds, from fevers to the knives of envious rivals, and made their fortunes.

These palaces were magnificent proof that this could be done. But although he admired their perseverance, he did not envy them their success. He would make his own way in the army. He might never become wealthy, but at least he would carry on his father's career. Maybe he could rise to heights denied to his father. If he could, he would not be doing this just for himself, but for his father who did not have his opportunities.

As he watched, he saw what appeared to be a long, brown log, floating downstream on the yellow current. On it squatted half a dozen kite hawks, sated with food and apparently dozing, with their beaks tucked beneath their wings. Then he realised that this was not a log, but the body of a native. Death, unknown and often terrible, was the obverse of the success exemplified by the proud mansions. He knew from Dr Kintyre how many more venturers had died of fever, plague, dysentery, or by more violent means, than the relative few who had survived to live in such style and state.

Anchor chains rang out with a roar of rusty links; the ship swung and half turned as the tide took her. Small boats were already putting out from the shore. In one, fluttering from the stern, he recognised the flag of the regiment he was coming to join. An officer about his own age stood in the bows, holding on to a varnished roofed section supported by four posts.

'Mr Bannerman!' he shouted. 'Mr Bannerman!'

'Here!' Ben called down.

The officer turned to four Indians crouched in the stern, gave them an order. They climbed up a rope ladder on to the deck. Ben went out to meet them.

'You have come for my baggage?' he asked in Hindustani. They looked at him in surprise. No British officer spoke their language well; most only understood a few basic words of command. Puzzled, they bowed acknowledgement. He took them to his cabin. They manhandled out his crates, climbed down the ladder, boarded the boat.

'Ben Bannerman,' he said to the officer, who had lit a long, thin cheroot.

'Bruce Deakin,' the other replied. They shook hands. 'Did I hear you speak their lingo?'

'Yes,' Ben admitted. 'I was born out here.'

'I would be quiet about that if I were you.'

'Why? My father was in the army.'

'Was?'

'Yes. He was killed in the retreat from Kabul.'

'Oh. A long time ago,' said Deakin without interest. 'That all your kit?'

'Yes.'

'Well, if you can speak the lingo, get these fellows

rowing. They're a sullen lot. This is the only boat I could find. They pretend they don't speak a word of English. Bloody liars, of course. They understand it as well as you and I.'

Ben addressed the oarsmen. They bent obediently to their task. The clumsy, creaking boat, scummy water swilling in her bilge, headed for the jetty.

Deakin explained that the regiment was encamped sixteen miles north of Calcutta in Barrackpore. They would ride there directly; baggage would be brought on by bullock cart.

'How long have you been out here?' Ben asked him.

'Couple of years. Not a bad life. Very good, in fact. You know the colonel?'

'No,' said Ben.

'He's my uncle,' Deakin explained.

'That could be useful.'

'As a matter of fact, we were expecting someone else, name of Grimsdyke.'

'I took his place,' said Ben.

'That must have cost something.'

'Only money,' said Ben, not wishing to elaborate. He did not want to admit he lacked private means.

'That's what I say,' said Deakin. 'Only money. And as long as there are other poor buggers to make it for you, life can be very good.'

'Anyone in the regiment speak the language well?'

''Course not. We have interpreters.'

'But how do you know what the men are saying or thinking? You only know what the interpreters care to tell you.'

'Agreed. But the system has worked like this for years. The sepoys are content. They have enough rice, a place to sleep, uniforms provided, pay every week.'

'I suppose you're right. But I would have thought it would help if officers could converse with them direct, not through an interpreter.'

'Well, you're wrong. What have we to talk to them about? Their ways are not ours, you know.'

Ben nodded. 'Any British regiments out here?' he asked, changing the subject.

'Oh, yes. One right next to us. The Golds. You'll meet the officers. A good crowd. Except for the CO. Dick Street is not quite – well, you know.'

'No, I don't know.'

'Oh. Well, you'll soon pick up what's what, and who's who. He has no money. Worked his way up, or pulled himself up by his bootstraps.'

'How, exactly?'

'By learning local languages, for one thing. When there wasn't any interpreter around, he would translate. And by reading every damn book he could find about past campaigns, how they were won, or lost. He made himself so knowledgeable that finally he was promoted on merit, not by purchase. That didn't make him too popular with our crowd, I can tell you.'

'Why not?'

'He and my uncle are both colonels, both level-pegging for promotion to brigadier. My uncle's got enough money to buy anything he wants, but unfortunately for him, lieutenant colonel is the highest rank offered for sale. Promotion to colonel follows automatically. But if he's promoted again, he loses his original investment because he can't sell it on. That would mean as much as twelve thousand pounds gone, while someone like Dick Street in the Golds wouldn't lose a penny piece because he hasn't spent anything on his promotion. Unfair, really, From a gentleman's point of view.'

'How long has your uncle been out here?' asked Ben.

'Over twenty years. By his own choice, of course.

Men serve ten years here, minimum. Usually a lot more. Sometimes they never go home. They get involved with native women, make their homes here. It's a better life than labouring in the shires, or no job at all.'

'I can see that. And the officers?'

'Most do go home, eventually. But they also like it here. So many servants. Such a good standard of living. One or two go *pagal* – mad – or native. They become mixed up with heathen religions. Most of the bachelors have Indian mistresses, anyhow, and I suppose if the women make a convert they believe they are guaranteed a place in Paradise. Rather like recruiting sergeants. The more they can bring in, the better they are regarded.'

For a time they rode in silence along the dusty track to Barrackpore. Nothing seemed quite as Ben had remembered it; the bright clear colours of childhood seemed to have faded. He did not remember so much dust, which now hung like an abrasive cloud above them, or the shrivelled shrubs, the dry, parched grass. And had there been so many wretched mud-hut villages, where young women carried burnished metal water pots on their heads, and old women, toothless and wrinkled, crouched over cooking fires of cow dung? He remembered a world of bright peacock colours, not dust and poverty under a burning sun.

Had he been wise to come back? Perhaps he was the one who had changed.

As Ben dismounted at regimental headquarters, an Indian came towards him from behind a clump of bushes and salaamed. He wore a white *dhoti* and a European jacket and held up a leather bag.

'I can give you money, sahib,' he said. 'As much money as you need. It will be my pleasure.'

'Don't touch that,' warned Deakin. 'If you get in the

hands of the *banyars*, you'll never be free. The interest can be exorbitant. I have known many good fellows ruined by having to pay it. As a matter of fact, an officer shot himself here only last week. Captain Jackson.'

'Not from me was the captain borrowing, sahib,' the Indian assured him earnestly. 'He was involving with *budmarsh*, bad man, sahib.'

'Get out!' Deakin told him contemptuously. 'Bugger off!'

'Salaam, sahib. I am just now quickly going.'

As they walked past the moneylender towards the mess, Ben turned. The man was standing where they had left him, watching them. Then he spat in the dust and walked away.

'He didn't seem too bad a fellow,' said Ben. 'But you certainly put his nose out of joint.'

Deakin shrugged. 'He asked for it,' he said shortly. 'Trouble is, we have some officers here who really can't afford to be in the regiment. There's one fellow, Ritchie, a major, been turned down for command for the umpteenth time, who can barely afford to buy a drink. Claims he has a bad stomach, so he only drinks water. Fact is, the poor devil probably can't afford anything else. How could a man like that possibly hope for command?'

'Is he a good officer?' asked Ben.

'What is "good"? You have to belong, be accepted. If you're worrying about money all the time you can't keep your mind on soldiering. He's competent in his way. But, rather like Street of the Golds, he's not, well, not one of us as far as means are concerned. I think he has quite a good background otherwise.'

Ben's quarters consisted of two rooms. In one was a narrow wooden bed with a rope mattress, a couple of easy chairs, a Kashmiri carpet on the stone floor, a desk with an oil lamp. In the next room, a tin bath hung from a nail on the wall. On a wooden table was a tin basin, a soap dish, a jug of yellowish water. A discoloured mirror was nailed to the wall above the basin. Behind the door hung two hogskins filled with water. The black hides glistened, as though varnished. Outside, through a back door, was a latrine. Behind the building, the plain stretched to infinity, shimmering in the sun like a hot-plate on a stove.

As Ben stood, breathing the hot, dusty air, bitter with wood smoke from cook-house fires, while vultures and kite hawks wheeled and turned hopefully in the sky, it seemed momentarily as though this empty plain had suddenly filled with marching men. They were moving slowly, inexorably, in a seemingly endless dark tide, towards the mess building. Ben closed his eyes and the sun blazed, red and angry, on his tired eyelids. When he opened them, the plain was empty again. But would it always be? He felt a vague, unfocused unease, just as he had experienced at Karim Khan's booth before the constables moved in to break up a riot that was not a riot.

He heard a slight movement behind him and turned. An Indian servant stood in the doorway. He wore white trousers, a long white jacket with a red and green striped belt. In the *pugri* on his head a brightly polished brass regimental badge shone like a captive star. He bowed and salaamed.

'I am Mohammed Shah, your bearer, sahib,' he said.

Ben held out his hand. For a moment, the Indian looked at him in surprise; officers did not usually shake hands with servants. Then he shook it. Ben spoke to him in Hindustani. The bearer's surprise increased.

'You speak our language, sahib?'

'I was born on the way from Kabul, and brought up here in Barrackpore only a mile or two away. And in

339

England I worked with an Indian. I speak a little of your language, yes. Can you speak mine?'

'Also a little, sahib.'

'Then perhaps we can teach each other to speak it better.'

By now, the bullock carts with Ben's baggage had arrived. Mohammed Shah supervised the unloading, opened the crates and cabin trunks, put away Ben's uniforms. Ben ate early in the mess, and alone; the other officers, including Deakin, were dining out in the Golds' mess.

Next morning, he appeared before the colonel. He had not expected Colonel Deakin to look so old. He had drunk too much claret in a hot climate for too long, and it showed in his face, flushed, puffy, unhealthy. There was a theory, to which the colonel subscribed, that claret was as much medicine as wine, that it fought all manner of tropical diseases, kept down fevers. Ben remembered Dr Kintyre once telling him about this. The doctor did not accept the opinion; there was overwhelming evidence that too much eventually affected the drinker's liver. Claret could kill as effectively as dysentery or malaria.

Colonel Deakin regarded Ben through narrowed, suspicious eyes. 'I understand you have taken the place of Mr Grimsdyke. You have held a commission for long?'

'No, sir. I bought it just before I sailed.'

'I see. Then you'll have a lot to learn about the army and about life out here generally.'

'I look forward to learning as much as I can, sir.'

'Doubtless. We have our traditions here. Your brother officers will tell you about them. I understand you speak the native language?'

'A little, sir. Yes. How did you know?'

'My nephew Bruce told me. And someone else heard

you talking to your bearer last night.'

'I learned it as a boy out here, sir.'

'Then you should forget it. Indians of all castes and classes and creeds learn *our* language. We do not learn theirs. That sort of thing leads to familiarity. Familiarity invariably leads to contempt, and who can say where that might end.'

'I would not have thought that if we can speak to them in their own tongue they would become contemptuous of us because of our ability, sir.'

'I don't give a damn about your thoughts on the matter. If you wish to succeed in this regiment, you will follow what I say. The colonel's wish is always interpreted as an order. A direct order. Do I make myself clear?'

'Perfectly, sir.'

'Right. A few thousand British-born officers and administrators keep India peaceful and the East India Company prosperous. The two aims are wholly complementary. We could not do this, obviously, without the respect of the native population, numbering three or four hundred million. They could rise up and wipe us all out within minutes if they chose. But they do not choose, any more than the elephant chooses to crush his *mahout* to death. He could do that just as easily, just as quickly, but he does not.

'You know why? Because he respects him. He fears his ability to strike back. Even if an elephant killed one *mahout*, as sometimes happens, others would instantly avenge the death. The elephant knows this. So do the Indians, as far as we are concerned. But it is a delicate, sometimes knife-edge situation. A balancing act more crucial than anything you will ever see in a circus. To keep the balance, we must eschew unnecessary familiarity with Indians. I make myself clear?'

'Yes, sir.'

'Good.' The colonel opened a buff folder on his desk. 'I have your particulars here. You are the son of a lieutenant, killed in Afghanistan, aged thirty-eight?'

'Yes, sir.'

'He had no private means, presumably, or he would at least have been a captain. Am I right?'

'You may well be, sir. I cannot say. My mother died shortly after my father.'

'I see,' said the colonel. 'So who brought you up?'

'A friend of my father's, sir, a surgeon with the East India Company. Dr Douglas Kintyre.'

'Kintyre. That name is in some way familiar, Bannerman. Why should I know it?'

'He was the only adult survivor of the retreat, sir. He brought me out literally on his back.'

'Of course. I remember him now. As a matter of fact, I interviewed him in this very office. Does he know you're joining this regiment?'

'No, sir. He does not even know where I am. I left home to make my own way. I did not tell him where I was going, what I was going to do. I will, of course, write to him when I have settled in.'

'He is still practising medicine?'

'Yes, sir. In Scotland.'

The colonel paused. How extraordinary that this young man should have been the baby boy brought out from the Kabul disaster. Of course he remembered Dr Kintyre very well. There had been some doubt about him, hadn't there, about the curious way in which he'd acquired someone else's horse and ridden to safety? He'd never heard anyone else cast doubt on the surgeon except his contemporary, the colonel in Jalalabad. And he was dead, years ago. Dropsy, as far as he recalled. Another name for drink. He'd taken to the bottle because he thought he should have done better in the service than he had.

Well, he was not alone in that, thought Deakin grimly. He should have done better himself. But he could not buy any further promotion and whenever a vacancy occurred, the next officer in seniority did not of necessity take his place. That could go to someone else, quite different, on any pretext. Damned unfair, of course. But then, so was life. Unfair.

He looked up at Bannerman. Mustn't let his mind wander. That was the difficulty. You had a couple of clarets with breakfast to sharpen your responses, and they did so very well for a time. And then somehow your mind became fogged. You'd look at someone, realise he'd said something to you and you hadn't quite heard him aright. Or maybe you'd said something to him, and for the life of you you couldn't remember just what it was.

He felt like that now, looking at this young man. How long would it take for his features to become dimmed by drink, by heat, by the constant inertia of India, the pounding drum of the sun every day, the wailing of jackals at night, the loneliness, the odd, uneasy feeling of self-delusion?

You were part of a company, running a country larger than all Europe from the Bosporus to the Bay of Biscay, dotted with indigenous rulers, each with immense power, prodigious wealth, with private armies and cannon sold to them by renegade Europeans. Any day, any moment, they might realise that, although relatively weak as separate princely kingdoms, their strength could be overwhelming if they united.

Deakin cleared his throat and tried to concentrate on the present, not the past or, worse, the future.

'Yes,' he said. 'We were talking about money, weren't we? Your father's lack of private means, I think. Well, money is not a subject gentlemen usually discuss, Bannerman. You either have money or you

343

marry it, and that's an end of the matter. I have to make it clear that in this regiment we expect all our officers, even the most junior like yourself, to take part fully in mess activities. We have a pack of hounds. We entertain all visiting Europeans as we would wish to be entertained in their homes. Messing expenses are therefore rather higher than in some other regiments. Do I make myself clear?'

'You do, sir.'

'I tell you this because I understand that, as usual with new officers, a moneylender approached you on your arrival. Keep away from such people. We had a regrettable occurrence recently. A captain, living hopelessly beyond his means, took his own life rather than face disgrace. He had lived like a gentleman. He took the only honourable way out, and died like one.'

'There was another way, surely, sir?'

'And what would that be?'

'To come to some accommodation with the *banyar* and eventually pay off what he owed, bit by bit. Then to follow your advice and keep away from them all in future.'

'So that is your view, is it? I can see you have much to learn about life here. Of course, we are having a whip-round for the widow. Minimum of two thousand rupees each. Voluntary, of course. But my wish. You will be debited with that on your mess bill at the end of the month. Any questions?'

'None, sir.'

'Right. I hope we will grow in confidence with each other.' Colonel Deakin's tone showed he doubted what he said. He nodded his dismissal. The interview was at an end.

When Ben went into the mess for breakfast the next morning, the room was empty except for an older

344

officer, a major, reading a week-old copy of the *Delhi Gazette*. The newspaper was propped up on a polished brass stand with clips that held the pages extended. A starched white cloth covered the table, laid with silver cutlery that shone in the morning sunshine. Bowls of mangoes, guavas, bananas stood on a sideboard.

Outside, the day was already gathering heat. Relays of servants carried shining hogskins full of water and dashed them on the woven rattan screens that half covered the open windows. The mess felt damp and musty. Its thatched roof had been soaked with water every day for weeks.

A waiter came forward, salaamed and asked Ben in English whether the sahib would like his eggs boiled or poached, and tea or coffee.

'Black coffee, please. And two eggs lightly boiled,' Ben replied in Hindustani.

The major lowered his newspaper, nodded brusquely to him. 'Don't often hear the local lingo spoken in the mess,' he said. 'Thought I was the only one who had that trick. Glad I've got a companion. I'm Ritchie, Douglas Ritchie.'

So this was the officer Deakin had mentioned, who could not afford to buy a drink. Ben introduced himself.

'Pleased to meet you, Bannerman,' said Ritchie. 'Heard someone new had arrived from home. Must all be very strange to you, I expect. We're into the hot season up here, you know. Those fellows out there with the water have the right idea, keeping us cool. But it's a war they can't win. This your first tour?'

'Yes. But I was born out here.'

'You were? Where?'

'On the retreat from Kabul. My mother and father both died then.'

'Did they now? Bannerman. That name rings a bell.

345

I knew a Benjamin Bannerman in Ferozepore before that fiasco. A lieutenant. Married a damned pretty woman. Anna was her name, if I remember right. Would have married her myself if I'd had the chance. But I didn't. So I married someone else, more's the pity.' He pushed the paper to one side. 'Not married, are you, Bannerman?

'No, sir.'

'Never mind the sir. We're in the mess now, not on parade. Can't say I recommend marriage myself, though some couples swear by it. But then my wife went off with someone else, a civilian, a box wallah, so maybe that influences my judgment. Some of these fellows make a lot of money. And you don't make money in the army, not these days. So you can't blame ladies for losing interest.

'When John Company was starting, of course, things were different. They wanted people to come out and run things, and promised them a share of the loot. They could go home after a few years, buy a country estate, and die like a gentleman on a couple of bottles of port a day. That's all gone. I've been in India longer than I care to say. I've been turned down for promotion and command three times, and that's enough.'

'I'm sorry to hear that.'

'My own fault, probably. I'm a difficult bastard.' Ritchie sipped his coffee as though turning something over in his mind. 'Bannerman, you say? An unusual name. Any relation to the Bannerman I knew, do you think?'

'Quite likely. I was named Ben after my father, and my mother's name was Anna.'

'That makes it clear then. You're Benjamin Bannerman's son. But how did you manage to survive when your parents didn't? You couldn't have been very old then.'

'I wasn't. A doctor carried me out. He told me he had brought me into the world, and he was determined to see I didn't leave it so soon.'

'Ah, yes. I remember. There was one survivor, a Dr Kintyre. The colonel and I have often had a ding-dong about him after dinner. Kintyre served here under him, when he came out. The colonel was of the opinion it was wrong he survived when so many others didn't. A doctor should save other people's lives, but not his own. Can't follow that line of argument myself, I must say. But then the colonel and I don't agree on so many things. He knows who you are?'

'Yes.'

'Your father was a brave man and a clever one. But he never had much of a chance to shine. Like me, he lacked enough money to buy his way up the ladder. A very great pity. Had he been in a position to make his views prevail, there might not have been a disaster at Kabul. Better still, we might never have got embroiled in the whole mish-mash of nonsense in the first place. But what's the use of saying "if only"?

'You're young, Bannerman, and I'm getting old. So let me give you some advice. There's only one worse thing in the world, as far as your superiors are concerned, than you being wrong, and that's you being right! They can't stand that. Too many of the men who come out to India now and buy commissions and promotion are little better than remittance men. They can't make a go of things at home, but their father has some money, so he buys them a commission, and goodbye. With any luck, they'll never come back. Out of sight, out of mind, for ever. Trouble is, when they're out here they can do a lot of harm. You know anything about the customs of the country?'

'I was brought up here in Barrackpore and Calcutta.

I learned Hindustani, but not much about the customs, no.'

'Well, you'll hear many people here going on about the iniquities of the caste system. And it is a very harsh system. If you're born an untouchable – they clean the shit out of the latrines – then that's the level you stay at all your life, and your children, too. No promotion. No hope of anything better. Or you might be a *bhisti* who carries water, like those fellows outside. And that's all they'll do as long as they live. There are others who do this or that or don't do this or that, and then there are the ones on top, the Brahmins. They control all the lower castes. They draw a ring round themselves and stay within that ring, untouchable in a different sense. They don't mix. Harsh, if you like. But at least everyone knows where they belong.

'The army has its own castes, too. Officers don't mix socially with sergeants. Sergeants don't go into the corporals' canteen. The fact is, the ranks come from a class brought up to respect and obey the class above them, from which the army draws its officers. All this means that too often we learn too little and too late about what's going on just outside our own little circle, what the men – and their wives – think of things. And the millions of Indians out there in the heat and the dust, what do *they* think? Do they think at all?

'We have our spies and police agents and God knows who else keeping an eye on some things, but my experience is that a spy generally tells what the person who pays him wants to hear. That's in his interest, if not in yours. So you end up paying him to reassure you that what you think is true. And sometimes it isn't.'

'You sound very adamant about this, Major.'

'I am. Years in the heat make you adamant. There's nothing else to be. Seen our weapons out here yet?'

'Not yet. I hope to.'

'You will. But they should be in museums, not in the hands of fighting men. Got a parade this morning?'

'No. Nothing at all.'

'Then come down to the ranges. I'll show you what I mean. But finish your breakfast first. I'll see you outside in twenty minutes. Have they fixed you up with a horse yet?'

'Not yet.'

'Then we'll walk.'

The sun was already halfway up the sky as they walked towards the ranges. On either side of the dusty path the dry earth had cracked like overbaked clay. Bullock carts moved slowly in the heat, wheels creaking, animals' heads well down, jaws chewing mechanically. Withered trees and bushes seemed to have shrunk in the heat. The hot wind dried Ben's nostrils and the edges of his eyes; he felt he was standing too close to an open furnace.

'Does you good to walk, shows you what the infantry have to put up with, in case you should ever forget, like the staff,' said Ritchie. 'This heat is why we start so early here, five o'clock first parade. Off at nine, do what you like. Early lunch. Get your backs down, what we call Egyptian PT, in the afternoon, and then when it's cooler, as the fancy takes you – polo, drinking, dinner in the mess, mess games. You know what they are?'

'I've heard about them,' said Ben.

'They're fun when you're young. But when you get older, they seem ridiculous – at least they do to me. Middle-aged men behaving like schoolboys, breaking up furniture, setting fire to tongas. They rig up an assault course over sofas. Some fellow will bring a bazaar pony in and everyone takes it in turn to ride. All the silver, of course, and the ornaments, anything breakable, is removed before these shenanigans start.

349

The mess servants bring out furniture made of bamboo, that's designed to be broken and cheap to replace.

'The youngsters may roll up someone they don't like in a carpet. Fellow suffocated like that last year. They clean forgot he was in the carpet. They got round that, of course, said he'd had a heart attack on service, sunstroke. Wangled his old parents a pension. He was another officer without private means, poor devil. Probably that's why they did it to him in the first place.

'We're all prisoners out here, really, Bannerman, and doing time, ten, twenty, thirty years. Like marriage – no remission for good behaviour. I suppose we try to forget the reality in these games – anything to take our minds off that basic fact. If we were emigrating to a colony, say Australia, the Cape, Canada, we'd intend to make whole new lives out there, live and die there. And if we had children they could follow on. But here, we're all on detachment.

'Then we go back to England, to the cold and the mists and the fog. And we find we don't really fit in there any more. We've been away too long. We're like these trees here that wither in the sun. Their roots aren't deep enough – if they've any roots at all.'

As they walked, vultures circled lazily in the sky, gliding down, flapping their wings to regain height. They centred above a group of brick and plaster buildings and next to them a mass of mud huts.

'What's over there?' Ben asked.

'Other ranks' lines. Come and see the soldiers' barracks.'

As they approached the lines, a faint smell of sewage and bad drains grew steadily stronger. The first barracks had small windows; wooden verandahs extended on ground and first-floor levels.

'Married quarters,' Ritchie explained.

'What's the smell?'

'What you think it is – sewage. If you look to the left you'll see a ravine. There's a trench dug from the quarters to this. That's the sewerage system.'

'It smells all the time?'

'Worst at midday. The flies are everywhere. Rats, vermin of every kind.'

Ritchie led the way up a short flight of wooden steps to the lower verandah. Half a dozen barefoot European children, three or four years old, dressed in short shirts or dirty vests, their legs stained with faeces, were playing with a homemade top. Their hair was matted, their faces had not been washed for days. A man wearing long underpants, a shirt, also barefoot, smoking an Indian cigarette of rolled-up leaf, came to the door.

'What do you want?' he asked belligerently, then realised who they were.

'Sorry, sir,' he said smartly. 'Making an inspection, sir? We weren't warned of nothing like that.'

'Not an inspection,' Ritchie assured him. 'Just showing a new officer how you live. Mind if we come in?'

'No, sir. A bit different from the mess, though.'

The room had a wooden floor. Crude seats had been made out of rough planks taken from crates and packing cases, still stamped with the names of the firms to which they had originally been consigned. Primitive cushions had been sewn together from canvas; bits of straw stuck out of holes. There was no glass in the windows, and no mosquito nets.

A sluttish woman, feeding a child at her breast, came out of a back room, stared at them with dull, lacklustre eyes. In the background a younger woman was keening over an ill child. The smell of unwashed bodies and stale food was almost overpowering. Ben felt relieved when Ritchie suggested they move on.

'Rankers' wives have a terrible time out here,' he

351

explained. 'They're here with their menfolk for ten years, living like you see, worse than many animals in England. When the regiment's on the march, they pack their gear, such as it is, a few pots and pans and more children than you can count, in bullock carts, and follow.

'A lot take to the bottle. Arrack, mostly. Native juice. They boil it up with spices and green chillis, even give it to their children to drink. Like children's nurses at home, who feed a teaspoon of gin or a few grains of opium if the child is teething and they don't want a disturbed night. This has the same effect, eventually. But first it makes the children drunk. I've seen kids rolling about in the dirt, drunk out of their minds, and aged only three or four. In a strange way it's a mercy, for quite a lot of children die young. What are they going to grow up to if they stay alive? To be camp followers, then maybe join up as drummers or bugle boys?'

'What do they eat?'

'Black bread, mostly. They buy fruit in the bazaar, but since they rarely wash it, they get fearful dysentery. The meat is the worst in the world – bazaar pork.'

He pointed towards half a dozen huge hogs, snorting and truffling in a pile of rubbish and sewage under a dark cloud of flies.

'That's your bazaar pork. Riddled with worms and every sort of disease. What can you expect? They live off shit. And that's what our rankers have for their Sunday joint.'

'How do the troops fight so well, and why, when they live like this?'

'A point I have often considered, Bannerman. I would say there are several reasons. First, the monarch. Queen Victoria believes in herself. We all believe

352

in her, and in our total superiority over an equal number of any other nation.

'These men are private soldiers, the lowest of our army's ranks, and regarded by civilians as not much better than lunatics and criminals. But that's not how they regard themselves. And look what campaigns they have won, with the wrong equipment, useless weapons, and idiots in command. Belief. That's what counts, especially belief in yourself.'

They walked on towards the native lines, rows of squat huts. Here, Indian women crouched, baking *badjares* cakes on small fires of chopped wood, or boiling curried meat in metal pots slung on tripods like those the stallholders used in King Drummond's fair. Everything was cleaner, healthier.

'Why?' Ben asked Ritchie.

'One reason I can think of is because this is their country. They don't get paid much, but they do get paid, which is probably more than they would be if they worked for a landowner in their village. And Indians are a martial race. We are not. We may be proud of our navy, even if most people never see the sea or a ship in all their lives, but our army has never inspired such feelings.

'When our soldiers are paid off back home, there's usually no work for them, nothing, only a pittance of a pension, pennies a week. So they have to wander the roads, not much better than highwaymen, violent beggars. If they come back from India, they've probably got wives with them little more than children. Had a case only last week, corporal up for beating his wife, knocked six teeth out.'

'Why? Unfaithful?'

'No. She was such a kid she was playing marbles with the other boys and girls when he wanted his supper cooked. So he set about her. There's not much young women like that can do for a living back home except become whores.

'Clever girls, if they decide to marry a soldier, often choose an old one, or someone about to go on service in a foreign war. If he's old, he's more likely to die of dysentery or cholera. If he's fighting, he can die from an enemy bullet.'

'How does that help them? They're widows then.'

'So they are. Which means they get six months' widow's pension, which is better than nothing. Women, my dear Ben, have a hard time of it. Can't wonder they'll do almost anything for money, can you?'

'No,' Ben agreed thoughtfully and realised he was suddenly thinking of one woman: Mary Jane. 'If I were wealthy, I'd do something to help the children of our rankers,' he said thoughtfully.

'How? What would you do?'

'Buy some big old houses – they're cheap enough in England these days because they're so difficult to run. I'd staff them with army widows and teach army orphans, boys and girls, a trade. Give them a future to look forward to. John Company or the Government, or both, should do that for them. But if they won't, someone else should.'

'A generous idea, Bannerman. But my experience of people is that they only suggest these charitable enterprises when, like you and me, they don't have any money themselves. Once they get rich, then these noble thoughts fly out of the window. They've something much more important to consider.'

'What is that?'

'Themselves. I'll tell you an odd thing about money. You either have none, or you can never have enough. Think about it.'

At the ranges, six huge plasterboard targets cut into

outlines to represent men were set up against a long ridge of earth about twenty feet high. In the foreground, half a dozen sepoys lay in the firing position, legs spread out, heels flat on the ground. Ben and Ritchie waited until they fired.

Each time they pressed the trigger, the musket's stock jumped back into their shoulders, no matter how tightly they held it. Ben could see that this hurt the firers; they winced slightly with each shot. Half the strength of the explosion, or at least a good proportion of it, was being lost. Was he the first to notice this and wonder whether anything could be done to harness the force in some useful way?

A *havildar*, an Indian sergeant, saluted them. Ritchie spoke to him in Hindustani. The *havildar* handed a pair of binoculars to Ben. He focused on the targets. All were clean, unmarked.

'No one's hit anything,' he said in surprise.

'Not to be wondered at,' Ritchie replied. 'These particular muskets they're using are known as Brunswicks, because they were designed by some German captain, a Brunswick Jäger officer. They underwent trials at Woolwich arsenal and the Board of Ordnance said they were wonderful. I think they're the worst weapon ever to come into the army. So does anybody who's been unfortunate enough to fire one. Above four hundred yards you can't hit the side of a house. The bullet just goes wild. To load you have to ram it down the bore. It's such a tight fit that, five years ago, a select committee on small arms said that so much force was needed that after a few attempts the soldier's hand would be too unsteady for accurate shooting.'

He turned to the *havildar*. 'Have the new rifles arrived?'

'Yes, sir. The Enfields.'

'We've been waiting years for these,' Ritchie

explained. 'The royal small arms factory at Enfield installed American equipment to produce them, and they're very good, with a barrel thirty-nine inches long, sighted up to nine hundred yards. But there's one big snag about the Enfield. I'll tell you about that afterwards, not here. These fellows understand English, even if they pretend not to.'

They waited while the sepoys fired half a dozen more rounds each. Again, none hit the target. Then they walked back to the mess anteroom.

'When I first came out here,' said Ritchie, 'we used flintlock muskets. You primed the flintlock with a little powder; if it was raining, the weapon was useless except as a club, because damp powder won't catch. A few years back, in the Sind campaign, the commander, Sir Charles Napier, gave two vital orders to his troops. "The first duty of a soldier is obedience," he said. "His second is *always to fire low*." No one heard of anyone being killed at even two hundred yards range by a flintlock musket. The bullets all soared up in the air like birds.'

'Like the Brunswick?' said Ben.

'Exactly. The Enfields are a great improvement, but they take a very close fit of cartridge – and here's the catch. The powder is issued in a twist of greased paper to keep out the damp. The soldier has to bite off the end, shake the powder down the barrel, push in the wad, and then ram the bullet down with a ramrod.

'The bullet's also greased, to stop it jamming. Even so, reloading is a slow business. The rifleman fires one round and then must roll over on his back and tear the corner of another paper. The powder stings his tongue badly – it could poison him if he swallowed too much of it. Then he hammers the rifle butt on the ground to get the powder down, and rams home the ball. He fumbles in the cap pocket for the percussion cap, and has to thumb that home before he can fire.

'After a few shots his thumbs are bleeding and his mouth is raw and bitter and burned with powder. And all the time he's aiming low for the guts or the balls because the bullets still rise like larks.'

'You don't have a high opinion of our equipment, Major.'

'I don't. I've served here for too long to be taken in by all the smooth claims the Government and the Company make, saying we're the best-equipped army in the world. That's just rubbish. I've seen too many good men die because their gear is so second-rate – and some of their officers not much better.'

'So what if we faced an attack now?'

'In Afghanistan, in your father's time, Bannerman, our potential enemies were the Persians and the Russians. If either of their armies came over the frontier now, we'd have to welcome them for we couldn't do a damn thing to stop them.'

Chapter Eleven

As the leading outriders passed the sixth milestone from Delhi on the Grand Trunk Road, they quickened their pace. On the far horizon, minarets and towers and white domes, like giant roc's eggs cut in half, shimmered like a mirage, or a glimpse of some strange celestial city.

On either side of the dusty road stretched plains of corn and rough grass where cattle grazed. From time to time, curious heaps of brick, like kilns or tumuli, erupted from the dried pastures. Mary Jane raised herself on the *doolie* and looked out across the flat expanse towards the city that would be her home, for how long she had no idea. She had not visualised such emptiness; the landscape stretched to infinity all around her without another person in sight.

By her side, still asleep, lay Captain Cartwright's four-year-old son, Paul, who was in her charge. She glanced down at his pale, puffy face. The muscles jerked slightly every now and then; one hand moved in an automatic reflex action to brush away a fly. The boy stirred uneasily in his slumber, but he did not awake.

In a *doolie* behind theirs lay Mrs Madge Cartwright, the captain's ailing wife. She had taken a strong sleeping draught late on the previous night and now she snored loudly. Soon, she would wake, thick-headed, dry-mouthed and still half-drugged.

The *doolies* dipped and rose and moved slightly, like the movement of ships in a restless sea. The eight Indians who carried the poles on their shoulders, two men to each corner, trudged on, heads down. Mary Jane could see their dark skins shine with sweat even at this early hour. They had been marching for hours, and still they appeared tireless. She could barely regard them as human; they seemed simply to be creatures of burden in human form. But then everything she had seen so far in this huge arid land seemed strange, unreal, grotesque.

She remembered beggars in Calcutta with legs swollen as thick as their trunks, dragging themselves along, leather pads on their hands, swollen shanks resting on a wooden trolley with small wooden wheels. A little boy, a relative or some other poor person's son, would hold out his hands calling out to richer passers-by: '*Baksheesh! Baksheesh!*'

She remembered hideously deformed lepers, faces fallen in, eyes rotting in their sockets, passing maharajahs' elephants, richly caparisoned in glittering cloth, with gold leading ropes and intricate patterns painted in pink and blue and white on their wrinkled foreheads.

Across the roads, against all traffic, moving ponderously between bazaar stalls, into the front doors of Hindu houses and through any open gates, sacred cows with white humps pushed their way, unmolested. Munching mangoes and vegetables taken from piles at street corners, they urinated and defecated with equal disregard for the pure white palaces of wealthy Indian merchants or the crumbling hutments of the poor.

The huge contrast between incredible wealth and starvation was something she had never imagined. Nor had she expected the total unconcern of rich Indians and British to others so much less fortunate. In

England, the gulf between rich and poor had seemed wide enough; here, it appeared totally unbridgeable.

As she pondered on this, she heard the clop-clop of a horse coming up on her right side. Captain Joseph Cartwright gave her a mock salute.

'You're awake early,' he said. He would have added 'Darling', but he was not sure whether the boy was really asleep or only pretending.

Mary Jane nodded.

'We're nearly there,' he told her. 'We'll be in our house near the King's palace within two hours. Then all this travelling and discomfort will be over. I look forward to showing you Delhi.'

'You know it?' she said.

'I have been here before on an earlier posting, yes.'

He winked at her and smiled. Under his topi his face was pale in the morning sun, unhealthy, like his son's. Mary Jane smiled, wanting to appear pleasant. On the captain's whim or his wife's mood her livelihood could depend. She did not like him, and she did not trust her. But she was in no position to pick and choose employers. She was fortunate to have this position and she knew it.

In England, she had read *The Times* and *The Spectator* and *The Enquirer* every day, poring over advertisements and applying to those that sought a nurse or a personal maid to accompany a family to India. Most of the advertisers did not even bother to reply. One or two who did were oldish men with narrow, foxy faces and hot, lecherous eyes. They did not really want a maid, they wanted a mistress, but a maid would be cheaper. Mary Jane declined their offers.

If she had wished to become a whore on those terms she could have stayed with Mrs Mentmore; her clients were richer than these old men. Mary Jane did not refuse on moral grounds but for sound commercial reasons. In the last analysis all she had to sell was her body or her mind; if she had to sell either, she wanted the best possible price.

Captain Cartwright was the fourth military man to whom she applied for a job, and the only one who answered. She saw him and his wife in the house they were renting, one of the new villas being built west of London on the road to Bayswater. Cartwright gave the appearance of being frank with her.

'My wife is in poor health,' he explained. 'However, she is a very brave person and she wishes to return with me to India where I have to go on an extended tour of duty. Her doctors advise that she should stay here, but she feels her place is with her husband, even though we have a child who, in my opinion, we would be better advised to bring up in the cool climate of England.

'However, that's as may be. I'm telling you this so you know our situation from the start. She is determined to go. I have agreed, reluctantly, I will admit, and only on condition she takes with her someone we can both trust to look after our dear son. Now, tell me about yourself.'

Mary Jane gave him an edited account of her life, leaving out her stay in Newgate, the visit to Mrs Mentmore's house, the actual nature of her work in King Drummond's fair. She said she had helped the owner of a number of fairs and other amusement establishments.

'I see,' said Captain Cartwright dubiously, as though this did not constitute the background he would have wished for his son's nurse. 'Why are you so desirous of going to India?'

'Since you have been good enough to be frank with me, sir, I will return the compliment. I am without a father or mother. In this country there are very few posts open to an unmarried woman without money or influence. I feel that in one of the colonies or in India the prospects, perhaps of marriage or of advancement of some kind, must be greater than here – for the good reason they could not very well be less.'

'So you have no intention of staying with us, provided, of course, that we find you suitable for the post?'

'I have every intention of staying with you, sir, for as long as you and your lady wife would wish to employ me. Assuming, as you say, that you wish to do so at all. But time passes quickly, and although your son is now four, I think you said, when he is ten, or eleven or twelve, you may not need me, but a *munshi* or a governess or someone of that kind. I would certainly wish, and hope, to stay with you until we mutually agreed that I should leave.'

'You take a very mature view of this, Miss Green.'

'I don't know that it's mature, sir. It seems to me to be common sense.'

'Anyhow, I appreciate it. Now, come and meet my lady wife.'

Madge Cartwright was in bed. The curtains were drawn. Her face was pale against white pillows, her hands thin and blue-veined on the white sheet. The impression was of a lying-in-state of the dead, not the afternoon nap of a young mother. She extended one hand towards Mary Jane, who shook it. The flesh felt cold, damp, unhealthy, as though she was touching the scales of a long-dead fish.

'I will hear about you from my husband,' Mrs Cartwright told her wearily. 'Let me just ask you a few questions, woman to woman. You are not engaged or promised?'

'No, ma'am.'

'You look clean in your person, I am glad to see.

363

You are not suffering, I trust, from any disease, contagious or otherwise?'

'Nothing, ma'am. Any doctor or nurse could examine me and assure you of that.'

'Good. Nowadays there is so much immorality. The young are not as chaste as when I was your age. Now tell me, have you worked with children before?'

Mary Jane took a deep breath. 'I know many children. I love children,' she said slowly, trying to gauge the woman. 'I believe they are grown-ups in miniature and should be treated as such. We must understand what makes them have tantrums perhaps, or appear unwilling to do something, to carry out our decisions. But equally we must be firm and never soft. And always fair in our judgments and decisions.'

Mrs Cartwright nodded. 'That equates with my thinking,' she said thankfully.

Mary Jane smiled. She had deliberately answered the question vaguely and ambiguously to make it appeal both to someone who favoured discipline and to anyone who felt that an easygoing approach to bringing up children was the correct one.

'I think that if my husband agrees, you will suit. What do you say, Joseph?'

'I think she's very good, Madge, my dear,' Captain Cartwright replied carefully.

'I think so, too. Then, to terms. I will give you twenty pounds to buy necessities for the voyage and the journey across India. I don't know whether my husband told you, but he is going to a position of very great responsibility. He will be commanding the British ceremonial guard to the King of Delhi, who I understand is the most important native in the whole of Hindustan.

'We will pay you a salary of one pound a week and, of course, your passage. Usually, for a servant, I would only pay a Third Class passage, but since you will be looking after dear Paul, and we will wish you to come through to the First Class with him, you also will travel First.

'Our ship is due to sail in two weeks. Can I take it you will be accompanying us? I would like your decision now.'

'You have it, ma'am. It will be my pleasure to come with you, and I will do my utmost to give total satisfaction.'

As Mary Jane replied, she happened to glance at the captain, who was smiling. His left eyelid drooped almost imperceptibly; if she had not been watching him closely she could have missed it. He was winking at her.

For the two or three days before the voyage, she stayed with the Cartwrights at their house in London. Their staff had been dismissed except for a maid of about her own age and a housekeeper in her forties who had been with Mrs Cartwright's family before she married. From her, Mary Jane found out more about her employers.

Mrs Cartwright had only become a semi-invalid after her marriage. As a single girl, she had been cheerful and healthy, and even enjoyed long walks and riding regularly to hounds. Now, she stayed in bed every morning until noon. Then she would get up, take a little walk in the park, have a light lunch, usually of boiled fish with seltzer water or a glass of warm skimmed milk, a peeled apple or pear, and retire to bed for the afternoon. She might get up for tea, or she might not. She and her husband took dinner together by candlelight. She retired to bed almost immediately afterwards. Her room was on the ground floor. Her husband slept in a room on the third storey on the far side of the house. The boy had his own nursery at the top of the house; Mary Jane used a bedroom next door.

'They're a strange couple,' said the housekeeper. 'They're young, but they never see much of each other. They don't occupy the same room at night, let alone the bed – you know what I mean? He's a funny bloke. He tried to touch me and the maid. She told me about it. I said, if he gives you a pound, let him have his way. But not the whole thing. It could be risky. You understand me?'

'Perfectly,' said Mary Jane.

'I think he's desperate for it. He's not getting anything from his wife, that's for sure.'

'Why not? Is she ill?'

'She pretends to be. I think it's because she can't stand him. He repulses her. She can't bear him to touch her, to be near her, even. It's all she can do to manage three meals a day at the same table with him. If you ask me, she doesn't like men. At least, not in that way. I think she's happier with women. There was a sort of companion here some months ago. They got on together like a house on fire. I'd hear them giggling and joking like two schoolgirls. Not all moping, like she is now. Why, she was quite cheerful, was Mrs Cartwright, like I remember her before her marriage.'

'What happened to the companion?'

'Oh, she went. The captain didn't take to her. They had words. Maybe he tried to have his way with her and she said no. She wasn't one for that, I can tell you.'

'But Captain and Mrs Cartwright have a child, despite what you say.'

'One. He wanted an heir. He's got an heir.'

'Is he very rich?'

'Very. And stupid. The family has estates in the Midlands and in the West Country. They own manufactories and rows of houses, whole towns, so I've heard.'

'And Mrs Cartwright?'

'I'm rather sorry for her, really,' said the housekeeper. 'She's not rich like he is. But she comes from a very good family. She's a decent woman in her own way. Deserves better than who she's got. I've heard him shouting at her. I think he beats her about. Some men do that to their wives. Makes them feel that they're important, powerful, when they're anything but. They're cowards, you see, bullies.'

'And is the captain?'

She shrugged. 'I have my own thoughts,' she said. 'I advise you to be very careful when you're alone with him. And if ever he makes any suggestions and takes a liberty, make him pay. He can afford to. And it's the only way he'll appreciate you.'

'You think Mrs Cartwright married him for his wealth?'

'I've no idea. That must have been an attraction. There's certainly not much else in the captain to attract any woman. And, to be honest, not much in her character to attract a man, if you see what I mean.'

The housekeeper and the maid accompanied them in the train to Southampton to see them aboard the *East Indiaman*, to check that everything in the cabin was to Mrs Cartwright's liking, that the bed provided for her was soft enough, with a basin by the side in case she was adversely affected by the motion of the ship. Then they curtsied and said goodbye.

Mary Jane's cabin was across a corridor. She shared it with Paul. The cabin contained two bunks; he had the top one, she the bottom. There was a ladder to climb up to the top, and a metal washbasin with a mirror. Mrs Cartwright had her meals served in the cabin – arrowroot, sago, and weak, salty broth. The captain sat alone at a table in the First Class restaurant.

There were two sittings for meals. He attended the first, Mary Jane and the boy the second.

The voyage was long and boring. She read to Paul, played Beggar My Neighbour and Patience with him. Tiny happenings that would be ignored on land assumed importance at sea, and became talking points for days. Two sailors caught a shark off Madeira; flying fish would dart from the waves like silver daggers and some even landed on the deck. Dolphins followed the ship. Young bachelors put out hooks and lines, and one caught an albatross. This proved inedible, and the superstition that to kill an albatross was unlucky worried the man who had caught it. He gave the dead bird to a sailor who was not at all superstitious. He cut off its feet, ripped out the guts, stuffed the inside with bran to dry it, then used the carcass as a tobacco pouch.

In the evenings, passengers usually sat on deck in basket chairs and watched the sun go down. On one such evening, several passengers who had brought musical instruments, horns, guitars, a violin, gave an impromptu recital. Mary Jane found herself sitting next to Captain Cartwright. Their chairs were very close together. He had a small leather case by his side. He opened it, took out a bottle of Madeira, filled two glasses and offered one to her.

'I don't drink,' she said.

'Just this once, as the sun goes down. Here.'

'I'd rather not.'

'I'd rather you did,' he said. There was a rough edge to his voice like a rasp. Mary Jane realised he would be offended if she refused. She raised the glass to her lips, sipped it, put it down on the scrubbed deck. The sun was a dark red ball of fire, sinking slowly beyond the horizon. Just for a moment, it turned the sea to blood, and then was gone. Its reflection hung for a moment in the sky and then the short tropical twilight gave way to the dark.

Everyone left the deck; Mary Jane and Cartwright were alone. The only sounds were the crack of sails above their heads and the thump of the engine; the *East Indiaman* relied on sails and steam. From somewhere deep in the heart of the vessel came a sound of distant singing and a round of applause; a violin stroked the night with music.

Mary Jane sat back in her seat, closed her eyes. The soothing motion of the ship, the music, the fresh air combined to make her sleepy. Then suddenly she was rigidly awake. She felt Cartwright's fingers stroke the back of her hand and move carefully up her arm to the elbow. She half opened her eyes. She could see him in the gloom. He was looking at her, wondering if she was asleep.

His hand moved on as though it had a mind of its own. It reached her shoulder, paused and then dropped down carefully, cautiously; with a light touch, soft as silk blown in the wind, his hand rested against her breast. His fingers moved expertly, encircling the nipple. She felt it harden beneath her cotton blouse. She opened her eyes, as though she had just awoken.

Cartwright did not remove his hand. Instead, he cupped her breast with it.

'Please,' said Mary Jane, suddenly nervous. He did not attract her; rather the reverse. She had not sought his advances, yet as his employee she could not afford to antagonise him. The situation was out of her experience. But maybe she should follow the housekeeper's advice and turn it to her advantage. She remembered Ivan once quoting an Eastern proverb: 'Even a thousand-mile journey starts with a single step.' She would never achieve her goal of making money if she baulked at the first step.

369

An older woman could have extracted herself with grace and charm. Mary Jane simply put up her hand and removed Cartwright's, gently but firmly. He appeared instantly contrite.

'I had no wish to offend or alarm you. I was simply so struck by your beauty in the light of the setting sun that I paid homage to it in the way a man does. Not just with words, but with honour.'

'Honour?' she replied.

He was peering at her in the dim light. His face was barely a foot away. For the first time, she realised how thick his nose was, how close together his eyes. Ivan had told her that while the hand is the map of everyone's future, with clear lines that represent health, wealth, happiness, long life, the face is the map of a person's past. Instincts, lusts, mistakes, all are written there indelibly. Looking at Cartwright now, Mary Jane knew that not only did she not like Cartwright; she distrusted him.

'You must have known my feelings for you, from the very first moment I saw you,' he said thickly. 'I hesitate to say this, because I am a married man with a son, but honesty is one of my traits, and in all honesty I have to say I loved you as soon as I saw you.'

Mary Jane drew back for a moment. 'You shouldn't say that. You're married. Your wife is lying here aboard ship, ill.'

'I am very well aware of that fact, my dear. Indeed I am constantly reminded of it. It is difficult for a man like me, in the fullness of vigour and manhood, to have a wife who, instead of being a helpmeet, in every sense of the word, is barely able, poor dear creature, to stay out of bed for more than a couple of hours a day.

'I want to love you, Mary Jane, in the fullest sense of that term. You may not wish to hear those words, and believe me it is not easy for me to utter them in my present situation. Were I single, I would have already declared my feelings for you in full, and would ask for your hand in marriage.'

'Please,' Mary Jane protested. 'You have said enough. I can understand frustrations in a man, but your wife is *here*.'

'She is here and she is not here. She is never with me when I want her, when I need her,' said Cartwright. 'I do not want to force my favours on you, and I am not so vain as to expect love from you, but perhaps you could like me and allow me to love you. You'll not lose by being kind to me.'

'What does "being kind" entail?' she asked him. 'I am in your employment to look after your son,' she went on without waiting for his response; she already knew the answer to her question. 'I am flattered and honoured by what you tell me. And I am disturbed, because I have to admit that I cannot help being attracted to you. I admit that openly, as you admit your need. But my upbringing is such that I could not allow myself to *love* you. However . . .' She paused, willing him to speak.

'However, what?'

'I have very little money, Captain Cartwright, otherwise I would not have accepted this job. But I wished to go to India, and I simply could not afford the fare. I am therefore willing to consider whatever you ask of me. But not for love, at least not yet.'

'You mean you'd do it for money?' he asked her crudely.

'Not for money as such. Not for five pounds, ten pounds, even a hundred pounds. Nothing like that. I'm not a whore, although what we are discussing could place me in that category. I believe you own property in England.'

'I do,' he agreed. 'In all honesty, I don't know just

how much, actually. Rows and rows of terraced houses in south London, in Manchester and Birmingham. Some of them only bring in a shilling or two a week, and others are in such bad condition that my agents say their tenants don't pay any rent at all.'

'Then make me a present of some of those houses. If they're not bringing in any money for you, you're not losing anything by such a transaction.'

'That's a bit irregular, surely?' Cartwright stared at her, trying to make out her face in the dim light. She was a cool one, all right. But my God, she was a good-looker. Those breasts, rising so tantalisingly just beneath her blouse. She had taken a deep breath, and they seemed to be standing out.

Cartwright was a vain man. No woman had ever refused him. This creature, young and beautiful, wayward as she might be, was not going to be the first. He smiled as though about to humour a child or someone of feeble mind.

'All right,' he said. 'How many houses?'

He expected her to say one. It might be amusing to make one little property over to her, and he would not miss it. And if the house didn't bring him in any rent, it might at least provide profit of a more pleasurable kind.

'Shall we say a round number?' Mary Jane suggested. 'If they're losing money, perhaps I'm even helping you. Say a dozen.'

'A *dozen*?'

This was not one little property; this was twelve little properties. 'For a start,' she said.

'A start?' he repeated in astonishment.

'Well, I think we had better make a start. We have sat here talking long enough.' Mary Jane put out her hand, let it run down his thigh. Cartwright gave a little shudder of delight, a tremble of anticipation.

'Twelve houses,' he said quickly, thickly.

'I hope you think it will be cheap at the price,' she told him and smiled. 'I think you may. But as you're a man of big affairs and, from what I can already feel beneath my fingers, equally big in more intimate parts, could we put this on a businesslike footing?'

'How do you mean, a businesslike footing?'

Cartwright drew back. The wind from the sea suddenly felt cold. This woman was hard, frighteningly hard. Could this be the same meek person who had appeared so grateful to be given a job and a passage East?

'A letter from you,' said Mary Jane, watching him closely.

'A letter? *Now?*' What the devil did she mean?

'Now,' she confirmed, and turned her face towards him. She kissed him gently on the lips, let her tongue dart out and seek his tongue. Just for a moment she held him lightly, slid her fingers into his flies, undid two buttons and stroked his throbbing phallus. She held it, feeling the beat of his pounding heart. Then she drew away.

'Let me go down below decks,' she said. 'You give me the letter when I come back. I will see you . . .' She paused.

'Where?' he asked urgently. 'Here?'

'Further up on deck, behind the wheelhouse. It's sheltered from winds and prying eyes there. I will change into more, shall I say adaptable, clothes and will meet you there. How long will you take to write the letter?'

'No longer than you take to change your clothes,' he said.

Once more Mary Jane let her fingers flutter over his trousers, and then she was gone. A faint whiff of her scent was briefly left behind before the wind blew it away. Cartwright sat for a moment on his own. A dozen houses seemed a lot for a short time with this woman, but not so much when measured against the hundreds, possibly thousands, he owned. He told himself he could get rid of some of the worst properties like this, the ones that needed reroofing or had appalling tenants who regularly intimidated his collectors when they called to demand the rent. Even when the tenants did pay, the sums only ran into shillings for each house. They weren't talking about houses any person of consequence would wish to live in; they were just hutches, shacks, crude shelters from the elements. He had inherited them, he had not bought them with his own money. He wouldn't miss them. In any case, it was only a paper transaction, nothing important.

He heard the bell sound to mark the end of the evening watch, stood up, went down to his cabin. His wife was in her bunk. An oil lamp burned on a wall bracket. The air felt stale and smoky, used up; not clear and fresh as it was on deck. He bent over her dutifully.

'Asleep?' he asked.

She did not reply. Cartwright looked at her without favour, or any feelings of warmth. Why had he ever married this weak creature? No doubt she had appealed to him in some way, maybe because she was so frail, although she had seemed fit enough before they married. Somehow she must have appealed to him then but he could not now recall in what way.

He went into the anteroom, opened a desk, took a sheet of notepaper embossed with the shipping line's name and address and a little flag above an anchor, and wrote the strangest letter he had ever been asked to compose.

'Dear Miss Green,' he wrote. 'As agreed, in view of the extra work you are being asked to undertake in connection, not only with my son, but in helping my wife and me in other ways, I make over to you the freehold properties Numbers 1–12 Bagshaw Gardens, Deptford, London S.E. Your ownership will commence as of the date of this letter.'

He added the address of his agents; she could get in touch with them whenever she wished. Then he read the letter again to satisfy himself it sounded purely impersonal, a straight business transaction – which, of course, it was. These crafty lawyers could read all sorts of implications into almost any communication. But not this one; he was too clever for those swine. He blotted the letter, folded it, put it in his pocket, then went up on deck.

Lying on her *doolie* now, Mary Jane remembered that first association with her employer. He had been remarkably easy to satisfy, and subsequent meetings made her realise he was incapable of a proper liaison. He just wanted to be stroked, manipulated, to squeeze a breast inexpertly and then, with a sudden gasp, he would bend forward as he came to a shuddering climax. She had sat back in the shadows, contemptuous of his pathetic performance, amazed at the ease with which she had extracted twelve properties from such a rich man.

That had been the first time. There had been others, of course, many others, sometimes several in a single day. Not all resulted in a new property, because she needed his good will. It was easier, and she judged, more productive to let him imagine she was growing to like him. Then he would become more receptive to her demands for a corner shop or six little cottages in a single terrace in some unfashionable suburb.

It all seemed so easy. Was it perhaps too easy? She did not like what she was doing, and she did not like herself for doing it. But she had learned how the key to many a man's moods, and to his purse, lay between his legs. She would be foolish not to capitalise on this discovery. But even as she did so, she realised she was paying a price that one day would be demanded. She was doing whore's work, if for huge rewards.

By the time the ship docked in Calcutta, Mary Jane owned forty properties. She had no idea how she could improve them, what rents they would bring in. But she owned them, that was the main thing. Their bricks, mortar, foundations and freeholds were hers. This was better than living in a caravan, travelling from fair to fair. She was a woman of property now; and this was only a beginning.

At first she had felt twinges of conscience about her behaviour when she saw Madge Cartwright propped up in bed or wrapped in rugs, spending afternoons out of the sun in the alcove where she met and pleasured her husband nearly every night. But after the first few meetings, these feelings of guilt, only mild at most, subsided. In their place came what she realised was an absurd feeling of resentment. Why should this plain, weak woman have access to her husband's wealth and give him nothing in return? She remembered a saying she had heard in Newgate among the whores: 'If washing isn't done at home, it goes out to be done.'

She was not sure how long she could continue the deception, or how long this vain, weak man would be willing to continue to surrender properties for a few moments of titillation, a brief fleeting satisfaction, followed by gnawing hunger until next time.

In the meantime, in Delhi there might be other wealthy officers, perhaps with equally unsatisfactory marriages. Or maybe she would meet rich bachelors and widowers, even Indian princes. She would put her skills to the test. All men had their weaknesses and she would exploit them. As Beatrice in Mrs Mentmore's house had told her most men had more between their legs than between their ears. She smiled at the recollection. And in remembering that brief unhappy stay, she realised she also extracted a strange sense of pleasure from what she did. There was no release in any sexual sense, but it alleviated some deeper need she scarcely realised was hers. She hated men and despised them. They could use her, betray her, but she would get the better of them all. She might arrive in India as little better than a serving maid. But by the time she left, she would be a woman of wealth and power . . .

Cartwright's voice scattered her thoughts. 'There's Delhi,' he said. 'Take a look at it.' His son Paul stirred beside her in the *doolie*.

Across a wide river, with a floating bridge that trembled under the hooves and wheels of passing carriages, Mary Jane could see the Red Fort. The vast structure loomed so large that it completely dominated the landscape. Its high dark red walls were scored by hundreds, maybe thousands, of narrow vertical slits through which snipers' muskets could be directed on any attackers. The walls soared up, sheer as any cliff. On top, they were crowned by battlements and minarets.

But as Mary Jane admired its size and impregnability, she suddenly had an uneasy thought. Most people, seeing Captain Cartwright, married and wealthy, with his wife by his side, would have imagined he would be difficult to seduce, an upright man of unshakeable honour. She had easily proved the reverse to be true. Indeed, he had instigated his own moral defeat. Could the same be said about Delhi?

The King of Delhi stretched his thin legs luxuriously beneath the silk coverlet and lay for a moment on his back, looking up at the tessellated ceiling above his bed.

Always in the early morning Shah Mohammed Abu Zuphur Saraz-o-Dain Mohammed Bahadur took a moment or two to focus his eyes. At eighty-two, they were not as bright and clear as they had been, and he had certainly endured enough troubles to cause them to lose the lustre and sharpness of youth. The wonder was not that they were so bad, but that they were so good.

He lay, puzzling for a moment over why he had woken so early, what was happening today of any special importance. Most days had the same dreary similarity; hours moved slowly, predictable as lazy cattle on a landscape. Then he remembered: the new Guard Commander was arriving with his family.

The East India Company provided the old King with a British officer and guard, more for ceremonial duties than for his protection. He took an interest in smart uniforms and parades and liked to see soldiers marching in drill formation. There was no doubt the British did this extremely well; so did the Indian regiments under their command. He had seen French and Portuguese detachments, and by comparison they looked slovenly and down-at-heel, not a patch on the British. He was looking forward to seeing how the new guard drilled.

Then, with a sigh of regret and acceptance, he realised a second reason for his early awakening; his bladder was causing him trouble again. It was bound to, so his English physician had told him. At his age, it was to be expected, especially after the debauched life he had led – so many women, wives, concubines, nautch girls. There was a price to pay and now he was paying it, although all those liaisons were many years past. Desire had long since overcome performance,

378

and now even desire was all but dead. What a terrible thing it was to feel so old!

He climbed slowly, stiffly out of bed, opened a sandalwood cabinet, took out a chamber pot inlaid with intricate ivory patterns and mother-of-pearl squares and crescents and diamonds, and made his water. Then he crossed over thick carpets, piled carelessly one on another, and stood for a moment at one of the high windows. The early morning sun dazzled his eyes. He closed them, unwilling to face its unwelcome brightness. From the mosque he heard the cry of the *muezzin* calling the faithful to the first prayer of the day: 'There is no God but Allah! Blessed be his name, and Mohammed is his prophet.'

The King peered over the wooden ledge. Far beneath the sheer wall of the Red Fort he saw the River Jumna, still grey while the sun slowly climbed the sky. By noon, the water would blaze like melting gold, but now its surface was flecked by ripples driven by a hard, unseasonable wind.

A mass of flat-bottomed boats, chained together like jewels in a huge, clumsy bracelet, formed a bridge linking both banks. The wind was forcing the bridge into the shape of a crescent. A good omen, he thought: the Muslim crescent. The chains that anchored the boats to huge stones in the river bed creaked and groaned in protest. The pontoons were so large that the bridge contained two broad tracks, one for carriages and carts approaching the city, the other for traffic leaving it.

At intervals, oil-lamp posts moved and dipped and rose again with the strength of the current. In the stern of each boat stood a wattle and mat hut for the men who tended the mooring ropes. This was a responsible job, especially in a high wind. He was glad it was not his responsibility – just as, presumably, these humble officials were thankful not to be King.

Some middle-aged Hindus were religiously completing their ablutions at the shallow edge of the near bank. One by one, they came up out of the water, dried themselves, and approached the master of their complex ritual, the *pujari*. He sat cross-legged under a pipal tree. In front of him, on the earth, he had set out three china saucers containing the sacred dyes of gypsum, sandalwood, vermilion.

As the men approached him, they bowed respectfully, and he repainted their caste marks in the centre of their foreheads, the coloured dot that marked one man, one caste from another. Then, chattering in shrill, high-pitched voices, the Hindus went off to begin their daily work as lawyers or professional pleaders for those who lacked the gift of eloquence. Most of them spent their working lives writing letters and petitions for people who could not write, to present to members of the King's court, who would not even bother to read them. But what did the writers care? They had been paid; that was what concerned them.

The old King watched the group flutter away like a flock of land-locked, wingless birds in white *dhotis* that reminded him of the shrouds used for Christian burials. Either directly or indirectly, the King probably employed most of them. Litigation interested him. He backed one cause against another, as lesser men might back racehorses. The lawyers encouraged his habit. They made great sums from him, and constantly urged him to engage in lawsuits on the slightest pretext, and often on no pretext at all. The old man imagined that he was somehow helping to enforce the laws of the land his ancestors had once ruled. In fact, of course, he was only helping the lawyers.

He turned away from the window. The view seemed stale and empty; he had seen it so often. A personal servant, waiting outside the carved and gilded door of his bedchamber, heard the slight movement and instantly tapped on the door. He came into the room carrying a silver tray. On this stood a beaker of hot water in which an emetic tablet had been dissolved, a single opium pill on a small gold plate, and a second plate of rice pilaff.

Forty years earlier, an English physician, whose judgment the King trusted, had assured him that such a diet every morning would assure anyone of a long life, personal contentment, and health beyond the normal span of men.

The man had not lied, the King thought now as he swallowed the pill and drank the bitter concoction. But somehow, when he felt old and feeble, when almost everything in his life lay in memory, when the slightest exertion seemed exhausting and the most trivial decision a matter of great concern, he wondered whether so long a life was really a boon or a burden.

All his contemporaries had long since died. He was a lonely survivor, thrown up by the tide of time, lacking anyone of his generation to share his memories and experiences. His wives were all much younger; he had grandchildren older than his youngest wife, Begum Zeenat Mahal, who had borne him an heir, now eighteen years old. She constantly plagued him with her ambitions for their son.

The East India Company had promised that the prince would succeed to his father's pension when the old man died, but not to what the Begum wanted most for her son, the title of King. The Company felt that the charade of maintaining a puppet king should end with his death. The arrangement had served its purpose. They could gain nothing more by prolonging it. But what might seem reasonable and totally rational to East India Company directors in London, over ten thousand miles away, seemed less than just to the Begum, as she frequently and petulantly made clear to the King. She did not seem to realise that her husband did not care to be so constantly and shrilly reminded of his age and the fact that soon he would die, and the King did not wish to tell her; such a rebuke would expose how old and vulnerable he felt. She had little tact or charm; he wondered frequently how and why she had ever attracted him. Whoever had written that a woman can have the face of an angel, the cunning of a serpent but the brain of an ass had doubtless written from experience.

King Bahadur Shah's ancestry stretched back for centuries. His forebears had all been emperors, conquerors, men of action, men of war. He was a direct descendant of the great emperor Shah Jahan who two hundred years earlier had built the Red Fort with stones red as rubies for his personal palace. Now Bahadur Shah was the last Mogul, the last Emperor, and that only in name, for he was without power or influence. He was really no more than an old-age pensioner of the East India Company, a senile actor playing the part of a king.

The Red Fort was a city within a city. Its eight-sided walls were a mile and a half round, a hundred and ten feet high. The two longer sides faced east and west; the six shorter ones, north and south. Thousands of slaves and prisoners had worked in relays for ten years through hot seasons, monsoon rains and dust storms to make the fort and palace impregnable to any outside enemy. The cost, even using such forced and unpaid labour who worked for their food alone, under the constant threat of death for any slackness, had exceeded ten million rupees.

A ditch thirty feet deep, seventy-five feet wide, was

dug round the base of the defending walls to make it impossible for any ladder or other known mechanism of war to be used to scale its heights. If an enemy force was foolish or desperate enough to attempt to cross the ditch, artillerymen with giant mortars and catapults capable of flinging rocks weighing half a ton a distance of half a mile could rain down a constant hail of missiles on them. Thousands of loopholes, narrow from the outside but much wider within, allowed archers and musketeers to fire on an enemy from positions of complete safety. And from larger openings set higher in the walls, the defenders could pour huge cauldrons of boiling oil on the heads of attackers.

Like the great Shah who had built it, everything about the Red Fort was much larger than life. Shah Jahan had decided to move his capital to Delhi from Agra because the climate was too hot and too dry there for his liking. When he arrived at the fort in 1648 to hold his first court, thousands of newly minted gold and silver coins had been scattered on the ground at his feet as a symbol of his wealth and prodigal generosity. For that occasion, the main courtyard, large as many a city square, was spread with Persian carpets and Afghan rugs. Silk curtains had fluttered over open windows and the Emperor sat on a throne built round two life-size peacocks carved from solid gold. Above his head hung a canopy of hammered gold supported by twelve pillars studded with huge emeralds and pearls.

The terrace of the Shah's audience chamber was built of white, unveined marble, with four white marble domes that could be clearly seen twenty miles from Delhi. Fountains of rose water, of lavender water, of water mixed with rare aromatic herbs, sprayed continually into sunken marble baths, sweetening the air with their scents.

Such ostentation, such public evidence of enormous, virtually uncountable riches, aroused envy and discontent. Shah Jahan's son seized power and imprisoned him in a cell at Agra. From its narrow windows he could see the sun rise and set on the Taj Mahal, the white marble tomb he had built in memory of the woman he had loved – and, ironically, the mother of his wayward son. Then the Persians marched on Delhi and carried off the Shah's peacock throne to Tehran. Twenty years afterwards, the Mahrattas arrived to seize treasures the Persians had left behind.

When King Bahadur Shah was still a young man, British troops of the East India Company engaged the Mahrattas, and defeated them. They marched into Delhi, but with no intention of humiliating the King; rather the reverse. They had come to India to trade. Conquest for its own sake paid no dividends, and was far more likely to produce a loss in a balance sheet than a profit. To make friends was more sensible than to make foes. You could trade with friends, not with enemies.

The Company knew that Muslims and Hindus alike held the King in high esteem, although by then he was only a harmless figurehead without power, a living totem, a reminder of a once omnipotent past. The Company calculated that if they treated him generously and ensured that his authority, shrunk to little more than commanding the servants in his palace, was not further curtailed, their own commercial activities might be helped. As a mark of respect, they therefore allowed him to strike his own coins for several years until they decided to mint their own. But while to the Company Bahadur Shah was simply a pensioner, and hopefully a useful remittance man, to millions of Indians of every faith he remained India's legitimate ruler. In any dispute or disturbance, he could be the last arbiter, the final judge, the focus of every loyalty, their King and Emperor.

The Company's directors installed a British Resident to check that the King did nothing that could harm the Company's commercial interests, and paid him a pension equivalent to a hundred thousand pounds a year, soon rising to a hundred and forty-five thousand. This enabled him to maintain the outward style of a sovereign, even if he did not possess any of the authority that accompanied kingship in the East.

This financial generosity, regarded by the Company's directors as a shrewd investment, almost the premium on an insurance policy guaranteeing peace and prosperity, had an important and unexpected side effect. It increased the King of Delhi's own self-esteem, and inflamed the greed of Indian lawyers who sensed rich pickings for themselves. They therefore urged him continually to seek even more attractive terms; each claim he made against the Company meant thousands of rupees in fees for them.

Without the ambitions of his youngest wife for their son and the avarice of his lawyers, the old man would probably have been content to lead what to him was a relatively simple life, without stress or turmoil of any kind. At his age, he valued companionship, peace, the pleasures of his hubble-bubble pipe more than political power. But he was one of very few in the fort content with such modest ambitions, Many around him, relations and courtiers alike, wished he could somehow regain the wealth and authority that earlier shahs had enjoyed; the richer he became, the richer and more influential they would also be.

The King had no clear idea just how many people relied on him for their livelihood. He would probably have been amazed to know that the number ran into hundreds. They included wrestlers, jesters, illusionists, conjurers, dancing girls who danced naked to inflame the weakened passions of old men. Forgers, thieves, dealers in stolen goods, distillers of illegal spirits, compounders of sweetmeats and opium also looked to him for sustenance and lodging. Scores of criminals sought refuge from retribution in the Red Fort.

The King was especially partial to watching exhibitions of sleight of hand, levitation and acts of magic for which there seemed no rational explanation. One room at the palace for which only he and his chief court conjurer held the keys was set aside for these performances.

The King's court was totally corrupt; almost everyone and everything was for sale or had already been sold. Here, wives intrigued against other wives, harlots against concubines, mothers against sons. Of them all the most assiduous intriguer was Begum Zeenat Mahal.

She was not with the old King at the moment, a mercy for which he gave silent thanks to Allah, the ever merciful. Her absence, if only temporary, allowed him the luxury of looking forward to whatever was happening this morning, knowing that her high-pitched voice would not spoil it for him.

But just what was due to happen? He had remembered only moments earlier, and now he had forgotten. He scoured his mind for what had momentarily cheered him and went to the window again to look out, hoping to see some sign that would stir his memory.

About half a mile away on the far bank of the river, he saw horsemen and bearers carrying two *doolies*, their side curtains rolled down. That could mean someone of importance was inside, a traveller who did not wish to be recognised, or perhaps a woman who hoped by this means to escape from the myriads of flies that would otherwise swarm about her and settle on her face.

Behind the *doolies* came a train of baggage animals, all heavily laden, with armed men riding on either side. Clearly, someone very important was arriving. Of course. Now, he remembered. This must be the new British commander for the ceremonial guard.

The King picked up a handbell and rang it impatiently. His servant must bring him his clothes at once. He would go down to meet the new commander, and he did not wish to be late.

Lieutenant Deakin leaned back on the feather-stuffed cushions of the cane chair in his uncle's drawing room and regarded the colonel solemnly.

Colonel Deakin poured two careful measures of whisky from a decanter into glasses of cut crystal and added seltzer water. They raised the glasses to each other, sipped their drinks appreciatively.

'So, how is young Bannerman settling in?' the colonel asked his nephew.

'Very well, with the natives anyway. He seems on unusually familiar terms with his bearer and other servants.'

'What exactly do you mean, unusually familiar terms?'

'He shakes them by the hand.'

'I see.'

'And then Ritchie has been pouring out his spite and bile. Someone overheard him in the mess the other morning. Ritchie thought he and Bannerman were alone, or he might have been more prudent. Anyhow, he was beating his usual drum. And Bannerman seemed to take it all in and agree with him. I think Bannerman could become a great nuisance to the regiment. More than that, a positive danger.'

'In what way a danger?'

'Continually taking the natives' side, sir. We're

wrong, they're always right.'

'You have an instance of this?'

'I have. He's told me how concerned he is that the new cartridge papers are being greased with animal fat because we cannot get any other grease.'

'As a matter of interest, why can't we?'

'I am told there's been some defaulting in the quartermaster's department.'

The colonel nodded. This was nothing new. All stores and rations, and as much military impedimenta as possible, were bought from Indian intermediaries known as army contractors. They acquired the items locally, perhaps from several sources, and as cheaply as possible. They then added a percentage as profit for themselves before offering the goods to the regimental quartermaster. Not infrequently, he added on a further totally unnecessary and illegal percentage for himself. Quartermasters were not gentlemen, of course; that was the difference. They had not been born to money, so many of them decided to make some themselves.

'We have a very ugly situation here already, as you know,' Lieutenant Deakin went on. 'A regiment is being disbanded because of trouble over the use of greased cartridge papers, and three sepoys have been sentenced to death for refusing orders to embark for an overseas posting to Burma. Last thing we want is Bannerman making more trouble for us.'

'Let's get rid of him, if we can, and the sooner the better. Ritchie, too.'

'I'm glad you take that view, sir,' Deakin replied. 'Providentially, this afternoon the adjutant was telling me of a request from the C-in-C for one or two officers to be posted from each regiment to some newly formed intelligence department. Other regiments are getting rid of their odds and sods in this way. Bannerman and Ritchie would suit very well, I think.'

The colonel drained his whisky, refilled the glasses. 'Good. That's agreed, then. Now to more important matters. The manoeuvres. We must beat Dick Street.'

Lieutenant Deakin nodded understandingly. His uncle and Colonel Street were almost evenly matched for promotion, but since only one could become brigadier, it was believed that the Commander-in-Chief would choose whoever's regiment did best on the manoeuvres.

Colonel Street had the better military record. Colonel Deakin, on the other hand, was infinitely richer, but since ranks above colonel could not be purchased, promotion to brigadier went to the best available candidate; or, as some put it more cynically, to the least unworthy.

'I suggest we discuss this with the adjutant,' said Deakin.

His uncle nodded. 'Please arrange it,' he said.

The manoeuvres would take the form of a simple test. Two attacks would be mounted on a ruined fort some miles out of Barrackpore. The first attack would be led by Colonel Deakin with his regiment, while Colonel Street commanded the defenders. Then the roles would be reversed. A team of umpires could assess how each regiment and their commanders performed in defence and attack.

'Now, anything else before I change for dinner?'

'Just one thing. Bannerman again. The question of money. He has no private means. When he arrived, he appeared contemptuous of money, so naturally I assumed he was rich. Far from it. I understand he has nothing whatever apart from his pay. Indeed he had to borrow almost as soon as he got here.'

'Not from another officer, I trust?'

'No. From a *banyar*. Two thousand rupees for the fund we're organising for poor Jackson's widow. He hadn't got even that amount in ready cash.'

'Really? He's not one of us then, clearly. He won't do any good in the regiment. We won't be happy with him and he won't be happy with us. This posting is, as you say, providential.'

'He could be a stubborn person. He may not like it.'

'In his situation, he has no option. Another whisky is called for. Your glass, Bruce, if you please.'

Ben saluted and stood to attention in front of Colonel Deakin's desk, eyes fixed on the colonel's bald head as he bent forward to sign a sheet of paper and scattered sand on the ink to dry it. The colonel looked up, almost as though surprised to see Ben standing there. He did not meet Ben's eyes, but directed his gaze a little above and beyond him.

'I asked you here, Bannerman,' be began, 'because a posting has come up which I think will suit you down to the ground. It is to a newly formed intelligence department. You speak the lingo, you seem concerned with natives' welfare. I am sure you will find the work congenial.'

'Thank you, sir, but if I had the choice I would rather stay with regimental soldiering, like my father.'

'Maybe you would. But you do not have the choice. You will be posted to Meerut, outside Delhi. I understand that this unit is starting from scratch. Prospects for promotion will no doubt exist.'

'The posting is irreversible, sir?'

'It is. Anything else?'

'One thing, sir. I was going to suggest this in any case, but in view of my posting to intelligence duties, it seems even more appropriate. The manoeuvres, sir.'

'What about them?'

'Since, as you point out, I speak the language and know the customs of the country because I was brought up here, I was going to suggest a way in which I could possibly help the regiment come out on top.'

'And that is, Bannerman?'

'This, sir. I dye my skin with strong tea, put on native costume, and go out, as a bearer or some such thing, to see if I can discover the opposition's intentions, how they plan to attack, and so on.'

The colonel put down his pen, sat back in his chair and regarded Ben with a mixture of astonishment and disbelief.

'Are you serious?' he asked him at last.

'Perfectly serious, sir. Since you think that I may have some aptitude for intelligence – or spying, which is the cruder word – I would be pleased to use the ability in a way that could also help the regiment.'

'I suppose you mean well, Bannerman, but I find your proposal totally unacceptable.'

'In what way, sir?'

'In every way. Do you mean to say that you, a British officer and a gentleman, would willingly dress yourself up in native costume, black your face like some buffoon in a music hall turn and hang about sepoy latrines and cook-houses, squatting in the muck, listening to bazaar gossip?'

'That is what, in essence, you are posting me to do in Meerut, sir.'

'It is *not*. In Meerut you'll be with other British officers. You will read documents, assess information and pass on your opinions to the Commander-in-Chief – through the proper channels, of course. You will not be creeping about like a bearer or a beggar, making a fool of yourself and lowering the standing of every British officer in the land.'

'It will probably be from informers, creeping about as you say, sir, that our information in Meerut will come, though I think it would be more valuable if we found the material ourselves.'

'I don't give a damn what you think, Bannerman. What you do in Meerut will be up to your commanding officer there. But I will not have any officer under my command dressing up in this ridiculous way and snooping on the plans of a fellow colonel. Now please leave before I lose my temper.'

Ben saluted and marched out.

Chapter Twelve

The adjutant informed Ben that since he was to be posted he would not take any part in the manoeuvres. He could go on local leave if he had anywhere to go, or he could stay in his quarters, but he had no official duties. Clearly, Colonel Deakin wanted nothing more to do with him. With unexpected time on his hands, Ben decided to visit the house where, as a boy, he had spent so many happy weekends with Dr Kintyre.

A low whitewashed wall still surrounded the property. Looking over this, Ben could see that, just as when he was there, a scrubby lawn was being watered from glistening hogskins by relays of diligent gardeners. Much seemed the same, but somehow the spirit was not. Other people with other lives occupied the place now; he did not belong here any more. He remembered it as home. Now, it was only another house.

Ben walked on, past the servants' quarters where he had enjoyed so many meals. In the compound, the cooks were preparing meals. He did not recognise anyone. What had happened to all those men and women who had so generously shared curry and rice with him years ago? He hoped they remembered him as warmly as he remembered them.

He walked on until he reached the small square house where the *munshi* had lived, half expecting it to

393

be empty, the *munshi* gone long since. But, to his delight, the *munshi* was sitting on the verandah in the rocking chair Ben remembered so clearly, his stick on one side, just as it used to be, so that he could prod the dusty floorboards and keep the chair rocking gently backwards and forwards as he talked or dozed.

The old man looked up when he heard Ben approach and peered in his direction, wrinkling his face. Then he put on a pair of steel-rimmed glasses.

'Ah, Benjamin sahib,' he said, his face creasing with pleasure. 'You have come home.'

'Yes, *munshi* sahib. You are right. Not back, but home.'

'Everyone who visits India from the West likes to think they have a home here. Something always draws them back. Come and tell me what drew you back.' He waved Ben to a seat, clapped his hands. A servant appeared, pressed his hands palm to palm in salutation, and bowed.

'*Salaamaji*,' he said.

'*Aleikum salaam*,' responded Ben and shook his hand.

'Two *nimbu panis*,' the *munshi* told him. 'No strong drink here. You know my rules.'

'And good rules they are,' Ben agreed.

The servant brought out two tall glasses of water with lemon juice, sugar and ice.

'Now,' said the *munshi*. 'You are here on business?'

'Not exactly. I am in the army.'

'Ah, the business of war. I did not think you were a martial man, Benjamin sahib.'

'I thought I would follow my father's career. But I am beginning to wonder if it is for me. The fact is, I had to leave home in a hurry.'

'Ah, a young man's troubles? A girl? A baby on the way?'

394

'No, *munshi* sahib. For a rather different reason.'

Ben explained about Bertha; how he had precipitately left home; how each day he meant to write and tell Dr Kintyre where he was but how he kept putting this off because he felt embarrassed.

'You must not put off writing any longer,' the *munshi* told him firmly. 'Write today. Dr Kintyre was as a father to you. Remember what the Prophet Mohammed said, blessed be his name: "A martyr shall be pardoned every fault, but debt." And you owe a great debt to the doctor.'

'You are right, *munshi* sahib. I will write.'

'Good. Now tell me, are you staying long in Barrackpore?'

'No. The colonel and I are not on particularly good terms. I am being posted away with Major Ritchie.'

'I have heard about him. A good man, I believe. Now, the colonel. He knows about Dr Kintyre?'

'Yes.'

'Then his attitude does not surprise me. He did not get on with Dr Kintyre either. The colonel is not a man of imagination. The doctor was. So are you. It is written, an hour's contemplation is better than a year's adoration. Colonel Deakin might not agree, or even understand.'

'I will have much time to contemplate, *munshi* sahib. I am being posted to Meerut. To join a new department being formed – intelligence.'

'Intelligence unfortunately is not always given in abundance to those who conduct our military affairs. Perhaps you can alter this? To waste knowledge on those who are unworthy of it is like putting necklaces of pearls, jewels and gold round the necks of swine.'

'I don't think I will alter anything,' said Ben. 'In fact, I feel a total failure. My father died in the service of his country – so he thought. But having heard more about the retreat from Kabul, I think his was like all the others in that army, a wasted death. Perhaps, even a wasted life.'

'So what do you learn from this, Benjamin sahib? Remembering, as always, the experiences of Alexander the Great.'

'I feel I am running away from events, or at the best just marking time. And all the while, like a river in flood, time is racing past me.'

'It is what the young often feel, my dear friend. And the old also. But it shows you have sensitivity, which is not given to all. No experience, however trivial or however sad, is ever wasted if we put it to use. When you see a person who has been given more than you in wealth or love or achievement, do not envy them. Look instead to those who have been given less.'

'I do not think that my experiences, vanishing in front of a crowd of yokels at a country fair, fencing with Karim Khan, have been much use to me, or will ever be of value.'

'I cannot say. But then neither can you – yet. The race is not over. Much of your life has still to be run. You may find that these experiences are vital milestones in your journey. As I say, no experience, of whatever kind, whether good or ill, is ever wasted. Every happening in your life is part of your life. If it had not taken place, your life would be diminished. Remember that, Benjamin sahib. God loveth those who are content.'

'You really believe that even totally unrelated experiences can be of ultimate value, *munshi* sahib?'

'Not only do I believe, I know. In your religion, the Lord Jesus Christ performed many miracles. He brought the dead back to life. He cured the incurable. He turned water into wine. You might say these actions were just tricks, examples of sleight of hand, like your conjurer friend.

'There may indeed be a simple explanation for these miracles, as no doubt there is for the tricks in which you took part. All things can seem simple when well-explained. But one's experiences are not incidents on their own. They are part of the whole pattern of each life.

'When the Lord Jesus Christ was crucified, it was not only this that was remembered, but also those other earlier happenings in his life.

'It was the same with the Prophet Mohammed, blessed be his name. His early life seemed full of sadnesses, but all worked together for his good. His father died before Mohammed was born. A Bedouin nurse Haleema cared for him from the time he was eight years old. When Mohammed was five, he was handed back to his mother, but she died within a year. Then his grandfather looked after him, until he died. Finally, it fell to an uncle, a merchant, to bring him up. Mohammed travelled with a caravan of merchants to Syria. There he saw the idolatry of the people, how badly they treated the poor and the weak.

'His uncle's business diminished, and Mohammed had to become a shepherd in order to eat. This experience gave him time to consider what he was doing with his life. When, like you, like all of us, he had doubts, he would retire to a cave in Mount Hira, outside Mecca, and ponder and pray.

'And one day God spoke to him, and Mohammed became the prophet of God. Then he realised that everything that had gone before had been a preparation for this. He began to preach and met tremendous opposition from those he sought to help. Attempts were made to murder him. For year after year, he was an outcast, a wanderer. But slowly, steadily, his followers increased, and before he died, thousands of people here in India, in Arabia, in Africa were all followers of his teaching.'

'Did this success change him greatly?' asked Ben.

'No. He was always a man of humility. He loved animals. In past times, the camel of a dead man would be tied outside his tomb to perish of hunger and thirst. Mohammed ended such a cruel and pointless custom. No longer would he allow living birds to be used as targets for marksmen. He proved that rain was not made to fall by the barbarous habit of tying burning brands to the tails of oxen. And always he was merciful, even to those who persecuted him.

'One day, in the hot season, Mohammed was sleeping under a palm tree. He awoke to find a sworn enemy, Du'thur, standing over him, sword drawn in his hand.

' "Oh, Mohammed," Du'thur cried. "Who is there now to save thee?"

' "God," replied Mohammed, for there was no one else.

'Du'thur laughed at this reply, and swung his sword to slay Mohammed. But as he did so he lost his balance and dropped the sword. At once, Mohammed seized it.

' "Oh, Du'thur," he said. "Who is there now to save thee?"

' "No one," Du'thur admitted, and prepared to die.

' "Then learn to be merciful," replied Mohammed and handed his sword back to him. They became true friends.

'In adversity, Benjamin sahib, have faith, courage, resolution. In victory, have mercy. Remember the words of the Prophet, "Whoever suppresseth his anger when he hath in his power to show it, God will give him a great reward." Now, let me see your hand.'

Ben held out his right hand to the *munshi*, palm uppermost. The old man put on a stronger pair of spectacles and examined the palm closely.

'What do you see, *munshi* sahib, for my future?'

'I see struggles. I see war and death, and out of these grows the flower of peace and kindness and love.'

He was about to elaborate when they both heard a cry from the road.

'Hullo! Didn't know I'd find you here,' and Ritchie came walking towards them.

'The *munshi* sahib taught me when I was a boy,' Ben explained.

'I have heard he is a good teacher,' said Ritchie.

The *munshi* bowed.

'Having your palm read, I see,' Ritchie went on.

'He had just begun.'

'What did he tell you?'

Ben shrugged. He was sorry Ritchie had interrupted the *munshi* before he could explain all he saw in his future.

'Have your hand read,' Ben suggested to Ritchie. 'Would you do that, *munshi* sahib?'

'It would be my pleasure.'

He examined Ritchie's plan. 'I see a struggle,' he said. 'I see a great surprise. And I see great happiness . . .' He paused.

'And then?'

'That is sufficient,' said the *munshi* quietly. 'The rest is lost in the mists of the mind. You must come another day, Major sahib. Then perhaps the clouds will have cleared. It is not always possible to see the future, as it is not always possible to see the hills from the plain.'

The *munshi* took off his spectacles.

'I am an old man,' he said. 'And you are both young. You must bear with me if I go to rest.'

'Of course.'

The *munshi* stood up, bowed and left the verandah. He sat down in his bedroom, his face in his hands. He had not told Ritchie sahib what he saw. It was not expedient to warn another man when he saw death in that man's hand.

The manoeuvres were due to begin in a week's time, but the adjutant and the colonel had been unable to devise any plan to attack the fort or to defend it.

'Trouble is, we don't know Street's strategy, how his mind is working,' said the adjutant. 'We can only guess what he is going to do and base our response on that. But that's risky. What we need is a damn good spy in his camp.'

The colonel coughed. 'Since we haven't one we will have to do our damnedest on our own.'

Ritchie saw Ben that evening. 'Whisky?' he asked him.

'Thank you, no.' He did not want to accept a drink when he knew he could not buy one in return until he was paid, and the regimental cashier was usually months in arrears.

'I know what it's like to be short of the ready,' Ritchie said sympathetically. 'But have one on me in any case.'

'I thought you didn't drink.'

'I don't when I'm out of funds. But an old aunt has died and most generously left me a few hundred pounds. So I'm drinking.'

The barman poured out two whiskies and water.

'I've been listening to our plan of attack,' Ritchie went on. 'That's why I feel I need a strong drink.'

'I'm not involved with the manoeuvres,' said Ben quickly. 'Should you tell me?'

'Why not? Everyone else will know it's a failure soon enough. Why shouldn't you?'

'Why do you say it will be a failure?'

'Because it's frontal. We march to the foothills and then charge uphill, bayonets fixed. The other side has only to wait until we're within easy range, exhausted in this heat, wearing field service marching order, best serge, red jackets, shakos – and then shoot us like rats in a barrel.

'The old Chinese strategist Sun Tzu laid it down that you never attack an enemy up a hill and from the front. You may put in a false attack that way, but your main one should be from the side, or the rear. Or maybe you launch a false attack in front and then retreat, blowing all your bugles. Down the enemy comes after you, to speed you on your way, and at once you close on him from both sides, like the jaws of pincers. But never a direct attack and nothing else.'

'Have you told the colonel this?'

'No. I asked to see him, to give him my opinion, but the adjutant said he was too busy.'

'A great pity,' said Ben.

For Colonel Deakin, the manoeuvres were more than that. His assault was a fiasco. The umpires, wearing blue and white armbands and riding white horses so that everyone would see their neutrality, shook their heads despairingly as his men came under withering fire from the fort. Had the defenders been firing live ammunition, the chief umpire ruled that all the attackers would have died. And when Colonel Deakin's turn came to defend the fort, the main attack came from the rear and Colonel Street's forces were successful.

A week later, the result of the test was announced. Two weeks later, Colonel Street was promoted brigadier.

Colonel Deakin realised that he had reached his highest rank. As he stood, pondering this bitter truth,

401

he looked out of his office window and saw Ben walking round the edge of the parade ground. It was forbidden for any officer or other rank to walk across the parade ground unless in column of route or in a drill parade.

The sight of Ben irritated Deakin to an extent he found almost unbearable. If he had accepted Ben's offer, would he now be brigadier instead of that upstart Street? If. If. *If*. That young fellow should have been in Meerut by now, anyhow. Why the hell wasn't he?

He banged the bell on his desk for his orderly and told him to give Mr Bannerman his compliments and would he attend at once in the regimental office. Ben came in, saluted, stood to attention. Usually, the colonel would give a junior permission to stand at ease while he spoke to him. But not today.

'What is the delay over your posting?' he asked Ben sharply.

'The adjutant was awaiting confirmation from Meerut, sir. It has just arrived by electric telegraph. Major Ritchie and I leave the day after tomorrow.'

'I see. Then there's one last duty you will attend to before you go. Not a pleasant duty, but then army life has many unpleasant facets in the cause of duty.'

He swallowed heavily, thinking how apt this was with regard to his own career. Was this young blade smiling at him behind his back? He would show him. He would give him something to remember.

'At oh-eight-hundred hours tomorrow, Bannerman, there is a parade on the square here in which you will take a crucial part. Before you arrived here, three sepoys were found guilty by court martial of mutiny. The punishment for mutiny, for the wilful disobeying of a superior officer's order, is clear and unequivocal. Death.

'Tomorrow morning this punishment will be carried

402

out, watched by their comrades. Their regiment is being disbanded in any case as a precaution.'

'What order did they disobey, sir?'

'They refused to grease their cartridges, and then would not embark for service overseas in Burma.'

'Having no duties to perform here, sir, while awaiting my posting, I looked through papers about the matter, sir. I saw that in January, four months ago, the Government of India made an order that these cartridges were to be kept for British troops only. Sepoys would lubricate theirs with beeswax and vegetable oil. In addition, rifle drill was to be changed. Instead of biting the paper with their teeth, they would tear it with their fingers. Was that not done, sir?'

'It would appear not,' said the colonel sharply.

'But, sir, surely if Government orders were given so long ago, some blame must attach to whoever did not act on them. Could not this be an extenuating circumstance? And on enlisting, all sepoys are assured they will not be asked to serve overseas. To cross the sea destroys their caste.'

'I don't want any barrack-room-lawyer talk here. I don't give a damn about what was or was not acted on, or what rubbish they affect to believe about crossing the sea. These matters do not concern us. What does concern us, and you especially, is what will happen on parade tomorrow morning. Here are your orders.'

As the sun climbed steadily up the sky, shadows shortened and heat began to beat back from the dusty surface of the barrack square.

On three sides of it, standing rigidly to attention, metal shackles around their ankles, were men of the regiment about to be disbanded. Ben picked up a pair of binoculars from a table in the mess anteroom and scanned their faces. Many looked old to be fighting soldiers, with grey moustaches and sideburns. Some were fifty, some sixty. From their teens they had served in the Company's army. This was, as they said with total truth, their father and their mother. Eventually, they had hoped to retire with pensions and return to their villages. As elders, men who had travelled, they would be deferred to, their opinions valued.

Now, they would go back penniless and disgraced, without one anna in pension, their lives in uniform wasted. Who now would listen to them, what work could they find to keep them, even in the slender necessities of food and shelter?

In the centre of the parade ground stood three siege guns, barrels polished, wheel spokes newly lacquered and shining black. The guns' muzzles pointed up to the sky at their highest elevation. In front of each stood a sepoy, and to one side a British soldier holding a crudely fashioned wooden cross in the shape of an 'X' as tall as a man.

Colonel Deakin, on his horse, was addressing the regiment. He spoke slowly and clearly in English, and an interpreter repeated every sentence. A slight breeze blew, and Ben did not hear all the words.

'A day of dishonour . . . You have eaten the Company's salt for years. Now you have forfeited the right to call yourselves soldiers . . . You have deliberately refused orders . . . Under the malign influence of agitators, you refuse to accept the assurance of your officers that the new ammunition is not greased with the fat of the cow or the lard of the pig. You believe lies. Worse, three have refused to embark on a ship for service in Rangoon. Since the army is engaged in operations in Burma, it is on a footing of war, not peace. The sentence for disobeying a direct order in war is death.'

He raised his sword. The sun shone brightly on the burnished blade. For a moment, Ben was reminded of Karim Khan and the fair in Scotland; he remembered his sword shining in the light of the oil lamps. How long ago all that seemed now! A different time, a different world.

'You are due out on parade now,' the adjutant told Ben sharply. 'Give the gunners the order to fire.'

'I cannot do that,' Ben replied flatly.

'What the devil do you mean, you cannot do that? It's an *order*. Get out there!'

'I cannot be ordered to commit murder.'

'It's not murder. It's your colonel's order. At this rate, you'd call shooting an enemy murder.'

'These sepoys are not our enemies. They have been bamboozled by clever people. We should be after *them*, not killing these simple soldiers.'

'I don't want a bloody dissertation on what we should or should not do. Are you going out there or not? The colonel's said his piece. You are to take over the parade, at once.'

'Not to kill those men.'

'Then say you're ill, for God's sake. A touch of the sun, fever, anything. You'll be court-martialled otherwise.'

'I am not ill, but maybe everyone else is ill who thinks this is right.'

'Right doesn't come into it. We must have discipline. Can't you understand that? Anyhow, we can't stand arguing here. For the last time, are you going or not?'

'No. I cannot. If you blow these men from guns, we're not only destroying their bodies, we're killing their souls. Hindus believe there is no afterlife for them, they will simply become ghosts, unless their bodies are burned to ashes or consigned to the River Ganges. Muslims believe that only those who die unmutilated as when they were born – unless they are injured honourably on the field of battle – will ever reach Paradise. Can't you see what we're doing?'

'I am not responsible for what they believe in their damned heathen religions,' replied the adjutant. 'I carry out my colonel's orders. If everyone started querying every order, we'd not have an army at all. You're a bloody stupid young pup. I wouldn't be in your shoes for a fortune when the colonel hears of this.'

The adjutant turned to Bruce Deakin.

'Ride out,' he told him brusquely. 'Take over the firing party. The colonel's waiting. You give the orders to fire.'

Deakin jumped on his horse. The sun glittered on his spurs, and on the polished jaws of huge metal pincers that two regimental blacksmiths were already carrying out to the centre of the ground. They saluted the colonel, then turned to the prisoners.

The pincers bit through their shackles. The blacksmiths picked them up, stood smartly to one side, saluted the colonel for a second time, then marched off the square. The sepoys were marched towards the guns, tied to the wooden crosses in front of their muzzles.

Deakin now saluted in his turn.

'Carry on,' the colonel told him shortly. Where the devil was that fellow Bannerman? He should be out here, not Bruce. But this wasn't the time or the place to start asking questions. On parade was on parade; here, nothing else counted.

Ben heard the gunners cry: 'Number one gun ready, sir!'

'Number two!'

'Number three!'

Then he heard Bruce Deakin's voice.

'Siege gun firing party, prepare to fire!'

A pause.

'*Fire!*'

The guns leapt up and back, digging their long metal trails into the hard surface of the parade ground.

The thunder of the explosions drove carrion birds out of the sky. The air was instantly fouled by the hot stench of gunpowder, burned human flesh, calcined bones. As pieces of the dead began to fall, the vultures returned to swoop greedily on red raw gobbets of meat.

The colonel rode back, dismounted. A groom led away his charger.

'Come into my office,' the colonel ordered Ben furiously. He nodded at the adjutant. 'And you, please. We have a serious problem on our hands.'

The adjutant followed them in.

'Why weren't you on parade as I ordered?' the colonel asked Ben.

'I could not give the order to shoot those men.'

'*Couldn't?* So you refused an order from your colonel? My God, Bannerman, if you were a ranker you'd be given field punishment. For refusing an order, any order, you'd be strapped to the wheel of a gun for a day in the heat of the sun, as well as receiving fifty lashes on your bare back.

'You have no defence, no extenuating circumstances. In full view of an entire Indian regiment being disbanded and dishonoured you deliberately dishonour your commission by disobeying orders I gave to you only hours ago, and the adjutant repeated minutes ago.

'I have no doubt whatever that a court martial will find you guilty of the most serious crime in the army. You will be cashiered and possibly after a period in prison have to re-enlist as a so-called gentleman ranker. You know what that means? A living hell.

Hated by the other rankers, and an object of contempt to your officers.'

Then suddenly the colonel paused. He disliked this young bastard for reasons he could not quite understand. Everything about Bannerman annoyed him. He had therefore deliberately sought to humiliate him and organised his posting almost as soon as he had arrived. Bannerman had offered to spy on the regiment's behalf to find out the plans of his rival for promotion to brigadier. He had refused the offer, and then been overtaken by the unspeakable bounder Street, who certainly was no friend of his.

The new brigadier might well wish to make a meal out of this episode simply to put Deakin in his place, show who was now in command. As brigadier he could even order a court of inquiry to discover why a junior officer, just out from England and new to the regiment, had been given this distasteful duty with a firing party. The court might also seek to discover why Bannerman was being posted away when he wanted to stay. Street might even find Bannerman congenial; they both spoke the bloody lingo well.

If he court-martialled Bannerman, then Bannerman would be punished, of course, but he himself could come in for criticism and, worse, public humiliation. He would do better to tread warily. The pup was being posted in any case. He would order him to leave at first light with that other misfit, Ritchie. Let him go. Good riddance.

The colonel cleared his throat. 'I'm disgusted by your performance, Bannerman. I will make the strongest comments about it on your personal report. But since you are being posted, I have decided it would be best for all concerned, not least the good name of the regiment, if you get out of here tomorrow at oh-six-hundred hours on the clear understanding I never see you again. Yours is not the behaviour of an officer I can trust, or of a gentleman in whom I can confide.'

He paused again. These words sounded curiously familiar. Of course, they were the same words he had spoken years ago to that doctor fellow, Kintyre, who came out of Kabul. A fishy business; one survivor and a baby who had grown up and was now standing in front of him. Well, he was getting rid of this man as he had got rid of the doctor.

He looked up at Ben. 'Well? Have you anything to say?'

'Only this, sir. I did not object, nor can any soldier, to a serious punishment for mutiny. It must be salutary, and be seen by everyone that there is no quibbling, no hanging back. But here, with feelings already very sensitive in the Indian community, I feel the sentence on the three sepoys was, on the most basic level, unwise. An entire regiment, nine hundred emissaries of revolution and discontent, are now leaving this headquarters for their villages all over India. They go as ambassadors of riot and resentment to spread the news that the British are punishing offenders not only in this world, but, according to their religious beliefs, also in the next.'

'You have had your say, Bannerman. Now I will have mine. I do not like you. You are a troublemaker. I have been lenient with you today because I want you out of my sight and out of this regimental headquarters tomorrow. I will then do my utmost to forget I ever had the misfortune to meet you. Do not come into the mess tonight, and do not mix with any other officers. If they learned the reasons you give for your unforgivable conduct, I could not be responsible for your safety. And believe me, I don't want to be.'

He turned to the adjutant.

'See the surgeon major. Have him put it about that

Bannerman has been taken ill suddenly. A touch of the sun. Fever. Anything. And refuse to say any more, no matter who asks you. Understood?'

'Perfectly, sir.'

'Good.' Colonel Deakin turned back to Ben. 'You heard that. Now *get out!*'

Ben went back to his bungalow. He was not thinking about the colonel, but about something he had seen in the instant when the guns fired. The explosions had released an enormous amount of energy, sufficient to dig the guns' trails deep into the hardened surface of the parade ground. That energy was being totally wasted, as when a soldier fired a musket or a rifle, as he'd first noticed at the firing range with Ritchie. Once again he wondered whether this force could not be utilised in some way instead of being dissipated.

He remembered the *munshi*'s statement: every experience can be put to worthwhile use.

If he could marshal his thoughts and find an answer to the problem, then maybe, just maybe, those three sepoys might not have died entirely in vain.

Captain Cartwright looked up irritably from his desk in the Guard Commander's office in Delhi as the British sergeant saluted.

'A *jemadar* outside, sir,' the sergeant announced. 'He'd like to see you on a personal matter.'

'How personal?' asked Cartwright bluntly. His wife Madge was lying in a darkened room complaining of an unusually bad headache. The long voyage and then the even more uncomfortable journey in a swaying *doolie* from Calcutta had weakened her. She appeared much more incapacitated than in London, and the surgeon major had been unable to prescribe any treatment that could help her.

And that delectable creature Mary Jane was not

responding to his advances as willingly as he had hoped – and expected. Damn it, he had made over goodness knew how many properties to her, but women were ungrateful creatures. He must not appear too eager; that would only make her realise her power, how much he needed her, and then she would increase her demands.

It was the devil of a situation to be in, two young women and no warmth, no passion, in a word *nothing* from either of them!

Cartwright did not speak any of the local languages or dialects, nor had he yet met the Indian contingent of his guard. He did not want to become embroiled with this junior Indian officer in some domestic matter. The sergeant guessed what Cartwright was thinking.

'He says it's about a military matter, sir. Not actually personal, as such.'

'Send him in then. With an interpreter.'

The interpreter was a thin, bald man with a wispy moustache and brass-rimmed circular spectacles. He bowed obsequiously and waited for the *jemadar* to speak first. Cartwright sat back, looking from one to the other as they jabbered away in an unintelligible tongue.

'Come to the point,' he told the interpreter sharply. 'What does the man say?'

'He says, Captain sahib, that a messenger has come to the King and shown him four chapattis dyed with red ochre, and an arrow dipped in oil.'

'Is this some sort of joke?'

'Not so, sahib. It is a signal. I have heard in the bazaar that other men are carrying these red chapattis. As they deliver them, they say: "From the north to the south. From the east to the west." It is a message.'

'Doesn't sound much of a message to me,' said Cartwright.

The interpreter put his head on one side in the Indian way to show that he heard this opinion but did not agree with it.

'He is also saying there are men who are willing to die for their religion.'

'Not surprising, surely?' Cartwright replied sarcastically. 'Men of good will in every nation are willing to die for their religion. It has been proved by the Christian martyrs time and again down the centuries. There is no reason Indians should be different. But what is the meaning of this message? Are they going to die now?'

'He says, sir, they are disaffected.'

'Who?'

'Sepoys, sahib.'

'Well, what can we do about it? We pay them, we clothe them, we feed them, we house them. What more do they want?'

'It is known you do these things, sahib. But I think they do not want to feel that their religious customs, ceremonies they have been brought up to from boyhood, are being taken away from them. Like suttee.'

'I wouldn't think the widows feel about that so strongly,' said Cartwright shortly. 'But thank him for coming to tell me. I appreciate it.'

'He says, sahib, that this message may seem obscure to many English people, but it really is very important. Would you please pass on this news to whoever needs to know? He says it is an urgent matter.'

'Yes, yes. Assure him all will be well. Now march the man out. And thank you very much.' Cartwright nodded dismissal.

The sergeant and the *jemadar* saluted and left. The interpreter paused for a moment as though he wished to say something more, but seeing Cartwright bent over his desk, apparently reading his papers, he bowed.

This sahib was not like the previous Guard Commander who had lived for years in India and had an Indian mistress. He would have listened sympathetically. But that sahib had been an officer of intelligence. This Captain Cartwright was a fool. His mind was asleep, and as the Prophet had said, sleep is the brother of death.

Mary Jane moved behind a curtain outside the door of Cartwright's office as the *jemadar* came out. She had overheard their conversation, and what the *jemadar* said held for her the hard stamp of truth. She had already heard rumours of discord and seen a telegraph message in Cartwright's room reporting that a regiment had been disbanded in Barrackpore, three sepoys shot from guns for mutiny, and trouble was likely elsewhere. Extra precautions should be taken, guards doubled on ammunition stores. Mary Jane sensed danger, a feeling she had already experienced three times in her life: when she and her mother had appeared before the magistrate; again with Mrs Mentmore; and then when she saw King Drummond outside Grimsdyke's house in Brighton. Each time, her presentiment had been justified.

She had intended going into Cartwright's office, but the sergeant was likely to return and what she had to say was for the captain's ears only. She went back to her own room. Curtains had been drawn across the windows to hold at bay the burning heat of noon. She lay down on the bed, kicked off her shoes and pressed both hands into her eyes as though she could physically blot out a vision of catastrophe that seemed imminent and unavoidable.

The house swarmed with Indian servants. She had only to clap her hands and one would come running to ask her wishes. The fact that there were so many would be dangerous in any emergency. The obsequity of these fawning creatures, bowing low as she passed by, squatting all night on the verandah outside her room in case she might call for a drink of water, could easily turn to rage. They knew where the captain kept his wife's jewels. There could be no secrets from them in this house, except, she hoped, the secret she kept strictly to herself but which she had meant to tell Cartwright that morning. She had not gone to his office in order to eavesdrop on a conversation with a British sergeant or an Indian *jemadar*; she had gone to tell him that the unthinkable had happened: she was pregnant.

She had thought she could avoid this. At Mrs Mentmore's, Beatrice had told her the value of a sponge soaked in vinegar, coated with butter and pushed into her vagina.

'That'll see you right, dearie,' Beatrice had assured her. 'Never known to fail. The tart's best friend, I call it.'

It had not proved to be hers; it had failed. Now she was at least six weeks pregnant. She had intended telling Cartwright and asking for money. Then she would leave on any excuse – illness, fever – and so save herself and him from social ostracism and disgrace. She could not stay and endure the indelible shame of an illegitimate child. Some of the odium that would surround her must brush off onto the captain. If he was not the father of her child, then who was? Mary Jane had been deflected by what she had overheard. Until then, she had tried to dismiss her feeling of impending doom, telling herself that the rumours of discord were exaggerated, untrue even, that her deep unease was due to her own most unfortunate condition. Now she realised it could also be due to a much wider, more important malaise.

She had felt so certain that she would be able to

continue exploiting the captain's weakness until she felt financially secure enough to be independent. She had never imagined such a setback. It seemed to her incredible that she should be with child as a result of Cartwright's pathetic attempts at lovemaking. It was manifestly unfair that she could apparently achieve motherhood so easily when it had never been contemplated and was not wanted, while childless wives would give anything to be pregnant. But incredible and unfair as this might be, she was with child and without any means of changing the fact.

Mary Jane desperately wanted someone in whom she could confide, a friend she could trust. There was no one. She could not very well tell her problems to Mrs Cartwright. And she guessed that as soon as she informed Captain Cartwright, he would immediately disown her and might possibly even cover himself by telling his wife he had reason to suspect Mary Jane's moral standards with other men; anything rather than become involved himself.

There must be someone, somewhere who could help her. But time was ticking away relentlessly. Every day meant one day nearer the eventual, inescapable discovery, unless . . . Unless what?

A servant tapped discreetly on her door.

'Come,' she called.

'Surgeon Major Evans, memsahib, to see Paul sahib.'

'Oh, yes.'

She had forgotten. The little boy complained of a sore throat which no amount of gargling with salt water seemed able to cure. Mary Jane swung her legs off the bed, put on her shoes and went downstairs to meet the surgeon major. He was a plump man, a widower in his fifties. He liked the company of pretty women and was known among officers' wives as a flirt, but quite harmless. He never touched them, never even attempted to, some of the older wives admitted in disappointed tones.

Like a night moth hovering around the globe of a lamp, he would flutter in and dart away again, making remarks that could be taken innocently or might have a deeper meaning, or again might mean nothing at all. He was a cheerful man. Sometimes patients consulted him, not because they were ill but because they wanted to hear his breezy comments on life and the human condition.

'Now,' he said, 'Miss Green. What's wrong with the young master today?'

She explained the symptoms. He nodded, followed her into the boy's room, opened his medicine case and took out a spatula.

'Open your mouth, my fine fellow,' he said. 'Ah, yes. Tonsils are a little red there. We should reduce those to the ranks, my boy. I'll give you something that will do the trick.'

He took a glass jar of pills from his black leather bag, shook some into a little wooden box and gave them to Mary Jane.

'Give him one three times a day after meals. Rest, warmth, and we'll soon have the young master on parade in fine form.'

'Thank you. That was very quick.'

'Well, it's not a very complicated matter. Infection's probably due to this damned country. Even the air is poisoned here. In England you can have a leg cut off and your wound will heal perfectly. Here, you cut a finger and it goes septic. Lucky if you don't lose your whole hand. Devil of a country. I don't know why it brought you here.'

'I thought it would be better than at home,' she replied simply. This seemed as a good a reason as any, and not so very far from the truth.

'You came out hoping to get married, did you? Like so many other young women?'

'No one's asked me so far.'

'They will, my dear. They will. You're a very handsome girl. Why, I had an enquiry about you only the other day.'

'About me? From whom?'

'One of the King's relations. Got so many he doesn't know who he is related to. Young Prince Munta Lal.'

'I don't know him,' she said.

'No. But he wants to know you. Wants to show you round the King's palace. All the sights of the city.'

'He is not British, then?'

'Hardly, with a name like that. One of the Leicestershire Lals, eh? Or maybe his seat is in Devon? He's Indian, of course. Very well-bred. Very rich, good-looking. Make a fine husband for someone.'

'Not for me, I think,' said Mary Jane.

'Well, you'll lose nothing by being civil to the fellow. I have a feeling we may need all the Indian friends we can get.'

'What gives you that feeling, Surgeon Major?'

'I've been out here all my working life. I know this country. I know the people. There's something happening in the army. They've always been loyal, always been good soldiers. Maybe our officers were a better type years ago than now. The present lot don't seem to understand the sepoys, and they're becoming restless.

'But that's by the by. I'll introduce you to the prince. I'm giving a dinner party tomorrow evening. He is among my guests. I'd be very happy if you would join us at nine o'clock. Have you a carriage?'

'No, I haven't. Captain Cartwright has, but . . .'

'Say no more. I will send mine for you. Half past

417

eight it will be here at the door. I think you will have an entertaining evening.'

Mary Jane had a most entertaining evening. The prince was all she had imagined an Indian prince would be: tall, broad-shouldered, handsome, with an aquiline nose, dark wavy hair, a small moustache. His clothes were of silk with gold buttons. He wore a turban with a jewel in front. He spoke perfect English.

'I have been to England,' he explained when she complimented him on this.

'You have?'

'Yes, I went on behalf of a relation of mine, the Nana Sahib, who lives in Cawnpore. You possibly have heard of him?'

Mary Jane shook her head. 'No, I haven't.'

'You must meet him. You would find him most charming. And now you are in my country, I would like to show you rooms in the palace that not many Europeans have ever seen. Or, except for you, are ever likely to see.'

'That is extremely kind of you,' said Mary Jane, flattered.

'It will be my pleasure. And I hope it will be yours. What time would be convenient to you, say, tomorrow?'

'I am looking after Captain Cartwright's son, who has not been very well. I don't think I could be away before the afternoon.'

'Shall we say about five, then? When the heat has left the day. This is the hottest time of year, and even palaces are better in the cool of the evening.'

They talked throughout dinner. Afterwards, Mary Jane could not remember what they talked about, but she had never met anyone who deferred to her opinion so readily, who clearly was so well read and far travelled that on any subject he had a point of view. He had been to this place or that, he had attended a royal garden party at Buckingham Palace, he had even been introduced to Queen Victoria. He had stayed with dukes and earls in England, travelled to France and to Italy where he had been the guest of counts and archdukes. Of course, the King of Delhi was one of his close friends; she must meet him.

She did so. She was rather unimpressed by the old man, with his toothless gums, lips sunk in on themselves as he sat, cross-legged, on a tasselled cushion on the floor, trembling in the odd way so many Indians had, as though his whole body must move in rhythm with every beat of his heart. The prince showed her the palace treasury: boxes of gold bars, each bar stamped with the King's crown; polished leather cases packed with diamonds and rubies that glittered and glowed against soft red plush as though they had a fierce, fiery life of their own.

She took tea with the prince. Not alone, of course. That would have been most indelicate, he assured her. But he had a sister who also spoke English and she appeared pleased to see Mary Jane and was a gracious and generous hostess.

Cartwright noticed this.

'I think I should warn you,' he said. 'We don't usually see too much of the prince. He's very close to the Nana Sahib.'

'He told me.'

'I would be careful in any dealings with Munta Lal. The Nana Sahib is not very friendly with the East India Company.'

'Why not?'

'The usual story. Money. If you're a maharajah, as he is, you've a number of retainers and pensioners you have to support. In his case he has fifteen thousand pensioners and probably half as many more servants he feels personally responsible for. He has to pay them all, feed them, provide them with living accommodation. That takes a lot of doing. And he's a generous man. He gives dinner parties and dances for our Commander-in-Chief in Cawnpore. He'll invite every officer in the garrison, and their ladies.'

'Is he very rich?' she asked Cartwright.

'Not by a maharajah's standards.'

'So how does he pay for all this?'

'Through loans. Moneylenders, banks, rich relations.'

'How is the East India Company involved?'

'In a rather complex way. The Nana Sahib is not a true son of the old Maharajah, Biji Rao, but an adopted son.'

Cartwright explained how the British had defeated Biji Rao at the battle of Seoni nearly forty years before. It was then agreed that he would give up his title in return for what the Company's lawyers carefully phrased 'a palace in Benares or any other sacred place in Hindustan'. More importantly, he was to receive an annual pension of 800,000 rupees, roughly £60,000.

'Biji Rao had no son to carry on. Two were born to him but died very young, one within days, the other before he was two. His wives, concubines and mistresses produced any number of daughters for him but not a male heir. Finally, he adopted two boys. The eldest, who inherited everything on the old man's death, is known as the Nana Sahib, a nickname meaning grandmother.

'Nana Sahib assumed that the Company would keep on paying the pension to him when the old man died, but they didn't. Their profits were down, and they said they couldn't afford to. He sent a couple of emissaries to London to try and persuade them to change their mind. One was your new friend, the other an employee, Azi Mullah. He'd been a servant, then a tutor. He told Nana he knew all kinds of important English people who had influence with the Company. So he did, but only through waiting at table or teaching their children. Neither of these emissaries managed to change the Company's view.'

'Will it ever be changed?'

'Only if they thought that to do so could be in their interests. It would certainly remove a longstanding point of contention if they did. But, enough of this talk. My lady wife is out for the afternoon, taking tea. One of the very few engagements she has felt well enough to attend. We have a clear hour.'

Even as Cartwright spoke, his hands were undoing the buttons on Mary Jane's blouse. She closed her eyes, hoping she could conceal the distaste she felt for this crude mauling – and for herself. If only she could tell him of her plight; if only she could tell anyone . . .

Mary Jane decided on her next move at a small party the Guard Commander gave for the handful of British officers in Delhi. Most were rather older than Cartwright. They pretended to enjoy themselves, but kept looking over the shoulder of the person to whom they were talking in case anyone more important or influential, who might help them to advance their careers, was approaching.

The only way out of her dilemma was by marriage. As she reached this conclusion she thought how her mother had also reached it before her. It had not brought happiness to her, and there was no reason to suppose it would have a different result now. But what else could she do?

As an unmarried English mother she would be an outcast. And how could she support herself and a

421

child? What folly to have allowed herself to fall into this ancient trap!

She did not know any Englishman she might marry. The only possible candidate was Munta Lal. At least he was rich and good-looking and kind. As she tried to list points in his favour, she realised one vital thing was missing: she did not love him, did not even care for him. And as she admitted this to herself, she suddenly thought of Ben. If only he were here, if only she could tell him. He would understand; of that she felt certain.

Surgeon Major Evans raised his glass in Mary Jane's direction.

'Avoiding the sawbones, are you?' he asked her jovially. 'I've been trying to catch your eye for ages.'

'I'm sorry. I was miles away.'

'How's the young musketeer? Throat on the mend?'

'He's quite all right now, thank you.'

'As I thought. Never known those pills to fail. Not for nothing am I called "Kill or Cure Evans".'

She smiled politely and then noticed that the surgeon major was not smiling.

'Come over here,' he told her in an uncharacteristically low voice. 'I'd like to speak to you in private if I can. Or as privately as is possible with all this talk going on.'

For a moment Mary Jane felt her heart sink. Could the doctor know she was pregnant? It didn't show yet, she was certain, but perhaps there was some medical sign in her face, her eyes, of which she was unaware? He couldn't know she was being sick every morning. No one would have told him. Or would they? You could never trust the maids. They were little better than domestic spies, passing on any absurd, apparently useless information to the servants of other families, who passed it on to their employers, who passed it back again. She smiled at the doctor mechanically.

Evans took her arm and guided her out of the main room into a small anteroom hung with curtains; brass ornaments glittered with coloured glass inserts. The room had a strong, not unpleasant smell of sandalwood and incense.

'That Indian prince I introduced you to,' he began, and then paused as though uncertain how to continue. 'I'd better come to the point right away in case we're interrupted,' he went on hurriedly. 'It's no business of mine, but as an older man who's been out here for many years, and a doctor, I think I may be forgiven if I offer you some advice. Unasked, and probably unwanted.'

Again he paused.

'Please go on,' she said.

'I can't help noticing, and some other people have also drawn the matter to my attention, that you see quite a lot of him. He's a charming man of honour and distinction. But he is an Indian. I don't know what his intentions are, but I am sure they are honourable in every respect.

'So I thought I should tell you, if he should ever ask you to marry him and you should feel disposed to accept his proposal, please realise there may be consequences that someone like you, just out from England, may not fully realise.'

'Such as what?' she asked him. 'Our children?'

'Oh, possibly. But that's something people soon get used to. A number of people here have an Indian father and an English mother or vice versa. Mostly, I must admit, in the other ranks, but that is by the by.

'If you marry him, you may have a Christian wedding, though as he is a devout Hindu I think it would be a native ceremony. Very colourful, very splendid. But once you are his wife, you may find you are not invited to English houses, or to Indian ones, either, for that matter.

'These things are important to both sides, you know. You won't fit in with their way of life, their culture and religious beliefs any more than he will fit into yours. You will both cut yourselves off from your own kind. It might even be a total break – on both sides. You have no relations here. He has dozens, so it could hurt him more than it would hurt you.

'Please forgive me for being so frank, but in my profession honesty is essential. Friendship with the prince is one thing. So is what I might call an *association*. Marriage is something quite different.'

'Thank you,' said Mary Jane. 'I will bear in mind everything you say. Now, I think we should rejoin the dancers.'

He bowed. 'Of course.'

As she came back into the room, Munta Lal approached her.

'I've been wanting to speak to you all evening,' he said. 'But you are in great demand.'

'It is very flattering to hear you say so.'

'I wanted to ask you something. I am going up north to Cawnpore. I have an invitation to visit my relation, the Nana Sahib. He has some problems with John Company. I think I can probably help to solve them – with your assistance.'

'Mine?' Mary Jane asked him, surprised. 'How could I possibly help?'

'First, you are English, and the Company is an English company. For another, you are here with Captain Cartwright, who holds a most important position as Guard Commander to the King. The captain is a wealthy man. He would not have chosen you if you were not high born. Maybe you know people who have the ear of the Company's directors. You could point out to your friends the injustice the Nana Sahib has borne without complaint, how his influence in India for peace and harmony could help advance the Company's commercial interests. If you could help the Nana Sahib, he would show his gratitude to you in a positive way.'

'What do you mean?'

'He would give you a present of jewels, diamonds, rubies. Or if you did not wish for jewellery, a large sum of money.'

'Are you being serious?'

'Of course. This is not a subject for jest.'

She looked at him sharply. Had he been cultivating her just for this? Did he really like her? Did either of these questions matter?

'I would be honoured to come with you,' she said. 'But would that not arouse comment? I am unmarried and unchaperoned, and I have my work here.'

'I will give you a guard to accompany you.'

'And what will you tell your relations in Cawnpore?'

'I will tell them a lie. It is sometimes expedient to lie when great issues are involved. In such circumstances, the value of the end excuses the means.'

'What is the lie?'

'I will say that we are married.'

'I am not going to live with you,' Mary Jane said coldly. She wanted no part in some illicit relationship.

'I am aware of that,' he replied. 'We would occupy separate rooms, perhaps even separate houses. The Nana Sahib is not a poor man by normal standards, although he complains of poverty.'

'Would he not think this suspicious if we are supposed to be married?'

'Not at all. You are English. What might be thought unusual with other people is generally held to be the natural thing for the English.'

'I must have time to consider your kind invitation,'

she told him. 'I would not want to accept your hospitality, and that of the Nana Sahib, unless I had some confidence I could help him in return.'

The offer was attractive, but was it feasible? She knew no one of influence, but equally saw no reason to admit this. And how could she possibly get away from Delhi for several weeks?

Next morning, she had her answer. Mrs Cartwright asked to see her. Mary Jane found her sitting on the verandah, fanning herself. She looked very pale; her face shone with unhealthy perspiration. Mary Jane had no idea why her mistress had summoned her so unexpectedly, and in the morning. Usually, Mrs Cartwright was not out of bed before eleven, and here at eight o'clock she was up and dressed. Surely she could not know she was pregnant?

Mary Jane stood, eyes downcast, so that Mrs Cartwright would not see the fear in them. Mrs Cartwright cleared her throat, fanned herself more vigorously.

'I called you here,' she said, 'because a distant relation of mine has just written to say she is coming to Delhi. She is what I would call a poor relation, and she has expressed herself willing to look after Paul in return for her keep.'

'You mean for good, ma'am?'

'No, no. For a few weeks, that is all. But if you have any friends you would like to visit, or sightseeing to do, or something like that, I thought she could have your room. This is rather a small house, as you know.'

'I could sleep somewhere else, ma'am.'

'Yes, yes, but I think that would not be convenient for you or for us. I suggest therefore that from Friday, when she is due to arrive, you make your own arrangements for the next three or four weeks. We'll be very glad to have you back, of course. You've looked after Paul very well, and he is extremely fond of you. But when you're in a place like Delhi, single, unattached, unencumbered, as they say, it is good to get about and see some of the sights. A remarkable city, Delhi, remarkable.' She smiled at Mary Jane.

Mary Jane tried to smile back. Their eyes met. Does she know about the captain and me? Mary Jane wondered. Does she suspect? Does she even imagine, which is probably worse than knowing or suspecting? It was impossible to say.

Mary Jane bowed. 'As you wish, ma'am.'

She left the verandah, went downstairs. Munta Lal was standing in the doorway.

'I was passing,' he said. 'I thought I'd call in. Have you thought any more about the trip to Cawnpore?'

'Yes. Quite a lot,' said Mary Jane. 'I've decided to accept your offer. I'd be very pleased to come with you. On the conditions we discussed, of course.'

'Of course,' he said, and smiled.

The Nana Sahib was a plump, shortish man who shaved his head in the fashion of the Mahrattas, one of India's most renowned martial races. There was, however, nothing especially military about the Nana Sahib. He was of a studious nature, quiet, well-read. He took very seriously what he considered his obligations to the thousands of people who relied on him for their food, their shelter, indeed their whole means of livelihood. Being adopted did not in any way diminish his sense of obligation and honour to those he knew depended on him.

For this reason, what he considered to be the deliberate parsimony of the East India Company was all the more unbelievable; he simply could not comprehend why, when his adoptive father died, the Company had refused to grant him the old man's pension. The Company was probably the richest in the East, possibly in the world, nor were they usually niggardly.

The ruler of Mysore had unwisely pitted his forces against the Company's army, and as a result had been decisively defeated. But on his death, the Company literally poured money upon his descendants and gave them a fine palace, bearing all expenses themselves.

Even the King of Delhi, a useless and enfeebled old man, was treated with honour and enjoyed a huge pension. The difference between their status and his coloured all the Nana Sahib's thoughts and actions. He continually sought for some way, any way, to persuade the Company's directors to change their minds.

The Nana Sahib kept on extremely good terms with the commander of the British forces in the area, General Sir Hugh Wheeler. In the hope that Wheeler could, or would, influence the Company, Nana gave lavish parties, dances and balls for officers and their ladies. He would invite as many as a hundred people to dine with him.

His guests noted that he served wine in a curious mixture of crystal champagne goblets and thick-bottomed tumblers which he had bought as a job lot from an American commercial traveller in glassware. Sometimes there were not enough table napkins to go round; instead, bathroom towels were cut into squares. The cutlery did not always match; side plates were stamped with odd regimental crests.

His guests, of course, thought that these eccentricities were the foibles of a very rich man. They found them amusing, almost endearing. They did not realise that the Nana Sahib could not afford to buy in such numbers plates or cutlery that matched, or the correct glasses for wine he did not drink himself.

When he sent his emissary, Azi Mullah, to London to try and plead with the directors face to face, he gave him fifty thousand golden sovereigns to cover his expenses and any bribes he felt might be necessary to pay.

In London, Azi Mullah realised very quickly that his master's case was hopeless; the directors would never change their minds. This knowledge he did not pass on to the Nana Sahib, nor was he in any hurry to return to India. Life in England was infinitely more agreeable.

He took on the title 'Prince', bought two large houses, one in Brighton and one in Belgravia. With his charm and obvious wealth, no one looked into his background. They accepted him for what he was, an Indian potentate loaded with money. He became very popular at fashionable dinner parties. Women were especially intrigued by his charm and sexuality. Was it true that Indians were masters in the Oriental arts of love? What exactly *was* the Kama Sutra? Azi Mullah was willing to explain by example; he could claim to have seduced nearly half of the titled younger hostesses in the kingdom. The others, he said modestly, had seduced him.

But finally Azi Mullah's money was all spent and he returned to India, leaving gigantic debts behind him. To excuse his prodigal expenditure to the Nana Sahib, he explained that in good faith he had given huge bribes to directors and their families. They had promised him all manner of things on the Nana Sahib's behalf, but they had not kept their word. The perfidious English had taken his money and dishonoured their bond.

The Nana Sahib was not a travelled man. He was so obsessed by what he felt was disgraceful treatment by the Company that he believed Azi Mullah implicitly. But where one had failed, perhaps another would succeed, so he sent a second emissary to England, Prince Munta Lal.

He fared no better. All that could be said in his

favour was that he spent only a fraction of the sum Azi Mullah had squandered, and punctiliously itemised all his accounts.

On this particular morning, the Nana Sahib paced up and down the marble floor of his palace overlooking the Ganges. His hands were clasped tightly behind his back. His soft leather shoes made no sound on the rich Afghan carpets that covered the centre of the vast room. Out beyond the coolness of this great and elegant room, the sun transformed the sluggish tide into a river of fire.

Pious Hindus believed if they could die on its banks they would be instantly transported to eternal bliss and walk for ever in the shady glades of Paradise. The river had many names that spoke of its magical powers and properties. It was Punya, the Auspicious; Ramya, the Beautiful; and Bhagya-Janani, the Creator of Happiness. Would that in some miraculous way the river, in which every morning the Nana Sahib performed his ablutions and said his prayers, could bring him happiness and release from his worries over finance!

As he came to the end of the hall and turned, he saw a man standing in one of the open archways, watching him. The man bowed low, pressing his two hands together in homage and greeting. The Nana Sahib recognised Azi Mullah, and his heart warmed to him. He was a loyal fellow indeed, a closer friend than many a brother.

'You wish to speak to me?' he asked.

'I have news for you, sir. Important news. Munta Lal is on his way here from Delhi. He has a wife.' Azi Mullah paused.

'Is that all your news?'

Azi Mullah smiled. 'Partly. But she is not of our faith. She is English. A Christian, apparently.'

'Why is he bringing her here?'

430

'She has been working for the British commander of the King of Delhi's guard, a nurse for his young son. I am told she is on the most intimate terms with this commander, one Captain Cartwright.'

'Does Munta Lal know this?'

'Only that she came out from England with the family. My understanding is that she is a spy for the Company.'

'What can she spy on here? We have nothing but debts and petitions from old retainers who have to live on a single bowl of rice a day. Would that this woman might tell the truth to her masters that to keep our honour bright we are reduced to borrowing from moneylenders.'

'I think this English woman is coming here to report to John Company on the style you keep. I would therefore suggest, Your Highness, that you are not too generous in your hospitality. If you appear to be rich, why should they give you a pension?'

The Nana Sahib nodded; Azi Mullah always made sense. He was a good man. The Nana Sahib was straightforward in his dealings with people. It never struck him that Azi Mullah could be envious of Munta Lal, who was a prince of the blood, and not, like Azi Mullah, only the hireling of an adopted prince.

'When will they arrive?'

'Very shortly. Relays of runners have brought me this news, so they will not be far behind them.'

'Did the runners bring other news?'

'Yes, Your Highness, and of events that could help your claim for fair treatment from the Company. They report a serious outbreak of unrest among the Indian troops in Barrackpore. They refused to accept cartridges which were greased, unbelievably, with pig's lard and cow's fat. The regiment has been disbanded.

As a warning, three sepoys who would not take ship for Burma were blown from guns. There have been stories of desertions elsewhere, of groups of deserters and soldiers from the regiment disbanded in Barrackpore drifting towards Delhi. They regard the old King as their sovereign.'

'How can this affect me?'

'Any insurrection must weaken and diminish existing authority. You are a loyal friend of the English, Your Highness. They will have few friends if insurrection spreads. So this is how I suggest we can turn these events and the visit of Munta Lal's English bride to your very great advantage . . .'

Mary Jane's first view of the Nana Sahib's palace was of a white building set in fields, yellow with mustard flowers, stretching unbroken from the Ganges to the foothills beyond.

The palace was surrounded by smaller buildings one storey high, all encompassed by a white wall. Outside this, a few goats were tethered and sacred cows moved slowly, languidly, without effort or purpose. The river ran heavy and flat and oily. On its banks stood temples, large and small; their tiny bells tinkled like tin cans in the hot afternoon wind. Steps green with slime led down to the water's edge, where the faithful would regularly bathe in the river which they hoped would one day receive them and bear them on to life eternal.

Mary Jane was in a *doolie* carried by eight bearers. The *doolie*'s canvas sides were rolled up for the sake of coolness; she felt relaxed and at ease. A man riding a white horse came out to meet them. Behind him rode six servants. He reined in as the caravan of horses and bearers and camels came to a halt.

'Greetings in the name of His Royal Highness,' said Azi Mullah.

'You do not seem surprised to see us,' replied Munta Lal suspiciously.

'I had news of your arrival only moments before,' he replied smoothly. 'A messenger from Delhi, bringing personal letters from the King, gave us the glad tidings of your visit.'

The Nana Sahib placed a small bungalow at Mary Jane's disposal. After the blaze of noon outside, it felt chill as a tomb within. The straw roof was kept damp by relays of *bhistis* throwing pails of water drawn from the river. Mary Jane thought that the house inside smelt stale as a stagnant pond.

It contained three rooms. In the largest were several heavy armchairs and a sofa. The table had a wedge under one of its legs to keep it level on an uneven floor. Carpets were faded and threadbare.

The next room contained a bed with a rope mattress, rather soggy pillows, sheets already folded down, a chest of drawers of unpainted wood, a table. A crudely framed mirror hung from a nail. Oil lamps stood on small tables.

The third room was a bathroom with a metal washbasin on a stand. A glass was inverted on a carafe of greenish water to keep out insects; a red enamel dish held a bar of cheap soap.

'This is the best guesthouse,' Munta Lal assured her. 'He has dozens and I know this is the finest.'

'Why has he so many guesthouses? Is he very hospitable?'

'Every November a religious festival is held here because in this place Bramah finished creating the world. Afterwards, he offered a horse in sacrifice, to mark the end of his grand design. During this ceremony a pin came out of Bramah's shoe. A disciple built it into one of the steps of the main temple. Now pilgrims come every November from all over India to worship here. They sleep in skin tents, in reed shelters, or out under the stars, anywhere. The most important and influential, of course, stay in houses like this. You are fortunate to be honoured in this way.'

'I don't like this house,' Mary Jane told Munta Lal bluntly when Azi Mullah had left.

'It may not be like a house in England, but it is as good as Captain Cartwright's in Delhi.'

'Possibly. But there's something odd about the atmosphere. It is evil.'

'Nonsense. You're just tired.'

'No,' she said. 'I cannot sleep here.'

'But you must. I'll stay here with you.'

She shook her head. 'No. That wasn't the arrangement. But where are you sleeping?'

'I have many relations here,' he replied. 'One of them has made a room available for me. His house is not far from here.'

'Was he surprised that although we are married we are not sleeping together?'

'As I told you, they expect odd things of the English.'

'Let me change places with you. I cannot stay here. Not for a day, not for a night.'

'But my relation might see you.'

'I'd come in late at night when it's dark. You sleep here.'

'The servants would know. They know everything.'

'Bribe them. But, whatever happens, I cannot stay here.'

Munta Lal looked at her closely, expecting her to change her mind; women were fickle. Mary Jane guessed his thoughts, shook her head firmly.

'All right,' he said reluctantly. 'But you will have to keep clothes here. If my relation finds out, he'll think I have made a mock of him. He will be dis-

434

pleased. Then he could tell the Nana Sahib that you don't think his best guesthouse is good enough for you. The Nana Sahib is always on the lookout for any insult or imagined slight.'

'When do we see him, anyhow?'

'I have to arrange this with Azi Mullah. You have a bath here now. I'll come back in an hour.'

Mary Jane took off her clothes, went into the bathroom. A *bhisti* had filled the tin bath with warm water. She climbed into it, soaped herself and then lay back thinking. Why did she dislike this house so much? Was it as eerie as she claimed, or was she imagining its malevolence because she was tired and felt alone and vulnerable?

A tiny scuttering sound broke into her thoughts. A rat was watching her with baleful eyes from a corner. The eyes reminded her of the rats in the pit at the Pig and Whistle public house near Bostal Heath.

She climbed quickly out of the bath, dried herself. Lizards hung motionless on the walls; cockroaches crawled across the damp floor. This might be the best house, but it was rarely cleaned. It probably had not been used since the previous November. She dressed and waited for Munta Lal to return.

'I've made arrangements to see the Nana Sahib tomorrow morning at ten o'clock,' he announced. 'He is most interested to meet you. We have a chance of doing something really worthwhile, not only for ourselves, but for both our countries.'

Mary Jane did not reply; she could not imagine what she could do to help anyone, let alone a maharajah. She knew no one of influence, and even if she met someone, how could anything she said help the Nana Sahib in any way whatever? Munta Lal was totally mistaken, but he was a pleasant man, and if he believed she could help his relation, then the least she could do was to listen to whatever proposal either man might make.

They ate that night in a small dining room, Azi Mullah, Munta Lal, Mary Jane, and two of Munta Lal's relations, Moti and Rajiv Lal, in whose house she planned to sleep. They spoke English, and she sensed their hostility: she was a stranger, a white-skinned foreigner. Why had Munta Lal married someone not of his faith or his race?

Azi Mullah's hostility was equally strong. Not only did she dislike him, she distrusted him. His eyes were too close together, he smiled too much, shrugged his shoulders too often. Her distrust of him was instinctive; the chemistry between them was wrong. As the meal progressed, she knew it would never improve.

She began to wish she had not accepted Munta Lal's invitation to accompany him. She had not been entirely at ease in Captain Cartwright's house, but life there was infinitely more pleasant than here. She began to suffer from a dull ache in her stomach and longed to be alone, in bed, not forced to make ridiculous conversation with people who disliked her so strongly. Was this pain due to her condition, or simply because she felt tired and, she finally admitted, afraid?

After the meal, she began to feel sleepy; the pain receded.

'If I may say so, Miss Green, I think an early night for you would be advisable,' said Azi Mullah earnestly. 'Coming from the heat of Delhi to our climate here often has a fatiguing effect on English ladies. In a day or two you will be acclimatised, and no doubt enjoy the recreations you ladies like so much, riding side-saddle, playing tennis, dancing.'

'Thank you,' she said. 'I am a little fatigued.'

She warmed to him unexpectedly. He was clearly doing his best to be friendly and considerate. The fact was, she felt exhausted. Probably being pregnant was the reason. She must do her utmost to impress the Nana Sahib; she desperately needed money from somewhere. She would go to bed right away and feel fresher and more alert in the morning.

Munta Lal jumped up. 'If you will excuse us,' he said, 'we will both retire. I will see you tomorrow morning, Azi Mullah, in the palace, just before ten.'

The others stood up and bowed courteously. Munta Lal escorted Mary Jane outside. The night was warm and the river moved slowly, sluggish now as mercury, under a rising moon. A bearer squatting outside the door of the guesthouse stood up to salaam as they arrived.

'You may go,' Munta Lal told him. 'We will want you here at eight o'clock tomorrow morning.'

They watched him walk away, his leather *chaplis* flapping in the dust of the compound, then went into the bungalow. Curtains had been drawn and candles lit. A few moths fluttered transparent wings around the flames; mosquitoes droned unseen and ever-present. Mary Jane picked up a small bag in which she had put her nightclothes and washing items. Munta Lal escorted her the short distance to his relations' home, a three-storey house. They went upstairs to his bedroom. It was on the second floor and opened onto a verandah. A candle burned on a bedside table.

'Wait here in the morning. I will come and see you before eight o'clock,' he told her. 'If my relation sees us together, he will think nothing of it. If he sees you on your own, he may. You understand?'

'Perfectly. And thank you for agreeing to this. I appreciate your kindness very much.'

'Goodnight,' he said.

'Goodnight,' said Mary Jane. As she locked her door, she thought that this was the first and only time a man had not sought to take advantage because she was on her own, had not sought to fondle her, kiss her, slip a questing hand beneath her skirt. Then she paused. No, it was not the first time, but the second. The first person who had never attempted to take any advantage had been Ben.

The sun peering through the bedroom window woke her early. Mary Jane sat up and looked out at the flowing river. On its banks, *dhobi* men were already pounding shirts and sheets on flat rocks, chanting as soapsuds swilled away in the tide. She felt heavy, listless, glanced at her watch: half past eight. Where was Munta Lal? He had promised to be here half an hour earlier. She had overslept. Had he arrived, found the door locked and gone away again? Perhaps he had knocked on the door, not loudly in case he woke his relation, and she had not heard him and slept on.

She washed and dressed hurriedly, sat waiting for him. Nine o'clock, five past nine. He must have overslept, too. Their appointment with the Nana Sahib was at ten. She could not wait any longer; she must risk being seen and go to the bungalow and wake him up.

Mary Jane gathered her belongings together, pushed them into her bag, opened the door carefully. The verandah was empty; it was safe to leave. Walking as quickly as she could, she went down the stairs at the back of the house, and made her way to the guest bungalow. This verandah was also empty. How odd! A bearer's duty, indeed his whole livelihood, depended on his obeying his master's commands, interpreting his wishes. She had heard Munta Lal tell the bearer to be there at eight o'clock. Where could he be? She turned the doorknob. It opened easily. She went into the main room, walked through it into the bedroom, pulled the heavy curtains. Then she screamed.

Munta Lal lay on his back on the bed with a fine silk cord round his neck. It had been drawn so tightly that his eyes had burst out of their sockets like huge onions. His mouth was open. His tongue protruded to an enormous and unexpected length. His face was purple, his hands locked, gripping the cord in a desperate attempt to loosen it. Flies buzzed greedily around his nose and lips. Had he killed himself? Impossible. He had been murdered.

A slight noise made her turn. For a second, she saw a dark face at the window. Then, like a shadow on a summer lawn, it was gone. She ran to the door. A man was disappearing round the side of the bungalow. She shouted: 'Bearer! Bearer!'

There was no answer. Who could have hated Munta Lal so bitterly that they had to strangle him? He appeared to be friendly with Azi Mullah, and he seemed on good terms with his two relations. Then the full horror of the situation struck her with all the force of a hammer blow to her heart. Whoever had killed him had done so by mistake. Munta Lal was not expected to be asleep in this house. *She was*.

The murderer had intended to kill her. Only the chance that she and Munta Lal had changed places had saved her. Someone in this palace hated – or feared – her so strongly that they had attempted to kill her. She must have sensed the danger, just as an animal, calm when it is driven a hundred times through the streets, will suddenly refuse to make the hundred and first journey because it senses that this time it is to the slaughterhouse.

She went back into the room, looked down at the dead body. She must keep calm. She must see Azi Mullah, but she did not know where he lived. As she waited, turning over in her mind how she might find him, going to the palace, asking for him, she heard

439

careful footsteps on the wooden verandah outside. They stopped outside her door. She saw the polished brass knob turn very slowly and the door open half an inch at a time. No one who had any right to be here would enter with such stealth. They would knock and wait for an answer.

She looked around for some weapon. She picked up a small hearth brush by the side of the brick fireplace. The door opened. Moti Lal came into the room.

'*You?*' he said in amazement and disbelief. She saw instant panic and horror on his face. He turned as though to run, as if he had seen an apparition, a ghost, then he steadied himself. She knew then that he had expected to find her dead. If he had not planned to kill her himself, he knew who had.

'I heard there was some trouble here,' he said unconvincingly, then glanced at the bed. 'My God!'

'Munta Lal has been murdered,' she said.

'By whom?' he asked hoarsely.

'I have no idea. I have just discovered his body.'

'But you were here all night?'

'No.'

'Where were you?'

'In his room.'

'Why?'

'Does that concern you? The point is, he was on his own here, and someone killed him.'

'There'll be an inquiry into this,' said Moti Lal grimly.

'Of course.'

'What have you got in your hand? A weapon?'

'A brush. I didn't know who was coming in. I was afraid. I picked it up in case the murderer was coming back.'

'How long have you been here?'

'Minutes.'

440

'I will fetch Azi Mullah. The police will have to be informed. This is terrible.'

He hurried out of the room. Mary Jane heard him run across the verandah. The police. If they discovered she had been imprisoned in Newgate for debt, or the business of Miranda, or about the houses Captain Cartwright had given her, she would be damned, her character ruined. But how could they possibly unearth the information out here, on the other side of the world? Then she remembered the electric telegraph. She had read how it could send messages across continents in a matter of minutes, men tapping keys, country to country. Nothing was secret any more.

She must get out of here while she could, find one of her own countrymen and appeal for help. She put down the brush, opened the door. The verandah was still deserted. She walked as quickly as she could, taking care not to run. People might remember a memsahib running, but not a memsahib walking. She came into a dusty street, with no clear idea where she was going. She must find a British officer, anyone who would believe her and help her.

A wave of nausea suddenly engulfed her; this wretched morning sickness. In the light of the new horror, she had forgotten she was still pregnant. She leaned briefly against a wall, retching, coughing, choking. Then she wiped her mouth, walked on more slowly. A four-horse carriage with a rider on one of the front horses, two footmen standing behind the carriage, came round a corner. A man and woman sat in the carriage. He looked old, at least in his sixties; the woman could be slightly younger. They had hard, unfriendly faces, but they were English. Mary Jane waved and ran towards them.

The man gave an order to the coachman. The carriage stopped with a rattle of bells on bridles.

'Yes? What is the matter?' the man asked her.

'You don't know me, sir,' she said. 'My name is Green. There's been a murder.'

'A murder, you say? Who has been murdered?'

'An Indian prince, Munta Lal.'

'Where?'

'In one of the palace guesthouses.'

'Who are you?' he asked dubiously. What sort of girl could this be, running through the streets dishevelled, claiming a prince had been murdered?

'I am English. I came from Delhi with him.'

'You are a relation?'

'I pretended to be married to him.'

'*Pretended?*' repeated the woman coldly. Under a coating of white powder, her face wrinkled in distaste. 'You've been sick. Your blouse is all dirty.'

Mary Jane looked down at her white blouse; yellowish streaks of bile stained it.

'Oh, yes. I hadn't realised. I do apologise. It was the sight of the body,' she explained unconvincingly as she dabbed the blouse with her handkerchief.

'I am Lady Greatheart. This is my husband, General Sir Richard. Deputy garrison commander. How long have you been here, Miss Green?'

'I arrived yesterday.'

'You came here for the ball?'

'The ball?' Mary Jane repeated vacantly. 'I don't understand you.'

'The Nana Sahib is holding one tonight. For the officers and their ladies. You haven't been invited?'

'I don't know anything about it.'

'I see.' Lady Greatheart pursed her lips. This girl was comely enough, if you liked her kind of looks, but clearly she was not a lady or she would have been invited. And what did she mean, saying she had pretended to be married to the prince?

442

'What can I do to help you?' the general asked Mary Jane brusquely. 'How did this happen?'

'I came back to the house. I had been sleeping elsewhere.'

'Alone?' asked Lady Greatheart sharply. You never knew with people nowadays; morals were not what they were.

'Of course.'

The general and his wife exchanged glances.

'I came into his room and there he was, strangled. The point is, whoever killed him meant to kill me. But I wasn't there. You see, I'd changed places with him, but the murderer wouldn't know that.'

'Quite so,' said the general soothingly. The girl was overwrought. That often happened when English girls became involved with Indians; East and West simply did not mix. The girls had to be highly strung or over-passionate ever to imagine such a relationship could be placid. She might even have taken a sniff of something. Drugs out here were more potent than strong drink.

'You'd better go back to your room. Wait there. I'll send an officer over to you who has legal experience. You'll have a fair trial.'

'A trial? For what? I had nothing to do with it.'

'But you were with the man, this prince. You found the body,' said Lady Greatheart.

'That doesn't mean I had anything to do with his murder.'

'Of course not,' said the general. 'It's just that, well, you admit you were involved with him, pretending to be married. It all sounds rather unsavoury, Miss Green. We'll get through the formalities as quickly as possible, I'm sure. The Nana Sahib is anxious not to antagonise the British, for reasons of his own. Equally, for reasons of our own, we want to keep things as friendly as we can with the Indians. You'll be all right.

443

You have my word, Miss Green.'

'I can't come with you?'

'That would be most unseemly. People could say you had run away, and that would look suspicious. I am sure you see that. No, no, you go back to your room. You've nothing whatever to fear if your story is as you say, Miss Green. My officer will be with you as soon as I have finished this drive.'

He nodded to the coachman. A whip cracked, the carriage moved forward. Mary Jane watched it go. Would they send an officer? Did they care? She turned. Azi Mullah was standing behind her. With him were three other men; one was Moti Lal, grim-faced.

'You had better come back,' said Azi Mullah gently.

'They're sending an officer to see me.'

'Possibly. But that is unnecessary. This is an Indian matter. A family affair. The British have nothing to do with it. First, we have our own inquiries to make.'

Mary Jane took a sudden step forward, as though to break and run or follow the carriage, but then realised she had nowhere to run to. She was on her own. No one else could help her now. Whatever officer the general sent could easily be fobbed off. This had nothing to do with the military. This was a civil matter. Of murder. And she was pregnant, unmarried and on her own.

Mary Jane buried her face in her hands. As she wept, the others surrounded her and walked her back quickly to the Nana Sahib's guesthouse.

Chapter Thirteen

Ritchie came into Ben's room.

'We're off early, I hear,' he said. 'The colonel wants us out as soon as possible. Sooner, if he had his way.'

'I know,' Ben replied. 'He told me.'

He was sitting in a canvas chair at the table, sketching with a pencil on a piece of paper.

Ritchie sat down on the edge of his camp bed, reached for the metal flask of whisky he kept in a leather pouch.

'Drink?' he asked Ben.

'No, thank you.'

Ritchie poured three fingers into a mug, drank it neat and leaned back, stretching himself. He had just returned from shooting practice on the range.

'Anything to report?' Ben asked him, shading in his drawing.

'Not really. We were trying rapid fire, but it's rapid in name only.'

'Even so, the Enfields we have now are much quicker than the old muskets,' Ben pointed out.

'Of course. So they should be. And the muskets they replaced were faster than bows and arrows. But we have to keep reloading for every round we fire, taking new aim. What we need is a gun one man can carry, no bigger than a rifle, that works automatically. Then we could pump out dozens of bullets in the time it takes now to fire a single round. The irony is we had one nearly a hundred and forty years ago. A man called James Puckle invented what he called the flintlock repeater.'

Ben looked up now, clearly interested. 'How did that work?' he asked.

'Ingeniously. It had a single barrel with a number of chambers for bullets mounted on a cylinder behind it. The soldier firing it revolved the cylinder by turning a handle. As he did so, each chamber locked neatly into the barrel. The whole thing was beautifully made. In tests, it could fire sixty-three rounds in seven minutes – nine shots a minute.

'As a refinement, Mr Puckle offered the weapon with two different barrels according to the targets expected. One barrel was round to fire round bullets against Christian enemies. The other barrel was square for firing square bullets at infidels!'

'What happened to the gun?'

'Nothing. I've only seen it in a museum. Poor Puckle never got it into production. Our generals are always reluctant to try anything new. The French are different. Napoleon the Third commissioned a scientist, Montigny, to make a gun to fire so quickly that one man using it could hold at bay an entire company of infantry armed with conventional rifles. That was his brief. Montigny produced a gun with thirty-seven barrels. But it was so heavy, four horses were required to pull the carriage on which it was mounted. Again, the gunner had to turn a handle, and each barrel fired in turn. The rate of fire was one hundred and seventy-five rounds a minute, but it was clumsy and complicated, and never used in anger, as far as I know, because it jammed so easily.'

'I'm drawing a plan for a much simpler and lighter gun,' said Ben. 'This won't need anyone to keep turning a handle. It works by itself entirely automatically when you press the trigger. I had the idea when I saw those three siege guns here recoil each time they were fired. A tremendous amount of energy was being wasted, so I thought why not use it to turn the equivalent of the handle? I suppose I had the basic idea before that, when you took me out to the ranges. Every time a soldier fired, he winced because the recoil drove the stock of his rifle back into his shoulder. Again, totally wasted energy.

'Look at this drawing. Here is a weapon that will take a rifle bullet. It has only one barrel mounted on a tripod so that it can be set up almost anywhere and moved by one man or, better still, two.

'Each time the gun is fired, the barrel and breech block move slightly backwards under the recoil. Then the breech block detaches itself from the barrel and a claw hooks out the spent cartridge case. A spring forces back the breech block and the gun fires a second time. And so on until the gunner stops pressing the trigger or he runs out of ammunition.'

'All right in theory,' said Ritchie doubtfully. 'But how are the cartridges introduced? In the guns I have described, there was a box, or hopper, for them. They dropped down, one after the other, under their own weight. One snag was that often they jammed and then the gun stopped firing.'

'That is not a positive enough arrangement,' Ben replied. 'My gun is fed by a belt or long strip of tough cloth at right angles to the gun. This belt has loops woven into it, and each loop holds a cartridge. As the breech block slides back, it moves a toothed wheel, over which the belt runs. The wheel revolves half a turn and pulls the belt on an inch at a time, enough to slip a new cartridge into the breech.

'Belts of cartridges would be kept in boxes, which

447

travel with the gun. Sick or wounded soldiers could be used to reload each belt, away from the firing line, so the gunners never run short of ammunition. What do you say to that?'

Ritchie poured himself another drink, swirled the whisky round his mouth as he considered Ben's plan.

'It's certainly a clever idea,' he agreed cautiously. 'It would revolutionise warfare – as long as the enemy didn't have a similar weapon.'

'I've read in the papers how scientists and inventors, working quite independently of each other, maybe even on different sides of the world, often announce the same discoveries within weeks of each other,' said Ben. 'Eventually, no doubt, every army will have them. But I mean to get in first, for ours. And each gun will have my name on it.'

He held out his left hand, palm downwards. The three-sided ruby in his mother's ring glowed red as spilled blood.

'This stone has three sides. My gun is mounted on three legs set in a triangle. I mean to call it the Fanfare Triangle.'

Five hundred miles north-west of Calcutta, on their march to Meerut, Ben and Ritchie reached the outskirts of Benares. To Hindus, this was the most important religious city in the world, the equivalent of Jerusalem to Christians and Jews, Mecca to Muslims. For two and a half thousand years Benares had been a centre of learning and pious faith, for here Buddha had preached his first message of enlightenment.

Originally it was called Varanasi because it had been built between two rivers, the Varauana and the Asi. But the third river that moved past the city in proud and sluggish flow with stone temples and great houses built along its banks was the most important in all

India: this was the holy river Ganges.

'I can guess what you're thinking,' said Ritchie as they passed small buildings huddled together on the edge of the city, with narrow alleys branching out from a single main street. 'Benares is going to look like Rome or Canterbury, for it's their equivalent. But it's nothing like that. This is one of the filthiest cities you could ever see. However, I've a friend here, Rodney Blake, who's just been appointed Commissioner. He'll be as glad to see visitors as we will be to see him. He has a fine house on the bank of the Ganges, beyond the burning *ghats*.'

'What are they?'

'You'll see,' Ritchie replied shortly. 'It's cremation, Indian style. Nothing quite like it anywhere else.'

As they rode on, the city gradually unfolded before them. Old, shabby houses leaned out across the narrowing road, louvred shutters closed tightly, secretively. The sun of unnumbered summers had dried and burned away all their paint, leaving only pale grey undercoat. The walls of the houses were streaked by rain and damp. Carrion birds, long-beaked vultures and others Ben had never seen before perched in rows on the rooftops, all watching the river.

A smell of rotting vegetation, human faeces and roasting flesh hung over the city like a foul fog. In a small courtyard to one side, a servant wearing a loincloth crouched on his haunches before a charcoal fire, stirring a sooty metal pot. At street corners, yellow-eyed dogs rooted in the debris of banana stalks and squashed, over-ripe mangoes. Blue clouds of flies buzzed busily about heaps of rubbish. The smells grew more oppressive, rich and sweet and somehow terrible. And then they saw the *ghats*.

Dozens of small boats bobbed, bow to bow, in the green water. Stone steps, like terraces, had been cut

449

into the bank to lead down to the water's edge. They were crowded with people, standing, sitting, lying. Birds dived and swooped and rose again above yellow blossoms floating on the water. Holy men crouched under umbrellas next to *dhobis* spreading out damp clothes to dry on the rocks; others beat soaking saris and shirts on flat stones to hammer out the dirt.

The windows of the houses overlooking the river were open here. Ben could see pictures of the god of good luck, Ganesh, the god with an elephant head. The whole area was crowded with people and yet appeared curiously derelict. Bushes, plants, even small trees sprouted from walls and between broken tiles on roofs. Across the river on the far side, shrouded in mist, he could see the spires of distant temples like a city seen in a dream.

A funeral procession came towards them. Ten men wearing *dhotis* carried a corpse on a stretcher, shoulder high. The body was bound in a white sheet, dusted with orange saffron powder. The chief mourners wore orange turbans and waved flags or beat drums. Slowly, the mourners carried the body down the bank, the doomed bearing the dead.

'There are fifty-two *ghats*, one for each week of the year,' Ritchie explained. 'Some are more holy than others. The Someswar *ghat* is said to cure all manner of diseases. The Dasaswamedh commemorates the fact that Bramah sacrificed ten horses on this spot. There is the shrine of Sitala, the goddess of smallpox, and so on.'

Corpses were arriving now in line, each one wrapped in sheets, bare feet sticking out at one end, the head at the other. Each *ghat* was little more than a flat space by the side of the river, thick with grey ash. Boys built pyramids of sandalwood for richer clients, mounds of green, raw branches for the poorer. With long poles, old men levered rigid corpses into position on the kindling wood. Others, the outcastes, the *chandals*, raked over ashes to prepare space for a new arrival. In the feathery ash, Ben could see a split and blackened skull, ribcages, the bones of a hand still with shreds of blistered flesh on the joints.

Someone began to chime a bell; at the sound, mourners raised their voices in a chant. An old man picked a blazing splint from a dying fire and thrust it beneath the latest corpse. There was a flare as oiled wood took fire. The sudden heat caused the muscles of the dead man to tighten. The body sat up as though it would be away. Ben remembered the corpse he had seen as a boy being burned outside Barrackpore. Boys beat the body back with poles until it collapsed in a great shower of sparks.

Worshippers were squatting on their haunches on the steps, others stood up to their armpits, washing themselves in the filthy stream. A leper, his face eaten away with huge pulsating, suppurating sores, raised both hands to dash sacred Ganges water on the most painful. Next to him, a man cleaned his teeth with a twig, rinsing his mouth with water scooped up in a metal cup. Only feet away, half-burned bodies of men, women, children, dead dogs, monkeys, some with vultures already perched on the remains, tearing at frizzled flesh, floated downstream.

Ben stared, fascinated yet horrified. Ritchie touched his arm, pointed towards a doorway. On the lintel he saw the red imprint of a woman's hand.

'A widow made that,' said Ritchie solemnly. 'Suttee. It's illegal now, but so are whisky stills in the Highlands of Scotland. When a widow knows she is about to be burned with the body of her husband, the last thing she does is to leave her handprint on the door of the house as she leaves. That is the only way she will be remembered. No gravestone, no eulogies, nothing but the print of a hand, not even a name.'

'Do they *want* to die like that?'

'Would you?' retorted Ritchie sarcastically. 'It's their religion. They have no choice. Sometimes they're doped, so they don't know what they're doing. They have to give their assent – what else can they do? Their parents don't want to keep them once they are widowed. They can't work. No man will marry a widow, so there's nothing left for them but death.

'I've seen them tied forcibly to the bodies of husbands dead for three weeks or more, rotting, stinking, crawling with worms, and the women screaming to be set free. Some actually jump free when the bonds burn through. And then their own families, even their own children, will drag them back and throw them on the fire!'

'But why is it so important that a widow has to commit suicide in this terrible and agonising way?'

'Religion, as I say. And belief. They are taught to believe that every Hindu wife must regard her husband as a god on earth. I must say, from a husband's point of view, that has a lot to commend it. My own lady wife would have been greatly improved, in my opinion, if she'd thought like that about me.

'They also believe that no woman who has been married can ever remain chaste. And if the husband was rich and old, as so many are, and his wife was young and beautiful, why should she be allowed to enjoy her life, and to make life enjoyable for some other man, when he is unable to enjoy her? Anyhow, economically she would simply be an extra mouth to feed. So they tell them that death is not an end but the beginning. It opens the gate to Paradise.

'If you believe in something strongly enough, no

452

one can shake your faith. Now, *I* believe we're almost there.'

They turned into the gates of a courtyard. A *chowki-dar*, a watchman wearing a well-pressed khaki uniform and carrying a long, metal-tipped stave, salaamed. Ritchie's friend Blake came down the steps of the house, eyes screwed up against the sunshine, wondering who could be arriving. His pleasure showed instantly as he recognised Ritchie.

'My dear fellow,' he cried enthusiastically. 'We haven't had guests here for six weeks. My wife will be delighted.'

He clapped his hands. Bearers came running and carried their baggage into the house, while grooms led away their horses.

Later that afternoon, the three men sat on the veran-dah overlooking the river. The setting sun hung low in the sky, turning it to blood. A pall of dark oily smoke hung above the burning *ghats*.

'They're very busy today,' said Ritchie.

'They always are,' Blake replied.

'We saw the red handprint on a house.'

Blake pursed his lips, nodded. 'The Governor General has tried to stamp that out,' he said. 'But it's damned difficult, although it's illegal. Apart from the economic burden a widow presents, there's another reason the Hindus favour suttee, but it's not talked about. Greed. If a married man dies childless, all his property goes to his widow – if she lives. No one else can claim a single anna. But if the widow also dies, then what he has left can be shared out among his relatives. So you'll find that the relations of rich and childless men are very keen on the custom.'

Blake picked up a pair of binoculars, focused them along the river, handed them to Ritchie.

'There you are,' he said. 'They're carrying a

wretched woman down now.'

Ritchie shook his head. 'I've seen too many of these terrible sights,' he explained. 'I can't bear to watch another.' He handed the glasses to Ben.

Ben could see a crowd of men, followed at a distance by women and children, half carrying, half dragging a young woman. She wore a white sari. Even at this distance, Ben could see her anguish. She was shaking her head, crying out, beseeching them to let her go free, but she was wrapped so tightly in the sari she could not move her arms.

They carried her down to a *ghat* and put her down on the ground beside a dead body, presumably her husband's. The wind changed and Ben could hear her screaming incoherently above the shouts and chants of the mourners, and the cries of the boys as they busily arranged the kindling sandalwood.

'We're watching murder,' he said hoarsely.

'Ever seen a man hanged?' Blake asked him. 'I feel the same about suttee as about hanging. But we Christians have killed a few in our time, too, you know, to encourage others to abandon whatever religion they followed and become Christians like us. We're really in no position to judge the morals of the custom.'

'I say we are,' retorted Ben, lowering his glasses. 'Can't we help her at all?'

'How would you propose to do that? Run along there and ask them to stop? You'd be cut down before you got within fifty yards. This is the most sacred moment in their lives – especially in hers, poor girl.'

Ben raised the glasses again. The woman was lying quietly now. She was either exhausted or drugged. Someone had drawn the end of her sari over her face so she looked already like a corpse. At least she would not have to see the *chandals* go about their grisly business, nor watch the flames leap for that tiny terrible instant before they scorched her flesh. Ben remembered how Dr Kintyre had told him that when Sir Alexander Burnes had gone to meet the armed Afghans who surrounded his house outside Kabul, he had covered his eyes so he would not see who struck him first.

As they stared at the distant *ghat*, the wind carried a great cry from the throats of hundreds of people. The widow had leaped up from the burning logs.

Their flames had burned through her bonds and she was running like a gazelle down into the Ganges. She had no chance of escape on land because of the huge crowds around the *ghats*. The river was her only hope. Men were shouting furiously, waving burning brands, throwing blazing logs at her. Several followed her into the water in a wild attempt to seize her, but the current whisked her out of their reach and carried her downstream. She would pass the Commissioner's house within minutes.

She was making no attempt to swim; perhaps she did not know how to swim or was too drugged to do so. She was being kept afloat by her sari which had filled with air like a balloon. Crowds were racing along the river bank, waving their fists at her, commanding her to come back to the side. The strong current carried her on serenely, easily outpacing the fastest runner.

'She's probably doped,' said Blake. 'Then she'll just drown and that'll be the end.'

'Bit of a mercy in a way if she can't swim,' said Ritchie. 'She'd have to be a pretty strong swimmer to go against that current. And if she reached the shore she'd be seized at once and carried back to be burned.'

'Have you got a boat?' Ben asked the Commissioner.

'No. Why?'

'I'd like to try and rescue her.'

'Don't be a bloody fool,' said Ritchie sharply. 'You

can't interfere in a Hindu burial ceremony. The mob would lynch us all. We'd never get out of here alive.'

'Fortunately for you, I haven't got a boat,' said Blake. 'Which has probably saved your life – and ours.'

'Not necessarily,' Ben replied. As he spoke, he tore off his shoes, ripped his shirt up over his shoulders and ran down the stone steps towards the river.

'Come back!' called Ritchie. 'You'll drown or they'll kill you. You'll die either way! Can't you see that?'

For a moment, Ben paused, facing the green scummy water with its yellowish froth and the debris of floating ash. Then he took a deep breath, closed his eyes, plunged in.

He felt unspeakable filth beneath the surface; unburned parts of half-seen, half-submerged bodies, brushed his flesh. Then he kicked out fiercely, shook water out of his eyes and swam steadily out to the centre of the river.

Ritchie was quite right. He was mad attempting to rescue some native woman, but he could not bear to see any living thing die unnecessarily. The animals in the cages at Barrackpore had been far better treated than this unknown Hindu widow. He trod water for a moment to establish his bearings. The tide was bringing the woman down towards him at unexpected speed. From the bank, it had been impossible to judge the sheer power of the river, which was tremendous.

He struck out towards her. As she passed, he grabbed the edge of her sari. The current swirled her round in a circle, her face still covered by the train of silk. She gave no sign of life or movement. She might already be dead.

He wound a yard of cloth from the sari round his right wrist and began to swim as strongly as he could towards the shore. He was unused to swimming against such a fierce current; his strokes grew slower and more

456

feeble. The woman was beginning to sink now as air escaped from the convoluted folds of her sari, and she still lay apparently insensible and incapable of helping him.

Blake and Ritchie were waiting for him down on the stone steps. Blake held a boat-hook towards him. Ben put out his hand, gripped it tightly. Slowly, the two men pulled him in.

Blake instantly handed Ben a mug of neat whisky.

'Rinse your mouth out with that at once,' he told him curtly. 'Spit it out, then drink the rest. Whisky has wonderful antiseptic powers.'

They bent down, pulled in the woman's body. She moved feebly.

'We must carry her up. We can't leave her here,' said Blake.

The three of them lifted the body up the steps to the courtyard. Two servants had seen the rescue and brought out a bed with a rope mattress. They laid her on this. Water poured from the folds of her sari down between the ropes. A small gold locket on a fine meshed gold chain dangled down onto the stone floor.

'Well, she's still alive,' said Ritchie. 'Let's have a look at her.'

He pulled the gold-edged cloth from her face.

At Ben's cry of amazement and disbelief, the woman opened her eyes.

Mary Jane looked up at him blankly. 'Where am I?' she asked weakly. 'Am I dreaming?'

'No,' he told her hoarsely. 'You are safe and with friends.'

'They were going to burn me alive,' she said in a faint voice. 'One of Munta Lal's relations gave me a glass of something that numbed my feelings. But I still felt the flames. My bonds burned through, so I ran.'

Haltingly, Mary Jane explained what had happened in Cawnpore.

'You're damned lucky to be alive, girl,' said Ritchie. He lifted the locket from the floor. 'I'm surprised they didn't take this. Usually they steal all ornaments from widows, on the basis that they won't need them where they're going.'

He pulled the thin gold chain over Mary Jane's head, wiped the locket with his handkerchief and opened it. Inside was a small brownish daguerreotype of a woman in her forties. She smiled out at them incongruously from behind the oval glass.

'My mother,' Mary Jane explained.

'Good-looking woman,' said Ritchie approvingly. 'Like mother, like daughter.' He closed the locket and put it on one side.

A servant came into the courtyard, approached the Commissioner, bowed.

'A big angry crowd just now gathering outside, sahib,' he said nervously. 'They want the widow.'

'So do we,' Blake replied. 'Tell them they can't have her. Anyway, she's English, not of their religion.'

'She was his wife,' said the man stonily. 'It is their custom, their right, sahib.'

The crowd began to shout angrily. From the noise, hundreds were waiting on the other side of the courtyard wall, with more arriving every minute.

'I was never his wife,' replied Mary Jane earnestly. 'I swear to you. I never married him.'

She sat up, and then, with a choking cry, pressed her stomach. She leaned forward in a sudden overwhelming paroxysm of pain.

'What's the matter?' Ben asked her.

Mary Jane could not answer. Her sari was suddenly stained by a wide crimson patch. Thick gobbets of blood dripped onto the stones beneath the mattress.

'We need a doctor,' said Ben. 'Quickly.'

'We'll never get one through this crowd,' Blake replied. He turned to the servants. 'Carry her inside to a bedroom. Get your wives to undress her, give her a clean shift. They will be able to help until we can get a doctor.'

'They will be afraid, sahib,' said the servant. 'They do not want to be killed.'

'They won't be. None of us will be if you act now,' Blake assured him with a confidence he did not feel.

The noise of the crowd had grown to a bellowing roar. They were shouting in English, in Hindustani. 'Open the gates! Deliver to us the widow!'

'How strong are the gates?' Ben asked the Commissioner.

'We have tree trunks that fit behind them,' Blake replied. 'Then it would take a battering ram to open them.'

'They won't need that,' said Ritchie grimly. 'Look at them.'

Heads appeared over the walls, staring at them excitedly, angrily.

'The danger is they'll bring up ladders. Once they're in, we'll never get them out,' said Blake.

The three men looked at each other. They all knew what Blake had not admitted. Once the crowd came into the courtyard, they could kill them all, loot the house and be away within minutes. There would be no punishment, no retribution. They were on their own, three men, an ill woman and the Commissioner's wife inside the house, plus three or four servants, against hundreds, possibly thousands of furious Hindus who believed they had deliberately interfered with this most important religious ceremony.

The three men felt a curious sense of being divorced from time and any involvement with danger. The shouts and rising anger of the huge crowd only feet away somehow did not affect them. They were watching something that concerned others, not them.

Then someone hurled a stone over the wall, missing Ritchie's head by inches. This broke the spell.

'Get me a table!' shouted Ben.

'What for?' Blake asked him.

'Just get it!'

Blake and Ritchie ran into the house and came out carrying a sturdy wooden table.

'Near the wall,' Ben told them.

They put it down six feet from the whitewashed bricks. Ben jumped up on it, so that all the crowd on the other side of the wall could see him. He raised both his arms above his head.

'Peace!' he cried in Hindustani. 'Peace be unto you all!'

He kept his arms raised while he surveyed the crowd. Hundreds of people were crammed into the street as far as he could see. They packed the open windows of houses on either side; they filled every balcony. Others stood on the flat roofs of houses, waving sticks, shouting. But gradually, as Ben stood facing them, arms outstretched, the commotion died and then ceased. It was obvious that this young man had something important to tell them. They would hear it – then they would kill him and his companions and seize the widow.

'You do well to wish the body of this woman returned,' Ben shouted. 'It is your faith, your sacred belief that every woman must treat her husband as a god. And when that god dies, so must she. Am I right?'

'*Ji! Ji!* Yes! Yes! You are right, sahib! Give us what is ours!'

'When a man dies, the one he has loved dies with him, as a gift to the gods. That is what your religion

460

says. And you believe and must obey. *Am I right?*'

'You are right, sahib! You are right!'

Now they began to cheer. This was not what they had expected him to say. How strange to hear such wisdom from one so young, and of a foreign faith.

'So when this woman's husband died and his body came to be burned with all your solemn rites on the bank of the sacred river, you wished to give her back to the gods who breathed life into her at the moment of her birth. This widow is your gift to the gods.

'But every gift, to be worthy of the name, must be accepted by the person, or the god to whom it is given. Otherwise, it is not a gift at all, but something thrust upon someone who does not wish to receive it, who would like to give it back. Tell me, *am I right?*'

'Yes! Yes!' yelled the crowd.

'So, after the ancient custom of your faith, you bound this woman with ropes to the body of the man who had loved her. Then you set fire to them both, so that her soul might join his soul in their journey through eternity. In death, as in life, they would be united. But the fire rejected her! The god of the fire gave back to you what you had given! The woman realised this at once and fled into the river.

'Now the river also sent her back. Thus the gift you gave was twice unwelcome, twice returned. She had been repulsed by the gods of fire and water! The message is plain. Her time to die is not yet!

'Who are any of us to go against the sacred wishes of the gods who rule our lives? If a friend rejects your gift, do you force it on him? Who will take responsibility for such an act of blasphemy against the gods? Answer me that! Let the man stand forth now who dares to go against the wishes of the gods!'

For a moment, no one replied. The men turned to each other and began to speak among themselves. This was a totally new and deeply disturbing point of view, and one that sounded true. If it were not, how could a widow possibly escape the embrace of fire *and* water? Then a priest came forward to the front of the crowd, an old man wearing a white *dhoti*, a white cap.

'Sahib,' he called. 'I did not expect to hear such wisdom from the mouth of one so young. Only the ears of fools are stopped against the words of truth. You are right in what you say. Let this miserable widow, this outcast creature the gods have rejected, go wherever the spirit takes her. She is not welcome to them. She is less welcome to us. Let her depart now in peace and return no more to this place.'

He raised both his hands, turned towards the crowd. At once there was a long murmur of agreement. Heads nodded. Men began to clamber down from the balconies and the rooftops. An exciting interlude was over, ended with honour to all.

Ben watched the crowd walk away. He was sweating. It had been a dangerously close finish; feelings could so easily have gone the other way. The servants came out of the house and bowed their grateful thanks to him.

'That deserves a whisky. A very large whisky,' said Blake. 'For a moment, I thought we were done for.'

'So did I,' Ben admitted.

'What gave you the idea to talk them out of it?'

'Alexander.'

'Who?'

'Alexander the Great. My old *munshi* used to tell me stories about him, how he always produced an unexpected plan when everything seemed against him.'

Blake raised his glass. 'To the *munshi*,' he said solemnly.

'Let's see how the lady is progressing,' said Ritchie. 'We can get a doctor now, surely?'

462

'Of course.'

Blake scribbled a note, handed it to a bearer to deliver to the local physician. While waiting for him to arrive and carry out his examination, Ben stripped off his soaking clothes and took a hot bath with strong disinfectant in the water.

The doctor joined them on the terrace overlooking the river.

'How is the patient?' Ben asked him.

'Recovering. And very fortunate indeed to be alive.' He paused for a moment. 'I would not usually discuss a patient's condition with anyone,' he said. 'But Miss Green has asked me to tell you the nature of her haemorrhage. As you may have already guessed, she was pregnant. Her terrible experiences on the burning *ghat*, and in the river, added to the soporific drug someone gave her, combined to bring on a miscarriage.'

'But if she was pregnant she should not have been compelled to suffer suttee,' said Blake. 'That is a very strict religious law.'

'So I told her. She said she had explained her delicate condition to her husband's relations, but they refused to believe her. Apparently, she and her husband had separate accommodation in Cawnpore, so the relations claimed the marriage had never been consummated. I suspect they would not listen to her because her husband was a wealthy man, and if she died they would share his estate. Not for the first time, gentlemen, the jingle of gold was louder in human ears than the voice of mercy.'

He turned to Ben.

'She is asking for you. But don't stay too long. Reaction will soon set in. After a short time here, I suggest she leaves Benares. It must have as terrible associations for her as Cawnpore, where she tells me her husband was murdered. I heard something about this. I believe the Nana Sahib or his creature Azi Mullah was involved in some way. I don't know quite how or why.'

'I will go and see her now,' said Ben.

He sat down by Mary Jane's bed. Her face and hands seemed very pale against the white starched sheets.

'You saved my life,' she said quietly and smiled. 'I wanted to thank you. It seems an inadequate sort of thing to say. But – thanks!'

'I didn't know it was you,' Ben admitted. 'If I had, I would have been in the water much more quickly, and swum twice as fast. Couldn't let a former tog lady go under.'

She smiled. 'Mine must have been a lucky number,' she replied. 'The doctor says I'll be all right soon.'

'I'm very glad. What are your plans then?'

'I'm going up to Peshawar, near the Afghan frontier.'

'That's a rough place for a woman.'

'No worse than a burning *ghat*. My husband owned a lot of property up there.'

'But you were not married to him. You told me that, although you didn't tell the doctor.'

'That's right. I wasn't married to Munta Lal. But his relations conspired to kill me. That is not something I am likely to forget. So publicly I call him my husband. And what are your plans?'

'Major Ritchie and I are on our way to Meerut. An army posting. I wish you were coming with us.'

'You like the army?' Mary Jane asked him.

Ben shrugged. 'In principle, yes. But some of the army people I have met so far have not impressed me.'

'I hear there's a very good fellow in Peshawar, John Nicholson, the Deputy Commissioner. I intend to see him as soon as I arrive and ask his advice on the property.'

'It was very lucky us meeting like this,' said Ben.

'For me, much more than lucky – providential,' Mary Jane replied. 'Especially since I heard in England you were dead.'

Ben flushed. 'You must not believe all you hear. I will tell you about that later, not now.'

'So don't let's wait for chance, or providence, to arrange another meeting.'

'You have an address in Peshawar?'

'Not yet. But I can let you know it if I decide to stay there.'

'And if you don't? If you move on?'

'Give me your address in Meerut. Then I can write to you.'

'It will simply be care of the Intelligence Department, The Garrison, Meerut. I don't know where I'll be staying. That should find me.'

'And if it doesn't?'

'Then I'll have to come looking for you, won't I?'

'Dear Ben. I hope you find me. It's just that . . .' She paused.

'Just what?'

'Oh, nothing,' she said quietly. 'Just that I'm still not quite myself.'

How could she open her heart and let all the terrible memories free? Newgate. Mrs Mentmore. Miranda. Captain Cartwright. And this almost miraculous escape from death by fire and water? She closed her eyes to try and blot out the fuming visions of violence and deception.

There was a gentle knock on the door. Ritchie came into the room, looked at her, then at Ben.

'I will leave you,' said Ben. 'The doctor advocates rest. And to make conversation to two people is more than twice as hard as talking to one.'

'Dear Ben,' she said again, opening her eyes. She

lifted her arms. He bent over the bed, kissed her gently on the forehead.

Ritchie waited until Ben had closed the door, then sat down on the cane chair by her bed.

'I will only stay a moment. Ben is quite right. Talking too much will tire you. But I thought you might want this back.'

He opened the locket, put it on the bedside table. Mary Jane picked it up and looked at the picture fondly.

'My poor mother,' she said.

'Is she alive?'

'Oh, yes. I saw her just before I sailed to India. Only briefly, but she was well.'

As Mary Jane spoke, she recalled their talk in a side road near her mother's lodgings, her mother's fear in case her husband returned too soon and saw them together. She tasted once more her mother's salt tears, and for a moment she almost wept herself.

Ritchie watched her face, saw the strength of emotion she was attempting to conceal.

'She'll be glad to know you are alive and well,' he said. 'Will you write and tell her? Or would you like me to do so?'

'I have her address, but her husband doesn't like me. He might take it out on my mother if I write. She specially asked me not to. In any case, she won't know what's happened to me here, and there's no need for me to alarm her.'

'So shall I write for you?'

'It is kind of you to suggest it, but I'd rather you didn't.'

'As you wish. Her husband is not your father then?'

'No.'

'Your mother was married before?'

Mary Jane shook her head. For a moment she

466

thought of saying nothing more about her past. But she had already been involved in too many lies and deceits, and she felt a deep need to confide in someone.

'It would all have been different if my mother had been married before,' she explained. 'She was a maid in a big house and the son of the house had his way with her. She found she was pregnant, just as I became. She had no one to turn to. She told the lady of the house and was put out. She was lucky to find someone who married her quickly.'

'Her husband did not know about this then?'

'No. He thought I was his daughter. She told him she was having a premature baby. When he discovered I wasn't his child, everything changed.'

'Where was this big house?'

'In Kent. Beechwood Hall. Ever heard of it?'

He nodded. 'Yes. A grand house in its time. And what about you, Miss Green? Were you married to this Indian? You told us you weren't, but the doctor assumes you were.'

'I told you the truth. I was not married to him. I have never been married.'

'But you were pregnant?'

'Yes. But not by him. There was nothing like that between us. He thought quite wrongly that I might know people who could influence the directors of the Company and could help his relation, the Nana Sahib. He promised me the Nana Sahib would reward me. I desperately needed money because I was pregnant so I did not admit I knew no one like that. I went to Cawnpore with him, but we slept in different houses. That's how he was murdered – in mistake for me.'

She explained how they had exchanged rooms; Ritchie nodded sympathetically. He knew what it was like to be without funds; he sympathised totally with her.

Mary Jane lay silent for a moment. 'I have told you

my mother's story,' she went on. 'Now I'll tell you mine, or at least some of it. I wanted to try one of the colonies, or India, but I had no money for my passage. I came out here looking after the young son of Captain Cartwright, who commands the ceremonial guard of the old King of Delhi in the Red Fort. Captain Cartwright has an invalid wife.'

'You had an affair with him?'

'Yes. But I was not in love or even greatly attracted. Quite simply, I needed money – desperately. I am sorry to have to admit this, but I made him pay me for his pleasure. I paid, too. In a different way. Now I hope I am out of debt.'

Ritchie nodded. 'I quite understand your motives and I will respect your confidence. Now, I think you are tiring yourself. You go to sleep. You are among friends. You are alone no more.'

I still remember the morning long ago when the village postie delivered two personal letters to me. In those days, a Scottish country doctor like me received very few letters carrying more than a halfpenny stamp. Most arrived in cheap brown envelopes from drug companies in Glasgow or Manchester, to advise me of some new preparation they were about to put on the market. They wished to offer free samples to try on my patients in the hope that I would then place orders with them.

The two envelopes that arrived that morning were of good quality white paper. One was postmarked Brighton; the other, Tilbury. I did not know of any drug manufacturer in either town. I opened the one from Brighton first, put on my glasses and sat down at my leather-topped desk to read the letter it contained.

The paper had a heavily embossed heading, 'Jonah Edwards, Solicitor & Commissioner for Oaths'. Perplexed, I read on:

Dear Dr Kintyre,

I must introduce myself at once. As a solicitor I have been favoured by the late Lady Victoria Beaumont to draw up her last will and testament, and, as her sole executor, to carry out her instructions.

She has left to you, as a token of her esteem, a painting of the chain-link pier at Brighton. I have had this valued, and understand that to a wholesale buyer it would fetch about £700. Consequently, I would suggest that its retail value must be more than £1,000. Pray give me your instructions, whether you wish me to send the painting on to you or to enter it at auction and forward the cheque to you.

Lady Beaumont possessed a number of other valuable paintings. These she has bequeathed to her nephew, Benjamin Fanfare Bannerman, refusing to believe that he is dead. Should his death be proved, her wish was that they would come to you as a memento of this young man who, I understand from her, you brought into the world.

I have had all these paintings valued and they are worth, wholesale, the sum of approximately £7,000, which means they might fetch £10,000 on the open market.

Lady Beaumont made the point to me most forcibly that she and her brother were possessed of very little money when they were young. As a result, she entered into a marriage to a man of means which, although it brought her a measure of material security, was never a union of love or like minds in the true sense.

Her brother lacked the wherewithal to buy himself promotion in the service of the East India Company's army. Consequently, he was passed over and perished in furtherance of his country's prosperity. I would therefore be obliged if you could kindly advise me whether you have heard any news of Mr Bannerman, since to a young man a capital sum can be of vital importance.

Assuring you at all times of my warm sentiments, I am at your command.

Jonah Edwards

I put down the letter, sat back in my chair, took off my glasses and wiped my eyes. Lady Beaumont had been the one remaining link with her brother, who had died by my side, and with her brother's son. Now she had gone, and I felt bereft.

I opened the second letter. The notepaper lacked any formal heading. Written in a full, round hand, I read, 'En Route to Meerut, India.'

Dear Uncle,

I feel very guilty at not having written to you before. Indeed, each day my guilt increased, so I kept putting off the prospect of writing. Now I feel I can delay no more. I have recently been in Barrackpore, where I visited your old house and had a talk with the *munshi* sahib. He was shocked at the fact I had not been in touch with you and insisted that I should write and explain my actions.

I have treated you very badly. I admit this at once and apologise for my behaviour, which was not intentional, but arose from a sudden decision to leave your house.

Like the Prodigal Son, I turned my back on your kindness, your love and your support, and went into the world to seek, if not my fortune, at least my own life. I wanted to find what I could do.

470

Perhaps I really also wanted to discover who I was.

When I left home I wrote a note to you giving one reason for my departure. Initially, I had no intention of staying away for a long time. I believed I would find a job locally and then I would return to see you, if not to live again at your expense, in your house.

But I found it more difficult to make a living than I had anticipated. I had a number of strange experiences, which taught me about life and my fellow men and women.

Finally, for reasons I can explain when we meet, I felt it prudent to pretend to die. To my great shame I did not at the time imagine that news of my death by drowning would grieve you because I did not think you would believe it. Now that I am better versed in the ways of the world, I realise that this was an absurd and selfish assumption, and I apologise most abjectly for any pain and grief I may have caused you, quite unintentionally.

As you will see from my address, I have travelled a long way. I am a lieutenant in John Company's army. I assure you that my warm love and affection for you is the same as ever, and I wish to offer you the opportunity of joining me in an enterprise which I hope may, at least in part, help to repay you for all you so generously spent over many years on my upkeep, clothes, education and my general well-being.

I am giving this letter to a missionary who is returning to England because of ill health. In these troubled times here it is safer to entrust a messenger with a letter than to risk using the postal service. He assures me he will post this as soon as his ship docks at Tilbury.

With this letter I am enclosing drawings of a gun I have invented. I am unable here to have even a model made of this weapon. I would therefore like you to show these drawings to any competent gunmaker, of whom there are a number in Birmingham and Coventry. Please be so good as to register the drawings first with the Patent Office in London, so that the design cannot be pirated. Of any money made from its manufacture I would like you to take fifty per cent, and arrange for the other half share to be sent to me care of Mr Grindlay's bank in Calcutta.

If you know a lawyer whose sagacity and integrity you can trust, it might be easier if you hand over to him the whole matter of patenting this design. It would be tragic if this weapon, which possesses the power of thirty infantry soldiers armed with conventional rifles, should fall into unscrupulous hands who might sell its secrets to foreign countries.

Having written now, and broken this long and disgraceful silence, for which I most sincerely ask your forgiveness and understanding, please be assured I will write again in the very near future.

I put down Ben's letter, picked up the second sheet of paper the envelope contained. It was covered with drawings of a gun of a type I had never seen before, but which, even in the sketches, looked formidable and eminently fit for its purpose.

How strange that these two letters should arrive by the same post, at the same time; one from across the world, the other from across the country. I felt that somehow this was providential.

For what inscrutable reason I could not even guess, a baby boy had survived the freezing wastes of the

Afghan hills. Providence had also saved me. I recalled my father's sermons on the Gospel according to St Luke, chapter 17, verse 36: 'Two men shall be in the field; the one shall be taken, and the other left.'

So many had been taken; two of us had been left. There *must* be a purpose. Sitting there, holding the letters and recalling those who did not survive, I felt the hand of the Almighty over the whole matter. What had happened was not simply by chance; it was all part of a pattern which one day would be made manifest.

I pulled a sheet of notepaper towards me, dipped my pen in the inkwell on my desk and began a letter to Mr Jonah Edwards.

Chapter Fourteen

At seventy-five years old and weighing twenty stone, General John Hewitt, military commander of Meerut, the largest and most important British garrison in India, could no longer mount a horse.

Because of his gross size he had for several years been obliged to detail a party of corporals to accompany him on all ceremonial parades and lift him into the saddle. But, as his weight increased inexorably, they had to engage others to help with this task. One day they all gave the general such a prodigious heave that he rolled right over the saddle and fell to the ground on the other side.

The garrison surgeon warned him that another fall like this could kill him, or at the least totally incapacitate him for even the limited service for which he was physically capable. The regimental carpenters therefore constructed a special buggy for him, like an invalid carriage, which was pulled by a pony led by a soldier. In this curious contraption, half wood, half basket work, with big, thin, spidery wheels, General Hewitt was being drawn away from the parade ground as Ben and Ritchie arrived in Meerut.

On their journey from Barrackpore they had averaged thirty miles each day. Their entourage – bearers, *bhistis* to draw water, grooms, camel wallahs for the camels that carried their heavy baggage, wives and families of these camp followers – extended for two hundred yards behind them. Except for their stay in Benares, they stopped at a *dak* bungalow every evening. *Dak* was the Hindustani word for mail, and these little buildings had been constructed at useful intervals along the Grand Trunk Road so that messengers and others in transit could spend one night there and then go on their way. It was not safe to pitch a tent by the roadside. Robbers prowling the countryside were as fierce as wild beasts and infinitely more unpredictable. They killed to live, and travelling in parties of a score or more, all heavily armed with swords and knives and pistols and muskets, it would need a strong group to stand up to their attack.

The general's adjutant had reminded him earlier that morning that two officers were arriving to join the new Intelligence Department, but he had forgotten. He found he forgot so many things these days. It was the heat, he said. Others thought his lapses of memory could be due, at least in part, to his habit of drinking a pint of claret every lunchtime and half a bottle of port or brandy as a nightcap.

The general nodded vaguely to Ritchie and Ben who stood at attention as he approached. An ADC came up to Hewitt, whispered in his ear who they were. The general nodded. Of course. Intelligence wallahs, misfits and throwouts to a man. Better see them now, though. Easier than seeing them later. Get it over with. He ordered his driver to halt the pony.

'You've arrived at a bad time, gentlemen,' he said. 'I understand from these new-fangled telegraph messages that you also left Barrackpore at a bad time. Men blown from guns, regiment disbanded. Things are no better here. Eighty-five men of the Ninth Native Infantry have just been sentenced to life imprisonment in the penal colony on the Andaman Islands.'

476

'On what charge, sir?' asked Ritchie, shocked by the news.

'The same as at Barrackpore. Bare-faced mutiny. Refusing to obey orders. God knows what we're coming to.'

Since these two newcomers were going to join this damn fool Intelligence Department the Commander-in-Chief had decided he needed, Hewitt thought he would be seeing a lot of them; too much, if first impressions counted. He didn't care for either of them, frankly. The old one looked tough and discontented. Good fighter probably, but that wasn't the only quality a soldier needed, not by a long chalk. General Hewitt had not seen any active service in fifty odd years of soldiering. He did not think it necessary for his staff officers to possess such military qualities. Good family was more important. A solid private income ran this requirement a very close second.

'Well, you've been some time on the journey,' he said in as genial a tone as he could muster. 'Since you are joining the Intelligence Department, what intelligence did you glean on your way?' He nodded towards Ritchie, for him to answer first.

'Nothing of comfort to any of us, sir,' said Ritchie. 'What struck me as most sinister is a prophecy made a hundred years ago about the English.'

'India is full of mournful prophets whose prophecies never come true, last year, this year, never mind what they said a hundred years ago.'

'It is the hundredth anniversary of the Battle of Plassey, sir. Clive, commanding an army of nine hundred Europeans and fifteen hundred sepoys, met the Nawab Suraj-ud-Dowla with fifty-five thousand men under French officers and routed the lot in one afternoon. The prophecy then was that British rule would only last for one hundred years after that victory.'

'I am well aware of the victory,' replied the general coldly, 'if not of the prophecy. Clive seized Bengal for the Company with the loss of only thirteen lives. The Indians would be almost bound to make some sort of forecast of our ultimate decline if only to save their face. Defeats of this magnitude can rankle.' He turned to Ben. 'And what did you find out, Bannerman?'

'The matter of the greased cartridges, sir, is the most serious cause of disaffection, to Hindus and Muslims alike. And several commanding officers on the way have told us how sepoys on guard duty had refused to wear uniforms, without giving any reason whatever. Others insisted on riding in bullock carts rather than march. The disaffection appears to be spreading. In view of this, I think the officers concerned acted harshly.'

'You have been in India for a few months at most, Bannerman,' Hewitt retorted irritably. 'I have served fifty years this summer. My view is we have not been too harsh but too soft with them. A woman, a dog and a walnut tree, the more you beat them, the better they be. My experience says that such treatment also sharpens up Indian sepoys, which, in all conscience, is essential. To see for yourselves, you two officers will check the mutineers we sentenced yesterday. Give you something to put in your first intelligence report.'

Hewitt smiled at his own proposal. What he wanted now was a large claret, and to keep out of the sun for the rest of the day. What a damn fool idea of the C-in-C to wish for an Intelligence Department, staffed by dolts like these who had no conception of the real problems of the country!

Ben and Ritchie were taken to their quarters, two small bungalows, about fifty yards apart, each containing a bedroom, a sitting room, and an anteroom in which the usual tin bath hung from a nail on one wall.

The roof was high for the sake of coolness. Birds flew in under the eaves to escape from the pitiless heat, and rested briefly on the rafters. Their white droppings splattered the shabby furniture, all of which had the same message burned into it with a branding iron: 'Property of the East India Company'. Like the occupants, thought Ben drily.

While bearers unpacked their gear, Ritchie joined Ben in his bungalow, followed by the regimental adjutant.

'I have orders to show you the prisoners,' he explained. 'Not a very happy sight. It was difficult to provide safe quarters for so many. They are being transported tomorrow, so we have shackled them and put them in the garrison hospital for the night. Fortunately, there are very few medical patients at this time of year and we've found other temporary billets for them.'

The hospital was a large building on the far side of the barrack square. It had few windows, very high walls, a thatched roof. Two British sentries with loaded muskets stood at the main entrance. Inside, the prisoners sat on the raw rope mattresses of locally made beds. Some were talking to each other in low voices, most were silent. Bright metal shackles on their ankles and wrists rattled and clanked as they turned to see who was coming into the building.

The Hindus had shaved heads, except for one long tuft of hair by which they hoped that, at the moment of death, their souls would be drawn up to Paradise. The Muslims had beards and moustaches. They stood up uneasily, but smartly enough, with a clang of manacles, as the officers approached them.

Ben spoke to several prisoners as he walked down the lines. They were glad to meet a white officer who could speak to them in their own language. He heard how wives and families relied on their incomes for survival. Several sepoys were supporting seven or eight people out of pay amounting to a few rupees a month. What would happen to those who looked to them for money and food once they were transported?

'You speak the language very well, Bannerman,' said the adjutant suspiciously. 'What are you talking about exactly?' He always distrusted officers who spoke these native lingos. Must be something odd about them; not quite straight. They were usually too keen to take the sepoy's point of view over anything; a dangerous habit.

'General things. Some tell me they've been ordered to scrve overseas in Burma, and they've refused, as in Barrackpore.'

'That's right. There's a short definition of that – mutiny. The judge advocate agrees entirely. He couldn't do otherwise, of course.'

'Of course not. But, with respect, the terms of sepoys' recruitment specifically states that they will never be required to serve outside India. The fact we try to force them to do so, just because we need men in Burma, does not alter that.'

'Words, Bannerman. If you want words, then the phrase "the exigencies of the service" cuts right through such claims. What else are they saying?'

'Brahmins believe they lose caste if they cross the sea. This is very important to them.'

'But not to us. What is important is that we maintain a strong presence in Burma. The sooner we get more missionaries out here and stop this damned heathen nonsense, the better it will be for everyone.'

'I don't quite agree with you.'

'I don't give a damn whether you agree with me or not, it's a fact, not a theory. The general was telling me you had quite an argument with him. A second lieutenant arguing with a general, the officer commanding! What is the army coming to?'

'I hope we are not about to discover the hard way,' Ben replied shortly.

They were nearing the end of the line when he saw one sepoy, older than the rest, standing with eyes downcast. As they drew level, he looked up at Ben and a look of amazement crossed his face.

'Karim Khan,' said Ben in Hindustani. 'What on earth are you doing with these prisoners?'

'You may well ask,' Karim Khan replied sadly. 'I never imagined we would meet like this, but I thank the ever merciful Allah we have done so. I see you took my advice and bought a commission.'

'I did. From the brother of the laird, out of what he paid me to take his place. And you?'

'I told you long ago, I come from a family of jugglers, illusionists. I went back to my village. I was quite a wealthy man – by their standards at least. Everything is relative.'

'So I am discovering,' said Ben. 'And then?'

'I found that my son Amin, my only son, had enlisted in the army. I followed him here. To my horror, I found he was under close arrest on a ridiculous charge of mutiny. He is a loyal fellow, he would never mutiny. There is no doubt he disobeyed an order and should be punished, but not with transportation for life. That is sentencing a young man to a living death until Allah in his mercy chooses to release him.'

'Where is he now?'

'Where I pray he will never be discovered.'

'And you?'

'I took his place. As you can see.'

'How?'

'To white officers who do not speak our language, who do not know the country or the customs of the people, one Indian looks very like another. It is the

481

same with Indians looking at you white people. But that is a digression. They only seek a body, to make up the numbers. Anyone will do, as long as the total is eighty-five. I am not Karim Khan, but Amin Khan.'

'And so, as Amin Khan, you will sail across the deep, dark water, *kala pani*, to the penal settlement in the Andaman Islands. There, still as Amin Khan, you will hack rocks every day of every week until death releases you. That is, as you say, a living death.'

Karim Khan shrugged philosophically. 'It is as you say. But I had no other choice. It was a matter of honour. My son is young. I am not. It is not meet that he should suffer when I can take his place. He still has his life to live. I pray he will use it to better advantage than I have used mine. In your religion, Jesus Christ died to save others. It is a far less thing that I do now.'

'But you are innocent.'

'So was He.'

'In Scotland you did not display this acceptance of a few hours in the local lock-up.'

'Ah, my friend, how right to remember! But that was in another country, in another time. And I knew that in my caravan I possessed the key to freedom. So I prayed that somehow I might get it in my grasp, and you appeared and brought it to me. Wonderful are the ways of Allah, the ever merciful, the all-seeing, the all-compassionate.'

'What are you two talking about?' the adjutant asked Ben sharply. 'You seem to be having quite a chin-wag.'

'He is telling me of his military service,' replied Ben quietly. 'Please don't wait. I will follow you out.'

'These fellows may attack you on your own.'

'I think not. But I am prepared to take that risk.'

The adjutant shrugged. 'As you wish.'

He and Ritchie walked on towards the door.

'We will now speak in English,' Ben told Karim

Khan. 'I do not want the other prisoners to hear that I still have a key to freedom.'

'What do you mean?'

'In Scotland you gave me a pair of laces as a memento, remember. They are in my boots now.'

Karim Khan's face lit up with unexpected hope. 'You are not joking?' he asked hesitantly, nervously.

'No.'

Ben knelt down, removed a bootlace, slipped the flexible saw from its cover, then threaded the cotton cover back through the eyelets in the boot.

'God will reward you,' Karim Khan assured him earnestly.

'When your disappearance is discovered, I may be much in need of assistance from whatever quarter,' Ben replied drily.

Next morning, before sun-up, the prisoners were paraded, still manacled. They could not march far in shackles, so a row of bullock carts waited in the shade of trees near the parade ground to take them on the first stage of their long journey into exile.

The general sat in his basket chair on the mess verandah, from where he could see this last parade. So that the full severity of the sentence could be witnessed by all Indian troops as a warning to any who might also feel disaffected, two sepoy regiments lined the barrack square. They were unarmed. Some paces behind them, in a second row, stood a line of British troops, muskets loaded.

The adjutant and another British officer were already out on the square, counting the prisoners. Interpreters followed them as the officers walked slowly up and down the line of sullen, dejected men. They did this several times. There seemed to be a discrepancy in the number on parade. After a brief discussion one of the officers marched smartly towards the mess.

'What's the matter?' the general asked him petulantly. 'Why can't you get on with it?'

'One prisoner is missing, sir.'

'Missing? You know who he is?'

'Sepoy Amin Khan, sir.'

'Well, he can't have got far,' said Hewitt irritably. 'That's one blessing. He was manacled. Is he hiding in the hospital?'

'No, sir. We have searched that thoroughly. He's not there.'

'You think he has got out of his chains during the night? Maybe someone helped him escape.'

The adjutant looked pointedly at Ben. 'You had a long talk with the man yesterday in his own language,' he said coldly.

'What the devil for?' asked General Hewitt in surprise.

'I had known him in England, sir. I was surprised to see him here – and a prisoner.'

'Known this sepoy in England? What are you talking about?' He turned to the adjutant. 'You have Amin Khan's record of service?'

'Yes, sir.' The adjutant picked up a folder, turned over the page, read from it.

'Enlisted 1853. Conduct good until this present disturbance. Never been out of India, but is prepared to serve overseas.'

'You hear that?' asked Hewitt.

'I hear that, sir. The man I talked to was not Amin Khan, but his father.'

'His *father*? What has he to do with this?'

'He is a former soldier, sir. He had taken his son's place, prepared to undergo years in prison. It seemed quite wrong to me, as I am sure it will to you, sir, that an innocent man should be so punished. I took it upon myself to help set him free.'

'Are you aware of what you are saying, Bannerman?' the general asked him slowly, his voice clotted with anger. 'You help to free a felon sentenced by court martial to life imprisonment on your own initiative?'

'No, sir. He was not a felon. He was an innocent man.'

'Where is he now?'

'I do not know, sir.'

'And Amin Khan. Where is he?'

'I have no idea, sir. His father did not tell me.'

The general turned to the adjutant. 'Confine this officer to his quarters immediately. Place him under house arrest. He is not to speak to anyone, or have contact with any other officer or anyone else unless on my direct orders. This is a most serious offence.'

He turned to Ben.

'In all my service, Bannerman, I have never heard of a more extraordinary action, or one so deliberately prejudicial to military discipline and good order. An officer conspiring to help free a prisoner – and readily admitting his part in it. Words cannot express my astonishment and disgust at behaviour you readily admit without a trace of shame or sorrow.'

The adjutant nodded to two lieutenants standing near them on the verandah. They moved towards Ben.

'Permission to march the officer prisoner off, sir?' asked the adjutant.

'Of course. Get him out of my sight! *Now*.'

Orders began to echo across the parade ground from the barrack wall on the far side.

'Prisoners and escort, atten-*shun*! Right *turn*. By the left, quick *march*.'

Round the rim of the parade ground the prisoners attempted to keep in step as they marched; years of army service were not easily forgotten. Their chains and manacles clanked with every pace. Some stumbled and fell and crawled on hands and knees until their comrades could help them to their feet. The Indian troops who ringed the square began to murmur. Some prisoners called out desperately to them: 'Remember us! For the faith, remember us!'

Men on the perimeter called back: 'We will remember you!'

As their cries increased, the captain commanding the British contingent called his troops to attention. They shouldered arms; everyone knew that their muskets were loaded and what the next command could be. The shouting died, but like the sound of a distant, angry, restless sea, the murmurs continued.

As the prisoners walked unsteadily towards the bullock wagons, the two lieutenants escorted Ben to his bungalow. Inside, he heard the key turn in the lock. The sound of their boots on the wooden floor of the verandah grew fainter and then died. He was on his own, a prisoner like the sepoys.

Ritchie walked slowly through the growing heat of morning to the room that had been allotted to the Intelligence Department. It contained half a dozen wooden chairs, a large table, and a smaller one. On this stood a beaker of yellowish water with a glass inverted over the top. He removed the glass, poured some whisky into it from the metal flask in his back pocket, added water, and drank.

Young Ben had meant well, but he had gone about things in the wrong way. If he had asked his opinion, he would have strongly advised him not to admit anything. He would be cashiered now, of course, at the very least. He might well be ordered to re-enlist in a British regiment as a private soldier, if he was not sentenced to years in gaol.

Ritchie sat down. He would like to help Ben if he

could, but how? He could apply to be his defending officer at the court martial, but he lacked the skill with words that a trained lawyer could command. He had no influential friends to whom he could appeal. In fact, he realised he had very few friends, and in Meerut not even acquaintances. He would miss Ben; they got on well.

A tiny tapping on the back door scattered his thoughts. Who the devil could this be? Probably some mendicant, a leper or hideously deformed cripple with a begging bowl; a carpet seller, a dealer in brass ornaments who wished to offer him rubbish at what he would claim was a 'special price'. But there were no bargains to be bought at special prices here, as there were none in life. The price of everything was always clearly marked – if you spared time to read it. And Ritchie had spent too much of his life engaged in futile arguments with superiors whom he felt were his inferiors.

He crossed the room, opened the back door. A *subahdar*, a senior Indian officer of many years' service, hair grey, face grave, saluted him smartly.

'Well?' asked Ritchie.

'Can I come in, sahib?' the *subahdar* asked him nervously.

'Of course.'

Ritchie opened the door. The *subahdar* closed it carefully behind him.

'I did not want to be seen,' he explained.

'Why not?'

'You are one of the few officers who speak my language. I wanted to warn you, because you may believe me when others would only scoff. There will be trouble in the lines as a result of today's parade.'

'You should tell the adjutant.'

'I have tried to see him, sahib, but he says he is too

busy. I felt I had to tell someone.'

'Thank you for coming to me. What do you want me to do?'

'You are a major, sahib. The adjutant is a captain. You are his senior in rank and service. Please tell him that the British troops will be attacked when they are in church tomorrow, Sunday. They will be unarmed then, and unable to defend themselves. At the same time, bungalows will be set ablaze and their families killed.'

'What good will that do?'

'No good whatever, sahib. None at all. But the sepoys are being taunted in the bazaar that although they outnumber you British ten, fifty, maybe a hundred to one, they meekly allowed their comrades to be sent into exile. They are being called eunuchs, not men, sir.'

'The prisoners, I am sure, had a fair court martial.'

'I do not dispute that, Major sahib. But they do.'

'I will do as you say,' Ritchie promised. He showed the man out, took another swig of whisky, and then walked over to the regimental office.

The duty officer told him that the adjutant was engaged.

'I have a very important matter to discuss,' said Ritchie.

'About Bannerman, sir?'

'No. Something much more important.'

'He's busy with the Bannerman case. He has asked not to be disturbed on any other matter.'

'I do not wish to disturb him, but to inform him of something that affects the entire garrison. A most vital matter. Please give him my compliments and explain this to him.'

'If you will wait a moment, I will see him, sir.'

The young officer went into the inner room. Ritchie

waited for three minutes by his watch before he came out.

'I'm sorry, sir. He cannot see you.'

'Not even for a moment?'

'No, sir.'

'Then you are witness I tried to see him. Please remember that.'

'I will, sir.'

Ritchie walked back to his bungalow. He knew he should not have drunk that second whisky in the heat, but now he felt so depressed, so miserable, that back in his room he poured out a third to cheer himself up.

The tolling of a church bell awoke Ben. For a moment he lay looking at a row of small birds perched in line on the rafter above the bed. The bell must be ringing for church parade. But where was his bearer? The man should have woken him at seven. Then he remembered he was under house arrest. The door was locked. His servants must be under orders not to visit him.

He pulled back the curtains, went into the bathroom. The *bhisti* had not drawn his bath. He had to bathe and shave in cold water. He tried the back door; it was locked from the outside. Then he heard distant cries and shouts and bugle calls, some far away, others near at hand. Against this unexpected Sunday morning disturbance, the bell kept tolling. Why? Church parade was not due for at least another hour. Had a special service been called for some reason?

He went back to the main room, and the key turned in the front door. The adjutant came in, closed and locked the door behind him.

'What's happening out there?' Ben asked him. 'What's all the noise?'

'The sepoys have rioted. I've never seen anything like it. They've freed all the prisoners and set fire to

489

the officers' bungalows. The whole garrison seems to be involved.'

'Is that why the church bell is ringing?'

'Yes. To warn everyone there's trouble. Apparently the sepoys planned to attack the British troops when they were in church, unarmed. There'd have been a massacre if they had. Luckily for us, they couldn't wait that long. They just attacked everyone in sight.

'I want you out there now to interpret orders, to try to get some sense into their leaders, in their own language, while there's still time. All the Indian interpreters have fled to save their skins, and I don't blame them. You and Ritchie are the only officers who speak Hindustani well. He's already out on the square, trying to calm them down.'

'The general, as you know, has put me under house arrest. If I come with you now, he could charge me with attempting to escape.'

'Don't be a bloody fool, Bannerman. It's desperate, I tell you. If we can't calm things down now, we won't have another chance.'

'And I'm desperate in here, believe me. Give me a note to say you drop all charges against me, and I'll come with you. Otherwise, I must obey the general's direct orders.'

'I can't give you that assurance. You know that. I haven't the authority. Only the general can do that.'

'Then if it's as serious as you say, get him to do so, or sign the note for him. On his behalf. As his adjutant.'

The captain hesitated, shook his head. 'No,' he said. 'I cannot. You must see my position.'

'And you must understand mine.'

As Ben spoke, the thunder of a cannon rattled the windows.

'They must have broken into the armoury,' the

captain said nervously. 'That's a big gun.'

Ben took a sheet of paper from the table drawer, handed it to the adjutant with a pen.

'There's an inkwell,' he said, pointing to the table.

'What d'you want me to write?'

'That of this day and hour all charges outstanding against me are dropped and will not be reconstituted. Signed for the general.'

The pen scratched on the gritty paper. Another cannon boomed.

'That do?' the adjutant asked him wretchedly.

Ben read the wording carefully. 'Yes,' he said. 'That will do.'

He folded up the paper, put it in an inner pocket. Then he buckled on his belt and pistol, and followed the adjutant out onto the parade ground. It seemed filled with cavalry riding to and fro without any apparent aim. Some men were in full uniform, others were half dressed. Yellow dust clouded the air like a fog. Riders waved swords, rifles, pistols. Flames and thick black smoke billowed up from bungalows burning on the far side of the square. As Ben stood with the adjutant, bewildered by the sight of such chaos, and the triumphant shouts of the sepoys, he saw Ritchie sprinting towards him, pistol in one hand, sword in the other.

'Get out! *Go!*' Ritchie shouted frantically, waving his sword.

Where to? What did he mean?

Then the ground trembled under Ben's feet. Through the haze of smoke and dust, he saw twenty horsemen galloping towards him. The sun glittered on twenty drawn swords. The adjutant fled.

Ben fired his pistol at the leading horseman, missed; the distance was too great. They charged. At that moment three other horsemen galloped towards

491

Ritchie from the side of the square. Leading them was the *subahdar* who had warned him of the impending unrest. He wheeled his two companions round to charge the other horsemen. At once they scattered and rode off in search of an easier target. The *subahdar* trotted his horse towards Ritchie, saluted with his sword.

'Thank you,' said Ritchie, much impressed.

The *subahdar* bowed acknowledgement. 'I could not stand by idly and see you murdered, sahib,' he explained. He turned his horse. 'Now my duty lies with my comrades.'

'But *we* are your comrades. You have just saved our lives.'

'My comrades are out there, sahib, fighting for theirs.' He galloped away, the other two riders behind him.

'Bloody close shave,' said Ritchie. 'I've been haranguing the rest in Hindustani, but they won't listen.'

'They've listened too much to other voices,' said Ben. 'Where's the general?'

The adjutant now reappeared. 'I left him in his house,' he said.

'We must get him to turn out the British regiments,' said Ritchie. 'They'll be in uniform for they were going on church parade. They'll only need to fetch their rifles. They can see off this rabble in minutes. If you could have spared me five minutes yesterday all this could have been avoided. But the duty officer told me you were too busy.'

The adjutant did not reply.

They ran across the parade ground; no need to walk carefully round the perimeter now. Flames lit up the huge square; thick black smoke darkened the sun as they reached the general's house. Two sepoys carrying unloaded muskets were usually on guard duty day and night at the front gate. Now, the gate was open. The guards had gone.

The three officers ran up the short drive and beat with their fists on the front door. The shouts and cheers and the booms of guns beyond the dark fog of smoke seemed somehow remote in this walled enclave.

'Who is outside?' an English voice called nervously from the hall.

'The adjutant and Major Ritchie. Open up!'

'The general is resting.'

'We *must* see him. The sepoys have mutinied!'

'I have orders not to disturb him, sir.'

'I am giving you orders to open up, man! *Now!* Or we'll shoot the lock away!'

The rattle of a chain, the squeak of a bolt being drawn and the three officers rushed through. The general's personal orderly stood to one side.

'Where is he?' Ritchie asked him.

The orderly pointed up a wooden flight of stairs. They ran up, beat on the nearest door. It opened at once. The three men stood staring at their commander. He still wore a grey nightshirt, a tasselled nightcap.

'Sorry to disturb you, sir,' said the adjutant. 'But there's chaos outside. We need the British regiments to put it down while they can. If we delay, it will be too late.'

'Their colonels will deal with that,' Hewitt replied.

'With respect, sir, they need your orders to turn out one regiment to engage another.'

The general looked at the adjutant, then at Ritchie, then at Ben as though he could not comprehend what the captain was saying. But when he recognised Ben his mouth tightened with anger.

'I put you under house arrest, Bannerman. What the devil are you doing here?'

'He and Major Ritchie are the only two officers who

493

speak Hindustani, sir,' the adjutant explained quickly. 'I took it on myself to allow him out in these very serious circumstances.'

'As you all know, I have served in India for fifty years,' retorted Hewitt, his voice charged with an old man's vehemence. 'Longer than all your service put together. I've seen uprisings come and go, for Indians are a volatile race. The heat and the hot curries they eat affect them. It will all be over by noon, mark my words. There is no need to cause further trouble by ordering British regiments to fight Indian regiments.'

'There is no other way of quelling the disturbance, sir, I greatly regret to say. Have I your permission to alert the British colonels, sir?'

'Do whatever you think necessary,' said Hewitt shortly. 'I bid you gentlemen good day. Pray do not disturb me again on a Sunday over such a trivial matter.' The general closed the door and locked it.

Behind the hospital building where Ben had visited the sepoys stood a second building of equal size, but without windows, and with a tiled roof instead of a roof of straw and thatch. This was the garrison armoury.

Solid double doors at each end were chained and padlocked. Behind the doors, inside the building, as a further safeguard, long iron rods fitted into metal hooks. Outside the armoury stood a small guardhouse from which relays of sentries, muskets loaded, constantly patrolled the building in pairs. Today, the guardhouse was empty; the guards, like those at General Hewitt's house, had disappeared.

The armoury was the heart of Meerut garrison. To its safekeeping all Indian troops had to deliver up their muskets every evening. Every musket had a serial number punched on the barrel. The muskets fitted into slots in the wall, each one bearing the weapon's number. Chains were then passed through trigger guards, and the muskets padlocked in groups of six.

Whoever could breach this armoury and seize the weapons would control Meerut. Whoever controlled Meerut could, by sheer fire power, control Delhi, and the greatest magazine of weapons and explosives in the world. And whoever controlled Delhi was on the way to controlling the entire Indian subcontinent.

Fifty of the strongest sepoys had now gathered outside the building. Each man was stripped to the waist, bodies shining like oiled ebony in the flickering light of the fires. They had torn a palm tree out of the ground, slashed off its fronds and roots with swords and axes. Then, using the trunk as a battering ram, they raced with it towards the armoury doors.

The huge wooden panels creaked and groaned under the ferocious impact. The men gave a cheer, drew back and tried a second time; then a third, a fourth. On the fifth impact, one door splintered and buckled, and the tree trunk went through. Now the men ran to one side with it, using the trunk as a huge lever. The planks split with a crack like a gun firing. They pulled out the trunk, flung it away, and crawled through the huge hole they had made.

Blacksmiths carrying huge pincers, with handles a yard long, followed them in to cut the chains that held the muskets secure. Sepoys formed up in line as they handed out two, three, four muskets at a time. Others passed wads, powder and ball to their comrades. Then came pistols, swords, fuses, mines. The whole operation was handled with parade-ground precision. Within minutes, the armoury was empty and the mutineers, now fully armed, swarmed away. They had found an armoury filled with guns and ammunition; they left an empty shell of a building.

Ben, Ritchie and the adjutant drew back into the

shadow of the guardhouse as the men raced past. It was impossible to stop them, and to be seen would be to die. They could only watch.

'Where do you think they're heading?' asked Ben.

'Delhi,' replied Ritchie at one. 'To the King. He is their sovereign. If this outbreak is going to spread, they will need him to give the appearance of a national uprising.'

'Can we stop them?' asked Ben.

'Use the telegraph,' Ritchie suggested.

'I know Morse,' said the adjutant.

They ran towards the telegraph house – little more than a whitewashed hut – about a hundred yards behind the armoury. As they ran, flakes of burning paper, straw, linen and tarred felt fell from the sky, brushing their faces.

They reached the telegraph office. The door was wide open. Near the Morse key, with its polished brass terminals, a manual of codes lay on a table. Thick copper wires, coiled like serpents, led up to china insulators in the roof.

The adjutant sat down at the table, threw the switches, and began to tap the key. He waited impatiently for an answering response. The flickering of a needle on a hairspring behind a glass dial would show that the message was being received. The needle did not move. He tapped again, furiously. The needle did not even tremble.

'Line's dead,' he said. 'You can send a message over ten thousand miles of wire, but if there's only half an inch gap somewhere, the message won't get through.'

None of them knew that by then mutineers on stolen horses had reached the telegraph relay station halfway between Meerut and Delhi, murdered the operators and cut the wires in a dozen places.

The adjutant stood up. 'My wife,' he said. 'I had

better go to her. I had to leave her in our bungalow when I came to see you. She's with three loyal servants, so she'll be all right. But she'll be wondering what's happening.'

'She'll be safe, I'm sure,' said Ritchie with a confidence he did not feel.

'Of course. But she's expecting. The baby is due next month. I wouldn't like to think she was alarmed by what's going on.'

'We'll come with you,' said Ben.

The adjutant led the way between the armoury and a blazing barracks to his bungalow. While they were still fifty yards from it, they could see that the front door was wide open and every window shutter had been smashed. They started to run.

As they approached, a yellow gout of flames burst through the doorway and the windows with a great roar. The straw roof took fire like a torch. The adjutant raced ahead of them, plunged into the blazing building. Ritchie pulled Ben back.

'No one can live in that,' he said shortly. 'Wait.'

They heard the adjutant's scream of indescribable agony, then nothing but a crackle of flames punctuated by sudden unexpected eruptions as some part of the furniture – a padded cushion, a horsehair sofa – flared up and burned with peculiar fury.

Then, almost as suddenly as the flames had risen, the fire died down. The roof and rafters were totally burned out, the little house gutted, simply four blackened walls. They went in over ash still glowing red, past metal strips from seats, the scorched frame of a cooking stove. A sword blade lay red-hot in the embers. Two corpses covered in shreds of calcined cloth crouched in one corner. The adjutant had died with his pregnant wife.

* * *

497

John Nicholson stood up as Mary Jane came into his office in Peshawar. They shook hands. She sat down in a stiff-backed wooden chair facing him. He thought she was an extremely good-looking woman, but a worried one. And with cause, of course. But she had a firm set to her jaw that showed she was also a determined person. She would get what she wanted, even if the price were high.

'I heard that you were arriving from Benares,' Nicholson told her. 'My colleague there, Mr Blake, informed me by telegraph of your remarkable escape.'

'Mr Blake was extremely kind and hospitable to me,' Mary Jane explained. 'A young officer, Ben Bannerman, on his way to Meerut, bravely dived into the river and rescued me. Then Mr and Mrs Blake looked after me. Without their generosity, I do not know how I could have coped. I have been ill, you know.'

'I heard,' agreed Nicholson delicately, not wishing to broach the subject of her illness about which Blake had already told him. As a bachelor, he felt embarrassed by gynaecological problems. 'If I can help you in any way while you are here, I will be pleased to do so. But I must tell you, I expect to be leaving for Delhi very shortly. I don't know whether you have heard, but there's been great unrest in that area. The commanders are all old and this sort of trouble can so easily overcome their declension of will.'

'I am beholden to you for seeing me at short notice, Mr Nicholson, and at a time of such tension. I came to ask your advice.'

'About what can I advise you?'

'I understand that if a Hindu wife does not die after her husband's death, then she inherits everything he owned.'

'That is so,' Nicholson agreed. 'As long as the marriage is childless.'

498

'I am without child,' said Mary Jane simply. 'I understand my husband owned a number of properties in Peshawar.'

Nicholson nodded. 'When I heard you were arriving,' he said, 'I made enquiries. Prince Munta Lal was a rich man. To such a degree, indeed, that if I may offer an opinion unasked, you may experience hostility from his relations. Suttee is popular among those who hope to inherit from a dead husband. They are therefore not always eager that his widow should enjoy a long life. Suttee is generally insisted on by richer Hindus, especially if the widow is young.'

'You mean there might be violence against me?'

'I have no evidence of that, madam,' Nicholson replied tactfully. 'But it is always a possibility when large sums of money are at stake. As the Bible says, the love of money is the root of all evil. I therefore thought it wise to warn you. I have heard of incidents where accidents have most unfortunately befallen young, rich widows.'

'Thank you for your frankness, Mr Nicholson. I appreciate it. Now I must be frank with you. I have no idea where my husband's property is in Peshawar.'

'I think I can help you. His agent is a distant kinsman of his, a Mr Koruna Lal. As a matter of fact, I rather anticipated your predicament, so I took it upon myself to invite Mr Lal here. He is in another room, waiting to escort you on a tour of the properties, to take note of your wishes.'

'That is most considerate and understanding of you,' said Mary Jane gratefully.

'There is one small formality I should point out,' Nicholson said. 'Before you inherit, you will have to produce documentary proof of your marriage. Your late husband's relatives will insist on that. You have a marriage certificate, of course?'

499

Mary Jane bowed her head. She had not expected this question and did not know how to answer it. Silence seemed to be her safest response.

'Then you have no problem,' said Nicholson. 'Simply produce the marriage certificate before a lawyer, or whatever legal figure the relatives require. In the meantime, I will introduce you to Mr Lal.'

He pressed the brass plunger on the bell on his desk.

The properties were larger and more extensive than Mary Jane had anticipated, or even imagined. Mr Lal had brought with him a plan sketched on oily parchment. Mary Jane studied the Indian names of streets and roads and alleys, counted the properties in each, noted Mr Lal's estimate of the worth of rows of houses, shops, a factory for producing blocks of ice, another to manufacture soda water, a flour mill, a small engineering works. They made a tour of them and walked for nearly two hours, until she had seen them all.

'What would you think is their total value?' she asked him.

Mr Lal inclined his head, bird-like, to one shoulder as he considered his answer. 'You are asking a difficult question,' he said. 'But their total value must be many lakhs of rupees. Many.'

She nodded. A lakh was 100,000 rupees, about £7,000 at the rate of exchange.

'I know it is difficult to be precise, but would you say ten lakhs?' she asked him.

'Twenty,' Lal replied so quickly she guessed the value was probably more. It was not impossible that Mr Lal wished to keep a small percentage for himself.

'What are your advices?' he asked her. 'I am asking you. You wish to sell one or all, yes?'

'I will think about it for the rest of the day,' she told him. 'Please call for me here at ten in the morning.

Then I will give you my answer.'

He bowed. 'Then I am saying goodbye,' he said.

Mary Jane watched him walk away, then turned in the opposite direction towards her hotel. She wanted to be alone to consider an answer to the question John Nicholson had raised. She had never been married to Munta Lal, so she was not his widow. She had no legal claim whatever on this estate, but she had every intention of seizing it if she could. But could she?

It only wanted one person to demand to see her marriage certificate, and her claim would crumble, like sand in a storm. Did John Nicholson suspect she was unmarried? How could she produce a certificate she did not possess?

She thought vaguely of consulting a lawyer and asking his opinion. Perhaps she could ask him to forge a marriage certificate. But if he were English, he would refuse. If he were Indian, he would probably also refuse – and he might tell Munta Lal's family. Corruption seemed to compound corruption, and she was in no position to accuse anyone else of dishonesty. There must, surely, be a way out of this labyrinth of deceit. But how could she possibly find it?

The hotel where she was staying had formerly been a private house and was still run by the Anglo-Indian widow of the original owner. Mrs Murison rented out half a dozen rooms to Europeans visiting Peshawar on business. It was a small, homely place. Mary Jane found herself looking forward to a cup of tea with homemade scones the landlady served.

As she came into the entrance hall, Mrs Murison, behind the reception desk, nodded to someone sitting on a settee to one side. He was an Indian of middle age, wearing a spotless *dhoti* and highly polished brown leather *chaplis*. He bowed obsequiously.

'You are the widow of Prince Munta Lal?' he asked

501

Mary Jane. She nodded. She had told so many lies, silence seemed somehow less distasteful. What should her title be now? Was she a princess if her husband had been a prince? 'I am just now hoping I might have a word with you,' the man continued.

'About what?'

'About the sad matter of your late husband's untimely death.'

'Who are you?'

'I am a lawyer. Mr Singh.'

'His lawyer?'

'Oh, no, though I am lawyer to some of his relatives.'

'I see.'

She should have guessed that as soon as she saw him. The man's narrow shoulders, his foxy face, the small eyes close together told their own story. He had a proposition to make – or a threat.

'What is the nature of your business?' she asked him, keeping her face devoid of any emotion.

'I am wanting to discuss this matter in private,' Mr Singh replied.

'Come into the sitting room,' she said.

The sitting room was across the hall. It contained half a dozen easy chairs, each covered in well-ironed white canvas. A sambur head hung from one wall; its glazed eyes seemed to regard them quizzically.

Mary Jane sat down and indicated that Mr Singh should do the same. She deliberately left the door open behind her. She did not trust this man. He believed she was a rich woman, or very nearly so, and she was on her own.

'Well?' she asked him brusquely.

'I have come to see you on behalf of blood relations of your dead husband. I expect you know that, under Indian law and Hindu custom, you inherit everything as your marriage was without children. Yes?'

Mary Jane inclined her head to show she knew this point of law.

'I am told,' the lawyer went on slowly, 'on what authority I cannot say, and whether the information is accurate or not I do not know, but I am told that you were with child when you escaped providentially in Benares. If this is so, then you cannot inherit. That is point number one. Also, your husband's relations can find no record of his marriage under either Hindu or Christian custom, with you or with anyone else. That is point number two.

'No doubt you have documentation, and possibly you were not with child when your husband died. But should either or both of these suppositions be true, Mr Lal's relations would have under English law – which of course is paramount in India – a very strong, I would say an unassailable, case for inheriting all his property. Am I just now making myself clear?'

'Perfectly,' said Mary Jane as calmly as she could. 'But, Mr Singh, I cannot believe you have come here just to tell me what is little more than bazaar gossip and rumour. Have you something more positive you wish to put to me?'

'I have, mem. A conservative estimate of the valuation of the prince's properties in Peshawar is fifteen to twenty lakhs of rupees, which is between one hundred and one hundred and fifty thousand English pounds sterling. He was a wealthy man. His relations, however, are not so fortunate. Such a sum would help them and their families immeasurably.

'They have asked me to see you, and have empowered me to make you a financial offer. Their proposal is that, to save time and money, with the involvement of lawyers and the long tedious process of the courts, the value of his properties is divided into two. One half would come to you, and one half would go to them. That is their proposal, mem.'

'It is one that favours them very greatly, Mr Singh. I would remind you, and them, that, as the prince's childless widow, I am entitled to all my late husband's estate.'

'Of course, as his childless widow. But if you were not in that situation, you would receive nothing.'

'I would defend such an accusation very strongly indeed, Mr Singh.'

'Doubtless, mem. But defence under the law can be very expensive. And the fact that you do not at once say you can instantly disprove this rumour by providing your certificate of marriage, here and now, but instead you talk of the law, inclines me to the view that at least one of these rumours may be true. And even if it is not, with appeals and counter-appeals, perhaps all the way up to the last arbiters, the House of Lords in London, it is not impossible that most, if indeed not all, of this fortune would be dissipated in legal and other disbursements.'

'No doubt you speak from experience, Mr Singh – on the right side of the law?'

The lawyer smiled with his lips; his eyes did not soften.

'I would expect that since the prince's relations have engaged you to state their case they would endeavour to cause me as much harassment and expense as is in their power, if we went to law. Having once attempted to murder me under the guise of a religious practice so that they could inherit, they might be emboldened to make another attempt.

'Therefore, I hear your argument. I appreciate my danger. My answer to their proposition is this. I am prepared to divide the inheritance, but in the pro- portion of one-third to them, two-thirds to me, on three overriding conditions.'

504

'And what are they?'

'First, Mr Singh, you will carry out all negotiations. I will pay your fee when they are concluded to my complete satisfaction. But not before.'

'And the second, mem?'

'That you draw up a document to give to them, which I will sign. This will state that I have deposited with several banks sealed letters to be opened should I ever suffer any accident or serious illness, or if I die. The letters will contain details of this arrangement and my own account of events leading up to it.'

'Your third condition, mem?'

'That my share of the money, or deeds to the properties to that amount, will be paid into my account with Mr Grindlay's bank in Calcutta before the bank closes for business today.'

'Your first condition, I can meet. Your second presents difficulties. The third is not possible. The properties will all have to be valued. The other parties will have to agree, and then they may need to borrow on the value to pay you out.'

'The harder the lawyer's task, Mr Singh, the greater is his fee. Those are my terms. I am not prepared to discuss them or to alter them. In our holy book, the Bible, we read that God made the world in six days and rested on the seventh. This small task can surely be accomplished by nightfall.'

It was. By seven thirty that evening, the electric telegraph from Calcutta to Peshawar clattered out an item of news from Grindlay's Bank for Mary Jane Green: 'Your account credited as of today's date with equivalent of one hundred thousand pounds sterling.'

After lunch, the main army trials were due to take place on a cliff top on the north Kent coast.

While officials from the War Office and the Board

of Ordnance and generals with red faces and red tabs on their lapels were lunching in the marquee, an unexpected wind sprang up from the sea. This flattened corn in the fields and spun the latticed sails of the windmills with unaccustomed speed.

A huge area on top of the cliffs had been roped off for the trials. Carriages and army carts were parked in neat rows. In front of them stood a line of tents, the canvas of each one stamped with the three arrows of the War Department, guy ropes scrubbed and pipe-clayed, tent pegs newly varnished. The tent flaps were tied open. Men stood talking animatedly outside nearly every one.

Some of the men wore frock coats, top hats or curly brimmed bowlers. For all of them the trials were of crucial importance. Others were artisans dressed in clean labouring clothes, corduroy trousers and collarless shirts. These men were the inventors of the ingenious weapons of war now on show and the craftsmen who had actually built them.

On this particular day they had an opportunity to display the weapons to the authorities in a final test. They had already passed earlier trials in the cellars of the War Office in Pall Mall, at Woolwich arsenal or on open patches of land, according to the size of the weapons under review. Now came the most important and final assessment. If their devices impressed the experts, then contracts would be drawn up for scores or maybe thousands of new weapons and pieces of accoutrement to be produced for issue to Her Majesty's Army. Everyone involved was tense and nervous; the results could have a critical effect on factories, large and small. For some, they could spell the difference between survival and bankruptcy.

That morning the observers had seen a hot-air balloon hover silently above the sea. It was linked by a thin wire to a post driven into the ground. An operator in the basket suspended beneath the balloon could tap out Morse messages along this wire to a colleague down below.

The value of such a balloon in warfare to gain a bird's-eye view of enemy dispositions was great, but so was the risk to the man in the basket. Critics pointed out that a single hostile bullet could puncture the skin of the balloon and cause the entire contraption, man and machine, to crash to the ground. The operator could be easily replaced. The balloon would be rather more difficult to replace, and much more expensive. The experts had therefore recommended that this device should not be proceeded with.

They had seen a heavy artillery gun that fired a shell like a torpedo. This contained in its tail a small propeller, whose blades could be set to keep the shell on course even when the initial thrust of the charge had diminished. This also had failed. The blades were found to be vulnerable to the explosion that initially propelled the shell.

There had been bayonets with serrated blades, a rocket of novel design, grenades, small bombs. Some passed, more failed. The senior officers were cautious men. Most had not seen active service for years; many on the staff had never seen any. They were reluctant to commit themselves to recommend the purchase of new weapons; what had served the army in the past might arguably be modified to a minor extent, but anything too revolutionary was not well-regarded. First, there was the initial cost to consider, and then the matter of its complexity. How could soldiers barely able to read and write possibly cope with complicated controls?

So, with muted enthusiasm, the experts gathered to watch tests of the last artefact on display, a quick-firing gun of a type never previously produced in any British ordnance factory. This in itself was a mark against it. How could private individuals design something that military experts had failed to produce? No one felt it opportune to remind these gentlemen that the only offensive weapons of any worth that Government factories had ever produced were the sword and the lance.

I stood with Mr Jonah Edwards, the lawyer, by the side of the Fanfare Triangle Machine Gun, which is how it had been described in the application to the Patent Office. The gun was mounted on a tripod in such a way that it could traverse over an area of forty-five degrees. Its barrel was about three feet long, finned for coolness. The rate of fire was said to be so high that, even with the fins, the barrel could glow red-hot. Its own success might well cause the gun to seize solid. Among the notes Ben supplied, he mentioned that he anticipated modifications to encase the barrel in a metal jacket filled with water for cooling purposes.

At the back of the barrel were two handles for the operator to grip, and a trigger which he could press with either of his thumbs, rather than pull. A canvas belt held cartridges half an inch apart, each one nipped in place by loops of cord. The belt was coiled in a wooden ammunition box on the right of the gun, went through the breech and, on firing the cartridges, could be stored in an empty box on the left. When the gun was firing, a clawed wheel would draw the belt steadily through the gun. A corporal of artillery stood at attention, waiting to carry out the demonstration.

As I stood in the sun, breathing the fresh salty air from the sea, I recalled the letter Ben had sent to me with his plans for this gun. I had at once contacted Mr Edwards and he instructed a firm of gunmakers in Birmingham, working under conditions of secrecy, to build a prototype. This had revealed some small flaws in Ben's original design, but nothing serious. Several examples were built and fired on the firm's ranges, before the directors pronounced themselves satisfied with the results.

Their representative was now in the marquee, talking to acquaintances from the War Office with whom he had previously dealt over other weapons. One by one the officers and the officials finished their coffees and brandies and filed out to watch the last demonstration of the day. They put on their hats, consulted folders that contained details of the Fanfare Triangle's weight and fire power. I could tell from their faces that several thought the claims made for it were ridiculously exaggerated. Still, it had apparently passed the earlier eliminating tests; they might as well see it now. After all, that was why they were here. One or two glanced surreptitiously at turnip watches. This was an agreeable interlude from office life, but even so, they did not wish to stay overlong; a fast train for London left within the hour.

The manufacturer's representative now addressed the civilians and officers who stood behind the gun. He was a tall man with a florid face, and the hectoring approach of a snake-oil salesman in a travelling fair.

'This is a weapon, gentlemen, which could quite simply revolutionise infantry battles in our favour,' he began confidently. 'It has a prodigious rate of fire, more than six hundred rounds a minute. This is twice as many rounds as may be fired by the Gatling, which, as you know, is a clumsy, heavy weapon.

'The Fanfare Triangle is in every way a very great improvement on the Gatling, which has ten barrels revolving round a central shaft. Cartridges are fed into the Gatling by gravity, from a hopper on top of the weapon. This can result in jamming. An automatic gun

509

that cannot fire presents an easy and possibly irresistible target for the enemy.

'The Fanfare Triangle has only one barrel, as you can see, in place of ten. It is therefore very much simpler in design and construction, and easier to use. It is fed by a belt of cartridges, worked by a simple mechanical device. Jamming is thus practically eliminated. You will observe, gentlemen, that the gun rests on a tripod. The legs fold up so that it can be transported easily.'

He turned to the corporal, who opened a wooden box and took out a folded tripod.

'We visualise two men working the Fanfare Triangle. One to fire it, the other to keep it supplied with ammunition. And if the gun needs to be moved in a hurry, one man can carry the barrel, the other the tripod. You will see that it is light, mobile and deadly.

'Are there any questions, gentlemen, before we start the demonstration?'

No one spoke.

The corporal sat down behind the gun, legs splayed out on either side of the tripod. While the representative had been talking, someone had fixed targets on posts along the edge of the cliff overlooking the sea. These targets were painted wooden cut-outs of soldiers wearing Russian uniform. The representative turned to the senior officer, a brigadier, touched the brim of his hat in a kind of salute.

'Have I your permission to begin firing, sir?'

'Carry on.'

The corporal pulled back the cocking lever, pressed the trigger. The belt jerked like a canvas snake with a chatter of small, repeated detonations as its belt whipped through the breech. Empty cartridge cases sprayed out on the grass in a hail of hot bright metal. The corporal traversed the gun slowly left to right. One after another, the targets disintegrated and fell. The air was suddenly sharp with the smell of burnt cordite and hot oil. As the last target dropped, the corporal stopped firing. My ears still rang with the noise.

'Any gentleman like to test the gun himself?' the representative asked.

The brigadier came forward, sat down, legs out, his right eye aligning the gun's two sights. He thumbed the trigger. Again, the gun chattered. The belt leapt, the pyramid of smoking empty cartridge cases grew. The brigadier stopped, stood up, shaking his head in wonder and surprise.

'Remarkable mechanism,' he said as he rejoined his colleagues. 'Amazing fire power. I've never seen anything approaching it.'

Several other officers and civilians now tried the gun. All were equally impressed. Then the company representative and the artillery corporal packed away the Fanfare Triangle in its boxes. The demonstration was over. The experts stood in a group discussing it, all thought of the fast train now driven from their minds. There was no doubt they were enormously impressed: they had seen a weapon that could revolutionise warfare. If only the British had possessed even one in Afghanistan, there would never have been a retreat!

Edwards and I walked slowly towards his carriage. We were in no hurry to leave, but stood in the sunshine, wondering whether we would know the verdict before we dispersed. We were not left in doubt for long. The representative ran after us. He was very excited.

'I've just been told unofficially by the brigadier, who is head of the War Office buying department, that it is absolutely certain they will take it,' he said. 'It could become the British army's main machine gun.'

'How many does that mean you will sell?' the lawyer asked him.

'At the very least, several thousand. And that is simply the initial order.'

'And what royalty will Captain Bannerman receive?' I asked.

'That has not yet been agreed,' the representative replied, looking at both of us in turn. 'I would say two pounds sterling on every Fanfare Triangle Machine Gun sold.' He turned to the lawyer. 'What do you say, sir?'

'I would say that is a starting figure on which we could base negotiations.'

Edwards opened the door of his carriage; we climbed inside. I knew then that Ben would soon be a rich man. If I accepted Ben's offer and took half of his receipts, I would also be wealthy. But I had no intention of accepting a penny. This was his invention, born out of his own experience. Whatever profit there might be in this belonged totally to him. I decided to write and tell him so that same evening.

This would only be the first order, of course. Other armies of the Empire, and perhaps of other countries, could not afford to ignore such a powerful weapon. The baby I had brought into the world, the boy I had watched grow to manhood and then lost awhile need never be poor again.

Chapter Fifteen

Ben sat on a wooden bench in a mess hut at the heart of the Delhi Magazine. Across the scrubbed table he faced two lieutenants, George Willoughby and George Forrest, of about his age, who were in charge of the Magazine. Beyond the forty-foot stone walls that ringed the enormous storehouse of gunpowder, shells, mines, fuses, and every known explosive instrument of siege or assault, they could hear a constant barrage of angry cries and threatening shouts from thousands of mutineers. Only the thickness of the wall separated them.

From time to time there came a fierce rattle of musket fire and screams of pain as people fell wounded, either by mutineers firing wildly and indiscriminately or from the shells of besiegers outside the city exploding in the narrow streets.

On the table in front of the three young men stood three empty bottles of India Pale Ale, the last in the Magazine store, and three almost empty glasses. Although none of them gave voice to their thoughts, the fact that the glasses now contained little more than a last swallow seemed uneasily symbolic. Was their time also almost up? Within minutes, would their souls be required of them?

They felt far too young to die, but if the mutineers came over the wall or swarmed through the gates, they knew they would be fortunate to survive for more than minutes.

Their orders were simple and unequivocal: to deny the contents of the Magazine to the mutineers. No retreat, no surrender, no excuses.

Ben scanned the faces of the others and guessed their thoughts. How strange to recall that only recently he had been under house arrest in Meerut. The outbreak of violence there, which he had used to secure his freedom, had died as quickly and unexpectedly as it had erupted, and for a very simple reason. Most of the sepoys simply marched out of the garrison, taking with them field guns and bullock carts piled high with supplies and ammunition. They all headed for Delhi, to the palace of the old Mogul King.

To Hindus and Muslims alike, Bahadur Shah represented leadership, the last of a long line of omnipotent emperors. He would lead them now in their crusade against changes to customs old as India, against rumours that the British planned to convert them all to Christianity. He would shield them from retribution for their acts of disloyalty. He would make up pay and pensions they had forfeited. He would redress all wrongs, all misunderstandings. If he lacked power to do these things, why was he still called King?

Plans for the Intelligence Department had been precipitately abandoned, and Ben's continued presence in Meerut was an embarrassment to General Hewitt. He and Ritchie had therefore been ordered to Delhi to join any regiment short of officers, of which the general did not doubt there must be several.

They had found the British regiments encamped outside the city, on and around an escarpment known as the Ridge, slightly north of Delhi and overlooking the city from a height of about forty feet. After an initial

514

successful engagement against the mutineers, when thirty thousand sepoys with thirty heavy guns had been routed (rather to the surprise of both sides), no one seemed clear as to their next step.

Younger and more vigorous officers were held back by the sloth and incompetence of their seniors, to whom inaction always seemed more attractive than attack. They counselled caution. It would be wiser to wait for reinforcements before any further attacks were contemplated. The monsoon was due soon. No one ever fought in the rainy season, when the dry parched earth turned to quagmire under months of ceaseless rain. Better to wait and see what the mutineers attempted before organising an attack themselves.

In the meantime, a group of British civilians, mostly women and young children, had taken refuge in the top floor of a four-storey building, Flagstaff Tower, also north of the city. This was a prominent lookout post, very popular with walkers on summer evenings. Its top room, about eighteen feet square, commanded a panoramic view over the River Jumna, Delhi, the Red Fort and the malarious swamps round about. It was a favourite place for Europeans with sketchbooks. Here, with varying degrees of success, they would try to capture the delicate tints of green and red, and the shimmering haze that always obscured the ultimate horizon.

Soon after Ben and Ritchie reached the British encampment outside Delhi, the commanding general ordered that these civilians must be rescued, but he did not propose any plan for this, nor did he say where the refugees should be taken if they could be extricated safely. He could not even provide a map of the city's maze of streets.

Equally, the Magazine, whose siting inside the city instead of outside it now seemed impossible to explain

515

or excuse, was in danger of falling to the mutineers. With the two young British lieutenants already inside the Magazine were three warrant officers, eight British private soldiers, and fifty Indian sepoys whose loyalty was suspect. Outnumbered both inside and outside, the British contingent's task of defending the Magazine was impossible. The only way to deny it to the insurgents was to destroy it. But it could only be blown up by those already inside, and how could they possibly hope to survive such a holocaust?

An officer was required to be detached to assist the two lieutenants, and another to lead the refugees to safety from the Flagstaff Tower. No officers already outside Delhi were keen to volunteer for either of these tasks. They had seen the ferocity with which the mutineers fought, and both assignments seemed equally hopeless. As new arrivals, Ritchie and Ben were detailed to decide between themselves which of these tasks they would tackle. They tossed a rupee coin. Ritchie called heads and won. He said he would attempt to rescue the women and children from Flagstaff Tower. So Ben was here in the Magazine, surrounded by drums and crates of explosives, pyramids of shells, wondering how long he had left to live – and how he had ever become involved in such a hopeless situation.

The Magazine was so full of explosives that the smell of gunpowder, packed in sacks in huge wooden crates, soured the air. Under the baking sun, cannons and piles of cannon balls gave off a constant smell of heated iron, reminding Ben of red-hot horseshoes on a blacksmith's anvil.

A rattle on the huge locks outside, the thunder of iron bars hammered against the foot-thick beams of the gates, scattered his thoughts. The shouts ceased for a moment, as an Indian called to them in Hindustani.

'This is the palace Guard Commander! Open in the name of the King!'

None of the officers replied; it would be pointless to indulge in a question-and-answer dialogue.

'I thought the Guard Commander was Captain Cartwright?' said Ben.

'He was,' Willoughby agreed grimly. 'But he was killed very early on with his wife and young son. They were horribly mutilated, so I heard. The carnage out there is absolutely indescribable. The Indians seem to have gone mad. They're not simply killing soldiers but anyone, male and female, of any age who has a white skin.'

'How trustworthy are the sepoys in here?' Ben asked him.

'Judge for yourself,' Willoughby said briefly, and nodded towards the Indians. They stood in a sullen group a few yards away, arms folded, watching the officers with hostile, wary eyes.

'They're only waiting their moment!' warned Forrest. 'I don't know why they haven't killed us already. Fourteen of us against fifty of them. We wouldn't have a chance. We could kill and wing a few, agreed, but the end could never be in doubt. So why are they waiting? If they attacked us, they could open the gates in minutes, and then the mutineers would have enough explosives to last them for a fifty-year war.'

'They all want to get out without suffering any casualties,' Willoughby said. 'That's why they're hanging back. As you say, we could kill and wing a few, but they don't know which of them would be in that number. And none are eager to put the matter to the test.'

At that moment a great shout of triumph came from outside. The end of a bamboo ladder appeared at the top of the wall. It fell back, then rose again, pivoted on the edge and fell down inside.

A second ladder followed it. They were long scaling ladders made of bamboo poles. Immediately, the sepoys in the Magazine propped them against the wall and swarmed up and over. They had all gone within a minute. Now the British defenders were on their own. The mutineers could bide their time; they had no hostages left inside the Magazine.

The officers jumped up, pulled away the ladders. If the mutineers were planning to scale the wall, they might think twice before they faced a forty-foot drop.

'Let's run through the orders again,' said Willoughby; anything seemed better than simply sitting and waiting.

Forrest brought the private soldiers into line, facing the table. Ben counted them – nine men. There should only be eight. Who was the ninth?

They numbered off from the left. The last man wore a civilian suit and trousers; he was slightly older than the others, and had thick-lensed spectacles with metal frames.

'Who are you?' Ben asked him. 'Are you a soldier?'

'No, sir. I'm a clerk. I work in the judge's office.'

'Then what are you doing in here?'

'Very simple, sir. I was carrying some papers for the judge and I got chased by a bunch of Indians with *lathis* – truncheons – and muskets. I had to drop the papers and run for my life. I saw the gate was open here, sir, so I came in. The Delhi Magazine is the biggest in the Empire, so I reckoned if any place was safe, this was it.' He smiled ruefully.

In the centre of the Magazine stood a single lemon tree, dried, withered, without fruit. Using this as a marker, the Magazine party decided to lay trails of grey and black gunpowder to the doors of the huge storehouse which contained the greatest concentration of volatile explosives.

A British soldier would stand at the end of each of these trails holding a lighted torch. If the sepoys outside succeeded in breaking through the gates, then Willoughby or Ben would immediately give the order to light the powder trails. Some of the soldiers might be shot by then, but the officers calculated that one trail, at the least, could be lit and would burn its way to the heart of the Magazine and blow it up.

To slow the advance of the insurgents as far as was possible, a seventy-four-pound howitzer was directed at the gates. A warrant officer, Conductor John Buckley, would stand against the wall, at one side of the gate, but beyond the arc of fire. If the gate was buckled by a battering ram and appeared likely to break, he would raise his hat as a signal and the howitzer would fire. The gunners possessed enough ammunition to fire until the barrel melted, but the defenders were so hugely outnumbered that they would be fortunate if they could fire half a dozen shells before they were overwhelmed. Nevertheless, the delay might be critical in ensuring the destruction of the Magazine.

Blowing up the Magazine was the ultimate deterrent. Unquestionably it would deny the contents of the Magazine to the mutineers, but it would probably kill everyone within the walls and unknown numbers beyond them. There would be the most powerful explosion ever deliberately set off in the history of warfare. The officers prayed that this suicidal plan would never need to be implemented.

If the mutineers decided to scale the walls, they would first have to throw over ladders or ropes, which would give advance notice of their intentions. Many could be picked off as soon as they put their heads above the wall, but not all. Two six-pounder guns, double-charged with grapeshot, were positioned to face the walls and gates. The guns were clumsy, but the defenders had just enough men available to swing them round to direct their fire in whichever direction the danger seemed greatest.

'Any questions?' asked Ben.

The men shook their heads.

'Then may God help all of us.'

They heard another roar from the crowd outside and a crash against the gates. The huge timbers moved slightly; dry crossbeams creaked in protest. Ben and Willoughby raced up the steps to a watchtower. They could see a hundred Indians outside, all stripped to the waist, bodies glowing with sweat like polished oak, manhandling a battering ram made from a giant tree.

Its branches had been lopped off close to the trunk to provide hand holds. They drew back twenty paces and then charged for a second time. At the third attempt, two planks splintered in the gate. The great iron hinges bent and buckled under the force of the onslaught. As Ben watched, half a dozen ladders with ropes tied to one end came over the wall. Indians appeared along the top of the wall, heads and shoulders dark against the blue sky. The soldiers aimed a six-pounder at them, fired. Two Indians disappeared, and with them two feet of stones from the wall. The gunners sponged out the reeking barrel, reloaded.

Again, the battering ram crashed. This time, the end of the tree poked in through the gate. Years of ferocious heat had dried the planks. The wood was breaking more easily than the defenders had expected. The next thrust with the tree trunk would punch a hole large enough to let the mutineers through.

Conductor Buckley raised his hat.

As though in slow motion, the howitzer gunner applied a lit taper to the port fire, a small hole through which the charge would be ignited. For a second that seemed endless and beyond all measurement to the desperate defenders, nothing happened. Then the gun fired with a roar that deafened them. The rush of the great shell caused a wind that sucked the breath from their bodies.

The giant charge blew away the gate and flattened a mass of wooden and mud buildings outside. Smoke and dust hung in the air like poisoned amber fog. Ben heard screams and cries of pain and terror. The gunners sponged out the barrel and fired a second time. At each side of the open gateway, men's heads now appeared above the wall. Over came more ladders and long, knotted ropes. Within seconds the sepoys were coming over in scores, a swarming dark tide of men in uniforms and *dhotis*, carrying muskets, swords, clubs, leaping down forty feet.

'Fire all guns!' shouted Ben. Both six-pounders now began to fire, aimed at the top of the walls. The grape-shot blew huge gaps in the stones and bricks of the walls. The compound was suddenly filled with broken, writhing bodies; fearfully wounded men with arms, legs, faces blown away, screamed in unbearable pain and bewilderment. Dust from whitewashed buildings within the Magazine yard fell like powdered snow, covering the dead and the dying. The air was so thick with the harsh stench of gunpowder that the defenders choked for breath.

As fast as they reloaded and fired, more Indians appeared. Then one gun suddenly stopped firing; the gunners had been cut down. Within seconds now it would all be over, and the Magazine in the hands of the mutineers. There was only one task left for the defenders: blow it up.

For a moment, Ben stood transfixed, as though somehow out of time, watching the terrible scene, but without any part in it. Was this how his life was about to end? Had he been born in the Afghan snows to die in a giant explosion set off at his own command? So much left to do, so little attempted – and now no time, no hope, not even a moment to pray.

In a daze, he shook hands with Willoughby and Forrest. Willoughby shouted to John Buckley. His voice was as calm, Ben thought with admiration, as if he was on parade. And so, of course, he was, possibly their last parade, and about to give the most important command of all their lives. He did not falter.

'*Now*, if you please!' he shouted.

Again, Buckley raised his hat. Through the thick, choking, eye-smarting mist of hot, swirling dust, Ben saw several soldiers light the tapers and bend to touch the powder trails. For a second, nothing happened, and then, like firework sparklers, the long lines of powder began to sizzle and flare. Flames raced on to the heart of the Magazine.

The defenders closed their eyes, covered their ears with their hands, crouching down, heads bent forward in a pathetic attempt to shield themselves from the force of detonation. Holding their breath, too exhausted to think, they waited.

The explosion was so loud it was heard clearly in Meerut, forty miles away. No one there knew the state of affairs in Delhi; they believed the noise must be a particularly violent pre-monsoon thunderstorm.

Inside the Magazine, Ben opened his eyes. He was lying on his back, half covered by rubble and dust. For a moment he was not certain whether he was alive or dead. Then he looked about him and knew that, miraculously, he lived. The Magazine walls had disappeared. Houses and other buildings for miles around had simply vanished. It took him several seconds to realise he was uninjured. His ears rang with the echo of the explosion. His nose and mouth were clogged with grit. Near him he could see Willoughby crawling on all fours towards the shattered gateway, then two or three others, their clothes torn, their faces so blackened with dust and sweat it was impossible to recognise them.

How many hundreds outside had died, Ben neither knew, nor, at that moment, did he greatly care. The size of the explosion and the casualties caused were beyond his dazed mind to calculate. Sufficient for him in that moment was the fact that no matter how many had died, he had not.

The few survivors crawled away, trembling with reaction, choking with dust and fumes and the terrible smells of violent death. They grouped together outside the shattered gates, momentarily too shocked to move any further. They stared at each other in amazement and disbelief that when so many others must have perished, they still lived. Then Ben saw the judge's clerk.

His clothes had been almost ripped off his body. He had lost his spectacles, and he sat, eyes closed, hair matted with sweat and dust, against a huge rock blown from a shattered building. Ben called to him.

The man opened his eyes, looked at him uncomprehendingly, and then smiled.

'You were right,' said Ben gently. 'You were safer in the Magazine.'

Ritchie had as little enthusiasm for his task as Ben had shown when he joined the Magazine party. It was unpleasant, quite likely impossible, but it was an order. He had to do his best.

He approached Flagstaff Tower from the south-west, leaving the dangers of Delhi well away on his right. This meant a long, hard march on his own in the ferocious heat just before the monsoon. He had decided against taking any British troops with him. They did not speak the language, and in their distinctive uniforms of red jackets and blue serge trousers they presented unmistakable targets to snipers. Also, the heat was such that in these uniforms he feared they might collapse and have to be left to their fate. British troops usually marched in the very early morning and the late evening because of the heat; Ritchie preferred to march on this occasion in the heat of the day. Time was not on the side of the refugees, and a noon arrival would be unexpected by their guards, who well knew how the British disliked tremendous and enervating temperatures.

Accordingly, Ritchie had stripped off his own uniform and wore Indian clothes. With a naked sword at his belt, two pistols and a water bottle, he felt more confident of carrying out his assignment. Because he had made a detour of several miles through the desert, he saw no Indians. The only sign of violence in Delhi was the constant pall of smoke that hung above the city, and the rumble of small-arms fire, the whistle of huge shells trundling through the sky.

An immense explosion from the centre of the city sent a huge orange ball of fire up into the air. Seconds later, the sound pounded his ear drums, and shock waves flattened his shirt against his body. That must be the Magazine going up, he thought.

He wondered how Ben had fared. He found it difficult to believe he could have survived unscathed, but long service in the army had hardened Ritchie to partings and death. You met someone and they became your friend. Then a posting or a bullet or an attack of fever meant that you had to say goodbye. You missed them and you remembered them, but men did not weep. The soldier's role was to follow the drum wherever its beat might lead him. Ritchie's task lay with the living, not the dead.

He reached the door of the tower easily enough. Then, drawing his sword, he began to climb the stone staircase. As he neared the top, he heard sounds of weeping, hysterical shrieks, the sobbing of little children. He reached the fourth storey and opened the door into the topmost room.

It was packed with people. Indian servants huddled on the floor. European women, hair matted, dresses torn and filthy, stared at him and drew back in terror as he entered. Then he realised why: they thought that because of his clothes and wild appearance he was an Indian come to kill them.

'I'm English!' he shouted. 'Do not be afraid! I have come to take you all away to safety.'

'How can we possibly go? And where to?' a woman asked him and pointed out of the window towards the cantonment. Groups of Indians were setting fire to the bungalows; some were already burning fiercely. Other mutineers were making away with whatever items they could remove; three men carried out a grand piano on their shoulders; others were carrying wooden chairs, vases, pots and pans. Behind the looters came the fire-raisers bearing flaming torches dipped in oil.

'We will go west,' Ritchie told the refugees. 'Then we will turn and cross the river, well out of sight of the cantonment. You will be all right. I give you my word.'

'How many men have you got with you?' the woman asked him.

Ritchie did not reply. To admit he was on his own could cause consternation. He counted the refugees: thirty, with ten Indian servants.

'Down the stairs,' he ordered. 'In single file. Follow me. No talking or crying once we leave the room.

Quickly and quietly is our motto now.'

There was something about his quiet confidence, his calm, unhurried voice, that comforted them. They followed him down the stone stairs. Little children held on tightly to their mothers' skirts, other mothers and *ayahs*, native nurses, carried babies too young to walk. An air of excitement, of expectancy more than relief, hung over them all. This was an adventure. Danger was past, or at least passing. Everything would be for the best. They gathered in the dust at the base of the tower, looking hopefully at Ritchie. What next? Where next?

Ritchie could not answer these questions because he did not know. All he did know was that they seemed a pathetic group, without food and water. Their clothes, and especially their shoes, were totally unsuitable for any exercise more arduous than an evening stroll before dinner. Now, they all faced a march to an unknown destination, and he had to lead them.

He formed them up roughly into two lines, and they set off through the scrub and dust. The women and children tried valiantly to keep pace with him. He was aiming for the house of a prominent judge, set in a park of a thousand acres. Here he calculated they could rest in the shade of the trees. Possibly they might even find food, and bullock carts for the oldest and the youngest, the pregnant and infirm. Then they could go on in the cool of the evening.

They reached the gates of the park, walked along its dusty drive towards the house. To Ritchie's surprise, as they approached it an Indian servant in uniform opened the front door, and bowed. They might be guests arriving for luncheon. The man showed no surprise. Nor did the under-butler and cooks who bustled about at Ritchie's orders. They were neither hostile

nor friendly, simply neutral, waiting to see which side
would win. In the meantime, they would obey his
wishes.

Ritchie told them to bring out any provisions they
had. They set loaves of bread, glass jars of potted
meat, bottles of beer and seltzer water on tables in the
garden. The repast had the grotesquely incongruous
air of a picnic. Yet a short distance away people were
killing and maiming each other with unspeakable ferocity.

The refugees ate and drank thankfully. It seemed
providential that they should have been met by such
servants, but something made Ritchie feel uneasy. He
did not trust them. The feeling of betrayal grew until
he had to put his fears to the test. He called to the
head butler. There was no reply. He shouted for any
servant, and when there was still no answer, he went
in search of them in the kitchen quarters. The kitchens
were empty. Everyone had disappeared.

This, to Ritchie, meant only one thing: the servants
had decided to join the mutineers, and as evidence of
their new loyalty they would tell them that a whole
group of unarmed mems and their children and servants were outside the judge's house. Within minutes
they could all be put to the sword.

Ritchie gathered everyone into the main hall and
addressed them.

'We must leave now,' he explained. 'The servants
have gone. I don't trust them. They may be back within
minutes, with others.'

'Where can we go?' someone asked him wretchedly.

'Towards the river. We will stay the night on the
bank and cross in the morning.'

'And then?'

'Then we will go to Meerut.'

'That's forty miles away. We can't walk that far.

There are ladies here in the eighth month of pregnancy.'

'We will make a camp,' Ritchie assured them, making up his plan as he spoke. 'Then several of the youngest and fittest among you will go on to Meerut and commandeer wagons to come back for the rest. There is no other way.'

'Then let us pray to God for deliverance,' said the woman quietly. 'There is no one else now who can help us.'

As she spoke, she knelt and began to pray. One by one, the others followed her, while Ritchie stood watching the gates for any sign of the servants returning.

Ben stood up slowly. He felt so weak, so shaken in body and spirit, he was glad to lean against the wall of a shattered house. The stones felt warm as fire bricks through his torn shirt. The others in the Magazine had gone, he had no idea where; the clerk had disappeared. Ben felt too dazed by the explosion, too disorientated to ponder the problem where they all might be. He closed his eyes, shook his head to try to clear his brain.

A huge pall of dust blew from the desert, obscuring the ruined buildings, the upturned carts, the dead and the dying. He took a pace forward and realised with horror he was like a man at the centre of a maze. He must escape, but how? And where?

He did not know the layout of the streets in Delhi and even if he did, the memory would have been useless, for so many had disappeared with the force of the Magazine explosion. He had no idea where he was, save that he was on his own. He heard cries of pain and grief and shouts of anger as he began to stumble away, half walking, half running. He had no plan; only the desperate knowledge that he must escape drove him on.

He saw a burst conduit pouring out a great shining gout of water and paused, held his face over it, gazing at its welcome coolness. But the water that revived him brought another, unexpected, danger. His face and clothes had been coated with red, sandy dust from the explosion; at a casual glance he could be taken for an Indian. Now, with his face washed clean, his clothes identifiable as uniform, he was unquestionably British. Within minutes, he would be recognised. Having escaped one death in the Magazine he did not want to die another far more painful at the hands of a lynching mob.

He began to walk as quickly as he could, trying not to appear to hurry. In a wall on his left he saw a wooden door studded with black bolt-heads. He passed it, then took a pace back, turned the handle. The door opened on oiled hinges. He went through it and, once on the other side, slammed the bolt shut.

He was in a narrow alleyway, running he knew not where, but at least he was away from the crowds and the carnage outside. He walked on, wondering where the alley led. A handful of white doves flew over the outer wall and strutted about on the pavement, cooing gently. Doors appeared on his left. He tried their handles as he went past. The first four were locked. The fifth opened. He walked through it, again bolted it behind him and stood for a moment, leaning thankfully against the warm wood.

He guessed he must be in some part of the palace complex, probably among outbuildings. He could smell cooking; that meant he was near one of the kitchens. If he could find a sheet, a long towel, a blanket, anything to conceal his obviously military appearance, he might succeed in bluffing his way out. Somewhere, behind one of these doors, could be a room containing something he could adapt as disguise. If anyone saw him as he was, he would not last a dozen paces.

Ben's ears still rang with the force of the explosion, and his brain still seemed numbed, his will atrophied. He knew what he had to do, but somehow lacked the impetus to carry out what his mind told him was essential. He must escape or he would die. These were the only two alternatives. There was no middle way, no other prospect. He must keep going, even though he realised that movement might only be an illusion of progress.

Fifty paces further on, he tried another door. This also opened easily. He was in a large room arranged as a lecture hall. Half a dozen gilded chairs like small thrones were arranged in a semi-circle on a dais. Facing them was a stage with curtains. He saw, to his astonishment, a white dove in a wicker cage, an English top hat upside down on a gilded table.

Next to this stood another table, larger and more elegant in gilt and white, with four legs and four candles burning beneath it. He had seen a table like that somewhere else, with candles burning beneath it instead of on top. But where, oh where? Then he remembered. Karim Khan had used a table like this in his booth; he had climbed on it many times, and then disappeared, apparently by magic, when a curtain was lowered round him. He glanced up at the ceiling of the room, painted blue like a summer sky and speckled with golden stars. And there, at the end of a rope, hung the familiar tube-like curtain required for this illusion.

A man was bending down, lighting the last candle. Ben took a pace towards him, meaning to stun him, seize his clothes, and then escape. But the man heard the movement and turned with animal swiftness, holding the lit taper above his head, peering at Ben.

'You!' cried Karim Khan in amazement. '*You!*'

Ben shut his eyes, shook his head again, in case this, too, was all illusion, an aftereffect of the explosion. He opened his eyes. Karim Khan was still there, staring at him.

'I was in the Magazine,' Ben explained. 'We blew it up. I'm not sure where I am now.'

'In the Hall of the Illusionists, in the King of Delhi's palace.'

'Maybe old General Hewitt was right,' replied Ben bitterly. 'He put me under arrest for helping you to escape, and you come right over to join the enemy.'

'You are not my enemy,' replied Karim Khan calmly. 'Nor am I yours. If I were, I would call the Indian guard now. But I will not. Yet you cannot stay here. If you are found, you will die.'

'Can you help me?' Ben asked him desperately.

'I will try.'

'What are you doing here anyway?'

'Following my trade. I am preparing to help the King's conjurer give an entertainment for His Majesty, and his wife the Begum and their son who will inherit when the old King dies. They are due any moment.'

Ben turned back towards the door.

'No, my friend, not that way,' said Karim Khan quickly. 'That is too risky. There is one other way out of this room that only the illusionists and conjurers know – under this table. Through a trap door like the one we used in Scotland. Go down through this trap, along the underground passage. It comes out near the city wall. There is a side gate. You will see no one. Once you are through the wall, you can be back on the Ridge in twenty minutes.'

'And you? You are staying here? With the enemy?'

'Not the enemy, Ben, but my own people. I served

your Queen and your Company for many years. This counted for nothing when my only son Amin was arrested on a charge of mutiny for which he could never be guilty. You saved me then. I can save you now – *I think*. At least I can offer you a start on your pursuers. But, hurry.'

Ben jumped up onto the stage, opened the trap door behind the two mirrors and beneath the table. As he eased himself through it, he heard the sound of distant trumpets, a wailing of flutes, the beat of drums.

'The King!' said Karim Khan. '*Quick!*'

The door closed above him. He was alone in a dark passage about four feet high, damp and foul-smelling. He stretched out his arms and felt the soft crumbling stone of the walls on either side. He began to walk forward carefully, counting each pace he took. Forty-five paces on, he walked into a solid wall.

He could not see anything. He could only feel the obstruction ahead of him. He ran his fingers carefully round the joints between the side walls and the obstruction. All the stones fitted tightly. He put all his weight against them, holding his breath until stars blazed against his closed eyelids. There was no movement whatever.

He pushed and heaved, searching desperately with his fingertips for any secret lock or lever that might conceivably cause the wall to move. He found none. He had to accept that he was trapped. Karim had deceived him. Whoever stood on that table in his act did not need to find a way out of the city; all he needed was sufficient space to hide until he had to reappear.

Ben retraced his steps, counting each pace until once more he stood beneath the trap door that opened onto the stage. He listened, sweating in the airless tomb. He could hear faint voices and then thin, sporadic clapping; then the braying of trumpets. He stood until at last there was silence. The King and his entourage must have left. He reckoned he had a few minutes, certainly no more, before the sepoys came down after him. He had to go at once or die where he stood.

Ben pushed up the trap half an inch with his outstretched hands. As far as he could see, the room was empty. He hauled himself up through the door, shut it carefully, went out into the corridor.

He still had a few moments' head start before they found he was not in the concealed underground passage. When they did so, they would follow him here because there was nowhere else for him to go. He began to run. The alley stretched on, it seemed, for nearly half a mile and then suddenly divided left and right. He approached the junction cautiously. Both sides were empty. He turned to the right. Three paces from the junction he saw, too late, a man, sword drawn, standing in an alcove. The man leaped out, barred Ben's way. He wore a shabby sepoy uniform, two pistols in his belt.

'My prisoner!' he cried triumphantly in Hindustani.

Ben said nothing: he had escaped from one trap to run headlong into another. The man put up his sword, drew a pistol. He put his other hand in his trouser pocket, took out a pair of handcuffs, snapped one on Ben's left wrist, the other on his own wrist. Then he smiled.

'We have not met, Mr Bannerman,' he said. 'My father told me he had made a mistake – he is under great strain – and he had forgotten the passage under the stage has been sealed off since the troubles. He guessed you would come out, and so you did.'

'Who are you?' Ben asked him weakly.

'Amin Khan. My father took my place in the hospital in Meerut. You saved him the indignity of being transported for life, as he had saved me. It is right that I

533

should help you now. It is written, "To gladden the heart of the weary, to remove the suffering of the afflicted, hath its own reward." This is my reward, sahib, to pay this debt of honour.'

They were walking in step along the tiled passageway.

'As I said, you are my prisoner,' Amin Khan continued. 'That is why I have handcuffed you. If I tried to disguise you, we might be caught, and then assuredly we would both die. Now, I am your guard and you are my captive. In this way we will both reach the gate of the city safely. And then, Englishman, you can go in peace.'

'As your father would say, you are my key to freedom, Amin. For which I thank you with all my heart.'

Amin Khan smiled. 'No man can claim to be a true believer, as I would wish to be, unless he desireth for his brother what he desireth for himself,' he reflected. 'My friend, I desire for you what I wish for myself, freedom and long life. And perhaps to meet once again, in happier times, at peace, all three of us.'

The next letter I received from Ben made me realise how the young man who had left me to seek his fortune had made a discovery of infinitely greater worth. He had found himself.

My dear Doctor,

I am giving this letter to an officer returning from Bombay aboard one of the new fast steamships. It should therefore reach you before any communication entrusted to the mails.

Months have passed since I last wrote to you, and for most of these months we were encamped as what we called the 'Relieving Force', outside Delhi. After some initial skirmishes and a pitched

534

battle six miles beyond the city, in which thousands of heavily armed mutinous sepoys were driven from their entrenchments, the impetus deserted our commanders. We waited then on a patch of high ground, known as the Ridge, a hill of quartz rock extending for two miles, and about forty feet above the city.

After our initial success we were commanded to burn all the native troop lines which had been built there. But when the monsoon came, and then the hot season, we had cause to regret these foolish orders, for we were now without shelter from the rain or the burning heat of the sun.

Our general, Archdale Wilson, a man in his sixties, was without stomach for attack. His subordinate commanders took their cue from him and lacked the zeal of younger men. So here we stayed, overlooking the city more as spectators than as an avenging army. We organised cricket matches and horse races. We entertained brother officers of other regiments. It was a time of make-believe. All the while we had the uneasy feeling that events were rushing past us until, finally, younger officers took the initiative. They disbelieved the mournful intelligence our seniors accepted, that tens of thousands of mutineers within the city, with no less than forty field artillery guns and more than three times as many mounted on the walls, were waiting to decimate us should we attack. Instead, they believed more optimistic reports. Many mutineers were growing disaffected; they had been told that the old king would make up their pay from his own coffers, but of course he could not possibly afford to do this. He is simply a Company pensioner. Their discipline was weakening, as was their resolve.

Our engineers prepared a plan for the city walls to be breached by batteries of heavy guns, and then they would blow open the great gates and we would surge through. They built scaling ladders, and throughout the nights of the first week of September, our big guns, each one so heavy they needed forty bullocks to pull them, were dragged from the rear and placed in position.

Relays of camels, bullock carts and mules brought in crates of ammunition. The noise they made was tremendous; there was no possibility of secrecy. Our casualties from sepoy riflemen on the walls of the city were high. But once our guns began to fire, the walls of Delhi fell like the walls of Jericho in the Bible story. The bombardment produced immense piles of rubble which would be difficult to cross under the fierce fire of the defenders. But we had waited for too long to accept any further postponement.

On the night before the attack, one of our number, a student of history, compared it to the eve of Agincourt. No one slept. Everywhere were signs and sounds of preparation; swords being sharpened, bolt actions checked, musket and rifle barrels cleaned with ramrods. We were so out-numbered, we could not afford any setbacks due to lack of preparation. This was a time when I wished the Fanfare Triangle Machine Gun was here in numbers, and not simply being issued to our army in England who had no active need of its fire power, as we had.

Our orders for the assault were simple and incapable of misunderstanding. Our column was to be led by John Nicholson, who had arrived from Peshawar, impatient of our delay and intent on victory. Such was the necessity of swift success that

Nicholson decreed that all wounded, of whatever rank, were to be left where they fell. No one must pause to help them. Inside Delhi, there would be no plundering and no looting. Any valuables discovered would be placed in a common pool and divided fairly at the end of the battle. Great care would be taken not to harm women or children. We officers drew our swords and pledged by them to abide strictly by these rules. The men gave their word.

As we were about to march off before dawn to take up our final positions before the assault, an old priest, Father Bertrand, addressed our colonel.

'We may differ, some of us, in matters of religion,' he said. 'But the blessing of an old man and a clergyman can do nothing but good.' He raised his hands to Heaven, and even the unbelievers among us were impressed by his obvious sincerity as he prayed for victory, and for divine mercy on the souls of those who might not live to see it.

A handful of brave men, British and Indian, prepared charges of powder and sandbags to blow open the great doors of the Kashmir Gate in the city wall. The sandbags would be placed on the charges to give each explosion added force. They ran forward with a bugler to sound the advance as the gate disintegrated. The defenders on top of the walls saw the men race towards the gate and instantly realised their intention. They poured a hail of fire on them, but by God's mercy the runners reached the relative shelter of the wall and set the charges.

The noise of the explosions and the subsequent confusion was such that the bugle was not heard.

We did not wait for it but poured through the open gateway in a human tide. From above, sepoys fired continuously at us. When their ammunition ran low, they flung stones, even their empty rifles at us in their fury.

I saw John Nicholson leading a charge up a narrow alleyway. At the far end stood two brass cannons, one a hundred yards behind the other. The men charged the first gun, captured it, but fire from the second drove them back. Nicholson urged them on. He was shot instantly, and lay where he fell. Later, a long time later, when the alley was cleared, we were able to carry him back to have his wound dressed. But his injuries were severe, and he had lain out in the fury of battle unattended for too long. He died a week later, a loss that Britain and India can ill afford.

Many other officers and men, British and Indian alike, fought bravely. This was a crucial test of the Indians' loyalty and they passed it with honour. They had friends and relations fighting with the mutineers but they stayed true.

'I have eaten the Company's salt,' one explained to me. 'I am a Company man.'

The carnage was indescribable. For days, dead bodies of men and beasts, many hideously and disgustingly mutilated, lay stinking under the burning sun, bursting with putrefaction. The state of wounded men, lacking any opium or laudanum to ease their fearful pain, was such that they begged comrades to shoot them and so end their agony.

I cannot describe all the acts of heroism, the sights of horror I saw. All of us who survived became so used to both that after a few hours they had no further effect on us. Our feelings were stunned by the size of the catastrophe. But two weeks after the first cannonade, Delhi was ours. On the 21st day of September, our artillery fired a salute of guns to mark the formal capture of the City of the King. Many officers and men found stores of wine and brandy in the cellars of palaces and private houses. Muslims, of course, would never drink alcohol and possibly the Hindus did not realise these stores remained. There was so much wine that a bottle of very good claret could be bought for three pennies.

There were celebrations, of course, but I was not the only one to feel that such were oddly out of place. I had seen too much slaughter, too much suffering, too many deaths. In any battle there must be casualties, but here they were all the more cruel because they involved defenceless women and children.

For example, a colleague, Major Ritchie, had personally brought out thirty or forty British women with children and some Indian servants from their hiding place in a high building known as the Flagstaff Tower. He had hoped to lead them to safety in Meerut, which was the nearest town of any size. But not one survived more than a few days in the desert. They suffered from fevers and plagues and died pitifully, and without purpose. Other women who escaped from Delhi were robbed by marauding bands of mutineers and then put to the sword.

All these unnecessary deaths and the pain and anguish that accompanied so many of them have had a profound effect on me. I had arrived in India with many misconceptions and preconceived ideas, and tried to fit events into the pattern I thought best for them. Now, the only thing I know is how little I know. I have decided to resign my commission as soon as may be practical, and relinquish for ever the profession of arms.

When I received your letter describing the success of the Fanfare Triangle Machine Gun at its tests in Kent, it seemed ironic that someone whose invention could kill and maim hundreds, possibly thousands, of people he will never meet should profit from this when he has become disenchanted with the whole art of war. As I read your letter, I recalled the plight of soldiers' children I had seen in the lines at Barrackpore. Their lives were miserable enough in peace, but as orphans now after this uprising, many will be infinitely worse. What is their future but misery in heartless institutions? What awaits them but sordid lives of crime, or as beggars by the roadside, cadging coins from those more fortunate, whose Company investments their fathers possibly died to save?

It came to me that a just and apt use of the money the Fanfare Triangle Gun will make would be to spend it on building a future for these boys and girls who, otherwise, have at best little hope, and at worst, none. Accordingly, I have come to two conclusions. First, you must take the half of the royalties as I proposed and which you have already declined. Second, my share should be placed in a fund to buy houses, possibly near the sea, to provide accommodation for as many boys and girls, sons and daughters of soldiers and sailors, as may require them.

You might care to help to run this charity, with a special responsibility for the health of the children. You speak highly of the lawyer, Mr Jonah Edwards. If you agree with my proposals, please instruct him to go ahead with these plans. No doubt he could also be a trustee and guide us through the quicksands of the law.

Now, I have written enough; words are no more substitute for deeds than are pious promises and intentions for acts of kindness. I am about to ride north to bring to justice a man held responsible for the massacre of many defenceless people in Cawnpore. He is the Nana Sahib, of whom you will have read in newspaper accounts of the uprising.

The feeling against this man is so strong and the revulsion against Indians in Cawnpore so great that the British commander now in control has made captured sepoys clear the remains of the dead from the places of their incarceration and murder. And to drive home to them the utter loathing we feel for their cowardly acts of torture and murder, they have been ordered down on their hands and knees and made to lick the blood-stains from the tiles on the floor with their tongues . . .

The go-between was a small man with large, worried eyes. He wore a loincloth, shabby *chaplis* on his feet, a ragged shirt on his back. It had no sleeves. His arms were thin, like the arms of a spider or some crawling insect. Ben did not like him, he did not trust him; but he needed him. He was the last in a long line of agents who had promised to lead Ben to the Nana Sahib, who was either to be brought to justice for the crimes he was accused of or to be killed if he should attempt to flee or resist arrest. Other officers had hoped to bepicked for the job of capturing the Nana Sahib. Such a captive would bring them fame: an instant decoration, perhaps even a knighthood. But they did not speak Hindustani; Ben and Ritchie did. At the last moment, however, Ritchie had been required to act as an interpreter during dealings with the King, now under arrest and due to be sent into exile in Burma.

Ben had come north with fifty British soldiers. It was not known how large the Nana's bodyguard would be, but fifty men seemed sufficient to deal with them. They had reached the foothills of a mountain in the north of India. As the troops made camp, Ben faced the go-between who, for an agreed sum, would betray his countryman.

'Where is he?' Ben asked him bluntly.

'Up this hill, sahib. He is with two others in a cave, with a holy man.'

'You know who I mean?'

'You mean the Nana Sahib. Two Muslims are with him. One is Sher Shah, a notable warrior against your people. I do not know the other. He is a young man, so I am told. Hindu and Muslim, like oil and water, snow and sun, they do not mix. But now in extremity they are together. You can catch them all. Three men with one bullet, three fish with one hook. You will remember me, then, sahib?'

'I will never forget you,' said Ben, and meant it. What infamies had this turncoat perpetrated when he thought he was on the winning side? But Ben knew now that in war, in mutiny, there was no winning side. Both sides had lost something more important than a battle. They had lost trust that could never entirely return.

He unbuckled his pouch, took out two one-hundred-rupee notes, handed them to the small man. The go-between looked at them closely, held them up to the firelight, pushed them into his loincloth. Blood money, thought Ben. But who is the worst, he who gives or he who takes?

He turned to his men. 'I'm going up alone,' he told the English sergeant.

'That wise, sir?' the sergeant asked him. He was an old soldier, cautious; he had survived many campaigns. Others, braver and more audacious, had not. He was determined to live long and to draw his pension.

'I don't know if it's wise or foolish, Sergeant, but it's what I'm going to do. If you hear shots, come up. If I am dead and the others are alive, kill them. If they are dead and I'm alive, we'll take them back together.'

The man smiled. 'You're a cool one, sir,' he said admiringly.

'Not really,' Ben replied. 'I've just had enough of fighting, enough of death. I'm becoming a fatalist. Whatever will be, will be.'

'I know how you feel, sir.'

Ben buckled on his pistol, checked that it was primed. If I had a Fanfare Triangle gun now, he thought, I could deal with the whole matter in minutes. As it is, events may take longer. But perhaps that is the better way.

'Goodbye, sir,' said the sergeant. 'Sure you'll be all right?'

'If it is written I die,' said Ben, 'I die.' They shook hands. Ben began to walk up the hill.

The cave where the hunted men had taken refuge was sheltered from wind and rain by an overhanging lip, like a huge eyebrow, of massive branches twisted together. The holy man, who had lived here for so long that even the oldest men in the village could not remember a time when he had not been in the cave, was squatting on his haunches in the mouth of the cavern. His hair and body were daubed with wood ash. He was lean, almost emaciated, and wore only a loincloth. He appeared oblivious of heat and cold and any discomfort.

In front of the fakir a few embers glowed beneath a metal pot. This contained herbs and strips of goat flesh. Another cooking pot was full of rice. He stirred the goat flesh slowly, his mind miles and centuries away, thinking of the abstracts, life and death, birth, regeneration, the fortunes of men that like a turning wheel rise and fall again. Sometimes, but seldom, had he ever seen them rise a second time.

I'll have no trouble with him, Ben assured himself. The Nana Sahib could be different; he had position, esteem, more to lose than simply his life. He might not give up easily. As for Sher Shah, Ben had never heard of him. The name meant Lion King and had first been used by one of the great Mogul emperors. If he lived up to his namesake, he would put up a fight.

So why was he going up the hill alone while fifty armed men waited below? Was not this a ridiculous and quite unnecessary risk? It was, but for reasons he could not explain, even to himself, this was what he wished to do. If he were in the Nana's situation, Ben knew he would rather be approached as a human being, a fallen ruler maybe, but one whose life had not been entirely without honour, than as a felon, a wild man to be taken roughly like a tiger in its lair.

Inside the cave, the Nana Sahib sat with his back against the wall of the cave. He was not an old man, but he felt old, a thousand years old. Like a demented gambler he had thrown all he possessed on the turn of a wheel, on the hope that an uprising in an army could bring him justice. The gamble had failed. Azi Mullah had been wrong in his forecast. The Nana still felt that the East India Company had treated him meanly, but no one and nothing could change that now.

He had hoped that if the Indians drove the British out, then they would treat him more generously. He had transferred his allegiance from one camp to the other, and the first had won. No doubt they would not let him forget this mistake. They would come after him, and extract their vengeance. He was blamed for the pointless and fearful massacre of women and children in Cawnpore. He would never go free; he was as good as dead if the British tracked him down.

He felt the earth crumble against the thin silk of his shirt, knowing that, like an animal pursued by hunters, he would be on the run until he was caught or illness or accident humiliated him and brought him down, like a wild deer with a broken thigh, helpless before his hunters. It must have been written in the stars that this was how he would end, miserably, a failure, lacking even a roof above his head, trapped in a cave.

If this was his destiny, he had to accept it. Tears were of no avail, nor were regrets. His path had been marked out for him. He had followed it. And this was where it had led him: to a dark hole, like a new-made grave, halfway up a hill.

Across the cave from him sat the Muslim, Sher Shah, and his son. He and the Nana had different backgrounds, different beliefs, they worshipped different gods. But in extremity they were like two sides of a melon joined, making one. They endured the same privations, feared the same future.

Sher Shah had come from Delhi to Cawnpore and had promised much. The Nana had welcomed him. By then, he had few other optimists around him.

Together, the Nana and Sher Shah had visited unimportant garrisons, largely military outposts, where sepoys chanted slogans and clapped hands as though already they were the rulers, Hindu and Muslim. And yet even then their welcome had seemed somehow hollow.

Azi Mullah had vanished long since, and the loyal Munta Lal had paid for his loyalty with his life. The rumour was that Azi Mullah had had something to do with this, that it was part of a complex plan to influence the East India Company in the Nana's favour. But like so much else in his career, it had not been successful. And now, what did rumours matter? Now, it seemed to the Nana, nothing mattered any more. Looking back, nearly everything had been wishful thinking, dreams instead of deeds.

The holy man turned to them. 'The meal is ready,' he announced briefly. He began to ladle it out onto crude, unglazed plates.

Suddenly, the bitterness of what had been, what might have been, almost overcame the Nana. He said, 'To think I used to eat off gold plates.'

'It is the food you eat, Nana Sahib, not the plate,' the holy man reminded him sharply. He cared nothing for these matters. All vanities were useless, to be avoided, snares and delusions for the unwary. He sought his reward in another world. In the meantime, he made do with what he had, without regrets, without grumbles. Life was a penance to be endured, like a thorny path with rough stones and cruel briars, because the wise knew it led to a bower of scented flowers that never would fade or die.

The Nana and Sher Shah, the Hindu and the Muslim, the two representatives of India's great religions, sat now on their haunches eating rice and goat flesh, using strips of oatmeal bread as spoons.

It had wanted only one man in any village to say that the Nana had passed through and the man would have received rupees enough to buy himself land and a new beginning in another part of India. At first no one had taken the blood money, but gradually attitudes had changed. Men came out with spears and sticks, not to greet the fugitives but to tell them to be on their way; it was not safe to tarry, not only for their own lives but for the lives of those who might shelter them. The British had long memories, sharp swords and new guns that could fire with the speed of a hundred Enfields. Go, said the villagers, or risk betrayal.

So they went, until finally they had retreated to this cave. They trusted the holy man. He would never betray them. He was not concerned about material possessions in this world. His thoughts were on the next.

Suddenly, the Nana Sahib put down his chapatti and listened.

'There's someone outside,' he said. He stood up, ready to fight or to run. Then he realised he could do neither; the time was long since gone.

'Who is there?' he asked.

There was no answer. He had not really expected one. The question had been a nervous reaction to an unexpected noise. And then he saw a man standing at the mouth of the cave, a dark outline against the dim blue of the sky.

'You are the Nana Sahib,' said the man. He spoke Hindustani, but he was not Indian. He had an English accent. There was no need now for the Nana to deny who he was. He must meet his destiny as a man, bear himself as a maharajah – or, he thought bitterly, as a maharajah's adopted son. In a curious way, he felt almost relieved. He had been hunted and now he was caught; the long chase was over, and he could rest. Death was surely only another name for sleep.

'I am the Nana Sahib,' he agreed quietly.

Sher Shah also stood up, and next to him his son, who had the build and bearing of a soldier. Together they watched the stranger come into the cave. They could kill him easily; a single shot from a pistol, a thrust from a sharpened sword. But they did not. They knew such a killing would not solve anything. It would not be a finite act, but only another in a seemingly endless chain of violent actions and reactions, as a cry can echo almost without end in the chasms of the hills.

'Do not reach for your weapons,' warned Ben. 'I am armed, and there are fifty armed men outside.'

The holy man went on eating. He had not stood up. Warnings and threats meant nothing to him.

Ben came further into the cave. He wanted to draw his pistol in case one of the three rushed him, but instinct made him stay his hand. He had not come to kill, at least not yet. Or had he? He was not quite sure. The fire was reflected in oil in a terracotta bowl with a floating wick. He bent down to the fire, picked up a burning twig, lit the wick.

The cave was very small, and in the gentle light of the oil lamp its crudeness was accentuated by the skin of some animal stretched on the earth in one corner as a bed, two wooden stools, a few beaten copper pots. Ben held up the light and looked at the Nana Sahib closely. He had expected to see a cruel face, hard eyes. Instead, he saw an ineffectual, disappointed man. In other circumstances, this man could have been his host at the balls he used to give for British officers and their ladies.

'You met someone once who I want to find,' he said. 'Mary Jane Green.'

'I am not remembering the name,' the Nana Sahib replied.

'She was married to Munta Lal.'

'Ah, yes. He went to England to try to persuade the directors to pay me a pension. It was my right. But they would not do so. He was a kind man. He died. I never met his wife.'

'I believe Munta Lal was murdered by mistake by people who resented him. He was honest.'

'Yes. An honest man.'

'And his wife?'

'She went away. I hope no ill befell her?'

Ben turned to the other man.

'There is no need for you to question me,' said Sher Shah.

Ben held the lamp close to his face. In the light of the tiny flame, Karim Khan smiled at him.

'You!' said Ben. 'I cannot believe it. I am looking for Sher Shah, the Muslim leader.'

'A man can have many names, my friend. I have been Karim Khan. Then I became Amin Khan. Now I am who you seek. And this other man here is my son. He tells me you have also met.'

'Why are you with the Nana?'

'We were drawn together by misfortune,' Karim Khan explained. 'I travelled to the West, and then came back to the East. I do not know whether I am a man of either world or of both – or of none.'

'You saved my life in Delhi,' said Ben.

'And you saved my liberty in Meerut. We are not in each other's debt. As you would say in your country, the slate is clean. You have your duty to do. We will not resist.'

'I hear that Queen Victoria has promised amnesty to all who surrender, who have not killed any British subject.'

'But who can say whether we have killed or not killed, directly or indirectly?' asked the Nana. 'Is the man who makes the gun, who manufactures the cartridge, not as guilty as the man who presses the trigger or the officer who gives him the order? All share in the guilt. But one man makes a profit out of the matter. If he makes a great profit he can also be honoured. In your country he can become a knight, a lord, an earl. But the man who presses the trigger may have to die for what he has done.'

'I came here,' said Ben, 'to take you both back to Delhi to stand trial, after which I don't doubt you would both be sentenced to die. But I have seen too many deaths, too much slaughter, too much cruelty on both sides. And now, too many turncoats, too much fake evidence. I am tired of the smell of the dead, of gunpowder, the sound of bugles and the crackle of guns. I have no quarrel with you. I owe one of you many debts. The other, in different circumstances, could have been my host – or my guest.'

The holy man now stood up, still holding his bowl of food.

'The young man speaks truth,' he said approvingly. 'The Lord Buddha said, "Victory breeds hatred, for the conquered is unhappy. He who has given up both victory and defeat is contented and happy." '

For a moment, no one spoke. Shadows thrown by the oil lamp danced on the walls of the cave.

'I have friends in Nepal and in Burma,' said the Nana Sahib at last. 'When I held court in Cawnpore, they visited me. Now I will visit them. Not as a maharajah's adopted son, but as a traveller in need. They will not turn me away. I will not return. You will be rid of me for ever.'

Ben nodded. He sensed that this intention was only another part of the Nana's dream. He would never reach Burma safely; someone on the way would recognise him and betray him.

Karim Khan held out his hand. 'You were the first Englishman to shake me by the hand,' he said to Ben. 'Now maybe you will be the last.' He took a more realistic view of their future than the Nana. They had been spared, but only for the moment. They would doubtless have to face further tribulations. But Ben would have his reward, of that Karim Khan was certain. God was never in any man's debt. As the Prophet had said, blessed always be his name: 'Whoever hath been given gentleness hath been given a good portion, in this world and the next.' Karim Khan turned away so that the others would not see the tears in his eyes; men did not weep.

'I am going down,' said Ben.

'You are sending the soldiers up to take us in?' asked the Nana; he wanted to make certain. He had been deceived too many times in his life by those he had trusted. Could this be another betrayal?

'No,' said Ben. 'Eventually we will all die. Let whatever gods we believe in choose that time, not us.'

'You speak truth, young man,' said the fakir. 'It is written, dust to dust, death to death, but mercy and love and peace overcome all things.'

Ben turned and began to walk down the steep slope. He could barely see where he placed his feet; his eyes were filled with tears. Once more he had failed in his duty, as before in Barrackpore he had failed to give orders to fire, and in Meerut he had released a prisoner.

He could be court-martialled for what he had done, and knowing the value placed on the capture of the Nana Sahib, his sentence could be severe. But he felt no shame. He had done what he did because he felt it was right. And was not the cause of right what the fighting had been about?

The sergeant came towards him. 'You are all right, sir?' he asked anxiously.

'Yes,' Ben answered him.

'Who's up there? Those Indians we're after?'

'Three old men, one a fakir, and a young fellow,' he said. 'Nothing to do with us.'

'So we got the wrong information from that spy, then, did we, sir?'

'That often happens,' Ben replied. 'We are told what

we want to hear, we believe what we want to believe.'

'Can't trust anyone, that's what I say. Are we staying here, sir, or going back?'

'There's nothing to stay here for,' said Ben. 'Get the men fell in.'

Up in the cave the holy man was scouring his cooking dishes. The go-between crouched on the other side of the fire, watching him. After a few minutes, he handed one of his hundred-rupee notes to the fakir. The holy man shook his head, pushed the money away.

'You keep that,' he said. 'You did your part well. As I prophesied, the young officer has let them go. They were not evil, only misguided.'

The go-between's astonishment wrinkled his face. 'They were very lucky,' he said.

The holy man shook his head. 'What is written, will be. Luck? That is only the unbeliever's word for Providence.'

Mary Jane entered the Commissioner's office in Peshawar and the clerk bowed an obsequious greeting. As she watched the familiar gesture – the man's two palms politely placed spatulate together beneath his chin – she suddenly wondered how many times since arriving in Peshawar she had seen this salutation, and whether it was as sincere as it seemed. The uprising appeared to have been quelled, but trust between Indians and British could take longer to return, if it ever would completely.

When Munta Lal's relations had agreed on the division of his estate, Mary Jane decided to stay on in her room in Mrs Murison's private hotel. It seemed possible that the unrest in Delhi might spread across India. Travel at such a time would be difficult and dangerous. And even if it were not, where could she go that was better than where she was?

For the first time in her life, she could do as she pleased. She had no one to consider but herself, and she had enough money to satisfy every reasonable wish. One town seemed as good as another, and she might as well stay temporarily in Peshawar as move elsewhere without real reason. When peace returned to the country, that would be the time for her to move – if she could decide where to go.

She had formed the habit of visiting the Commissioner's office every afternoon to learn the latest news of the fighting. In a back room, telegraph operators worked in shifts, transcribing Morse messages that came in regularly from Delhi and Calcutta.

'What is the news today?' she asked the clerk now. He put his head on one side as though the effort of pondering a satisfactory answer felt a physical weight.

'Nothing new, memsahib,' he said at last. 'But this is good news, yes?'

'Yes,' Mary Jane agreed. She had not heard from Ben or from Ritchie, but then they did not know her address, so there was no way they could communicate. She realised it was quite unreasonable to suppose she would have any message from them or about them, but still, quite irrationally, she hoped to hear. Now that the siege of Delhi seemed to be over, perhaps they would travel north. She found herself missing them both, and especially Ben. He had a cheerfulness and resourcefulness she found most appealing. And but for him she would either have drowned in the Ganges or been dragged ashore and burned alive.

She worried that in one of the forays on the Red Fort, about which she sometimes read briefly in the transcripts, he might be wounded, or, unspeakable, unbearable possibility, he might even be dead.

Every day the electric telegraph produced the names of officers and men who had died: Lieutenant Morris, of wounds; Captain Jones, of fever; Colour Sergeant Ansty, killed on patrol. She did not know any of them, and now she never would, but she could imagine wives, mothers, fathers, sisters, brothers, all hundreds, maybe thousands of miles away, imagining they were still alive, still writing to them. They might not know the truth for weeks or even months.

When Mary Jane returned to Mrs Murison's house, Mr Singh, the lawyer, was waiting for her. She had not seen him since she had paid him for drawing up the agreement between Munta Lal's relatives and herself.

'What brings you here?' she asked him. She neither liked nor trusted the man, but she had no wish to antagonise him.

'To arrange a further meeting with you and your husband's relations.'

'I have nothing more I wish to discuss with them,' Mary Jane told him. 'They have received their share of the money. As far as I am concerned, that is the end of the matter.'

'I understand your feelings, mem, but for their part they feel they have not been very sympathetic to your situation. You have lost a dearly loved husband and have generously allowed them a share of the prince's inheritance. They have undergone a total change of heart and attitude in the last few weeks. They would like to renegotiate the agreement.'

'I would not,' Mary Jane replied. 'What we have agreed, we have agreed.'

'I understand that perfectly, mem. But if you will permit me, you might change your mind when you hear their proposal.'

'What is it?'

'In these unhappy times, when life is cheap, several of their relations have most regrettably died as a result of the insurrection. They were bachelors of

554

considerable wealth. Thus, your late husband's relatives have unexpectedly inherited important sums of money. In these circumstances they feel that it would be inappropriate for them to accept a portion of your inheritance in addition.'

'A most unexpected development,' replied Mary Jane cautiously.

'Mercy and generosity are sometimes unexpected, mem, but they are none the less welcome for that.'

'What is their proposal?'

'They wish to discuss giving back to you what you have given to them. You would then receive everything your late husband possessed.'

'If they wish to do that, why do they not do it? I am hardly likely to disagree with their proposal, am I? If that is their decision, what is there for us to discuss? Please draw up whatever letter of agreement is required.'

Mr Singh bowed. 'I will do so, mem, but there are matters concerning it – where and when and how the money should be paid – that would be most speedily agreed at a meeting between you. I would advise you, mem, in your own interests, to see them. One would not wish them to take offence and then perhaps change their minds, with consequent embarrassment to both parties.'

'Where do they want to meet me?'

'At any place convenient to you.'

'Then tell them to come here tomorrow morning. Ten o'clock will suit me.'

'If that is your wish, I will so inform them.' Mr Singh bowed and went out into the street. He left behind him in the hall a faint scent of the rich jasmine oil he used as a hair lotion.

The offer seemed unlikely, and yet it could be a prudent move on their part, in the nature of an insurance premium. If Munta Lal's relatives paid back their share of the inheritance, which apparently they could now well afford to do, Mary Jane might feel more ready to speak for them should they be arraigned and charged with disaffection to the Company or the Crown after the present insurrection was crushed. She could not believe they were making the offer simply out of friendship, but self-protection seemed a plausible reason. It also suggested to her that they had something to hide. She smiled to herself; at least they did not know the secrets she had to conceal.

Next morning, she saw Mrs Murison. 'I am expecting Mr Singh and two strangers,' she explained. 'I will see them in the lounge. I would appreciate it if you could come into the room from time to time as we talk.'

'You do not trust Mr Singh?'

Mary Jane shrugged. 'I have had experiences that make me reluctant to trust anybody,' she replied. 'I trust you, however, to be within earshot. I may have to sign some papers. Perhaps you could witness my signature. I would, of course, make that worth your while.'

'You are very kind,' said Mrs Murison warmly.

No, thought Mary Jane, not kind; just cautious.

At ten o'clock she was sitting in the main room opposite the sambur head above the mantelpiece. The hotel was quiet, the street outside almost empty. She wondered what Ivan would be doing now and King George Drummond, and where the circus and the fair were playing. Ten o'clock here in Peshawar would be about four o'clock in the morning in England, so they were probably asleep. She was so lost in thought that she only realised that Mr Singh had arrived when he coughed gently. He appeared very grave.

'Where are the others?' she asked.

'There has unfortunately been an accident,' he said

556

slowly. 'I am sorry to have to tell you that Mr Rajiv
Lal has broken his leg. He is in bed at his home. He
sends his most sincere apologies for any inconvenience
this might cause you, but perhaps you could come with
me and see him there. I have a tonga waiting outside.'

Rajiv Lal's house stood a little way out of the bazaar.
Strings of camels padded their stately way past its shut-
tered windows; the owners of sweetmeat stalls cried
their wares at the roadside. On a wooden table, an old
woman sliced water melons to sell at half an anna a
sliver to thirsty travellers. Flies swarmed greedily over
the juice that spilled onto the table top.

A servant opened Mr Lal's front door, showed them
along a narrow hall into a room overlooking a central
courtyard. Water from a fountain trickled and tinkled
into a stone basin, bearded with green weed. They
could be miles away from the bustle and rush and
smells of the frontier town outside.

Mary Jane and Mr Singh sat down on two wooden
chairs inlaid with ivory carvings. Carpets hung from
brass rails on the walls. A curtain parted at the far side
of the room. Moti and Rajiv Lal came into the room.

'I thought you had broken your leg?' she said
accusingly to Rajiv Lal.

'To think is not to know,' he replied quietly, and
smiled. 'It was fortunately not a break, as we had at
first thought. Simply a sprain.'

'Well, now I am here, I agree to your proposition
and thank you for your kind offer. I have asked Mr
Singh to draw up an agreement.' She looked round for
Mr Singh's confirmation, but he was no longer there.

'I think he has gone to fetch it,' said Rajiv Lal.

Mary Jane stood up. As she did so, hands gripped
her from behind. Someone she could not see held a
soft pad, soaked in chloroform, over her mouth. She

struggled and kicked and tried to scream, but to no effect. Gradually, the two brothers, the inlaid chairs, the carpets on the walls, fused and merged, and then died as darkness fell quietly from the air.

Chapter Sixteen

Ben and Ritchie thankfully dismounted from their horses outside the Commissioner's house in Peshawar.

Ritchie had heard that on John Nicholson's death his friend Blake had been promoted to Peshawar from Benares. It would be more agreeable to spend a few nights with him and his wife here than in some hotel.

Grooms led away their horses, while servants unpacked their kit. Others of Blake's staff made arrangements for the accommodation of the bearers and camel boys who travelled with them, and to feed the horses and camels that had carried their baggage.

For most of their first evening at dinner, as giant night moths flung themselves with trembling wings against the globes of the lights, they discussed events in Delhi and Cawnpore, and the future of the British in India.

'You may remember that after the battle of Plassey a rumour spread that our rule would last for one hundred years,' said Ben. 'We have just had that anniversary, and the prophecy came true. I hear that the Company's suzerainty is going to give place to proper governmental rule. India will come under the British Crown. Now another prophecy is going the rounds. British rule in India will not last for another hundred years, but for ninety.'

'That takes us up to 1947,' said Blake musingly.

'Well, whatever happens then will be out of our hands. It's what happens between now and then that is important to me.' He turned to Ben. 'What are your plans? Staying in the army?'

'I think not,' Ben replied. 'I only came out to India because I wanted to leave England in a hurry for reasons of my own. I admire the bravery of the rank and file Indians and the British. I do not hold the same admiration for their leaders on either side.'

'So what do you plan?' asked Ritchie. 'You're well set for promotion now.'

'Yes, I suppose so. But I feel I've seen enough killing. I would like to do something to help people instead, if I can.'

'I understand from the telegraph messages here that there's a gun named after you, the Fanfare Triangle,' Blake commented. 'People say they've never seen such a deadly weapon. Is that so?'

'I invented it, I suppose, yes. I first started to think about it when I was in Barrackpore. I noticed that both rifles and cannon have a considerable recoil. I worked out a way to use this wasted force so that one shot could load the barrel with another, and so on, virtually *ad infinitum*.'

'Fortunate man!' said Ritchie. 'You will now leave the club of the impoverished.'

'I never thought I would,' Ben admitted. 'But if so, I'd like to use the money for something I think worthwhile.'

'Which is?' asked Blake, passing the port.

'Some people like to collect stained glass, or to endow a chair at a university. I would like to pay something back to people who have had no part in any of our wars and yet who lose almost as much as those who have, through the loss of fathers, husbands, their homes. I would like to help children orphaned in war.'

560

'How?'

'I'm going to start homes for them.'

'And call them Fanfare Homes?'

'Why not? I will be making the money out of Fanfare guns, so let me do something to help those that other armies' guns have orphaned. Educate these boys and girls, give them a chance in life. At present, they've no hope at all. At Barrackpore I was shocked to see how wretchedly they lived when their parents were alive. I can't imagine how terrible it must be if they've no parents or their fathers are killed.'

'I admire you for that,' said Bake. 'But it's not often someone who makes money gives it away.'

'Well, you asked me what I'd do. I'll do that. In the long term.'

'And in the short?' asked Blake.

'I want to find Miss Green. We last saw her in Benares.'

'I've dined out often on that story,' said Blake.

'I hope you dine out on the sequel. How I found her.'

'That should be easy to do. She has been staying at a private hotel run by an Anglo-Indian lady, Mrs Murison. She has been coming in to my clerk's office nearly every day, asking for news of Delhi. The casualty lists were sent by electric telegraph. She read these most assiduously. She was sad to learn of the death of Captain and Mrs Cartwright and their small son. And every day she was very obviously relieved that your names weren't on the lists.'

'Is she in the hotel now?' Ben asked him.

'You had better find out.'

'Can I help you?' Mrs Murison asked Ben with the air of someone who believed that a stranger would only call to bring bad news. Ben introduced himself.

561

'I hope so. I am looking for Miss Green. I understand she is staying here. I knew her back in England, as well as here in India.'

'Miss Green was staying here, but she left one morning last week.'

'You have an address for her?'

'No. She went out unexpectedly. I do not think she intended to stay away. Her clothes are still in her room. And she owes me one week's board and lodging which is quite out of character.'

'How much would that be?'

'Thirty rupees.'

Ben took three ten-rupee notes from his pocket. 'I would not like you to be owed money. Now, Mrs Murison, have you any idea where she is?'

'None. All I can say is that Mr Singh came to see her. He is a lawyer here in Peshawar.'

'What did he want?'

'You are a friend of hers, Mr Bannerman?'

'I am.'

'Then I must tell you this. Miss Green asked me to stay nearby while Mr Singh introduced two strangers to her. She said I might be needed to witness a signature. I formed the impression that she did not trust Mr Singh. For some reason, she did not want to see these men on her own.'

'You heard what was said?'

'Yes. Only Mr Singh turned up. He told her that one of the others had broken his leg. He asked her to come with him to this man's house. She had not expected this. She had arranged to meet them here at ten that morning.'

'And she has not been back?'

'No.'

'Has she been abducted, do you think?'

'I could not say that.'

'But you feel suspicious? You think that something odd has happened, Mrs Murison?'

'Anything involving Mr Singh gives me disquiet. I have to admit that.'

'Why? Is he dishonest?'

'When my husband died, he left me this house. We have no children or other relations. I have no money except what I can make from guests like Miss Green. I thought the house was freehold. But Mr Singh insisted he held a mortgage on it at a high rate of interest. He threatened to seize the property. Almost everything I earn goes to Mr Singh until that is paid off.'

'You have seen the deed of mortgage?'

'No. I have asked for it, but he always has some excuse for not producing it. He was my husband's lawyer and he says that I also owe him money for work done for my husband. I find that difficult to believe. Apart from making a will, my husband had no need of a lawyer and neither did I. We were not rich.'

'I will see Mr Singh,' promised Ben. 'I have your permission to examine the mortgage deed, if need be?'

'Of course. I would appreciate your help very much. It is difficult when you are a woman alone, without money or influence or friends.'

'You have a friend in me, Mrs Murison,' Ben assured her.

Mr Singh's clerk was a tall, thin Hindu.

'Mr Singh is engaged,' he said when Ben came into the front office. 'Can I help you, sir?'

'I would really like to see him on an important matter.'

'Important, sir? Relating to what, may I ask?'

'You may. Regarding the whereabouts of a friend, Miss Green.'

563

'I will inform him again.' He went into the inner room, came back in a moment. 'He is free now, sir.'

Ben walked past him into Mr Singh's office. The air smelt sweet with jasmine hair oil. The lawyer's desk was piled with papers written in copperplate, bound in pink ribbon.

'I understand you wish to discover the whereabouts of a Miss Green,' said Mr Singh. 'I am sorry but I know no lady of that name, sir.'

'Then, as you lawyers say, let me refresh your memory. You called to see her in Mrs Murison's hotel. She expected you to bring two other men to discuss some matter. But you went alone to tell her that one of these men had broken his leg. She went with you to his house. Since then she has not been seen.'

'Ah, you mean the widow of Prince Munta Lal? The English lady who most unhappily disturbed the religious ceremony involving the funeral of her late husband in a most unseemly way? I took her to the house of her late husband's relation. I have not seen her since.'

'Nor has anyone else, Mr Singh. This country has gone through great turmoil these past few months. Now, at last, I hope there is peace. But I must tell you this. There will be no peace for you unless you answer my question. For the last time, where is she?'

Mr Singh stared at Ben as though daring him to carry out his threat. Ben stood up, turned towards the door.

'Wait,' said Mr Singh quickly. 'Now I remember that Mr Moti Lal, the relation of the late prince, said he was taking her over the border into Afghanistan. He had a friend he wanted her to meet there.'

'Unusual, to cross the frontier, surely?'

'Not at all, I assure you.'

'Why did his friend want to meet her there?'

'To discuss the matter of her inheritance, I believe.'

564

'You have an address over the border?'

'The name of the village, yes. Kantara. No other address. A day's ride north. She may well be back here by now.'

'She is not back here, so I will ride to Kantara and see if she is there. In the meantime, I will inform the Commissioner of our conversation. One last thing. I am told you have a mortgage on Mrs Murison's property. She, and I, would be obliged if you could cancel it.'

'That would be impossible,' Mr Singh protested. 'There is no doubt whatever that the mortgage is legal.'

'I will also ask the Commissioner to look into this matter on her behalf. She is a widow woman and needs someone to safeguard her interests. You understand me, Mr Singh?'

'I understand you, sir.'

For a few moments after Ben had left, Mr Singh sat at his desk, considering his situation. If this Englishman did bring charges or persuade the Commissioner to look into his dealings, there would be no shortage of people in Peshawar eager to testify against him. He was not known as a friend of the fatherless and the poor.

On the other hand, Afghanistan was a wild, rough country, and no doubt this officer would ride north almost immediately, as he claimed was his intention. Mr Singh realised that, as a matter of self-preservation, it was incumbent upon him to see that he did not ride south again.

He pressed the brass bell-push on his desk. His clerk came into the room. Mr Singh scribbled a note, dashed sand on the paper to dry the ink, folded it in an envelope, sealed it.

'See that this is delivered immediately by rider to Mr Moti Lal in Kantara,' he told the clerk.

He paused for a moment. Something might still go wrong; nothing was ever totally certain. As an act of apparent good will, he would deal with the matter of Mrs Murison's mortgage; it would not bear any examination whatever, and he had already extracted a lot of money from the old woman. This act would surely tell in his favour if the Englishman did raise the matter with the Commissioner.

'And another thing,' he told his clerk. 'Look out the deeds of Mrs Murison's property. Return them to her today. Explain her husband's mortgage has been fully repaid.'

The clerk bowed and went out of the room. All his working life he had been at Mr Singh's command: go here, go there, fetch this or that, take a message to someone, collect a note from someone else. He had no hope of advancement of any kind, and he disliked Mr Singh intensely. But, as an unqualified clerk, there were few openings for office employment in Peshawar. However, he made full use of whatever opportunities presented themselves to make a few extra rupees.

He had listened outside Mr Singh's office to the conversation, because often by this means he had learned little items which he could translate into money. He thought he could do so on this occasion. He had been impressed by the English officer's bearing. He stood and spoke like a man. His eyes were direct, his skin burned brown by the sun. But, most important, most surprising in a European, he was wearing a ring with a ruby of peculiar, almost unique, shape. He had seen only one other ring with a stone cut in this triangular form. He wondered whether Mr Singh had noticed it, but in view of his instructions, he doubted it. Mr Singh was not observant. He was a clever man, as everyone agreed, but it was often the case that those with sharp minds, like those who meddled with

566

sharp knives, could easily cut themselves.

The clerk smiled at the thought, went into a small room in the rear of the house. The air felt heavy with the smoke of cheap cigarettes, simply a rolled-up leaf, that three men in rough khaki clothes were smoking in the room. They sat on a bench without a back. They were Mr Singh's messengers. He treated them as creatures rather than as humans. If he had provided a back to their bench they might loll against it and sleep in his time. Such behaviour was not to his liking.

The clerk handed Mr Singh's note to the first messenger, and told him to deliver it to Mr Lal in Kantara. The second messenger he took outside and gave him private instructions of a different sort, with a second sealed envelope. He watched the two men go their separate ways.

When they were out of sight, he went back to the narrow hutch he dignified with the name of his office, and wondered just what the information he had would be worth to the person to whom he had sent it. He hoped he had just made himself at least a hundred rupees – maybe even a thousand if he was lucky.

Mary Jane was lying face down on a rough wooden raft that dipped and rose and shuddered alarmingly with every beat of an angry, thundering sea.

As it moved, she stretched out her arms desperately, palms flattened against the boards, to try and hold herself steady, to keep her face above swirling blankets of seaweed that threatened to choke her. She gasped desperately for air, and sat up.

There was no raft; that was the dream of a mind fuming with drugs. She was being tossed from side to side on the rough floor of a bullock cart. The seaweed was a thick brown blanket that covered her face completely. She threw it to one side and thankfully gulped down mouthfuls of fresh air. Then she peered over the edge of the cart at an infinity of dust and desert, broken here and there by huge outcrops of amber rock.

Where was she? What had happened to her?

Ahead, she could see the hunched back of the driver, goading his two bullocks with a pointed stick. A man on a horse trotted on one side. He wore a white shirt and jodhpurs, now grey with dust. He had seen the movement in the cart, and looked at her. With astonishment, she recognised Rajiv Lal.

She looked to the other side. Moti Lal bowed ironically to her from his horse. Now she remembered. Mr Singh had told her these men wanted to pay her back their share of the inheritance. She had gone to their house. She remembered the sweet smell of some soporific spirit.

'Where are we?' she called out weakly.

'In Afghanistan,' Rajiv Lal replied. 'Over the border. Where the British can't get you.'

'But why? I came to your house with Mr Singh. He said you were going to give up your share of the inheritance.'

'A mistake, dear lady. You misunderstood him. *You* are going to give up *your* share which is rightfully ours.'

'What do you mean?'

'Precisely what I say. You see that village ahead?'

Mary Jane screwed up her face against the sun. In the distance, like a mirage trembling with heat, she could make out earth walls, a few scrubby trees.

'You will stay there until you agree.'

'And if I refuse?'

'You will still stay there, alive or dead. I do not think it will prove a very friendly village. The Afghans are not a friendly people, especially not towards you British. I think you will soon agree to our proposal. Then you can go back to India, unharmed but perhaps wiser. And certainly poorer!'

As he spoke, they both heard a faint cry from far behind them. It sounded like a warning, borne on the wind, diminished by distance. The wheels of the wagon and the horses' hooves had set up a drifting cloud of dust. Through this and beyond it she could see vague figures on the landscape, strung out, galloping towards them. Rajiv Lal also saw them.

'Quick!' he shouted to his brother in a voice sharpened by terror. He whipped his horse. The beast reared up as he dug in his spurs. The two men raced ahead of the cart.

The bullock driver began to shout in alarm. He flogged the thin shanks of his beasts mercilessly. Then he turned, pulled the blanket over Mary Jane's head again and pushed her down on the floor. She lay there, face pressed against the dry warm planks. She heard a crack like a whip or a twig breaking, and then a scream and the thunder of hooves all around the cart.

She lay, dry-mouthed and sweating with fear. The cart stopped. She heard shouts. Someone ripped off the blanket. She sat up.

Half a dozen riders on dark, well-groomed horses surrounded her. In contrast to their neat horses, the men were dirty, unshaven. They wore rough clothes, leather bandoliers crammed with cartridges across their chests. They held the reins in one hand and distinctive long-barrelled muskets in the other.

A riderless horse stood, head down, fifty yards away to the right. Near it on the ground lay a crumpled mass of a once white shirt and jodhpurs, now reddened with blood. Rajiv Lal had been shot as he tried to reach the safety of the village.

Moti was still riding ahead, presumably unaware, or uncaring, that his brother was dead. As he neared Kantara, three men rode out towards him. One fired a musket over his head. Moti threw up his arms in surrender. Immediately, they closed in on him. One seized the reins of his horse. They all trotted back towards the bullock cart.

The tallest of the Afghans questioned the driver. He shrugged his shoulders, answered in a whining, apologetic voice. Mary Jane could not understand a word either said, but guessed he was asking who they were, who she was. When Moti Lal came back, he began to talk rapidly in the same language. The riders all took part in the conversation, nodding towards her, then towards the village, once towards the dead man.

'What's happened? Who are these people?' she asked Moti Lal in English.

'Afghan robbers,' he replied tersely. 'This area is full of them. They will either kill us, as they have killed Rajiv, or hold us prisoner and send someone back over the border for a ransom. Even if the ransom is paid at once, it won't mean we go free. They'll probably go back for more. And even if more is paid, they might still kill us simply to stop us remembering their faces. I have told them you are a very rich and important English lady. That may delay things for a while. If they think you're worth a huge ransom alive, we may have a chance.'

One of the Afghans gave a sharp command to the driver of the cart. He prodded his animals. The cart moved forward slowly, with Afghans now riding on either side, close to it. They stopped by Rajiv's body. The leader ordered Moti and the bullock driver to lift the corpse up and put it on the cart behind Mary Jane. Then they approached the nearest building and stopped outside it.

Moti Lal and the bullock cart driver carried Rajiv's body towards a low circular wall surrounding what appeared to be a well. They balanced it on top and then heaved it over. There was no splash as the body landed, only a heavy thud; the well was dry.

One of the Afghans now gave a sudden cry of surprise and pointed across the desert behind them. In the distance, Mary Jane could see a swift horseman riding towards them at a great pace, trailing behind him a huge frond of amber dust. He rode bent low over the horse's neck. When he raised his head, he saw for the first time half a dozen Afghans riding out purposefully to meet him.

He reined in his animal, would have turned and fled, but they seized his bridle, brought him over towards the group. He was a young Indian, clearly frightened. He glanced from one to the other in bewilderment. Then he recognised Moti Lal.

'Do you speak English?' Moti Lal asked him.

'A little.'

'These people don't. What brings you here?'

'This. To deliver to you personally.'

The young man unbuttoned a leather pouch, took out a note, handed it to Moti Lal.

The Afghan leader seized it, peered at the paper, turning it up and down and sideways. Clearly, he could not read. After a few moments, he gave it to Moti Lal, who read it aloud in Hindustani.

'It says two British officers are on their way here.'

'Nothing more?'

'It is signed, Singh.'

The messenger raised his right hand in a hopeful gesture of farewell. He had carried out his commission; there was nothing left to do. As he turned the head of his horse, the Afghan shouted an order. The man next to him drew his sword and struck the messenger on the side of his head with the flat of the blade. The young man was not expecting the blow and fell heavily on the hard earth, one foot caught in the stirrup. The swordsman cut the leather and whipped the horse away. The messenger collapsed in the dust, lay for a moment, and then crawled up wretchedly to his feet. He looked beseechingly from one Afghan to the next.

The leader shouted an order to him. The man shook his head, cried out in alarm and fear, held out his hands, begging for mercy. The Afghan drew his sword. At this, the man began to rip off his clothes. He let them fall in a pile on the sand, made no attempt to fold them. Within seconds, he was standing naked as the day he was born.

'They can't let him go back,' Moti Lal explained to Mary Jane in a whisper. 'He'd recognise them. Maybe he even knows them. So they're going to kill him. They're discussing how. But they don't want to spoil his clothes. They can use those.'

The Afghan leader took a wide-mouthed metal flask from his saddle bag, unscrewed the top. He flung the contents over the young man's chest. A thick, golden stream of honey flowed down slowly over his stomach, his genitals. The Afghans roared with laughter at the sight. The leader buttoned down the empty flask in his saddle bag and rode a few paces to one of the scrubby trees.

He stopped, thrust his sword into the mass of thick, dusty leaves, hacked off a branch. He carried this back, holding it well away from his body. His horse was clearly terrified, for the leaves hummed and throbbed with angry life – a huge cluster of desert bees.

The Afghan rode up to the messenger and threw the branch into his face. The man screamed in horror, then in agony. He put up his hands instinctively to protect his eyes as his face and body crawled with a thick brown mantle of thousands upon thousands of furious bees. He choked with the agony of innumerable stings, then collapsed. For a few moments he writhed in unspeakable pain, and then he was still.

He lay on his back, naked and dead. A thatch of swarming bees covered his sweating flesh and gorged themselves on the honey and his blood.

Ben and Ritchie rode out of Peshawar together, going north.

Blake had not been able to provide them with accurate maps of Afghanistan; there were none. It was too dangerous for any mapmaker to attempt more than an approximation of villages, hills, rivers, although in years past many British and Indian officers had made valiant attempts to do so, often travelling in disguise as itinerant traders.

They had therefore memorised known landmarks; a cairn of stones here, a black flag marking the grave of a holy man further ahead. They brought a third horse with them to carry food, water, bedding rolls and, Ben hoped, Mary Jane on the ride back to Peshawar.

At first they chatted to each other as they rode, but soon the effort of talk became tedious. Heat pressed down on them like a physical weight. Their mouths felt dry as gourds; their lips cracked, rimmed with white salt. They kept silent to conserve their energy for whatever might lie ahead.

Their plan was to reach Kantara at dusk. They both wore Indian clothes and had darkened their faces, hands and arms with tobacco juice boiled in a pan. They decided that if they only spoke Hindustani to each other, they might just pass as Indians, possibly Kashmiris who had lighter skins.

Not all Afghans, of course, were dark. Many were almost as white as Europeans, with reddish hair and light blue eyes. These Afghans were said to be in line of descent from Greek soldiers of Alexander the Great whose armies had marched through these same deserts and gorges more than two thousand years previously.

Heat drained slowly, reluctantly, from the day as the sun moved across the sky and slid down behind the mountains. All around, the earth lay grey as spent ash. Huge rocks littered each side of the camel track. Here and there, small patches of dried dung showed that camel caravans had recently passed this way before them. A faint fog began to roll towards the riders from the foothills. The air, which moments before had felt hot and dry as the blast from an open furnace, suddenly turned chill, damp, gritty. They shivered in their sweat-soaked shirts.

Ahead of them lay the village of Kantara, little more than a huddle of small buildings, many roofless, some fallen in on themselves. Generations of tribesmen passing through had carried off stones and beams to build anew elsewhere.

They halted about fifty yards from the nearest building. This was larger than the rest, with a wide archway, lacking a gate. They dismounted. The horses moved towards a brackish pool of water, edged with reed, and drank greedily. Ben and Ritchie looped the reins over the stump of a dead tree. Then they drew their pistols from the leather holsters in front of the saddles, loaded and primed them and walked slowly towards the building. Shadows stretched long dark fingers across the desert in the brief, tropical twilight.

They paused outside the building, listened. They could hear nothing except the wind of evening that lifted dust and blew it with a faint, rasping sound away towards the hills.

They went on, side by side, very slowly and cautiously, through the archway. The building was roofless, just four stone walls. Stumps of broken beams and rafters pointed to the umber sky. Suddenly, Ben gave a cry of amazement, disbelief. Standing against the far wall opposite them he saw Mary Jane.

Both men stood still. Was this an illusion, caused by tired eyes and heat and dust, and the sudden chill of evening? No. This was real. Mary Jane was staring at them, shaking her head.

Ben took one tentative step towards her.

Immediately, three men jumped on his back, brought him down with a blow to the side of his head. Ben could see Ritchie fighting three more men who had attacked him in the same way. Like idiots, with confidence born of a ridiculous belief in their own superiority, they had walked right into a trap of childish simplicity. Then the weight of the world fell in on them and all was dark.

Ritchie regained consciousness first. He was lying, wrists and ankles bound by thin leather thongs, on the dirt floor of the building. Mary Jane was still standing where they had first seen her. He could see her more clearly now; torches made of branches bound together and dipped in oil had been pushed into holes in the wall. By their smoking, flickering flames he saw that her hands were bound behind her back. She was tied to a ring in the wall once used for tethering horses.

Ben still lay unconscious. The bruise on his head was bleeding slightly, but Ritchie could see he was breathing. The leader of the Afghans crossed the floor, kicked him playfully in the groin.

'You speak Hindustani?' he asked.

Ritchie nodded.

'Who are you? English officers?'

For a moment Ritchie thought of denying this, then changed his mind. They would find out soon enough; better admit their identity right away.

'Yes.'

'What are you doing, Englishmen, coming armed into our country with your faces darkened? You planned to seize your countrywoman, yes?'

'We wished to find her,' Ritchie corrected him carefully. 'How did you know?'

'A messenger came from Peshawar. A lawyer called Singh sent him. The messenger wanted to rush back to him, but we persuaded him to stay.' The man jerked his head towards the low circular wall beyond the archway, grinning widely. 'He will not be returning. He is down there. The question now is, what to do with you? Do you join him? Or do we ask your friends for money to release you?

'The woman should fetch a ransom if she really is rich, as her escort claims. We must find out. Or maybe we could sell her to one of the King's sons who likes women with fair skin. She has a value, either way. But you two? I am not sure yet. We will keep you until I decide.'

'Where? Here?'

'No. You would have to be looked after, guarded, if you stayed here, otherwise you might be tempted to try to escape. We have better things to do than guard the faithless and unbelievers. You will join the messenger. That's where we throw all the rubbish – dead dogs, cats, sheep bones when we've eaten the meat, and people for whom we have little use.'

He called one of his men who brought a wooden bucket full of water, and a knife. He cut the ropes round Mary Jane's wrists, then those that bound Ben and Ritchie. He dashed the bucket of water over Ben. The shock made him sit up suddenly, then he gripped his head. It was pounding like a demented drum.

'Get up!' the leader ordered him in Hindustani.

He led them out across the hard, baked earth to the well. Behind the wall Ben saw a small well also ringed by a low stone wall.

'Down there,' said the leader.

Ben climbed over the wall. A wooden ladder was fixed to the vertical side of what appeared to be a secondary well shaft. Mary Jane followed him, then Ritchie. They went down slowly, reluctantly, hand over hand into the dark, dank pit.

The hole grew so narrow that their shoulders brushed its sides. Dried earth fell into their eyes, and down their backs. Finally, they reached the bottom, where a doorway opened into a larger pit. They could hear a slithering of serpents. The moon shone through the opening at the top of the well and was reflected in dozens of pairs of bright green eyes that watched them warily. Ben realised what Jed must have felt in the pit of rats at the Pig and Whistle inn outside Plumstead. He had not survived that experience. Would they be any more fortunate? Then he drove the thought from his mind.

An Afghan threw down a torch made of thin strips of wood tied together and dipped in sheep fat. They jumped to one side to avoid the falling flame. The smoky glow lit up skeletons of sheep, Lal's broken body and the messenger's, glistening with honey, and crawling, creeping horrors feeding on the dead: snakes, worms, rodents so bloated and gorged they could scarcely drag themselves along.

The door suddenly slammed shut behind them. Then came a harsh squeal of rusty bolts, and they stood imprisoned at the base of the main well. Their flesh revolted at the sight, the sounds, the smells of putrefaction and decay.

The Afghan had been quite right when he said there was no way of escape. The walls were smooth and so high it would be difficult to scale them, even if someone threw a rope down from the top. And no one was going to do that.

577

Ritchie was the first to speak, slowly, softly, as though thinking aloud.

'When I was young,' he said gloomily, 'I used to think I was going to live for ever. Others would grow old, or fall ill, or be wounded and die. But not me. Never me. Now, I'm not so sure.'

'I am,' replied Ben confidently. 'We are going to escape.

'When I was a boy,' Ben continued, 'I didn't think I'd live for ever, like you, but I liked stories about people who had overcome what seemed insurmountable obstacles. It started with one Dr Kintyre used to tell me, a Bible story his father, the local preacher, often used in his sermons.

'There were three men, Shadrach, Meshach and Abednego. King Nebuchadnezzar seized them for some reason, bound them hand and foot, and threw them into a furnace. Just to make certain they could not possibly escape, he had the furnace stoked up to seven times its usual temperature. And still, by what seemed a miracle, they got out.

'We're not bound and we're not burning – two points in our favour. Now for the third. We cannot climb the walls, and we cannot open the door to the other well shaft. Since we cannot go up, we will have to wait until someone comes down, either to feed us, if they think we could be useful, or to kill us if they don't. And when they come through that door, this is what we do . . .'

Back to back, arms linked, they dozed on their feet like horses, waking up suddenly as their heads drooped. Tired as they were, it was unthinkable that they should lie or even sit on the floor, alive with worms and putrescence. Time passed slowly, painfully, in their uneasy hinterland of weariness, lost somewhere between slumber and wakefulness.

Ben was the first to hear footsteps on the ladder of the smaller well shaft. He squeezed the arms of the other two, held a finger to his lips for them to keep silent. Quietly, Ritchie and Mary Jane moved to each side of the door as Ben had proposed in his plan. Ben stood several feet from the door, facing it. He slipped his belt from the loops on his trousers and stood holding it loosely in front of him.

A rattle of bolts and the door burst open. A bearded Afghan came through the doorway holding a smoking torch above his head in one hand, a drawn sword in the other. Behind him, a second Afghan carried a bucket and a sword.

'Food!' shouted the first man in Hindustani. 'We have brought you food!'

He looked around him, unable to see anyone; his eyes had been dazzled by the light on the climb down. He blinked hurriedly to try and accustom them to the gloom.

'Where are you?' he called through the smoky, stinking air.

'Here!' Ben replied. As he spoke, he whipped the belt above his head and tugged on both ends. The hidden magnesium flare with which Karim Khan had dazzled the constables in the field near Ardrey in Scotland blazed with the blinding and unexpected brilliance of a captive meteor.

The Afghans cried out in terror. The man dropped the bucket, staggered back. His companion thrashed the air uselessly, blindly, with his sword. Ben brought one knee up into his groin, looped the belt round his neck and pulled with all this strength. The Afghan's head snapped down onto Ben's other knee. His nose broke like a dry branch. He collapsed, unconscious. Ritchie dealt with his companion. Mary Jane picked up the burning torch and led the way through the door.

Ben strapped the belt round his waist, bolted the door behind them. Then they all began to climb the ladder. At the top, they snuffed out the torch, paused for a moment to regain their breath, and stood listening, breathing deeply, thankful to feel fresh cool air after the foetid stench of suppuration and decomposing bodies.

The only sound was the blowing of a horse, the rattle of a bit, and the constant abrasive rasp of dust being lifted by the wind.

Their horses were where they had left them; they had found some scrubby grass and were munching it steadily. Ben unstrapped the bedding and saddlebags from the third horse, helped Mary Jane up into the saddle. Then he and Ritchie mounted their own horses. Within seconds they were away, riding south and riding fast.

From time to time Ben looked over his shoulder. Under the moon the ruined village seemed peaceful. They could not see any sign of life; it could be totally deserted. He calculated that they had possibly an hour's start on any pursuers. It must surely take that long for the two men at the bottom of the well to raise the alarm. With any luck at all, they could be in Peshawar by morning, their experience simply a terrible dream safely behind them.

If the experience had any value – as Ben believed the *munshi* might claim, if ever he heard of it – then it must be that now he would value his liberty above all else. Wealth, success, they were of little worth when weighed in the balance against freedom.

The hills ahead loomed up grey and carved with shadows by the moon. Nothing moved, nothing seemed even to live on those cruel slopes with their jagged edges and huge promontories, peaks lost in perpetually drifting cloud.

'Keep close together,' said Ritchie warningly. 'We're coming to the gorge.'

By some volcanic split or earthquake aeons of time earlier, the mountains had moved apart by a matter of twenty feet. Sheer walls of greyish-brown rock, scored with veins of mica and minerals that by day glittered like fool's gold, now soared dark and sombre on either side.

They rode three abreast, Mary Jane in the centre. The sound of their horses' hooves echoed and re-echoed hollowly from the walls. High above them, saplings and small bushes, seeded by eagles, sprouted from cracks and fissures, temporarily blotting out the moon.

Ben glanced behind him. There was still no sign of pursuit. They were safe. Even if a horse went lame, they surely had too great a lead to be overtaken.

They came through the far mouth of the gorge, out into the open desert. Mist billowed across the empty landscape in drifting waves, as though clouds had fallen from the sky. One moment all seemed chill and damp and opaque. The next, they were through the patch of fog and under a bright, clear moon. They breathed more freely.

The gorge had been the most dangerous part of the journey, the perfect site for any ambush, and there had been nothing. They felt as safe now as if they were riding in Rotten Row. They spurred their horses on, looking ahead to a bath, a clean bed, a meal – and total freedom.

And then, even as they relaxed and their pounding hearts slowed, Ben had a sudden sharp presentiment of danger.

'Stop!' he called out.

The others reined in their horses. For a moment, the only sound was the panting of the tired animals. Then, in the distance far behind them, probably miles away but rapidly approaching, he heard the faint alarum of horses' hooves he had sensed, rather than heard, before.

They were being pursued after all. Their captors must somehow have freed themselves. Their horses would be faster and fresher than their tired mounts. They could still be overtaken and captured.

'Gallop!' said Ben grimly, and dug his spurs into the heaving sides of his weary horse.

They rode on through another wide stretch of mist that muffled the sound of their pursuit. Then, out of the gloom on the other side, they saw twelve riders in a line, facing them.

It was an illusion, of course, a fantasy born of fear and tired eyes and reaction from their escape. They could be ghosts, or carved men on carved horses, stone figures from some ancient kingdom. But they were none of these things. Unbelievably, they were real. The man in the centre drew his sword.

'Halt!' he called in Hindustani. 'Halt, or you die!'

Enemy ahead of them, enemy behind them. They had escaped from one danger simply to meet another at least as deadly.

For a second, Ben thought of charging, but the odds were far too great. Such folly could have only one outcome. He reined in his horse.

'Who are you?' asked the man who had stopped them.

'We are English,' Ben replied in Hindustani. 'A lady and two officers. We have come over the frontier in error. We are riding back again, now.'

'You are a long way from the border,' said the man. 'What brings you so far? You have no beasts of burden,

582

no equipment. No one comes into Afghanistan without a tent or a blanket, and no European without servants.' As he spoke, he reached down into a leather pouch on the horse's pommel, struck a lucifer and lit a hard twist of oiled rope. He held it up like a torch. 'Raise your hands above your heads,' he commanded.

They did so. The man looked closely at them.

'We conceal nothing,' said Ritchie. 'As you can see, we are unarmed.'

'You speak truth, Englishman. Now you are our prisoners.'

Ben groaned in dismay. Were these men with the group from whom they had just escaped? Or could they be hostile to them? He did not know, and somehow he felt too weary to care.

'You will come with us,' the Afghan continued. 'We have a camp five miles from here. Do not make any attempt to break away. If you do, you will die before you have gone ten paces. You understand me?'

At that moment they all heard a thunder of approaching hooves echo and re-echo against the vertical rocks of the ravine. Half a dozen riders suddenly charged towards them through the mist. In an instinctive reaction, their leader swung up his long-barrelled rifle, fired.

Ritchie gave a great cry and fell forward across his horse's neck. His right foot slipped from the stirrup, and he rolled over onto the ground. Around him, muskets crackled like a summer brushwood fire. The pursuers had not seen the Afghan escort. When they did, they instantly wheeled round and fled back through the gorge, three riders chasing them. The hills echoed with the sound of drumming hooves.

Ben jumped off his horse, knelt down by Ritchie's side. Mary Jane joined him, and the Afghan with the twist of rope came close, holding it up so they could see how badly Ritchie was injured. Under a thick layer of dust his face was already damp with the sweat of approaching death. The front and back of his jacket were soaked with blood. The bullet had apparently gone right through his body. Ben ripped open his jacket, but it was impossible to staunch the pumping flow of blood.

Ritchie opened his eyes, blinked up at them weakly in the unexpected glare of the smoky flame. He tried to speak, but for a moment all Ben could hear was blood bubbling in his throat. Then Ritchie coughed, began to speak very slowly and faintly in a whisper they could scarcely hear.

'Mary Jane,' he said. 'I wanted to tell you before. I lacked the courage. But if I don't speak now, you will never hear.' He paused. His chest heaved as though he had been running a long way uphill.

'Your mother,' he went on, gasping now for breath. 'You have her picture in the locket. I recognised her as soon as I saw it in Benares. Jane was a maid in our house, Beechwood Hall. She left. I didn't know why then, but my parents did. They sent me as far away as they could, to India, to avoid any scandal. My father bought me a commission in the Company's army. They wanted me to forget her. But I didn't. I wrote to her, but the only address I had was my home. I don't expect they ever forwarded the letters. So she never knew. But you must tell her, and that I'm very proud of our daughter. My father lost everything gambling in Monte Carlo. He couldn't face ruin, so he blew his brains out. That's why I could never buy any promotion.'

His voice was fading now, like someone calling softly against a great and rising storm.

'You only love once, my girl, and I loved her. I wanted to tell you. And I want you to tell her.'

Ritchie's lips moved again, but now no sound came

from them. The heaving of his chest slowed, and then was still. Ben and the Afghan stood up. The Afghan gave a sharp order. His men unstrapped small shovels from their horses' panniers and began to dig.

The three others now rode back through the ravine and spoke excitedly to the leader. He turned to Ben.

'They caught up with them,' he explained. 'And killed them all. They were only robbers.'

Ben nodded. This was the law of a land beyond laws. Both sides did what they were trained to do: to kill, then to kill the killers. But nothing could bring back the dead. A hundred might die to avenge Douglas Ritchie's death, but he would lie here for ever.

Gently, they lowered his body into the shallow grave. Ben saluted. As they shovelled earth on top of him, he repeated the only words of the Burial Service he could remember: 'The Lord giveth and the Lord taketh away. Blessed be the name of the Lord.'

He remembered the *munshi* in Barrackpore reading Ritchie's palm and suddenly refusing to say what his future held. Had he seen death written on his hand? Ben glanced at Mary Jane, wondering at her thoughts after Ritchie's admission. She had just seen her father shot dead. Was there no end to such pointless killings, seemingly repeated time and time again, a death for a life, a death for a death?

The Afghans surrounded Ben and Mary Jane, and they rode across the desert in a group. Their horses were weary; they travelled slowly. The night felt chill, and as the sweat dried on Ben's body, he shivered, and not entirely from cold. Nothing lay ahead of them but interrogation and, very probably, death at the end of the questions.

Finally, they saw a ring of flares lit round a cluster of tents. A sentry challenged them; the leader answered.

'Dismount,' he told Ben and Mary Jane.

They climbed down stiffly and stood, flexing their muscles. Someone led them to a large tent, lifted the entrance flap. They went inside. Lights were burning. Chairs and a table had been set out on huge rugs; the air smelled of musk and wood smoke. The tent was the size of a small house, divided into four sections. Ben and Mary Jane stood at the entrance, realising for the first time how exhausted they were.

A small man, with the plump, soft face of a eunuch, came in, bowed to Mary Jane. He spoke to her in Hindustani. She did not understand and looked questioningly at Ben.

'Follow him,' he told her. 'He says there is warm water ready for you to wash, and new clothes.'

'Is this a trick?' she asked him nervously.

'I don't think so. We've been fairly treated so far,' said Ben. 'We just have to trust them. We have no other option.' He watched her go.

A male orderly led him into the fourth room. Here, a metal bath was half full of steaming water. He stripped, bathed, dried himself on a rough towel the orderly provided. The man handed him a pair of leather *chaplis* and a loose-fitting jacket and trousers. Then he took him back to the main room.

Mary Jane came in, also dressed in fresh clothes. They smiled at each other's appearance in Afghan clothing.

'Did you know Douglas Ritchie was my father?' she asked Ben.

He shook his head. 'No. I had no idea. He never mentioned the matter to me.'

'I saw him looking at the locket in Benares as though he recognised the face,' said Mary Jane. 'What a sad thing, my mother married the wrong man, and my father the wrong woman. I'm never going to make that mistake, never.'

'I won't let you,' said Ben simply.

'How can you stop me?'

'Very easily. You're going to marry me.'

'*You?*'

'Of course. What d'you think we've been through all this for? Just to meet again and then say goodbye? First of all, we meet in Scotland. Then, it's hail and farewell. At Bostal Heath we meet and part again. In Benares, I swam out into the river to meet you. If I hadn't, we wouldn't have met here in Afghanistan for a fourth time. We've said goodbye three times. I'm never going to say goodbye again. And that is final.'

Mary Jane paused. 'You mean that?' she asked at last.

'Of course I do.'

'About wanting to marry me?'

'I will repeat it. You are *going* to marry me.'

'But you don't know me.'

'I intend to rectify that by spending the rest of my life getting to know you. And one lifetime will barely be long enough to tell you how much I love you. We haven't endured all this just to part again. It's fated that we should stay together.'

'Do you believe in fate – kismet?'

'I believe in myself, in my stars, and also I believe that we're going to get out of here. Because we have to before we can marry.'

'You called me a philosopher once,' said Mary Jane, smiling wryly.

'And so we both are. Look at the facts. If these people here meant to kill us they'd have done so by now, maybe out by the gorge, maybe even here. Or they'd have kept us in some cage or cave as the others did in the well. Instead of that, they've treated us with civility. They have made arrangements for us to bathe, even provided a complete change of clothes.'

'You're not just trying to cheer me up? You really believe we will get out?' asked Mary Jane, looking at him closely.

He saw fear in her eyes.

'I'm certain of it.'

'You know, whenever we did say goodbye, I always missed you. I didn't realise just how much until I saw you again next time. But I'm going to be honest with you. I've done some terrible things you know nothing about.' She paused.

'Haven't we all?' he said. 'We can only do what seems best at the time. Looking back, it often doesn't seem as good as it did then. But you should never look back. The old *munshi* taught me, you can only go on. And we're going on – together.'

'You say such kind things, I *want* to believe you,' she said. 'I'm ashamed of the things I've done now. But I wasn't when I did them. Perhaps that's the most shameful thing of all.'

'That's all in the past,' he said. 'Here and now, today and tomorrow, not yesterday, is what concerns us.'

She shook her head miserably, remembering how she had robbed Sir Martyn; how she broke into the laird's house and cheated Francis Grimsdyke in Brighton. Miranda, indeed! She recalled her affair with Captain Cartwright that left her a woman of property; her pregnancy – and something else.

'I lost my baby,' she said tonelessly. 'And I wasn't married to the father. Doesn't that alter your opinion?'

'No. It doesn't make a damn bit of difference. We all do foolish things, wrong things, sometimes, for all sorts of reasons. We don't know the consequences when we do them. And there are no rewards or punishments for whatever we do, only consequences.'

'There is also something else,' Mary Jane went on. 'When I lost that baby, the doctor in Benares told me

I could never have another child. That means I could never give you an heir, or an heiress. If we married, we would never have children.'

'Nonsense,' Ben replied. 'I don't need any. I plan to have hundreds, boys and girls.'

'Whatever do you mean?'

'Exactly what I say. The money I make from the sales of a machine gun I have invented I am putting into a trust to buy big houses along the south coast of England. I mean to fill them with orphaned children of service families who have lost their parents in war. I was an orphan of war myself, remember. Dr Kintyre helped me. I want to help them.'

'It's a wonderful idea,' said Mary Jane. Tears were now running unchecked down her face.

'We haven't any houses to start with yet, of course.'

'I've got a number Captain Cartwright gave me. They're small, according to him, but they might help us on the way.'

'So you see, it was all predetermined, predestined. You have the houses, I have the idea. Now, have I answered all your objections, or is it that you just object to me, but don't want to say so? But remember, whatever you say won't change how I feel. I love you.'

'Dear Ben. No one ever said that to me before. And I love you.'

He took her in his arms then. As they kissed, Mary Jane remembered the tears her mother had shed as they said goodbye. Now the tears she tasted were her own.

The Afghan leader came into the room.

'Come with me,' he said curtly, ignoring their embrace.

They followed him outside. The moon had risen fully and bright stars prickled the sky. Their breath fanned out as they followed the man between other tents, past hobbled horses that snorted uneasily at their approach. They reached a much larger tent. Two guards stood outside it with swords drawn. They followed the leader into a canvas anteroom.

'Wait here,' the Afghan told Mary Jane. 'His Highness wishes to see the Englishman alone.'

He lifted a heavy curtain so that Ben could go on into the main part of the tent. He followed him. The curtain fell into place behind them. The room was empty. Carpets and rugs were strewn on the floor, two and three deep. Silk, striped in red and white, lined the walls. At the far end, on a raised wooden dais, stood a chair with gilded arms and crimson cushions. The back was carved into the shape of an eagle with spread wings.

'Wait,' the man told Ben and went out, leaving him on his own. Ben stood, watching flickering smoky flares that lit up the tent; the smell of burning animal fat was very strong. A man entered the tent from behind the chair. He was in his fifties, wearing a brocaded jacket and white pantaloon trousers. He crossed the carpet and stood looking at Ben, eye to eye, without saying a word.

He was powerfully built with a broad forehead. His dark beard was flecked at the edges with grey. His eyes were bright, clear, piercing. He had a silver dagger in a curved silver sheath at his belt. Rings on his fingers reflected the flames around the walls, green, blue, ruby-red.

'You are English?' he asked Ben in Hindustani.

'Yes, sir,' said Ben.

'What is your name?' he continued in English.

'Ben Bannerman.'

'You are an officer?'

'I am. A lieutenant in the Company's army.'

'I am told you claim to have crossed the frontier by

mistake. I might believe that if you were near the frontier. But we are nearly thirty miles away. How do you explain that?'

'A brother officer and I crossed the frontier from Peshawar because an Englishwoman had been kidnapped in India and brought here.'

'By people of this country?'

'No, sir, by two Indians. They brought her over the border against her wishes. They felt it would be safer for them in this territory than in British India. They wished to extract money from her.'

'So far, you speak truth, Mr Bannerman. One of these Indians died at the hands of robbers. The other escaped but my people captured him. He was persuaded to tell the real reason for his presence in our country. It was as you say. Unfortunately for him, he told us many lies at first. He is no longer with us to tell any more. Did you find this woman?'

'By the grace of God, we did, sir.'

'By the grace of whose god? Yours or mine, Englishman?'

'Ours, sir. I believe there is only one god with many names. We all worship the same god. He has been good to me. As it is written, "God's kindness towards His creatures is more than a mother's towards her babe." '

'It is also written, "If the unbeliever knew of the extent of the Lord's mercy, even he would not despair of Paradise." Who wrote that, and the words you quoted, Bannerman?'

'The Prophet Mohammed, sir. I learned a little of his teachings from a *munshi* in Barrackpore.'

'So he taught you the rudiments of faith, and the words of the Prophet, blessed be his name always.'

'He did, sir.'

The man took a pace backwards from Ben so that

he could regard him more clearly. 'Hold out your hands, palms uppermost,' he ordered.

Ben did so.

'Now turn them over.'

Ben obeyed. The man peered at the ring with the ruby triangle which Ben wore on the little finger of his right hand. For a moment he did not speak. Then he looked up at Ben's face.

'An unusual stone,' he said. 'Where did you get it?'

'It was left to me, sir, by my mother.'

'Left? What do you mean?'

'She died shortly after I was born, sir. She left it with the physician who attended her.'

'What was her name?'

'Anna, sir. Anna Bannerman.'

'And do you know where she got it?'

'My father gave it to her.'

'And where is your father?'

'He died shortly before my mother, sir. They were with the British Army of the Indus, retreating from Kabul.'

'I watched that army come north over the border,' said the man reminiscently. 'I knew several officers and their ladies in Kabul. We played games of tennis and chess and cards together. We watched horse races they organised. We even played your English game of cricket. We had no hostility towards them, rather the reverse. We had not invited them into our country, agreed. But since they were there, we enjoyed each other's company. It was only when we began to realise they did not intend to leave that our attitudes altered. We were surprised to discover they wished to stay and perhaps even attempt to colonise Afghanistan. Then feelings changed towards them. It was a very sad situation. I heard only one European survived that retreat. A doctor. Is that correct?'

'Yes, sir. A Scottish doctor, Douglas Kintyre, in the Bengal Army. He is still practising as a physician in his native Scotland. As a matter of fact, he brought me into the world. My mother gave this ring to him to keep for me.'

'Tell me, where did this happen?'

'Somewhere on the road to Jalalabad, sir. My mother was being carried in a *doolie* with other sick or wounded people, soldiers and civilians. My father, Lieutenant Ben Bannerman, saw an Afghan patrol about to shoot them up. He attempted to beat off this attack and was killed. My mother was greatly weakened by the retreat and shocked by the loss of her husband in front of her eyes. When I was born shortly afterwards, complications set in almost immediately and she died.'

'And then? What happened then?'

'Dr Kintyre reached Jalalabad, carrying me on his back. Later, he left the Bengal Army and practised as a civilian doctor in Calcutta. He fell ill with fever and returned to Scotland. He brought me up in Calcutta and Barrackpore, and took me to Scotland with him. He was, and is, a bachelor. His housekeeper in Scotland resented my presence so I ran away. I took the place of a British officer who did not wish to serve in India and I brought the ring with me. I look on it as a talisman. It is the only link I have with my mother.'

'Take it off your finger,' the man said roughly. Just for a moment, Ben paused. Then he removed the ring.

The man clapped his hands. A servant came in carrying a small wooden table which he set down by their side. The top was covered by a white cloth. On this lay a pair of silver bent-nosed pliers. The man held out his hand for the ring. Ben put it into his palm. The man picked up the pliers, carefully loosened the tiny delicate hoops of gold that held the stone in place. He took out the triangular ruby, turned it over on the cloth.

'What do you see, Bannerman?' he asked.

Ben picked up the stone, held it towards the nearest flare. Engraved in the back of the ruby he could see the crescent of Islam, the cross of Christianity.

'I never knew anything was carved there,' he said in surprise.

'There may also be other things you do not know,' said the man gently. He held out his left hand. On the little finger, in an identical gold ring, glowed an identical triangular ruby.

'There are only two stones cut in this shape in all the world,' he said. 'You have one, and I have the other. They have been cut in the shape of a triangle for two reasons. It represents the shape of the island off the Burma coast from which the rubies came, Akyab Island. Akyab is also my name. And the carvings show that, as you say, God has more than one name. The cross and the crescent have much in common and their union can be blessed. The teachings of both religions are not dissimilar. Fear God. Keep His commandments. Love thy neighbour.' He paused for a moment. 'Did your mother leave you anything else?' he asked.

'Not that I received, sir.'

'What do you mean by that?'

'I mean that Dr Kintyre told me how when my mother realised she was dying, she asked for a piece of paper and a writing instrument and she wrote a note. She handed this to him and asked him to give it to me when I was old enough to understand what she had written.'

'And he gave you this note?'

'No, sir. The note was lost. It must have fallen out of the doctor's pocket. He could not go back to look for it. He felt very guilty about this, for he had no idea what it contained. He told me so openly. He brought me up so that if I made a mistake, or did a foolish act, I should always admit it. He lived by his own precepts.'

The Afghan put his hand in his jacket pocket, took out a folded, crumpled envelope ingrained with reddish dust. Its edges were brown from dried blood. He handed it to Ben. On the outside, one word was written: *Ben*.

'Read it,' the man commanded him.

Bewildered, Ben opened the envelope, unfolded the single sheet of paper it contained. It was creased and tattered; the writing was spidery and tailed away, without any punctuation. Words were smudged and difficult to decipher, but Ben could just make out each letter, formed painfully by a dying hand.

'My son,' he read aloud. 'I will not see you grow up and you will never know me. Always remember your father was a brave man. He was not of our faith, but his faith was one of honour. I admired my husband but I did not love him. The man I loved but could never marry was Akyab Khan, the second son of the Afghan King.'

'I don't understand,' said Ben, but even as he spoke he knew that he did.

He realised now why he could always see the Indians' point of view, why he felt in sympathy with them. He knew why he could let the Nana Sahib, possibly the most hunted man in all India, go free when he held him in his power and to capture him would have brought him a decoration, perhaps even a title. Half of him was always on their side. He was a man of two worlds, able to understand both viewpoints, East and West, always attempting to arbitrate fairly. Now he understood so many things. Now, at last, he knew who he was, why he was.

'But how did you know I was here in your country?' he asked. 'You must have done, because your men were waiting for us beyond the ravine.'

'We learned you were being held prisoner in Kantara. I thought we would have to attack the brigands there who were holding you though I felt it would be better if you came to us rather than for us to go to them. If you had not managed to escape, then we would have had to rescue you. But I thought you would not be my son if you stayed a captive for long. I had faith in your energy and ability. And it was not misplaced.'

'But how did you know I was in Afghanistan at all?'

'Because of your ruby ring. I maintain emissaries in Peshawar and elsewhere. Years ago, I heard of an English boy in Barrackpore who possessed a valuable and most unusual ring that Dr Kintyre kept in a safe. Then you both went home to your own land, and I heard no more – until you returned.'

'This is also my land.'

'It is now, but then it was not.'

'The *munshi*, he must have told you.'

'He has been helpful. And so have others, including Mr Singh's clerk. It was a matter of following you and bringing you here. But I had to make sure you were who I thought you were. You might have been someone else who had simply stolen the ring.'

'And in that case?' Ben asked him.

'In that case,' Akyab replied quietly, 'we would not be talking like this now.'

He replaced the triangular stone in the ring, bent back the prongs that held it safely, handed the ring to Ben.

'Every man would live long, but no man would be old,' Akyab continued. 'Similarly, every man wishes to sire a son to whom he can teach the lessons of his own

596

life, and guide to the peaks of honour and happiness. No man yearns more strongly for a son to bear his name and his sword than the father who has begotten one and lost him, and whose seed since will only flower with daughters.

'I am proud to say I loved your mother, although she was married to another man. I liked him whose name you bear, Ben Bannerman. I admired him. But of all human emotions, love is the strongest. And I loved your mother above all women.'

'I had the feeling that Dr Kintyre also held her in the highest regard,' Ben replied, remembering the lock of his mother's hair in the doctor's possession.

'Yes, I think he did.'

'The doctor said you tried to shoot them, my mother included.'

'That is not so. Numbers of Afghans, not owing allegiance to the King of those times, were indeed attempting to pillage and murder the retreating army. They wanted their guns, their clothes, jewels, whatever they might possess of use or value. It is the nature of victorious fighting men to strip those they have defeated. I rode in to try and stop this orgy of looting. The situation was confused and dangerous. There was firing on both sides. Lieutenant Bannerman was killed. I was wounded. It was then my turn to retreat. I did so.

'After the *doolies* had gone on, I ordered the area to be searched. Not much of value was found, but this note was brought to me by someone who knew of my friendship with Lieutenant Bannerman and his wife and the doctor. I knew then that I had a son – Ben.

'I believed that this knowledge had been vouchsafed to me and that one day, when the moment was opportune, Allah, in his all-embracing mercy, in his infinite compassion, would grant me a meeting with my son. And now he has given me my heart's desire.'

Akyab Khan held out his hand.

As I explained in the beginning, this has been Ben's story, not mine. But I played a small part, in that I introduced him to the world first of all. Events then took over in a way and on a scale I had never envisaged, or even imagined. Now, as I look back across those years, I marvel how incidents, which at the time seemed in total isolation from each other, meshed together, like pieces in a jigsaw, each with its own importance.

Questions pursue answers, like the painted horses on roundabouts in King Drummond's fair.

If Karim Khan had not befriended Ben when they first met at dusk in Scotland long ago, would he have lived out all his days on a prison island in the Indian Ocean?

If the *munshi* in Barrackpore had not lit Ben's imagination with stories of Alexander the Great's astute tactics, would Ben have ever persuaded the angry mob in Benares to disperse peacefully?

If Bertha, poor woman, who lived and died a spinster, had not made life unpleasant for Ben in my house, would he not have stayed there, perhaps followed my career, and now be the village doctor in my place?

I do not know, but I have no doubt that Anna would have been proud of her son. She would have loved him as deeply as she loved his father.

Whenever Ben was in Scotland in latter years, he came to see me and we would recall old times, and like so many older people, I would live my life again at secondhand through his experiences, his adventures. He was due to spend New Year with me, but he did not arrive. I assumed that he had been forced to postpone the visit through pressure of so many other more important matters.

I read, without much interest, how the bridge across the River Tay, nearly two miles long, boasting eighty-four huge metal spans and only opened a year earlier, had collapsed in an unprecedented gale.

Then, by chance, I saw a copy of *The Enquirer* newspaper, a journal I did not read regularly, and I realised with sadness why Ben had not kept our last appointment. It contained this article:

More details are now becoming available about some of the passengers who perished in the train crossing the Tay Bridge when it collapsed in the violent storm of December 28 last.

One whose loss will be greatly felt was Sir Benjamin Fanfare Bannerman. Sir Benjamin had little formal education, but he rose to become one of this country's most generous philanthropists. He will best be remembered by the charity known as Fanfare Homes, which he founded to help children of soldiers and sailors, killed or severely incapacitated in the service of their Queen and country. These homes have provided sound basic education and a Christian upbringing for thousands of boys and girls who have since found useful and worthwhile careers in this country and abroad.

Sir Benjamin, who was born, and orphaned, during the retreat from Kabul in Afghanistan, had a remarkable early life. He worked in a fair-ground, became an officer in the East India Company's army, and served with distinction throughout the Indian Mutiny. During this campaign, he observed the recoil of big guns when firing, and subsequently patented an ingenious method of using this wasted energy to power the automatic machine gun that bears his name – the Fanfare Triangle. This machine gun has been widely adopted by regiments of the British Army, and by many other armies around the world.

From this enterprise grew the immense manufacturing concern that bears his name, designing and producing weapons of many kinds. He has devoted its profits to the upkeep of Fanfare Homes around the country.

Sir Benjamin had a natural affinity with Eastern countries and their peoples. It is largely due to his extraordinary influence that relations between the present King of Afghanistan and this country are now at their most cordial for more than a generation. And his frequent visits to India, his friendship with Indians of all classes, Muslim and Hindu alike, have also played an enormous part in the present prosperity and tranquillity of that vast country, the jewel in our Queen's imperial crown.

Sir Benjamin used to say that the question he was most often asked concerned his middle name – Fanfare. This came from lines quoted by his mother shortly before her death, describing a celestial fanfare on the death of Mr Valiant-for-Truth in John Bunyan's classic, *Pilgrim's Progress*: 'And so he passed over and all the trumpets sounded for him on the other side.'

Sir Benjamin's view of dying was strongly influenced by Muslim teaching, especially the saying of the prophet Mohammed: 'Death is a bridge that uniteth friend with friend.'

Sir Benjamin, who always preferred to be called by the abbreviation 'Ben', was knighted for his services to philanthropy. He married Mary Jane Green, who survives him.

There were no children of the marriage.